PRAISE FOR *NEW YORK TIMES* BESTSELLING AUTHOR BARBARA DELINSKY AND HER MARVELOUS NOVELS

THE WOMAN NEXT DOOR

"Delinsky's adept and compelling exploration of the inner workings of the modern upper-class American family makes for one of her best books to date."

—*Booklist*

"Spellbinding. . . . Delinsky carefully peels away the surface facades of [the women characters] in a process that's both riveting and painful. Thanks to Delinsky's poignant prose, it's also wonderfully unforgettable."

—Barnesandnoble.com

"Delinsky's latest novel is like a murder mystery, with clues and even red herrings thrown in along the way, but Delinsky surprises the reader in the end."

—*Library Journal*

"Delinsky peers into the dark corners of ideal marriages, loving families, and ideal neighborhoods and makes you realize that 'the woman next door' could be you."

—*Roanoke Times* (VA)

"*THE WOMAN NEXT DOOR* . . . has something in it that will stir everyone who reads it. . . . Likely to go down as one of [Delinsky's] best."

—*The Anniston Star* (TX)

THE VINEYARD

"High drama, beautiful scenery, and resilient yet sensitive characters make this a must for all Delinsky fans and a perfect introduction to her work for new readers."

—*Booklist*

"Another enjoyable novel."

—*Library Journal*

LAKE NEWS

"[An] engaging tale."

—*People*

"Delinsky spins another engrossing story of strength in the face of cataclysmic life changes."

—*Library Journal*

"Delightful. . . . Readers will be sorry to reach the end of *Lake News* and yearn for more about its cast and characters."

—*The Pilot* (Southern Pines, NC)

"An enjoyable novel. . . . Delinsky is one of those writers who knows how to introduce characters to her readers in such a way that they become more like old friends than works of fiction."

—*Flint Journal* (MI)

"A gripping tale sure to please."

—*BookPage*

COAST ROAD

"A winner. . . . Delinsky delivers an emotion-packed journey . . . firmly cementing her status as a bestselling writer of top-notch books."

—*Booklist*

"Heartwarming."

—*Star Tribune* (Minneapolis)

"A remarkable journey. . . . Delinsky delves deeper into the human heart and spirit with each new novel."

—*The Cincinnati Enquirer*

"Beautiful. . . . Delinsky is one of the twentieth century's best writers."

—Amazon.com

THREE WISHES

"[A] heartwarming, tear-jerking small-town romance."

—*Kirkus Reviews*

"Touching and delightful. . . . A story of genuine love, sacrifice, redemption, and the cohesiveness of life in a small town."

—*Chattanooga Times* (TN)

"Delinsky's prose is spare, controlled, and poignant."

—*Publishers Weekly*

BOOKS BY BARBARA DELINSKY

The Woman Next Door
The Vineyard
Lake News
Coast Road
Three Wishes
A Woman's Place
Shades of Grace
Together Alone
For My Daughters
Suddenly
More Than Friends
The Passions of Chelsea Kane
A Woman Betrayed

BARBARA DELINSKY

THE WOMAN NEXT DOOR

A NOVEL

POCKET BOOKS
New York London Toronto Sydney Singapore

POCKET BOOKS, a division of Simon & Schuster, Inc.
1230 Avenue of the Americas, New York, NY 10020

Originally published in hardcover in 2001 by Simon & Schuster, Inc.

ISBN: 0-7434-1125-0

First Pocket Books printing July 2002

10 9 8 7 6 5 4 3 2 1

Printed in the U.S.A.

Acknowledgments

Some of my books require extensive research. *The Woman Next Door* did not. Years of watching people, of observing their interactions, and of talking with friends about their lives' quandaries prepared me well for this book. That said, I am not a professional counselor. If school psychologists existed when I was a student, they were a well-kept secret. I was therefore particularly fortunate, during the writing of *The Woman Next Door,* to have the help of Ann Cheston. A school psychologist at the Fay School in Southborough, Massachusetts, she helped me wade through the quagmire of day-to-day dealings with teenagers in a small school setting. I thank her for her time and expertise. My thanks also to Bonnie Ulin for talking me through the basics of landscape design.

What about infertility? you ask, and rightly so. I learned about this subject for *The Woman Next Door* by reading books and working the Web, which means that I have dozens of nameless, faceless women (and men) to thank for teaching me the basics. For those of you currently dealing with fertility issues, please know that the scenario encompassed in *The Woman Next Door* is but one of many—and that my heart and hopes are with you!

As always, my family was wonderful. I thank my son Andrew, who listened through hour after hour of plot twists and turns, and then, using his own experience as a teacher, offered the most insightful advice. I thank my son Eric for feedback on bluegrass music, and my son Jeremy for feedback on corporate names and business dealings. I thank Eric's wife, Jodi, and Jeremy's wife, Sherrie, for sharing their thoughts with me as part of my target audience. And my husband, Steve? Poor guy. During dinner after dinner each night after work, he suffered through the growing pains of this book. For that, he deserves a literary medal of honor!

I thank my friend and fellow writer Sandra Brown, who gave me invaluable writing advice. I thank my agent, Amy Berkower, and my editors, Chuck Adams and Michael Korda. Mostly I thank you, my readers, for your undying support. You have never let me down; I promise to do my best to return the favor.

THE WOMAN NEXT DOOR

Prologue

Given their druthers, Amanda and Graham would have eloped. At thirty and thirty-six, respectively, all they wanted was to be married. But Amanda's father insisted that his only child have a big wedding, her mother delighted in spending his money, and Graham's family loved a party.

So they had a lavish June wedding at the Cape Cod country club to which Amanda's father belonged. The ceremony was held overlooking a salt marsh, with willets, terns, and three hundred guests bearing witness. Then, led by the bride and groom, who walked arm in arm, those three hundred guests trooped across the eighteenth green and around the clubhouse for a buffet dinner in the garden. The place was lush with greenery, vivid with lilacs and peonies, scented with roses, all of which was appreciated far more by the bride's guests, who were into form, than the groom's, who were into fun. Likewise, the toasts ran along party lines, starting with that of the best man.

Will O'Leary was the next older brother to Graham, who was the youngest of eight siblings. Champagne glass in hand, he directed an O'Leary grin at his wife and four children before turning to the groom.

"No matter that I'm the older of us by a year, you've been a tough act to follow, Graham O'Leary. You always did better in school. You always did better in sports. You were always the one elected class president, and boy, there were times when I hated that." There were chuckles. "Not now, though, because I know something you don't." His grin turned mischievous. "You may have gotten the family's looks and brains, but that doesn't mean much in the dark of night. So. I wish for you and Amanda everything I've had these past fifteen years." He raised his glass. "To you both. May your lives be filled with sweet secrets, hearty laughter, and *great sex.*"

There were hoots and cheers, the clinking of glasses, the downing of drink.

When the noise subsided, Beth Fisher stepped to the microphone. One of three bridesmaids dressed in elegant navy, she spoke softly. "Amanda was single a long time, waiting for just the right guy to come along. We used to commiserate about that, she and I. Then I met my guy, and Amanda got busy with work and put her own search on hold. She wasn't looking when she first saw Graham, but that's how some of the best things in life happen." She lifted her glass. "To Amanda and Graham. May you love each other forever."

Amanda hadn't put her search on hold, so much as despaired that she would find a man she could trust enough to love. Then, one unsuspecting August afternoon, she sought refuge from the heat of Manhattan by visiting her former thesis advisor in Greenwich, and there Graham was, stripped to the waist and sweating beautifully as he planted junipers on a hillside by the woman's home.

There were six men at work. Amanda had no idea why her eye was drawn to Graham rather than to one of the others.

No. That wasn't true. She knew very well why her eye was drawn to him. He was riveting with his dark hair and close beard, taller than the others and more finely muscled, though she later learned that he didn't often do the digging. He was the brains of the operation. She claimed to have been drawn by that, too.

And how had she known anything about brains from the distance of a hundred feet? His eyes. They had found hers over the slant of that dug-up hillside, and had held her gaze in a way that suggested either total brashness or supreme confidence. Both were foreign to her experience with men, and one as titillating as the other. Then, barely fifteen minutes into her visit, he knocked on the door with a drawing of the landscape plans for another part of the yard.

The interruption was deliberate. He admitted that right from the start. He had wanted an introduction, and he got it.

The groom's oldest sister, MaryAnne O'Leary Walker, came to the mike wearing a green suit that had fit her better before the last three of her five children were born. Undaunted and confident, she turned to Graham, who stood surrounded by friends, an arm around his blond-haired, white-laced-and-beaded bride.

"I was twelve when you were born," MaryAnne blurted out, "and changed more of your diapers than either of us cares to admit, so it's your turn now." She raised her glass. "May you have *lots* of babies, and lots of *patience!*"

"Hear, hear!" chorused the crowd, echoing itself in diminishing degrees until another bridesmaid in navy stepped up to the mike.

"Amanda and I met in graduate school," said Gail Wald, her tone genteel. "We were psychologists in neighboring schools in New York before Graham stole her away, and I'm not sure I'll ever forgive him for it. But the fact is that Graham has been a smile in Amanda's eyes since the day she met him. In a world where smiles often come hard, that means a lot. When you do what we do for a living, you understand this. You know how precious smiles can be. You also know how to spot a real one, and that's the kind my friend wears." Holding her glass high, she faced the beaming couple. "To Amanda and Graham. You may have happened fast, but you're the real thing. Here's to thousands and thousands more smiles, and a life filled with health and prosperity."

Amanda didn't usually like things happening fast. She far preferred to explore, ponder, and plan. When she dated, she wanted to know almost everything about a man well ahead of a first kiss, because she was seriously jaded. She had seen the downside of mismatched couples in her own home, long before she began hearing tales complaining about parents from the students she counseled, and she certainly didn't believe in love at first sight. Lust, perhaps, but not love. The therapist in her wanted reason and rhyme.

Her attraction to Graham O'Leary made a mockery of that. He turned her into a sushi lover on their first date the day following their meeting in Greenwich, and when they went dancing the night after that, she was lost. Graham was an incredible dancer. He led with fluidity and grace, and she—independent soul though she was—followed his lead.

One song became the next, and then the next. When he tucked her hand close to his heart, she felt the rest of her being drawn closer as well.

For Graham, that was a defining moment. He didn't need a woman who fit the image of his mother or his brothers. He'd already been there. This time, he needed a woman who fit him. *Something about the way Amanda settled into his body said she did—and it went beyond the physical, just as he needed it to. He was thirty-five. He knew what physical attraction was about, but there was more to Amanda than just physical appeal. She was a pedigreed lady, classy and reserved, but she seemed to feel the spark between them as strongly as he did. The surprise he saw in her eyes when he drew her close, seconds before she sank into his body, said that though she didn't trust easily, she trusted him.*

He would remember that moment until the day he died. He had felt strong. He had felt unique. He had felt needed.

Dorothy O'Leary, mother of the groom, didn't raise her glass in toast. Her smile was wooden, her eyes glazed. She stood off to the side with her brother and his family, seeming distant from the party until her third oldest son approached the mike. Only then did her eyes clear and her features soften.

Peter O'Leary was a Jesuit priest. Possessed with a remarkable charisma that was only enhanced by the Roman collar he wore, he easily quieted the crowd. To the bride and groom, he said, "I might've worried when you chose a country club wedding over a church one, had I not spent so much time with the two of you these last couple months. If ever a relationship seemed right, this is it." Leaving the mike, he approached the newlyweds. With a hand on Graham's shoulder, he lifted his glass. "Love shines from your faces. May it always be so. May you live long, may you give more than you take, may you serve our Lord in wondrous ways." He paused, let a twinkle enter his eye, and succumbed to the O'Leary in him. "And, yes, may you reproduce well!"

Amanda didn't sleep around. She'd had two lovers before Graham, had dated each for several months and given due thought to time, place, and precautions before shedding her clothes.

With Graham, everything was different. He had suggested they go hiking, which sounded wonderfully adventurous to Amanda, who envisioned a day trip, only to have Graham show up with sleeping bags, food and drink, and the key to a friend's cabin, four miles up in the woods.

It never occurred to her to say no. She wasn't a hiker, hadn't owned a sleeping bag in her life—at least, not the kind that could insulate a body in the chill of a mountain night, which was the kind Graham had brought. But he was capable and coordinated. He liked explaining things to her and did it well. He had no qualms about asking questions when they got to talking about things she knew more about than he, and then there was his smile. It was relaxed, wholehearted, and wide enough to cut a crease through his beard on either side. All told, being with him was the most exciting thing that had ever happenedto her.

The mountain they hiked was lushly green, with clear streams, sweet birdsongs, and breathtaking vistas making it a heady climb from the trailhead on up. He knew where they were going, leading as skillfully as he had on the dance floor, and she put herself in his hands as she had done then.

They didn't make it to the cabin. They had barely finished lunch when he stretched her out in a sheltered glen just off the path and made love to her, right there, in broad daylight.

They were sweaty and dusty and—she thought—tired, but once started, they couldn't stop. She remembered thinking that if he hadn't taken the responsibility for birth control, she would have done without. She needed him too badly for caution, felt too whole when he was inside her to care.

"My family is incorrigible," declared Kathryn O'Leary Wood from the mike. Her eyes touched briefly on Megan Donovan, Graham's childhood sweetheart, first wife, and still a dear family friend, before settling on Graham and Amanda. "This message is from me and Megan. Amanda, my brother is the best. In addition to being positively gorgeous, he is smart and sensitive and special. It looks to me like you're all of those things, too." She paused and smiled. "So we can expect gorgeous *babies* that are smart, sensitive, and special. I wish you and Gray all the happiness in the world." Her eyes narrowed on the groom, her junior by three years. "As for you, Graham O'Leary, this is the very last time I'm doing this for you!"

The applause was long and loud, ebbing only when Amanda's maid of honor came to the mike. Tall, slim, and shy as she looked over a sea of faces with their wide O'Leary smiles, she said a soft, "I don't have children, or brothers and sisters like you. But I do have a history with the bride. I know her parents, and would like to thank them now for such a beautiful party." She lifted her glass to Deborah Carr on one side of the room and William Carr on the other, and waited for the applause to end before speaking again. "I'm Amanda's oldest friend here. We met in kindergarten and have stayed close all this time. Amanda has been there for me over the years in ways only she and I know. She is the best listener, the clearest thinker, the most loyal confidante. It's no surprise to me that she's so good with teenagers. I've often envied those kids. Now I envy Graham."

Graham would have envied himself, if that had been possible. He knew what it was like to stand at an altar and look down a flower-strewn aisle toward the back of the crowd at the moment when his bride appeared. What he didn't know was what it was like to have everything else . . . totally . . . fade away. He wasn't prepared for that, or for the little catch deep in his chest that actually brought tears to his eyes.

He was that taken with her, felt that privileged to have her. She was smart and cultured and fine—everything he had always admired but never felt that he was, coming from the family he did. For all their differences, though, he and Amanda had yet to have an argument. They liked the same furniture, the same food, the same music. They wanted the same house, the same big family. From his first sight of her back on that Greenwich hillside, he'd had the absurdly sentimental belief that the single, best reason for the demise of his marriage to Megan was that Amanda was waiting for him.

This day, all else had indeed faded. He had seen only her, walking toward him down that grassy path, and when his heart shifted in a way that he knew would be permanent, he let it be.

Concluding her toast, Amanda's maid of honor caught Graham's eye. "My friend is precious. Take good care of her, please." She raised her glass. "Here's to you both. Let the wait have been worth every minute."

There were sighs and soft words of assent, then a deep-voiced, "Speaking of the wait . . ." and the inevitable approach of Malcolm O'Leary to the mike. The oldest O'Leary sibling—proprietor, along with the second oldest, James, of their late father's hardware store and father of five himself—raised his glass. "I have one piece of advice for my handsome brother and his beautiful bride. Go to it, Amanda and Gray. You're starting late."

Amanda and Graham celebrated their first wedding anniversary by looking at a house. They had seen others before it, but none as large or as handsome, none in as upscale a community, and none that excited them as this one did. The asking price was definitely a reach. But Graham's work as a landscape architect had grown enough for him to hire a full-time assistant, and Amanda had just been appointed school psychologist in the same town as the house.

That town was Woodley. Prosperous and pristine, it lay in a cluster of rolling hills in western Connecticut, ninety-some minutes by car from New York, and counted among its fourteen thousand residents half a dozen CEOs of Fortune 500 companies, innumerable lawyers and doctors, and a growing list of the Internet-riche. The population was increasingly young. As new, large homes sprang up on wooded lots, or older residents retired and moved south, the town's streets were seeing a growing parade of Expeditions.

The house itself, barely ten years old, was the first in a circle of four Victorians that had been built around a wooded cul-de-sac. With its generous yellow body and white trim, wide wraparound porch, quaint picket fence and gaslights, it was as picturesque as its neighbors—and the beauty didn't end at the front door. The entry hall was open and bright, flanked on either side by living and dining rooms with carved moldings, mahogany built-ins, and high windows. At the back of the house was a large kitchen with granite counters, wood floors, and a glassed-in breakfast area. A winding staircase, replete with window seats at each of two landings, led to four bedrooms on the second floor, one of which was a lavish master suite. As if all that weren't enough, the real estate agent led them to a pair of rooms over the garage.

"Offices," Amanda whispered excitedly when the woman turned away to take a cell call.

Graham whispered back, "Could you counsel people here?"

"In a minute. Could you draw landscape plans here?"

"Big time." The whispering went on. "Look at the woods. Smell the lilacs. If not here, where? Did you see the bedrooms?"

"They're *huge.*"

"Except for the one right next to ours. It could be a nursery."

"No, no." Amanda envisioned something else. "I'd put the cradle in our room and make the little room into a den. It'd be perfect for reading goodnight stories."

"Then we'll give Zoe and Emma the room across the hall, and put Tyler and Hal at the end."

"Not Hal," Amanda begged. It was a long-standing debate. "Graham, Jr. And if they're anything like you and your brothers, they'll be into mischief, so they should be closer."

"Hal," Graham insisted, "and I want them farther off. Boys make more noise. Trust me on this." Slipping an arm around her waist, he drew her lower body close. His eyes grew heavier, the color on his cheekbones warmer, his voice deeper, a whisper. "Diaphragm put away?"

Amanda could barely breathe, the moment was so ripe. "Put away."

"We're makin' a baby?"

"Tonight." They had deliberately waited the year, so that they could have each other for an uninterrupted time before their lives inevitably changed.

"If this house was ours"—his whisper was more hoarse—"where would you . . . ?"

"In the breakfast nook in the kitchen," she whispered back. "Then, years from now, we'd look at each other over the heads of the kids and have our little secret. What about you?"

"The backyard. Out in the woods, away from the neighbors. It'll be like our first time all over again."

But it wasn't their first time. They had been married a year, and they had pressing dreams. "This house is perfect, Gray. This *neighborhood* is perfect. Did you see the tree houses and swing sets? These are nice people with kids. Can we afford to live here?"

"No. But we will."

They celebrated their second anniversary by seeing Amanda's gynecologist. They had been making love without benefit of birth control for a year, and no baby had come of it. After months of denial, months of reassuring each other that it was only a matter of time, they were starting to wonder if something was wrong.

After examining Amanda, the doctor pronounced her healthy, then repeated the verdict when Graham joined them. Only when Graham flashed Amanda a broad smile and pulled her close did she allow herself to be relieved. "I was frightened," she told the doctor, sheepish now that the worst had been denied. "People tell awful stories."

"Don't listen."

"That's sometimes easier said than done." The worst storytellers were her sisters-in-law, and what could she do? She couldn't turn and walk away when they were talking, and it wasn't as if they spoke from personal experience. Their stories were about friends, or friends of friends. O'Learys didn't have trouble making babies. Amanda and Graham were an anomaly.

The doctor sat back in his chair, fingers laced over his middle in a fatherly way. "I've been at this for more than thirty years, so I know what problems look like. The only one I see here is impatience."

"Do you blame us?" Graham asked. "Amanda's thirty-two. I'm thirty-eight."

"And married two years, you say? Trying for a baby for just one? That's not very long." He glanced at the notes he had scrawled earlier. "I'd wonder if it was stress, but you both seem happy with your work. Yes?"

"Yes," they both said. It had been another banner year.

"And you enjoy living in Woodley?"

"Very much," Graham said. "The house is a dream."

"Same with the neighbors," Amanda added. "There are six kids, with great parents. There's an older couple—" She stopped short and gave Graham a stricken look.

He pulled her closer. "June just died," he told the doctor. "She was diagnosed with cancer and gone six weeks later. She was only sixty."

Amanda still felt the shock of it. "I barely knew June a year, but I loved her. Everyone did. She was like a mother—*better* than a mother. You could tell her anything. She'd listen and hear and make solutions seem simple. Ben's lost without her."

"And what did June say about your getting pregnant?" the doctor asked.

Amanda didn't deny having discussed it with her. "She said to be patient, that it would happen."

The doctor nodded. "It will. Truly, you do look fine. Everything is where it should be. Your cycle is regular. We know you're ovulating."

"But it's been a year. The books say—"

"Close the books," he ordered. "Take your husband home and have fun."

For their third anniversary, Amanda and Graham drove into Manhattan to see a specialist. He was actually their third doctor. The first had fallen by the wayside when he kept insisting that nothing was wrong—and it wasn't that Amanda and Graham were convinced that there was, just that they thought a few tests were in order. So they met with the second, a local fertility specialist. He blamed their problem on age.

"Fine," Graham said, voicing the frustration he and Amanda shared, "so how do we deal with it?"

The man shrugged. "You can't turn back the clock."

Amanda reworded the question. "How do you treat . . . older couples who want to have kids?"

Graham gawked at her. "Older couples? We average out at thirty-six. That's not old."

She held up a hand, bidding him to let the doctor answer.

"There are definitely things you can do," the man said. "There's AI. There's IUI and ICSI. If all else fails, there's IVF."

"Translate," Graham ordered.

"Yes, please," Amanda added.

"Haven't you read up on this yet?" the doctor asked. "Most couples in your situation would have done research."

Amanda was taken aback. "The last doctor we saw kept saying nothing was wrong. He told us just to keep on doing what we were doing and not to worry about special procedures."

"Do you want a baby, or don't you?" It was less question than statement, and wasn't spoken harshly, but it had that effect.

Graham stood. "This isn't a good match."

Amanda agreed. They needed someone who was understanding, not judgmental.

The doctor shrugged. "Go to ten others, and you'll hear the same thing. The options are artificial insemination, intrauterine insemination, intracytoplasmic sperm injection, and in vitro fertilization. The procedures get more expensive as you progress from one to the next. Likewise, you get older and less apt to conceive."

When Graham caught Amanda's eye and hitched his chin toward the door, she was by his side in a flash, which was how they found themselves in New York on their third anniversary. Seeming empathetic and resourceful, this newest doctor started with a battery of tests, some of which, for the first time, were on Graham. When the immediate results showed nothing amiss, he gave them a pile of reading matter and a folder filled with instructions and charts. Assuring them that he didn't expect any surprises from the results of the remaining tests, he sent them home with a regimen that had Amanda identifying her fertile periods by charting her body temperature, and Graham maximizing his sperm count by allowing at least two days to pass between ejaculations.

They joked about it during the drive back to Woodley, but their laughter held an edge. Inevitably, making love wasn't as carefree as it used to be. Increasingly, the goal of making a baby was coming before pleasure. With that goal unrealized month after month, their uneasiness grew.

They spent their fourth anniversary quietly. Amanda was recovering from minor surgery performed by yet another doctor. This one was female, and ran a fertility clinic thirty minutes south of Woodley. She was in her forties, mother to three children under the age of six, and disgusted with colleagues of hers who blamed things they couldn't diagnose on emotions, as finally the doctor in Manhattan had done. This one insisted that they call her by her first name—Emily—and not only asked questions none of the others had, but did different tests. That was how she noticed a small blockage in one of Amanda's tubes, and while she wasn't sure that it was severe enough to be causing the problem, she advised a precautionary cleanup.

Amanda and Graham readily agreed. By now they had hoped to have three children—Tyler, Emma, and Hal—born in three consecutive years. As things stood, the house that they loved for family space was starting to feel too large and much too still. And though they tried not to obsess about it, there were times when each wondered whether children would ever come.

There was no lovemaking on this fourth anniversary. Amanda was still too tender for that, and even without the surgery, the timing wouldn't have been right for sex. So it was a morning for gentle exchanges. Graham brought her breakfast in bed and gave her a pair of heart-shaped earrings; she told him she loved him and gave him a book on exotic shrubs. Then he went off to work.

Indeed, work was the good news on their fourth anniversary. O'Leary Landscape Design flourished. Graham now rented a suite of rooms in the center of Woodley to house two full-time assistants and a business manager. He was given preference for the best materials in the three largest nurseries in western Connecticut, had ongoing relationships with tree farms in Washington and Oregon, and shrub farms in the Carolinas. He kept two of Will's crews busy planting on a regular basis.

For her part, Amanda had been named coordinating psychologist for the Woodley school system, which gave her the power to bring a slightly antiquated system into the modern day. That meant getting to know students in nonthreatening situations such as leadership seminars, lunch groups, and community service programs. It meant opening the door to her office, allowing for five-minute sessions as well as forty-five-minute ones, and communicating with students by e-mail, if that was the only way they could handle a psychologist. It meant working with consulting psychologists on difficult cases and with lawyers on matters of confidentiality. It meant forming and training a crisis team.

So she and Graham had their house, their jobs, their neighborhood, and their love. The only thing that would have enhanced their fourth anniversary celebration was a child.

Two months shy of their fifth anniversary, with Amanda feeling more like an egg-producing robot than a woman, she and Graham met for lunch. They talked about work, about the weather, about sandwich choices. They didn't talk about what Amanda had done that morning—which was to have an ultrasound that had measured her egg follicles—or the afternoon's activity—which would entail Graham producing fresh sperm and Amanda being artificially inseminated. They had already failed the procedure once. This was their second of three possible tries.

A short time later that day, Amanda lay alone in a sterile clinic room. Graham had done his part and gone back to work. Emily had poked her head in with a greeting on her way down the hall. After what seemed an interminable wait, a technician Amanda didn't know entered the room. Amanda figured she couldn't have been more than twenty-one, and "technician" was the proper word. The girl had neither social skills nor personal warmth, and Amanda was too nervous to make more than a brief attempt at conversation. When that attempt got no response, she simply stared at the ceiling while the girl injected Graham's sperm. Once that was done, she was left alone.

Amanda knew the drill. She would lie there for twenty minutes with her pelvis tipped up to give the sperm a nudge in the right direction. Then she would dress, go home, and live with her heart in her mouth for the next ten days, wondering if this time it would take.

But today, lying there alone with Graham's silent sperm, Amanda felt a pang in her chest. She wanted to think it was a mystical something telling her that a baby was at that instant starting its nine-month intrauterine life, but she knew better. This pang came from fear.

Chapter One

Graham O'Leary shoveled dirt with a vengeance, pushing himself until his muscles ached, because he needed the exertion. He was filled with nervous energy that had no place to go. This was Tuesday. That made it D-day. Amanda would either get her period or miss it. He hoped desperately that she would miss it, and only in part from wanting a child. The other part had to do with their marriage. They were feeling the strain of failing to conceive. A wall was growing between them. They weren't close the way they used to be. He could feel that she was pulling away.

For Graham, it was déjà vu.

Grunting at the unfairness of that, he heaved an overloaded spadeful of dirt from the hole, but when he lowered the shovel again and pushed in hard, he hit rock. Swearing angrily, he straightened. Sometimes it seemed that rock was all he found. Forget the historic bit about stone walls marking one man's land from the next. He would bet that those walls were built just to get the damn rocks out of the fields! *Put 'em over near the other guy's land,* he imagined the old-timers saying. Only they'd missed a few.

Annoyed, he bent, worked his shovel under the rock, levered it up, and hauled it out. Clear of that impediment, he tossed spadefuls of dirt after it, one after the other in a steady rhythm.

"Hey."

Oh, yeah, he knew what pulling away looked like. He had seen it in Megan, building slowly, mysteriously, reaching a point where he had no idea what she was thinking. With Amanda, he knew the cause of the problem, but that didn't make it easier to take. They used to be on the same wavelength on everything. Not anymore.

Grunting again as he dug deeper, he remembered the tiff they'd had the week before when he had tossed out the idea that she might be more relaxed, and therefore more apt to conceive, if she cut back on the hours she spent at school. She didn't have to be the head of a dozen different programs, he had said in what he thought was a gentle tone. Others could do their part. That would allow her to come home early one or two afternoons each week; she could read, cook, watch *Oprah*.

She had gone *ballistic* over that. He wasn't suggesting it again.

"Gray."

Gritting his teeth, he hauled out another rock. Okay, so he was working longer hours, too. But he wasn't the one whose body had to provide a hospitable environment for a child to take root. Not that he would even breathe that thought. She would take it as criticism. Lately, she misinterpreted lots of what he said.

"Hey, you."

She'd actually had the gall to accuse him of being absent for the second artificial insemination—like the thing could have been done without his sperm. Okay, so he'd gone back to work after producing it. Hell, she had told him to leave. Of course, now she was claiming that what she'd *said* was that he didn't have to stay if he was uncomfortable.

"Graham!"

His head flew up. His brother Will was squatting at the edge of the hole. "Hey. I thought you left." The crew worked from seven to three. It was nearly five.

"I came back. What are you doing?"

Planting his shovel in the dirt, Graham brushed spikes of wet hair back with an arm. "Providing a hospitable environment for this tree," he said with a glance at the monster in question. It was a thirty-foot paper birch that would be the focal point of the patio he'd designed. Not just any tree would do. It had taken him a while to find the right one. "The hole is crucial. It has to be plenty wide and plenty deep."

"I know," Will replied. "That's why I have a backhoe coming tomorrow morning."

"Yeah, well, I felt like getting the exercise," Graham said offhandedly and went back to it.

"Heard from Amanda yet?"

"Nah."

"You said she'd call as soon as she knew."

"Well then, I guess she doesn't know yet," Graham said, but he was pissed. They hadn't talked since he had left the house early that morning. If she'd gotten her period, she was keeping it to herself. His phone was right there in his pocket, silent as stone.

"Did you call her?" Will asked.

"No," Graham said, pedantic now. "I called yesterday afternoon. She said I was pressuring her."

"Moody, huh?"

He sputtered out a laugh and tossed up another shovelful of dirt. "They say it's the Clomid. But hey, it's not easy for me either, and I'm not taking the stuff." Under his breath, he muttered, "Talk about feeling like a eunuch."

"No cause for that," Will said. "You haven't lost it. You have an audience, y'know."

Graham paused, pushed his arm over his brow again, shot his brother a wry look. "Yup." He went back to digging.

"Pretty lady."

"Her husband's an Internet wizard. They're barely thirty and have more money than they know what to do with. So he plays with computers, and she watches the men who work on her lawn. It's pretty pathetic, if you ask me."

"I'd call it flattering."

Graham shot him another look. "You talk with her, then."

"Can't do. I gotta get home. Mikey and Jake have Little League. I'm coach for the day." He pushed himself up. "Don't stay much longer, okay? Leave something for the machine."

Still Graham dug for a while more, if only to bury the idea of Little League under another big mound of dirt. By then his muscles were shot. Tossing the shovel out first, he hoisted himself out of the hole and made for his truck, a dark green pickup with the company logo in white on the side. He took a long drink of water from a jug in back, doused the end of a towel, and did what he could to mop sweat and clean up. A short time later, he pushed his arms into a chambray shirt and set off for home.

* * *

"Your move," said Jordie Cotter from the edge of the deepest armchair in the office. He was fifteen and as sandy-haired as his three younger siblings, which Amanda knew not because she kept detailed files on every student, but because the Cotters lived two doors away from Graham and her. In fact, she had no file on Jordie at all. He wouldn't be in her office playing checkers with her if he thought he was being counseled. For the record, he was here to discuss his community service requirement, since she headed the program. This was the third time he'd come, though. There was a message in that.

Grateful to be distracted from thinking about the baby that was or wasn't, Amanda studied the checkerboard. There were five black pieces, four of them kinged, and three reds, all single. The reds were hers, which meant she was definitely losing.

"I don't have many choices," she said.

"Make your move."

Picking the lesser of the evils, Amanda moved in a way that she figured would sacrifice only one piece. When Jordie jumped two, she sucked in a breath. "I didn't see that coming."

He didn't smile, didn't pump a fist in the air. He simply said again, "Your turn."

She studied her options. When she looked up at the boy, he was somber.

"Do it," he challenged. When she did, he jumped her last checker to win the game and sat back in his chair. Still, though, there was no sense of victory. Rather, he asked, "Did you let me win on purpose?"

"Why would I do that?"

He shrugged and looked away. He was a handsome boy, despite the gangliness that said he was still growing into his limbs. But his T-shirt and jeans were several notches above sloppy, his hair was clean and trimmed, and he didn't have acne, not that many students here did. In affluent towns like Woodley, dermatologists did as well as orthodontists.

"You want to be liked," he answered without looking at her. "It helps if you lose."

Amanda drew in a deep breath. "Well, I do know how that is. I used to do it in school sometimes—you know, deliberately blow an exam so that I wouldn't look like a geek."

"I wouldn't do that," Jordie said.

Amanda didn't believe him. Oh, maybe it wasn't the geek factor. With Jordie, there were other possibilities, not the least of which was the tension she knew existed at home. But something was definitely going on with the boy. His grades had taken a dive at midterm, and the expression he had taken to wearing around school was the sullen one he wore now.

His eyes met hers. They were dark and wary. "Did my mom say anything to you?"

"About the grades? No. And she doesn't know we've talked."

"We haven't talked. Not like, *talked.*" He glanced at the checkerboard. "This isn't talking. It's just better than doing homework."

Amanda touched her heart. "Ach. That hurts."

"Isn't that why you have things to do here? To make kids want to come?"

"They're called icebreakers."

He snorted. "Like Harry Potter?" he said with a glance at the book on her desk.

"I think Harry's cool."

"So do the twins." His twin brothers were eight. "I tell them Harry flies through our woods on his broomstick. That keeps them from following me in there. Our woods are cool. They're real. Harry's not." Sitting forward, he began resetting the checkers on the board. "About the CS requirement? I'd do peer counseling if I thought I could, but I can't."

"Why not?"

"I'm not good at talking."

"Seems to me you talk with your friends."

"They talk. I listen."

"Well, there you go," Amanda said in encouragement. "That's what peer counseling's about. Kids need to vent, and you're a good listener."

"Yeah, but sometimes I want to *say* things."

"Like what?"

He raised unhappy eyes. "Like school sucks, like home sucks, like *baseball* sucks."

"Baseball. I thought you liked baseball." He had just come from practice. It must have been a rough one.

"I'd like it if I played, but I don't. I sit on the bench all the time. Know how embarrassing that is? With all the kids watching? With my *parents* watching? Why do they have to come to games? They could miss one or two. I mean, my mom is *always* at school. Julie loves it, but what does she know? She's only six."

"Your mom does good stuff for the schools."

"Know how embarrassing that is?"

"Actually," Amanda said, taking a calculated risk, "I don't. My parents were too busy fighting with each other to have the time or energy for either my school or me."

Jordie lifted a shoulder. "Mine fight. They just do it when they think we can't hear."

Amanda made a noncommittal sound, but didn't speak. Taking the moment's space to gather his thoughts, Jordie went off in a direction that was slightly different, but clearly upmost in his mind.

"And even if we can't hear, we can see," he said. "Mom hardly ever smiles anymore. She doesn't plan fun things like she used to. Like sleepovers for all our friends." He caught himself. "I mean, it's not like I want those anymore, I'm too old, but Julie and the twins aren't. Mom used to have twenty of us over at once with popcorn and pizza and videos, and I didn't even care if the little kids were bugging me and my friends, because that was all part of it, y'know?"

His enthusiasm gave way to a somber silence, then anger. "Now she just pokes her head in my room asking nosy questions."

"Fuck it," came a high, nasal voice.

Amanda frowned at the neon green parrot in a cage at the end of the room. "Hush up, Maddie."

Jordie stared at the bird. "She's always saying that. How come they let you keep her?"

"She only swears for kids. She knows better when it comes to Mr. Edlin or any of the teachers. She's perfectly polite when they're in here."

Like checkers, Maddie was an icebreaker. Some students stopped by daily for a month to give the bird treats before they felt comfortable enough to talk with Amanda.

"She's a good bird," Amanda cooed in the direction of the cage.

"I love you," Maddie replied.

"She flips?" Jordie asked. "Just like that? Is she a good guy or a bad guy?"

"A good guy. Definitely. Good guys can say bad

things when they're upset. Maddie learned to swear from someone who used to chase her with a broom, which was how I came to adopt her. She knows what anger sounds like. She gets upset when kids get upset, like you just did about baseball."

"I wasn't talking about baseball when she swore," Jordie said.

No. He had been talking about his mother. But, of course, he knew that, which was why he was on his feet now, hoisting the backpack to his shoulder. Talking about parents was hard for kids like Jordie. Talking about feelings was even harder.

Jordie needed an outside therapist, someone who didn't know his family. For that to happen, though, either he or one of his parents had to take the initiative. None of them was doing it, yet. So Amanda went out of her way to be there when Jordie came by. Unfortunately, she couldn't make him stay. Before she could utter a word, he was out the door and tromping down the empty hall, lost again in whatever dark thoughts were haunting him.

Wait, she wanted to say. *We can talk about it. We can talk about moms fighting with dads, how you feel about it, what you're doing when you're supposed to be studying, what you're thinking when you're blue. I'm free. I can talk. I can talk as long as you want. I have to keep my mind busy.*

But he was gone, and as they had been doing all day, her eyes went to the desk and Graham's picture. It was in a neat slate frame, his smile beaming at her through his trim beard. It was a face that many a female entering this room had remarked upon. Graham O'Leary was an icebreaker, too.

She had to call him. He would be waiting to hear.

But she didn't know anything yet, and she might not for hours.

Besides, lately it seemed that the only thing she and Graham were about was having a baby—and, oh, did she feel the pressure of that. He had done his part successfully, and more than once. Her body was the problem. Of course, he didn't say that in as many words, but he didn't need to. She felt his impatience.

But what more could she do? She had followed Emily's instructions to the letter—had eaten well, rested well, exercised in the most healthy and normal of ways, except for today. Loath to do anything that might bring on her period, she was moving as little as possible.

It was nonsense, of course. Normal physical movement wouldn't wreck a normal pregnancy. At this point, though, she was desperate. She hadn't left her office since lunch, and though she might have liked to use the bathroom, she quelled the urge. As a diversionary measure, she sat back in the sofa, checked her watch, and thought about Quinn Davis. It was five-thirty. She had told the boy she would be in her office until six, and so she would be.

His notes unsettled her. They had come by e-mail, the first sent early that morning saying, "I need to talk to you, but it's private. Is that okay?"

"Private is definitely okay," Amanda had written back. "What you say is between you and me. That's the law. I'm free third period. Would that work?"

He hadn't shown up during third period, but another e-mail arrived during fourth. "Would my parents have to know that we met?"

"No," Amanda replied. "That's part of the confidentiality rule. They wouldn't know unless you sign a form saying it's okay. I have a free half hour right after school, but if you have to be at baseball practice, we could make it later. I'll stay until six. Will that work?"

She hadn't heard back. Nor had she heard footsteps in the hall to suggest that Quinn had come while Jordie was there, and she'd been listening. Something was up with Quinn. Her instincts told her so, and it had nothing to do with the fact that he approached her by e-mail. Many students did that, precisely because it was more private. She often suggested meeting times, often never heard back, and other than keeping an eye on the student or perhaps sending a follow-up note, there was nothing she could do. She couldn't force the issue.

But Quinn Davis wasn't her usual case. He was a star. In addition to being sophomore class president, he was a peer counselor, high scorer of the varsity basketball team the past winter, and now he was the wunderkind of the baseball team. Two older brothers, both leaders at Woodley High, were currently at Princeton and West Point. Their parents were local activists, often in the papers, forever in Hartford lobbying for one cause or another.

Amanda wondered if Quinn would show and, if so, what he would say. It could be that he wanted to tell Amanda about a student who needed help; part of the point of the peer leadership program was to identify problem students before they exploded. Student referrals were responsible for easily a third of the students she regularly saw. But she doubted that was the case here, with the student insisting on confidentiality from his own parents.

Slipping off her shoes, Amanda folded her legs beside her. She was tired emotionally; that was a given. She was also physically tired, though if she dared think that it might be the earliest sign of pregnancy, she got a nervous knot in her belly. In any event, she was grateful that her job allowed for casual dress. Allowed for? Demanded. The students had to perceive her as both professional and approachable, no mean feat for someone like Amanda, whose small size and wayward blond curls made her look more like she was twenty-five than thirty-five. The challenge was to appear more sophisticated, yet not formidable.

Today's outfit worked. It was a plum-colored blouse and pants, both in a soft rayon.

A noise came from the hall—a muted sound that could have been an anguished shout—then silence. Fearing that it was Quinn and that something was terribly wrong, Amanda jumped up from the sofa and went to the door. Down the hall, immobile and alert with his mop protruding from a pail-on-wheels, was the janitor.

"Heeeere's Johnny," sang out Maddie from the depths of her office.

Amanda let out a breath. "Mr. Dubcek." The man was white-haired and stooped, eighty if he was a day, but he refused to retire. He was remembered not only by parents of current students, but by grandparents as well. That gave him clout in the respect department. He was never spoken of as Johann, always Mr. Dubcek—except for Maddie, but then, Maddie didn't know about respect. She only knew that the old man fed her and cleaned out her cage and took her every night to his small apartment in the basement of the school.

"I was listening for voices," the janitor told Amanda

in a rusty voice. "I'd'a gone away if you had someone in there. I didn't want to interfere."

"No one's here," she said with a smile, but the smile faded when, standing now, giving gravity its due, she felt an unwelcome rush.

Heart pounding, she went down the hall to the lavatory. Well before she closed the stall door and lowered those soft plum pants, she knew. In that instant, pummeled by a dozen emotions, not the least of which was a profound sense of loss, her mind closed down. Sinking onto the toilet, she put her elbows on her thighs and her face in her hands and began to cry.

She must have been there a while, because the next thing she knew, there was a loud knock on the outer door and the janitor's frightened call: "Mrs. O'Leary? Are you all right?"

Mrs. O'Leary. Ah, the irony of that. Professionally, she had always been Amanda Carr. She had surely introduced herself to the janitor that way four years before. At the same time, though, she had introduced him to Graham, who was helping her set up her office. She had been Mrs. O'Leary to the proper old gentleman ever since.

And what was wrong with being Mrs. O'Leary? On a normal day, nothing at all. She was proud to be married to Graham. She had always believed that once they had kids she would use O'Leary more often than Carr.

Once they had kids. *If* they had kids. And that was what was wrong with being Mrs. O'Leary today. Without the kids, did she have a right to the name?

Tears came again.

"Mrs. O'Leary?" the janitor called again.

Sniffling, she wiped the tears with the heels of her hands. "I'm fine," she called in an upbeat, if nasal, voice. "Be right out."

After dealing with necessities in the stall, she washed her hands and pressed a damp paper towel to her eyes. A headache was starting to build over the right one, but she didn't have the wherewithal to pamper it here, much less the strength to deal with whatever was ailing Quinn Davis. Praying that the boy would not show up, she returned to her office, repaired her face in a hand mirror, shut down her computer, locked up her files, and, waving at the janitor's distant figure on her way down the hall, left school.

Graham considered prolonging the trip home. There were places he could stop, ten minutes here, ten there, giving Amanda more time to call. But the suspense was too much. He kept the truck on the highway and his foot on the gas.

The phone rang. His heart began to pound.

"Hi?" he answered as much in question as greeting, but it wasn't Amanda. It was a woman who owned a real estate firm and had hired him to redo the office grounds. The job was small, the potential large. The woman's clientele was high-end. If she liked what he did, she would recommend his work, and while he had plenty to keep him busy, he always welcomed more. Lately, given the tension between Amanda and him, his work was his salvation.

"I was just wondering when I'll be seeing you," she said warmly.

He drove with his left hand while the right opened his little black book. "You're on my call list. I'll have your plans ready by the first of the week." He flipped several pages, darting glances at each. "How does a week from today sound? Say, four?"

"Perfect. Next Tuesday at four. See you then."

Graham barely ended the call when the phone rang again. Again, his heart began to pound, but it wasn't Amanda this time, either. It was his brother Joe.

"Any news?"

Graham let out a breath. "Nah. I'm headed home."

"Mom was asking."

"I'll bet she was. I have to tell you, there are times when I wish I hadn't said anything to anyone."

"We asked."

So they had. The questions had started one month into his marriage, and they hadn't stopped. In hindsight, he should have said that he and Amanda didn't want children, and would they please bug off. Having his entire family know what they were going through was nearly as humiliating as jerking off into a jar. O'Leary men didn't have to do things like that. Hell, Joe had recently had his fifth child, and Graham suspected he and Christine weren't done yet.

"She's beginning to despair," Joe said now of their mother, Dorothy. "Says she wants to see your kids before she dies."

"She's only seventy-seven."

"She says she's growing frail."

Graham felt a cursed helplessness. "What more does she think I should do?"

"She says this is her last wish."

"*Joe.* Come *on.* This isn't what I need right now."

"I know. I'm just putting you on notice. She keeps saying it should have been Megan."

That was nothing new. "Well, it isn't Megan—it

can't possibly *be* Megan—I don't want it to be Megan," Graham declared. "Help me out here, Joe," he pleaded. "Remind her I'm married to Amanda. If I'm going to have a baby, it'll be Amanda's. Hey, there's my call waiting," he lied, but he couldn't keep this particular conversation going. "I'll get back to you later."

He disconnected without another word and drove on in brooding silence. This damned day was nearly done. He didn't know why Amanda was keeping him in the dark. Even if she didn't know anything yet, she could have called and told him that. She knew he was waiting.

Turning off the highway, he drove along roads that he knew now like the back of his hand, and there was some solace in that. He loved Woodley, loved the way the town roads twisted and climbed through forested hills. A map of the town was like a tree—a trunk that rose from the highway and forked way up at the crest of the hill, spilling off in two directions with limbs bearing town buildings, offices, and stores, branches off those limbs for houses, and, farther down the branches, neat cul-de-sacs like the one he and Amanda lived on.

No road in the town was barren. Each was bounded by white pine, beech, and hemlock, or maples, or birches, or oaks. Climbing into a curve now, he passed a meadow of red trillium. Farther on, he saw yellow trout lily, and beyond that, a dense stand of mountain laurel with its perfect white blossoms. A less-knowing passerby wouldn't have picked out the jack-in-the-pulpit with its maroon hood from the shade at the side of the road, but Graham did. Likewise, at a glance, he could differentiate maidenhair fern from oak fern or bracken, or lichen from moss.

These woods had them all. Graham took pride in that. His own hometown, where much of his family still lived, lay only fifty minutes to the east, but the two towns were worlds apart. That one was a working-class enclave filled with good folk who dreamed of living here. For Graham, the dream had come true.

At least, one part of it had. They were still working on the other part, and if the news was good today, he would be doubly thankful he lived here. When it came to hospitable environments in which to raise kids, Woodley took the cake.

The town center was nestled around the fork in the road at the top of the hill. The three streets intersecting at its core were lined with beech trees, wood benches, and storefronts that were as inviting in winter white as they were now in May. The smells were as rich as the populace—hot sticky buns from the bakery, a dark roast blend from the café, chocolate from fresh dipped fruit at the candy store. Give or take, there were a dozen small restaurants on side streets to serve an upscale population of fourteen thousand, but the food staple was on the main drag, a chic little eatery that served breakfast, lunch, and dinner at wrought-iron tables in a glassed-in patio in winter and an open one in summer. Several doors down, past an art gallery and an antiques store, a bookshop was stocked to the eaves, and what parent in his or her right mind would go elsewhere when this one employed a full-time storyteller for kids? There were boutique-type clothing stores scattered around, a drugstore whose owner cared enough about his clients to advise them when medications clashed, a hardware store, a camera shop, and—the latest—a tea café.

Some of the stores took up the two floors that the town fathers had decreed would be the height limit, but those second-floor spaces also housed lawyers, doctors, interior designers, and the like. Graham's office was over a housewares store that had sent more than one newcomer to Woodley his way.

He didn't stop at the office now. Nor did he stop at Woodley Misc, the general store, though an SUV pulled from a spot right in front. Not so long ago, he would have swung in and run inside to buy an Almond Joy for Amanda. Amanda loved Almond Joys.

This day, though, he didn't have the patience for chitchat, which was what one could count on getting at Woodley Misc. Besides, he was annoyed at Amanda for not calling, for not thinking about him for a change. He was annoyed at her for not being long since pregnant, period.

That thought stopped him cold. He knew it was unfair, but his mind didn't take it back, which left him feeling more than a little guilty.

It was with a deliberate effort that he propped his left elbow on the open window, draped his right wrist over the back of the passenger's seat, and made like all was well and that he was cool.

Amanda's numbness wore off during the drive home from school, and the enormity of the situation sank in. There would be no baby. Again. No baby. She felt empty, barren—frustrated, bewildered, sad.

She and Graham had been so cautious this time, not daring to get carried away. Still, they had talked of hanging a stocking on Christmas Eve for the baby about to be born, and of having something new to toast this New Year's Eve. They had talked about how much easier the O'Leary holiday bedlam would be if they were about to have a child of their own.

Pulling the tortoiseshell comb from her hair, she shook her head to spread out the curls and tried to relax with positive thoughts. She had plenty to be grateful for, plenty that others didn't have. For starters, she had a beautiful house on a charming wooded cul-de-sac in an upscale neighborhood—a perfect place for kids.

Only she didn't have the kids yet.

But she did have three neighbors, two of whom had become close friends. The third, Ben's young widow, kept to herself, but the others more than compensated with front-yard visits in spring, backyard cookouts in summer, leaf-raking parties in fall, and Sunday-night pizzas in winter. More important, there were countless woman-to-woman talks on the phone, on porch steps, or by the Cotters' pool.

She could use one of those talks now. Either woman would tell her how envious they were. Neither of them had the kind of career she did. Karen worked hard without benefit of either a paycheck or respect, and the trade-off for Georgia, who got a large paycheck indeed, was being out of town and away from her family several days a week.

Amanda wasn't paid a lot, but her career wasn't about money. She simply loved the work—and talk about convenience? The school was ten minutes from her home. If she had a baby, she could exchange her full-time position there for one as a consulting psychologist. She would have as large or small a caseload as she wanted, and could see students right at the house. The office over the garage had its own entrance. If she had kids, it would be perfect for that.

She even had a car for kids, an SUV that was *de rigueur* in Woodley. Granted, it was four years old and starting to show its age. In the past few months, they'd had to replace the fuel-injection system, the suspension, and the battery. They talked about getting a new car, but then month after month passed without her conceiving, and it seemed foolish.

The car purred happily enough now as she turned off the main road and drove through a gently winding stretch of wooded land. A final turn, and the cul-de-sac came into view.

Graham's truck was not in the driveway.

Not quite sure how she felt about that, she opened both front windows and, with the flow of warm air through the car, let the circle soothe her. With May just days old, the landscaping around the four houses was coming to life. The grass had greened up and just been cut, leaving horizontal swathes and a lingering scent. Huge oaks ringing the dead end had leafed out into a soft lime shade; paper birches with curling white bark were dripping with buds. The crocuses had come and gone, as had the forsythia blossoms, but patches of yellow daffodils remained, and tulips were starting to bloom. Clusters of lilacs stood tall and fat at each porch rail; though still a week shy of full bloom, they were budded enough to perfume the air.

Turning into her driveway, Amanda breathed it all in. Spring was her very favorite season. She had always loved the freshness, the cleanness, the sense of birth.

Sense of birth. Shifting into park, she stepped on the emergency brake and wondered why it always came back to that. Many people went through life without being parents. Some women she knew were actively choosing not to have kids, and they were perfectly satisfied with their lives. The thing was that she *did* want them, only it wasn't happening, and she didn't know why.

Was this her punishment for wanting a career of her own? For keeping her maiden name? For delaying parenthood? Yes, she would have had an easier time conceiving ten years before, but she hadn't been ready to have a baby at twenty-five. She hadn't even known Graham then. And he had been worth the wait. She still believed that.

Her mother believed otherwise. She believed that the genetic differences between them were simply too great for conception. Graham was tall, solid, and green-eyed; she was small, lean, and brown-eyed. He had straight dark hair; hers was curly and blond. He had seven siblings; she was a lonely only child. He was athletic; she was not.

As far as Amanda was concerned, her mother was a snob, and her theory was hogwash. But that didn't lessen the pain she felt now. They'd had such high hopes this time. Graham was going to be upset.

She should have called him. Cell phones, like e-mail, were less intimidating than having to say some things face-to-face. She might have broken the news that way. Shared the sorrow. Confessed to failure.

She could still do it. But her courage failed her.

Disheartened about that failing on top of the other, she gathered up her briefcase and had straightened when a movement in the rear-view mirror caught her eye. It was the widow, Gretchen Tannenwald, wandering along her newly edged flower beds. She had spent long hours the fall before putting in bulbs, working with her back to the neighbors, keeping to herself even when others were out and about. Attempts at friendliness on their part were met with the briefest possible response. Even Amanda, who was supposedly good at it, had made a try or two, but Gretchen was no talker. Hard to believe that she had been married to the ever-genial Ben.

Then again, not hard to believe at all. Gretchen was barely half Ben's age and the total antithesis of June, but he had needed a drastic change to pull him from his grief.

The neighborhood men were sympathetic. "You can see she idolizes him," said Russ Lange, the romantic. "Any man would love that."

Leland Cotter, the dot-com chief, was more blunt. "What's not to love? She's a looker."

Graham suggested that Ben loved her energy. "She has him traveling and hiking and playing tennis. He and June led a quieter life. Gretchen opens new doors."

The neighborhood women were less generous. As far as they were concerned, the Tannenwald marriage was about two things: sex for Ben and money for Gretchen.

Of course, that didn't explain why Gretchen was hanging around without Ben. Amanda had thought she would sell the house, take the money, and run. But here she was, wearing a short, swingy dress that made her look even younger than thirty-two.

Actually, Amanda decided with a start, the dress made her look pregnant.

Unsettled by that, she twisted around to look out the rear window. It was a minute before the light caught Gretchen's body in profile again, and there it was, something that did indeed look like a belly—

which was a curious prospect. Ben had been gone a year, too long to be part of it, and Gretchen had been a virtual shut-in since his death. She didn't date; surely they would have noticed. To Amanda's knowledge, the only men who had been in the house for any period of time were the plumber, the carpenter, and the electrician—and, on one mission or another, Russ Lange, Lee Cotter, and Graham O'Leary.

Chapter Two

Amanda was twisted around, looking out the back window of her car, when Graham's green pickup came into view. Heart leaping, she forgot about Gretchen and climbed from the car.

He drove typically loose, with one hand on the steering wheel, the other out the window. When she had first met him, the car had been a Mustang convertible, and he had looked so cool with the wind in his hair that she had fallen hard for that, too. Watching him now, she felt a glimmer of the old excitement, the old yearning. Then she remembered what it was that she had to say.

He slowed as he approached and raised his left hand in greeting to Gretchen, who turned briefly. Then he pulled into the driveway beside Amanda.

Leaving her car door open, she walked around to his truck. His eyes held hers the whole way, asking, then knowing. Visibly deflated, he sank against the back of the seat.

"You got your period."

She was grateful not to have to say the damning words herself. "Half an hour ago."

"Are you sure? Maybe it's just spotting."

She shook her head. What was going on wasn't spotting. Besides, the cramps in her belly had a familiar feel.

"Maybe you should try a test."

"I'd have to miss my period for a test to work."

He hung his head. Then he dropped it back, sighed wearily, and opened the door of the truck. Eyes filling with tears, Amanda turned away and went for her things. By the time she had closed the car door and gone up the flagstone walk to the breezeway between the house and garage, Graham was already there, slouched against a pillar, looking out at the backyard. He hadn't only designed the landscape here, he had done the planting himself, right down to the very last shrub, and the care showed. Even this early in the season, the yard was a dozen different shades of green.

Their yard was the envy of the neighbors—actually the envy of the whole town—but Amanda suspected he saw none of it now. His voice held defeat. "I thought it would take this time. I thought for sure it would."

Amanda leaned against another of the pillars. "So did I. So did the doctor. We had the timing down pat."

"What is the *problem?*" he asked in frustration.

Clenching her arms to her chest, she said, "I don't know. There were eight eggs. That's two more than last month. It's seven more than most women produce." Her own frustration caught up with her. "I'd have thought at least one of the eight would be fertilized. My God, it's our turn."

Still staring at the yard, Graham muttered a bleak, "Seems like our turn came and went." His head came around, beautiful green eyes challenging. "What's not working?"

Amanda was heartsick. She hated their being adversaries. She needed Graham with her in this. "I don't know, Gray. *They* don't know. As many as fifteen percent of infertility problems are unexplained. You've heard Emily."

"Yeah, and she says that as many as sixty percent of those couples will conceive on their own within three years, so what's our problem?"

Amanda didn't know. "I'm doing everything they tell me. You see me taking my temperature, keeping my charts, taking my Clomid. I even had an ultrasound this time to make sure we did the insemination on just the right day."

"Then why aren't you pregnant?"

She told herself that he was upset with the situation, not with her. Still, she felt she was being attacked. "I don't *know.*"

"We waited too long," he decided. "You were thirty when we got married. We should have started right away."

"And a year would have made the difference? Come on, Graham. That's unfair."

"The older you get, the harder it is. They've told us that."

"Uh-huh, a million times. What they *said,* to be exact, was that fertility rates drop dramatically at thirty, then again at thirty-five, and again at forty, so since we got married when I was thirty, maybe it was already too late. And if we're making accusations, I want to know why *you* waited so long. Where were you when I was twenty-three?"

"I was in the Pacific Northwest learning my trade."

It was an evasive answer. She knew about those years and pressed on, having a dire need to share the blame.

"You were on the rebound from Megan. You were twenty-nine and playing the field. You didn't want to be tied down. You were off climbing mountains and rushing rapids, having a grand old time with your buddies. Sure, it would have been better if we'd started earlier, but if you and I had met back then, you wouldn't have been interested in getting married, much less having a baby."

He didn't reply at first. Her argument seemed to have calmed him a little, which was reassuring. One of the first things she had loved about Graham—after the way he looked in that Mustang—was his ability to be reasonable. He could listen and hear. For someone in her profession, that was a must in a mate.

Reasonably indeed, he said, "We don't know what would have been if we'd met back then."

"Exactly." She rubbed a burning spot between her breasts, a pain that, were she more of a romantic, she might think was a crack in her heart. "So please don't say it's all my fault. This hasn't been easy for me. There are times when I feel like I'm doing all the work and you're the one who wants the baby."

"Whoa." He held up a hand. "Are you saying you don't want one?"

"You know I do. I want a baby more than anything, but you were the one who was up for it from the day we were married, and I understand that." How could she not? Graham had grown up thirty miles away. Most of his family still lived in the same town. They got together often. "You have seven siblings, who now have twenty-seven children between them."

"I love children," he said.

"So do I, but I'm not a brood mare."

"Obviously," he remarked, and suddenly the space between them felt like a chasm.

"What does that mean?" she cried, and, to his credit, he gentled.

Bowing his head, he rubbed the back of his neck. His eyes were tired when they met hers again. "This is going nowhere. I don't want us to fight."

Neither did Amanda. She hated that chasm, hated feeling alone. She hated the pressure she felt and the toll it was taking. Mostly, she hated feeling like she was wholly responsible for their failure to conceive. She hated feeling that this was her fault, her problem, her body gone bad.

Close to tears again, she waited a minute before speaking. But the tears remained, and her thoughts spilled out. "I just need you to understand what I'm feeling. I'm doing everything I can, everything Emily tells me to do. So maybe she's the problem—"

"No no no." That fast, Graham was fired up again. "This is doctor number four. We agreed we liked her."

"We do, but she isn't the one producing eight eggs, and she doesn't know why all those sperm of yours can't fertilize a single one."

He seemed taken aback. "It isn't my fault."

"I know, but this is hard for me, Gray. It's hard emotionally, because my hopes soar and plummet, soar and plummet. It's hard physically, because the medication makes my breasts sore and bloats my stomach and makes me sweat—and don't say I'd have the same symptoms if I were pregnant, because if I were pregnant, I wouldn't mind. This is even hard professionally. Half of my referrals lately seem to be pregnant teenagers."

Putting his back to the column and his hands in the pockets of his jeans, Graham stretched out his long legs and snorted. "*There's* an irony. They have sex once and—voom—instant baby. We've been trying for four years."

"Irony" was one word for it. Amanda could think of others, like "unfairness," even "cruelty." And while she was on the topic of everyone else having babies but her, she said, "Gretchen's pregnant."

He didn't seem to hear at first, lost in what well might have been self-pity—which, Lord knew, she was feeling enough of herself. After a minute, though, he looked up, startled. "*Ben's* Gretchen?"

"I saw her in the garden just now." Amanda saw the image again, clear as day. "She's pregnant."

Graham made a dismissive face. "I saw her, too. She's not pregnant."

"You didn't see her in the right light. It had to hit her a certain way."

He sighed, closed his eyes, rolled his head on his neck. "Come on, Mandy. We've talked about this before. You see pregnant women where there aren't any."

"No, I don't. Now that it's spring, coats are coming off, and those pregnant bellies are real. I see them in the supermarket, I see them at the mall. I see them at the drugstore, the library, the school." She heard her voice growing higher, but couldn't hold it down. "I swear there are times lately when I wonder what God wants. Is He sending us a message? Is He saying this wasn't meant to be?"

What she wanted, of course, was for Graham to deny it quickly and vehemently.

But he didn't. He just eyed her warily. "What wasn't meant to be? Us?"

She felt the same fear then that she had felt lying in that clinic room the last time. She was losing Graham. Life was pulling them apart. "Babies are supposed to be made by love. They're supposed to be made in the privacy of a bedroom. What we're doing is a mockery of that. The most precious part of our lives is a mess of doctors' appointments, pills, charts, and timing. It's taking a toll on us, Graham. We aren't . . . *fun* anymore."

She was in tears now, physically shaky and feeling so isolated that Graham wouldn't have been Graham if he hadn't been touched. Coming close, he took her in his arms and held her, and for a minute, enveloped by his arms, his earthy scent, his solidity, she remembered what they'd had. She wanted it back. Wanted it *back.*

Too soon, he released her. Facing the yard again, he once more slid his hands in his pockets. "About Gretchen?" he said. "You're wrong. It was a trick of the light. She isn't pregnant. Her husband's dead."

Amanda wiped tears from her cheeks. "It isn't always the husband who fathers the child."

Graham turned to her. "Are you talking about us, or her?"

"Her. *Her.*"

"So if she's pregnant, who's the father?"

"I don't know. But I know what I saw." Needing to be right about this—more, needing to escape what was happening between Graham and her—she went down the back stairs and onto the flagstone path.

Graham's voice followed her. "Did you call the doctor?"

"Tomorrow."

"Do we try it again?" he called.

She called back without missing a step, "I don't know."

"Where are you going?" he shouted, sounding annoyed now.

"Next door," she shouted back. "I'm asking Russ about Gretchen. He's around during the day. He'll know if she has a guy."

Leaving the flagstones, Amanda crossed a carpet of grass, slipped between bristly arms of junipers and yews, then cut through the pine grove that separated the Langes' house from hers. The scent of moist earth and pine sap, so strong here, was a natural sedative. Or maybe it was the physical movement—or the distance from home—that eased the ache in her belly. Whatever, she was calmer by the time she reached her neighbors' back steps.

She started up, stepping quickly aside when the door flew open. Allison Lange, newly fourteen, passed her in a blur of long dark hair and gangly limbs.

"Sorry," the girl said with a breathless laugh.

Amanda caught the door in her wake. "Everything okay?"

Already down the steps, Allison jogged backward across the lawn. "Fine, but I can't talk now. Jordie needs algebra help." Turning, she ran off into the Cotters' yard.

Jordie Cotter was Karen and Lee's oldest son. He and Allison had been best friends since grade school. They were freshmen in high school now, and though Allison was a year younger, an inch taller, and more academically inclined than Jordie, they were as close as ever.

Amanda loved Allison, who was warm and decidedly open for a girl her age. Jordie was a tougher nut to crack.

"I'd greet you at the door," Russell Lange called from inside the kitchen, "but this sauce needs stirring." Russ, a tall, lanky guy with auburn hair that was rumpled, if sparse, was at the stove, his small, round, rimless glasses perched halfway down his nose. He wore an apron over his T-shirt and shorts, and nothing at all on his feet, which was largely how he went about his day, regardless of the temperature outside. He liked to say that living barefoot was a major perk of being a househusband, but Amanda had always suspected that he simply hated caging his feet, which were huge.

Russ was a journalist. The better part of his income came as a book reviewer, but his joy was writing a weekly column on parenting. His wife, Georgia, was the CEO of her own company, an operation that required she be on the road several days a week. That made Russ the children's major caretaker. From what Amanda had observed, he had become a commendable parent. He had also become a marvelous cook.

"Something smells wonderful," she remarked.

"It's veal marsala, light on the vino given the presence of these two kiddos, though I think I just lost the girl."

Eleven-year-old Tommy, who had the same thick black hair as his mother and his sister, put in his two bits from the table, where he was doing homework. "Allie said if you added more wine she'd be back."

Amanda squeezed the boy's shoulder. "What do you know about wine?"

"Just that Allie likes to drink it."

"And where does she do that?"

"Right here," Tommy said with an innocent look. "She sips from Mom's glass."

"How is your mom?"

"She's cool. She'll call later."

Amanda amended the question. "*Where* is your mom?"

"San Antonio. She'll be back tomorrow." The boy slipped from his chair. "I have to go in the other room, Dad."

Russ aimed his long wooden spoon toward the den. "If it's to chat on-line with Trevor and John, forget it."

"It's to pee."

"Ah." Russ shot Amanda a dry look. "I asked for that. Okay, pal. But come right back. You need to finish your essay." He watched until the boy disappeared. Stirring his sauce again, he gave Amanda a questioning smile. "How are you?"

"I've been better." She went to his side and peered into the saucepan. What simmered there looked every bit as wonderful as the veal that waited, lightly browned, in a pan on the next burner, and suddenly she felt guilty about this, too. She never cooked anything fancy. Graham was a meat-and-potatoes kind of guy, an easily pleased, grilled-whatever kind of guy. When they ate at home, they cooked together, but they went out as often as not.

This night she wasn't sure she could eat at all. "I need your help. Gray and I are having an argument. I say Gretchen's pregnant. He says no. What do you say?"

She would have sworn Russ went red. Then it occurred to her that it was heat from the stove.

"Pregnant?" he echoed. "Wow. I don't know anything about that."

"You haven't noticed her shape?"

His color deepened. No cooking heat this time. His glasses weren't steamed in the least. "Her shape?"

Of *course* he had noticed her shape. He, Graham, and Lee were *abundantly* aware of her shape. "Her stomach?" Amanda prodded. "You haven't seen the change?"

"No. I haven't noticed anything." But he didn't tell her she was imagining things. "Pregnant? How could that happen?"

Amanda would have laughed had her life been different. "The normal way, I assume. I told Gray you'd have seen if someone had been coming around to visit."

Russ stirred diligently. "Not me. I'm glued to my computer all day."

"Wouldn't you notice if a car came down the street?"

"I used to, but the parade got boring—mailman, exterminator, UPS guy. I don't bother looking anymore." He chewed on the inside of his cheek, pondering something.

"What?"

"Just thinking about Ben. He'd have loved fathering a child at his age."

Amanda suspected that men loved fathering children at *any* age. It was a sign of virility. She wondered how much that bothered Graham.

"Ben's kids wouldn't have liked it much," she said. "They had enough trouble accepting Gretchen. A baby would pour salt on the wound. But this can't be Ben's. The timing's wrong."

"Are you sure she's pregnant?"

"She sure looked it."

"How far along?"

"Five months, maybe six." Amanda paused. "Just a guess. I'm not exactly an expert."

Russ was silent. Softly then, he asked, "Anything doing with you?"

Amanda studied his sauce. "No. Maybe I need cooking lessons. I've never made anything like this. Maybe cooking is the key to fertility."

"Home and hearth?"

"Mm." She went to the door. She was suddenly feeling guilty about having walked out on Graham. He was suffering, too.

"I could run over and ask Gretchen," Russ offered. "Maybe I'll do that after the kids are fed and settled in. I haven't talked with her in a while. You don't see people in winter the way you do in summer, and summer was eight months ago. Besides, I'm always inside working, then taking care of the kids, and romancing my wife when she stops in at home." The phone rang. "It'd be really interesting if Gretchen's pregnant."

Having mixed feelings about that, Amanda went out the door but had barely reached the bottom step when Russ stuck his head out. "That was Graham. He wants you home. You have an emergency call."

She nodded, setting off just as Karen Cotter came across the grass carrying a foil-covered tray.

Karen was of average height and weight, a woman who rarely bothered with makeup and routinely used headbands to keep her brown hair off her face. On all physical counts, she was more neutral than bright, but that had been secondary once. When Amanda had first met her, what she had lacked in appearance, she had more than made up for in energy. Back then, she rode the perpetual high of a busy life, buoyed by running yet another of a series of successful charity events—and still she'd had time for the occasional night out with Georgia and Amanda. They hadn't done that in a while, and through no lack of interest on either of the other women's parts. On each proposed evening, Karen either had a meeting, a sick child, or a headache. Lately, all that remained of her smiles were lines that left her looking tired and tense.

"There's a bake sale at the school tomorrow," she explained now. "I told Russ I'd save him the worry and make extra cookies for Tommy to take in."

"You're a good soul," Amanda said in what was probably the understatement of the year. Karen was the designated driver of the parent community, as well as perennial room mother, yard sale chairman, art-day coordinator, PTO head. What with handling all that, plus four children between the ages of fifteen and six, she worked as hard as any woman Amanda knew. Amanda looked up to her for that. She hoped that as a mother she would have half the stamina Karen had—or used to have.

"How are the kids?" Amanda asked.

"The twins' asthma is kicking up because of the pollen, but otherwise we're fine. How are you?"

"Not bad."

Karen raised her brows, inviting news.

Amanda shook her head. "It didn't take."

"Oh, Mandy. I'm sorry."

"Me, too. Getting pregnant is so easy for some people. Speaking of which, have you talked with Gretchen?"

"Talked? Not quite. We wave when we pass. That's about it."

"I think she's pregnant."

Karen recoiled. "Pregnant? Oh, no, I don't think so. She can't be pregnant. She isn't seeing anyone. She doesn't *go* anywhere. She's still mourning Ben." Her voice went lower. "What makes you think she's pregnant?"

"I saw her earlier, and she looked it. She's always

had great breasts, but her stomach used to be flat."

"Yeah. Like a model. Lee tells me not to compare myself to her, but how not to? Our men drool when they look over there. They fall over themselves volunteering to help her with chores. Is that because she's a riveting conversationalist?" Slowly she shook her head. "I don't think so." She looked suddenly worried. "I've never seen a car there overnight, but someone might have parked in the garage."

Possibly, Amanda reasoned. "But wouldn't one of us have noticed a car coming or going?"

"Maybe not. Maybe he parks elsewhere and sneaks in." Looking a bit pale, Karen insisted, "Gretchen can't be pregnant. She really can't be."

"Mandy," Graham hollered across both yards.

"Emergency call," Amanda explained and gave Karen a quick hug. Her heart went out to this woman who was so unappreciated by those she catered to most—her husband, Lee, being the major offender.

But Karen insisted that he had his good points, and Amanda could do nothing but give her support. Just then, though, a hug was all she could spare. Graham sounded impatient.

She would have jogged home if her stomach hadn't been cramping again. She didn't often get calls at night, though between the tension of upcoming exams and end-of-the-year transition issues, the time was ripe for it. And then there were the usual family traumas—domestic violence, parental separation, even death. Affluence didn't exempt Woodley from those. If anything, their presence in such a privileged population was all the more stark.

She went up her back steps and into the kitchen; Graham was leaning against the counter, not far from the phone. The look on his face said that he hadn't appreciated her running out on their conversation—at least, that was the reading her guilty conscience gave it. He seemed upset. He was uncharacteristically idle, as if he didn't know what to do with himself. She would swear he had been standing in the same spot the whole time she was gone, grappling with their problem, waiting to continue the discussion.

"So is she?" he asked.

It was a minute before Amanda followed. She had been thinking of her own pregnancy, not Gretchen's. But Gretchen was indeed where they'd left off.

"No one knows for sure," she said and glanced at the slip of paper in his hand.

He held it out. "It was Maggie Dodd."

Maggie was the vice principal of the school, but the number on the paper was for the office of the principal himself. Lifting the phone, Amanda punched it in. After barely a ring on the other end, a male voice said a low, "Fred Edlin."

"Fred, it's Amanda Carr. Maggie just called."

"Here she is. I'll let her explain."

Maggie came on the line. "I hate interrupting your evening, Amanda, but we have a problem here. There was an incident at baseball practice this afternoon. Quinn Davis was involved."

Amanda's insides twisted—guilt telling her she should have more actively followed up on his e-mail, sought him out, stayed longer at school.

"Quinn Davis?" she repeated for Graham's benefit. He would know the name. Hard not to, living in a town whose weekly paper loved a hero, and Quinn was currently that. It helped that his family was so visible. One Davis or another was mentioned in the paper each week.

"He and a little group of friends showed up at practice drunk," Maggie said.

Amanda let out a breath. "Oh no."

"Oh yes. The coach marched them right over here. I'd have called you sooner, only it was a while before we reached Quinn's parents. They were at the statehouse canvassing for wetlands regulations and weren't pleased to have been called back. They're in the other room arguing with the coach and Fred about what the punishment should be. We need your input. His parents want the thing hushed up. They say that their son does too much for the school to allow him to be used as an example. The problem is that the whole team saw him drunk. If there's no punishment, what message does that send to the others?"

Amanda knew what message it sent. She didn't want to give that message to them, any more than she wanted to give it to Quinn. He had to be responsible for his actions, all the more so for the exalted position he was in.

That said, she had to wonder why he had contacted her that day—had to wonder what was going on with him that he would drink after school.

"Have the others been punished?" she asked.

While Maggie gave her the peripheral information, Amanda held Graham's gaze. He was struggling to be patient, but barely succeeding. Many times he had indulged her in student emergencies; this wasn't one. His eyes were ink green and intense, demanding equal time. The conflict was tugging at her. There was a crisis right here in this house that needed tending. He wanted her to deal with their own problem first.

But she had her period. No amount of "dealing" would change that, and she didn't know where to go from here. She hated what the medication was doing to her, hated living life on a closely timed schedule, hated the agony of the wait each month. She hated going to the clinic and feeling like a machine that wasn't working right, hated feeling like a failure yet again. She was sick of the whole thing. She wasn't ready to think about the next step.

She needed to feel useful. Working with Quinn and his parents would give her that. Besides, given the notes he had sent, she wanted to see the boy. His being with his parents was all the better.

"I'll come down," she told Maggie.

Graham set his jaw and looked away. When Amanda hung up the phone, he looked back with clear reproach.

Wanting him to understand, she filled him in on the immediate situation. "The other boys were suspended from the team for the season. Quinn's parents don't want him missing one game, much less six. My worry is why. They may be taking a stand for reasons that have nothing to do with Quinn."

"They're his parents," Graham argued. "They should be able to take whatever stand they want."

"True, but someone has to take the stand that's best for the boy."

"Can't Maggie do that?"

"They need an arbiter."

"Do you know what's best for him?"

"No. I can't know until I get there and hear more."

"Those are powerful parents. They've spearheaded drives that have run teachers out of town. We've both read those stories. Edlin and Dodd may be using you as the bad guy. You're putting yourself in an untenable situation."

"But what choice do I *have,* Gray? Quinn's the important thing here."

"Tonight? Right now? Can't it wait until morning?"

"They want it settled now. The parents don't want rumors floating around."

"What about us?"

"I won't be long."

He shot her a doubting look.

"I won't," she insisted, reaching for her purse. Confiding in Graham as she often did, if for no other reason than that he would know to get her quickly if one of her clients called the house, she added, "Something's up with Quinn. He was trying to reach me this morning, but we missed each other. I need to see if I can help him now."

"He's a strong kid. My Lord, look at all he does."

"Maybe the image is weighing heavy. He also has two superstar older brothers in whose footsteps he has to follow, and parents with egos the size of Texas. I've met those two. They're tough. We don't know, Gray. It could be that life at home is a nightmare for that boy."

"And you know how that is."

"I do," Amanda conceded, choosing to believe that he wasn't mocking her. "My situation was different. I was caught in the crossfire. Right now, Quinn *is* the crossfire. He's his parents' current cause. That isn't fair."

"Lots of things aren't fair," Graham muttered, turning away again, and suddenly she did want to talk about it. She wanted to talk about what was fair and who deserved what, what it took to be a good parent, and the fact that she and Gray would be the best parents ever. She wanted to talk about the things that could ruin relationships and how to nip them in the bud. She wanted to talk about dreams that seemed to be going up in smoke.

But she didn't have the strength. It used to be that talking with Graham was as easy as breathing. Now it involved greater thought and heart. It also involved greater time than she had just then, what with a student in need.

"I won't be long," she repeated and went out the door.

Chapter Three

Amanda had barely driven away when Karen walked out the back door of her own pretty Victorian, this one white with gray trim. She held another foil-covered plate of cookies, but not for the bake sale at school. This batch was for the widow, and while a peace offering would have been in order, it wasn't that, either. It was a bribe.

Karen wanted information. She had to know if the widow was pregnant, and, if so, by whom.

Russ claimed ignorance. Karen had grilled him, but, if he knew anything, he hadn't cracked. He maintained that Amanda's mention of Gretchen's pregnancy was the first he had heard of it, and that even if it was so, out of respect for Ben he wouldn't begin to speculate on the identity of the father. His response was a cop-out if ever there was one, which made Karen fear that his refusal to speculate had less to do with the dear departed Ben than with Russ's friendship with Graham and Lee. Of course, he would protect them. It was a male thing.

Gretchen Tannenwald's Victorian, very similar in design to the other three houses on the cul-de-sac, was pale blue with white trim. It had the same wraparound porch as the others, the same gaslights, the same dormers and eaves. Unlike the others, Gretchen's had a widow's walk at the top. Karen, Amanda, and Georgia had occasionally wondered about the significance of that. Ben and June used to go up there. After June died, Ben had gone there alone from time to time. It struck the others as a quiet, contemplative place. The fact that they had never seen Gretchen there, with or without Ben, was another strike against the woman.

The house was the fourth and last circling the cul-de-sac, which made Gretchen the Cotters' immediate neighbor. It took no time for Karen to cross from one yard to the next and hook onto the bluestones that led to the back door. She climbed the steps and knocked, thinking of the many talks she'd had with June on this porch. June had been a mother figure for the three other women. She was dead three years now. Karen missed her.

When no one answered, she rang the bell, then shaded her eyes and peered through the mullioned glass. While June's kitchen had a country feel, with patterns and prints and grandchildren's drawings, Gretchen's was stainless steel and sleek. The same was true of Gretchen herself, as far as Karen was concerned. She was cool, state-of-the-art chic, and standoffish.

Karen was about to ring the bell again when Gretchen appeared. She was wearing leggings, a loose man's shirt that was spattered with paint, and a look that became guarded when she saw who was at her door. The two women had never been exactly close.

Crossing the kitchen without hurry, she opened the door.

Karen extended the dish. "Double chocolate chip cookies. To celebrate the coming of May."

Gretchen gave the dish a cautious look. In a voice that was quiet and as wary as everything else about her, she said, "That's nice." *Why now, why you, why at all?* she might have said.

Feeling fraudulent, Karen shrugged. "I had to make batches for the bake sale at school and I overbought ingredients, so I made extras for Russ's kids, and extras for *my* kids, and then there was still chocolate left over, and it seemed silly to save it, so I just kept going."

"Ah," Gretchen said, though she sounded far from convinced.

Karen gave the dish a little nudge. "You'd be doing me a favor by taking them. I have more than I know what to do with. If they stay in my house, I'll eat as many as the kids, and they'll go straight to my hips. You aren't on a diet or anything, are you? You're so slim." It was the perfect excuse to glance at the widow's middle, which Karen promptly did, but the shirt gave nothing away.

Gretchen took the plate. "I've never had to diet. I'm lucky, I guess."

"I'm envious. You name it, I've done it—Atkins, Pritikin, Weight Watchers, Jenny Craig. It's not that I've ever been *fat,* just that I'd always look better if I could just lose ten pounds, if you know what I mean. Do you work out?"

Gretchen shook her head.

"I suppose you don't have to. You're naturally athletic. You kept Ben going. I really do miss Ben."

The phone rang. Gretchen said a quiet, "Excuse me," and went to answer it.

Karen kept an eye on her stomach, but if anything was there, the shirt hid it.

Gretchen said hello, paused, said it again, then hung up the phone.

"Solicitation?" Karen asked. "Boy, this is the hour. Sit down to dinner and *rrrrring*, there they are. If it weren't for the fact that Jordie's always getting calls, I'd put on a recording warning solicitors off. You could do that."

"It wasn't a solicitor," Gretchen said. "No one spoke."

"That can be just as bad. Does it happen often?"

Gretchen thought a minute, shook her head, and turned to put the cookies on the counter. Only then did the shirt brush close enough to her body to tell tales.

"Oh my," Karen murmured, raising her eyes a second too late.

To her credit, Gretchen didn't deny it. Rather, she put a hand on her belly. If there had been any doubt left, it was gone then. The bulge was unmistakable.

Still, Karen said, "Are you . . . ?"

Gretchen nodded.

"How far along?"

"Seven months."

"Seven." Karen scrambled to do the figuring. If this was May, seven months would put conception in November. No, October. "You don't look seven months pregnant." October would mean that the culprit could as easily be Graham as Lee. Graham had redone the landscaping for Gretchen last fall, and had spent a fair

share of time inside with her reviewing the plans. October would also mean that Russ had to be a suspect. By October, his wife would have been at work, the kids back at school, and no one other than Karen around to see what he did. But for Karen, October had been a hellish month, crammed with new-school-season events that kept her away from home much of the day.

"Is not looking it good or bad?" Gretchen asked.

"Good. Definitely good. It means less worry afterward. Not that you'd have any worry at all. Pregnant. Wow." She paused, giving Gretchen time to remark about the father. When she said nothing, Karen gestured at the paint-spattered shirt. "You're decorating a nursery."

"Uh-huh."

"Navy and yellow?"

Gretchen nodded.

"That's nice. You can do it the first time around, with no other little ones tugging at you. I loved being pregnant with my first. It was harder after that, especially the last time. Lee wasn't good about taking the three boys off to do things, so I had to juggle their schedules around a huge belly. You get bigger with each child. The muscles lose their tone. But I do love having my girl. I don't care what they say, there's a difference. Genetically. Uh, do you know what it is? Boy or girl?"

Gretchen shook her head.

"I guess you wouldn't," Karen reasoned. "They don't start talking about amniocentesis until a woman is thirty-five. You're still young. They wouldn't do an amnio unless there's cause for worry, like the possibility of passing on a congenital disease that runs in your family or in the family of the baby's father." Again, she paused. Gretchen remained quiet. "Was this . . ."—she searched for the word with studied nonchalance—"uh . . . planned?"

"No. Definitely not."

Well, that was something, Karen reflected, though it didn't tell her what she needed to know. "But you want the baby."

"Oh, yes."

Karen smiled. "So, what do you think Ben would say?"

"He'd be pleased. He knew I wanted a child."

"And the baby's father?" There it was. Finally out. Totally natural. Totally appropriate.

Gretchen let the question hang, arching her brows as if to ask, *What about the baby's father?*

"Is he pleased?" Karen prompted.

"He doesn't know."

Oh Lord. "Will you tell him?"

"I'm not sure."

"Don't you think he ought to know?"

"No. He has other obligations."

Karen didn't like the sound of that. It fell too close to home. "And here we all thought you were sleeping alone," she teased.

Gretchen didn't crack a smile. "I am," she said with quiet finality.

Not knowing what to say to that, Karen simply added, "Well, enjoy the cookies." With a backhanded wave, she left.

But she didn't head home. She strode straight through her own yard to Russ's, thinking as she did that Gretchen was the most unfriendly neighbor she'd ever had, that neighbors didn't answer kind gestures with monosyllabic answers, that the woman had to be guilty of something.

Concerned that the something had to do with her own husband, Karen walked right into the Langes' kitchen and started in on Russ, who fortunately was alone there.

"She's seven months pregnant. She just told me so."

"Seven?" he asked, turning from the sink where he was washing dishes. "Whew. We've been kept in the dark."

"We still are. She wouldn't say who the father is. Wouldn't give a hint. You had to have seen something, Russ. You're here more than any of the rest of us. You have to know something."

Russ raised soapy hands in denial, distancing himself from the fray. "Not me."

"Not you being the father?"

"Not me knowing anything." He pushed up his glasses with the back of his wrist, returned his hands to the water, and scrubbed a pan. "I don't watch. I don't see cars out there. Really I don't, Karen. I have better things to do with my time. Besides, it didn't have to happen here. She goes out."

"Not for long."

"It doesn't take long."

Karen wasn't buying it. "Graham was working with her all fall. He was in her house a lot."

"Graham loves Amanda. You're barking up the wrong tree."

"But they're having trouble. You know, the infertility stuff. Things are tense."

"Not that tense."

"Then Lee," Karen said with her heart in her throat. When Russ shot her a fast look, she lowered her voice.

"You know about that little dental hygienist he was playing with last year, and you know that I know about her. His latest playmate could be Gretchen."

"I don't think so."

"But you don't know for sure."

"I haven't asked him, if that's what you mean." He unstoppered the sink. Soapy water swirled away. "Last I heard, the hygienist was ancient history. He swore he was a reformed man." He ran water to rinse. "Besides, he wouldn't fool around with the woman next door, not right under our eyes."

"Why not? His hygienist worked on my teeth, too."

"You know what I mean, Karen."

"Then if it isn't one of you three guys, who is it?"

"Beats me."

"You have to have some idea," Karen pleaded. She wanted to know that it wasn't Lee. She didn't really care who it was, as long as it wasn't her husband.

Russ looked at her then. "Did you ask her directly?"

"I couldn't. She wasn't very friendly. I brought her cookies. She didn't even thank me."

"She was probably shocked that you'd visit at all. You ladies haven't been very friendly toward her."

"We've been fine."

"Fine isn't friendly."

"Gretchen isn't June."

"So you all keep reminding her."

"We've never said that."

"Not in words."

Karen pinched the bridge of her nose. It wasn't just that Gretchen wasn't June. It was that she was thirty-two to Karen's forty-three, and beautiful to Karen's mousy. Gretchen was the kind of woman that men went for, especially men in their upper forties who didn't want to *be* in their upper forties. Lee was forty-seven. And he had a history of fooling around.

Suddenly weary, she let her hand drop. "Well. No use standing here. You won't tell."

"I don't *know,*" Russ insisted.

Karen didn't believe him for a minute, but she knew better than to try to milk a stone. She had dinner in the oven. It would be done soon, and the kids would be hungry. Lee might even be home in time to join them.

Walking back to her own house, she half hoped that he would phone with another of the lame excuses he used—that he was waiting for a call, or was needed in a meeting, or obligated to take his A-team of programmers to dinner because they had just met deadline on a job. Let him give her a line. She welcomed an opportunity to confront him.

Lee was a computer genius. At least, Karen assumed he was a genius, since his company was doing well, but whether the success was due to his own brains or the brains of the people he hired, she didn't know. She wasn't into computers, and he discouraged her from using them. He said that if she got involved, they would become a boring couple. He said that he lived and breathed computers at work and didn't want to talk business at home.

In her most suspicious moments, she wondered if he was hiding something, wondered what she would find if she could turn on the computer in his den and read his e-mail. In her most guilty moments, though, she hated herself for thinking that way. He was her husband. They had been married for seventeen years. When she had confronted him about the hygienist and threatened to leave, he had broken down in tears and sworn that it was over, that he loved her, Karen, and that he would be faithful.

But the hygienist wasn't the first. He had sworn that before and broken his word. Karen didn't know what to believe anymore.

Letting herself in the back door, she found her kitchen empty of all but a neatly set table and the smell of a meaty lasagna. By the time she had fixed a salad, her daughter, Julie—six years old and her little helper—was at her elbow. Karen sliced bread; Julie put the slices in a basket, then, standing on tiptoe, put the basket in the microwave oven.

The twins, Jared and Jon, appeared moments later. They were eight and had identically tousled hair and allergy-stuffed noses that gave their voices a nasal quality. That said, she might not have caught what they said even if their voices had been clear. They had a way of talking to each other that was unintelligible to others. It wasn't a different language, exactly, just a kind of run-on murmur. They had been communicating with each other that way since they were old enough to talk. A tight twosome everywhere they went, they were as self-reliant as eight-year-olds could be. Though Karen drove them places, cooked their food, cleaned their rooms, and bought their clothes, they made her feel superfluous. That was one of the reasons she cherished Julie. Julie needed her. Julie adored her.

The three younger children were barely seated when Jordie came in. Again—still—Karen was startled when she looked at him. At fifteen, he was finally shooting up, seeming suddenly to be making up for lost time. He was now taller than she was. Between that and the change that puberty had made in his features, he was starting to look so much like a man—like Lee, actually—that Karen never failed to be jarred. Then again, the jarring was likely because he was in his usual rush, reaching for bread and digging into his lasagna as though he was late. No doubt he had evening plans.

She was losing him. It was so clear to her that he wanted to be anywhere but here, doing things that she couldn't see, and it made her nervous.

But she couldn't make him stay home. Boys his age needed to be with their peers. That didn't mean she was comfortable with how much he was gone from the house, however.

She asked about his day. He mumbled an answer between mouthfuls. She teased him about sounding like the twins, who protested in a way that was perfectly articulate because they chose it to be. When they lapsed into murmurs, she returned to Jordie, but she had barely gotten out a question about baseball practice when Julie howled. She had touched the hot lasagna pan and burned her finger. Karen rushed her to the sink, held the finger under cold water, gave her an ice cube to hold, and guided her back to her chair. By then, Jordie was wolfing down seconds.

She told him to slow down. He said that the guys were already at Sean's house. She asked what they were up to. He said they were listening to a new CD. She asked if he had finished his homework, and he said he would finish it there. She said she wanted him home by ten, and, with a look of dismay, he asked her why. When she said it was a school night, he said he never went to bed before midnight, so why did he have to be home so early. He insisted that Sean's parents would be there, that no one was leaving to go anywhere else, and that he *hated* that she didn't trust him.

Then Lee walked in, all sandy-haired and handsome, long-legged and oh so smooth, and with a genial smile asked what the argument was about.

Annoyed at her husband for being late without a call, for giving her cause to wonder where he was all the time and then showing up with that innocent smile, she cut a slice of lasagna, shoved it onto a plate, and pushed back from the table to heat it in the microwave. The conversation behind her was increasingly lively, which annoyed her all the more. She was the one who spent her days doing things for and with the children. It was unfair that they were so obviously pleased to see Lee.

To his credit, he was good when he was with them. He listened and teased and played good cop to her bad cop. Even now, as she returned to the table, wasn't he telling Jordie that he could stay at Sean's until ten-thirty just this once? Wasn't the smile Jordie shot her a defiant one? Wasn't that her own faithful little Julie, sitting on Lee's lap with an arm around his neck?

Setting the plate in front of him with a thunk, Karen returned to her own dinner, but she didn't join in the talk, only listened, and with half an ear at that. Her mind was on other things. She kept seeing Gretchen's belly and wondering when Lee might have been with her. There were dozens of opportunities, of course. Karen always marked her own meetings on the large calendar by the kitchen phone. Lee would know when she was out, where she was, and how long she would be gone. He would know when the kids would also be gone, when there would be no one to see if he ran next door. There had been times—at night, no less, in the *dark*, when no neighbor would see either—times when he had pleaded one work-related excuse or another and skipped an event involving Karen and all four kids. Several of those times, they had returned home to find him there.

"Just walked in," he always said with a big smile, tousling the twins' hair and catching Julie when she catapulted into his arms.

Well, he might have just walked in. But whether he had walked in from work or from Gretchen's was anybody's guess.

Grinding her teeth in a way that the dentist had warned her about but that she simply couldn't help, Karen pushed away from the table and took her plate to the sink. The plate was empty. She had eaten everything without tasting a bite. Rinsing it now, she yanked the dishwasher open and dropped it inside, swearing, *swearing* that if Lee was the father of Gretchen's baby, it would be one affair too many. Seventeen years of marriage would go right down the drain. They would be done. Finished. If he was the father of that baby, Karen didn't want to feed him again, sleep with him again, wash his socks again. If he was the father of that baby, she didn't want to *see* him again.

Yes, she was being emotional about this. Given his late nights at work, the phone calls he took but never identified, the expenses on their credit card bill that she couldn't explain—and couldn't ask about, because she wasn't supposed to be seeing them, since Lee insisted that paying the bills was his job—she couldn't be objective. She just couldn't. At that moment, chafed raw by Lee's history of infidelity, she couldn't imagine that the baby's father could possibly be anyone but him.

The phone rang. Pushing a last piece of bread into his mouth, Jordie jumped for it. "Hey," he said in his new deep voice to whomever was at the other end, likely a friend, to judge from his tone. He listened, frowned, and listened more.

Drawn to his silence, Karen looked back at her son just as his color drained away.

Chapter Four

Georgia Lange sat alone in her San Antonio hotel room, only vaguely aware of her surroundings. After spending so many nights of the last few years in hotel rooms, one blurred with another. She rarely unpacked other than to hang up wrinkled clothes; as odious as living out of a suitcase was, it felt better than making herself at home in a place that wasn't. Likewise, she had taken to pretending that the rest of the house she loved was right outside her door. That helped ease the isolation—until she found herself waiting for Russ and the kids to come in, which was usually at the hour when their dinner was done and the evening began settling in. That was when she picked up the phone and called home.

This evening the line was busy on her first few tries, which meant that her daughter was using call waiting to switch back and forth between calls. Sure enough, when the phone finally rang, Allison picked up in a rushed voice. "Hello?"

"Hi, sweetie."

"Mom," the girl said with the deep-voiced awe she

typically used to suggest something big afoot, "Quinn Davis is being kicked out of school."

"He's what?"

"He went to baseball practice totally sloshed. His parents are having meetings with Mr. Edlin right now, but Melissa, Quinn's girlfriend? She said they're gonna expel him. Melissa called Brooke, who called me and Kristen. They want me to call Jordie, because he may know something, but Alyssa's on the other line. Hold on, let me get off." There was a click, then silence.

Drunk? Georgia felt a chill.

Allie returned. "They can't expel Quinn. He's the president of the class."

"Was he really drunk?"

"Staggering."

"Why?"

"Why was he drunk? Why does any guy get drunk? I don't know. But if they expel Quinn, they could expel anyone."

"Well, they *should*. Where was he drinking?" Georgia pictured Quinn alone at his house, while his parents were off championing their latest cause. Worse, she pictured their *garage*, where a boy could drink himself silly, not unlike two boys destroying everything in sight before going to school and opening fire with shotguns. "Was it beer? Hard stuff? Where'd he get either?"

"Come on, Mom. If you want it, you can get it. This'll totally screw up the baseball season. I mean, we were up to win the division—"

"Allison, forget baseball. What possessed him to drink?"

Allison sighed. "Kids drink, Mom. It isn't the first time Quinn's done it. And he doesn't stop at booze."

"What else is there?" Georgia asked, holding her breath.

"Pills."

"Quinn?"

"He's not a saint. He isn't all that different from the rest of us."

"You don't drink. Do you?"

"*God,* no. We've talked about that. You know I don't. But guys do. Look, Mom, I'm sorry I said anything. It's not that big a deal."

"Big enough," Georgia said. Allison was fourteen and young for the grade. Most of her friends were fifteen. A few were even sixteen and driving. "I wish I was there." Her daughter was growing up too fast. "Where's your dad?"

"Downstairs. Don't worry. He knows about this. But I can't stay on now. I have to go see if Jordie knows anything more than we do. Want to talk to Dad?"

Georgia did. Definitely. "First your brother."

"Okay— *Tommy!* Bye, Mom."

"Allie, call me later. My number's on the board."

But the dead silence said that Allison had already gone, and within seconds, Tommy picked up. "Hi, Mom. Everything's okay here, but I'm IM-ing with the guys, so I can't talk long. When'll you be home?"

"Tomorrow afternoon." She figured that either he didn't know about Quinn, or he was too young to care, which was probably all for the best. She wanted to talk him through things like this herself. "How was school today?"

"Good, but I can't talk now, so can I tell you tomorrow?"

"Is there something to tell? Did something happen?" She waited, but all she heard were computer keys clicking in Tommy's typical hunt-and-peck style. "Tommy?"

"School's school, school's always school, but I can't type and talk at the same time, and the guys are waiting, Mom."

"Are you ready for the math test?"

"I guess. Will you be here when I get home from school?"

"Definitely. I love you, Tommy. I miss you."

"Me, too, Mom. I'll see you tomorrow. Bye." He hung up, just as Georgia was about to ask for Russ. Closing her mouth, she stared at the receiver, then punched out the number again.

When Russ answered, she felt instant relief. He was her anchor. She could never do what she did professionally were he not at home in her stead. She couldn't begin to imagine what it would be like if Russ went to work in the city and the kids spent their afternoons alone. If she was worried now, she would be a total basket case then.

"Russ," she said with a sigh. "Allison told me about Quinn. Was he actually drunk? In the middle of the day? In the middle of the *week?*"

"Looks that way," Russ said calmly.

"It doesn't fit the image."

"Nope."

"Allison was at the same party as him two weekends ago. This doesn't give me a good feeling."

"She's okay, Georgie."

"Does she understand that what he did was wrong—unhealthy—*dangerous?*"

"She will. This is still hot off the press. No one knows the facts for sure. Right now, the girls are just into gossip."

"Do you think Allison drinks at those parties?"

"She comes home sober. We know that. We see her."

"Not always. Sometimes she goes to Kristen's house. Or Alyssa's. We don't know if other parents look for things like that—and anyway, soon these kids will be driving. What happens if there's drinking then?"

"I'll write a batch of columns on designated drivers."

"I'm serious, Russ."

"So am I. I don't want them drinking any more than you do, but so many of them do it at some point that we'd be fools to bury our heads in the sand. You agree with me on this. You're just feeling removed right now."

"I'm feeling hamstrung. I liked it better when we took our kids everywhere, so we knew that they arrived safe and sound. I want those days back."

"You wouldn't say that if you were the primary chauffeur," Russ remarked. "It'll make my life a whole lot easier when Allie can drive herself around. I trust her."

"So do I," Georgia said. "It's her friends I worry about."

"They're good kids."

"So's Quinn."

"You're blowing this out of proportion."

Maybe she was. But it was hard not to, being several thousand miles away. Was this only Tuesday night? She had been home yesterday morning, but yesterday morning felt at least a week away. "Is Tommy ready for his test?"

"As ready as he ever is. I checked his homework. He did it right."

"He was in a rush to get off the phone. I thought he might be hiding something."

"Nah. He's just chatting on the computer. He probably figures he can tell you everything when you get home. What time are you due?"

"Three, give or take."

"At home? Or are you stopping at the office first?"

"Home." She felt a yearning deep in her gut to be there. It was coming more often lately, and stronger. "I don't like this life, Russ. I feel like I'm missing too much."

"I'm on top of things."

"I know. But I want to be there, too."

"You wanted to work. You can't have it both ways."

Coming from someone else, the comment might have sounded snide. But Russ said it gently. Besides, he was the first to admit that her working eased the pressure on him. He had juggled many more balls, professionally speaking, when he was the sole breadwinner. He made no bones about preferring the life he had now.

And what was there not to prefer? He was home with the kids, involved with their lives in ways that she used to be—and wasn't now, and missed. "What else is happening?"

He made a dismissive sound. "Not much."

"Did the lawn guys come?"

"This morning."

"Are the tulips up?"

"More for Gretchen than the rest of us. She has a green thumb."

Georgia didn't doubt it. Gretchen also had a big bust and a bad attitude, but Georgia didn't want to discuss either with Russ. He saw things from a male point of view—be it Gretchen or drinking—and she'd had enough for now. "Anything else new?"

"Not since we talked yesterday. Except that Amanda isn't pregnant."

"Oh, God." Georgia felt the pain of that. "Poor thing. She must be discouraged."

"She is."

"What'll they do next?"

"I don't know. I didn't ask."

Georgia would have, but that was because in the last four years Amanda had become a close friend, and they often discussed whens, whys, and what ifs. It was one of the perks of being a woman. Russ might be a marvel at most every aspect of raising kids and taking care of a house, but he would never be one of the girls.

"I'll ask tomorrow," she said, thinking that here was another reason why she needed to be home. She missed spending time with friends. "How's Graham taking it?"

"I don't know. It'd be a good topic for a column—the male side of all that— *Be right there,*" he called. "I have to go, hun. I'm driving Allie to Brooke's house. They're doing a history paper together."

"A history paper? Really."

"Okay. They'll talk about Quinn. But that's fine. *Coming, Allie!* Georgie, I gotta go."

"Nothing else new, then?"

"Nah. I'll see you tomorrow."

"What'll you do after you take Allie to Brooke's?"

He sighed. "Watch the news looking for an idea for my next column, then get Tommy ready for bed, then go pick up Allie. Just think. If she had her license she could do this for herself. Bye, hun."

Georgia hung up the phone only because he had.

She would have liked to linger. But the kids were in a rush to get her off. Russ was in a rush to get her off. How could she not feel shunted aside?

It hadn't always been that way. Not so long ago, she had been the hub of their daily lives.

She tried to remember those days—in particular, tried to remember the negatives, so that she could appreciate being alone now. She tried to remember feeling tired, harried, and bored. She tried to remember the frustration of endlessly washing clothes, picking up toys, scheduling the kids into playgroups, music lessons, and soccer games. She tried to remember the long, hard struggle to admit that she needed something besides child care to give direction to her life.

But the negatives eluded her. She could only think about how nice it had been.

That said, she wouldn't turn back the clock. Seven years had passed since she started the business, and, to this day, she was amazed by its growth. If she were to give a motivational talk on the key to success, she wouldn't know what to say. She had stumbled into something. Luck probably had as much to do with it as anything else.

Vegetable juice wasn't a new thing. It had been around for ages. But it never had been dubbed Beet Beer before, or been smartly packaged, with five varieties beyond beets, each one as delicious as the next. At first, it was a cottage industry housed in the commercial kitchen of a local caterer, with sales to a handful of local stores. Now, it had processing plants on both coasts, produce coming from a dozen different states and half a dozen different countries, and sales in every major supermarket chain.

People called her an entrepreneurial whiz, but she wasn't. The business had taken off on its own, and she'd been pulled along in its wake. Yes, she knew how to get things done; motherhood had trained her for that. But had she begun with a vision? No. She had targeted her product for the workout crowd. To this day, she didn't quite know how mothers had taken to the drink for themselves and their kids.

She did see the big picture now, though. A major food manufacturer was courting her in hopes of buying the rights to her product and its name, and the figures being tossed out were mind-boggling. That kind of money would pay for the childrens' educations and a lot more. It would pay for family vacations for years to come, plus a beach house, plus a comfortable retirement. Not that retirement was imminent. Georgia was barely forty. Her suitor wanted her to stay on as CEO. It was part of the deal.

She didn't know whether she liked that idea, particularly on a night like this. She felt too far from home, too removed from the lives of her husband and children. She was with them every weekend, but it wasn't the same. Nor was talking with them on the phone each night.

She had come a long way. Everyone said it, and they weren't only talking about her business. Seven years ago, she had been a frumpy mother with flyaway hair, hiding her stomach under loose sweaters and, tired of being humiliated at the gym, trying to shape up by drinking carrot juice. Now she was twenty pounds lighter, with short, sleek hair, a daily makeup routine, and a wardrobe of chic business suits.

Oh, yes, she had come a long way. But there'd been a price to pay.

* * *

Amanda was at the high school for two hours. By the time she drove back down the street, it was nearly eight, and she was thinking that she might not want to be a parent at all, if it meant waging wars like the one she'd just been through. Granted, she and Graham would be more reasonable than the Davises had been—hopefully more understanding of their own child and his needs, and Quinn Davis did have needs. She had seen the chink in his armor tonight. He sat there looking sick, grinding each thumb against its forefinger while his parents argued on his behalf. Apparently they chose not to see the nervous gesture. When Amanda had dared suggest—gently and privately at the end of the session—that she would be happy to talk with Quinn, they had jumped down her throat. There was nothing wrong with *their* child, they said.

The whole thing left her weak.

Having her period didn't help. It drained her.

But enough. Taking a deliberate breath, she focused on releasing the tension.

The setting helped. Darkness brought its own serenity to the cul-de-sac. Gaslights glowed at the head of each walk, while softer lamplight spilled from the houses. A television screen flickered in the Langes' first-floor den, saying that Russ was there. Likewise, next door and one floor up, twin lamps in twin windows, coupled with twin shadows cavorting, vouched for the presence of the Cotter twins. And, yet another house over, where was the widow? Her front windows were dark; it wasn't until Amanda reached her own driveway that she saw the light at the back of the living room. Gretchen was in the library, as she often was at night.

Amanda wondered what she did there. June used to read every bestseller she could get her hands on—fiction, nonfiction, whatever. She had belonged to three book groups that took her beyond the cul-de-sac, and she often replayed those groups' discussions with Amanda, Georgia, and Karen. June's two sons, both over forty now, had always known that books were a sure winner as gifts. Ben knew it, too, and indulged her.

Was Gretchen reading books from June's collection, then? Amanda doubted it. On the occasions when Amanda had mentioned a book in an attempt to make conversation, Gretchen looked totally blank.

So maybe she was reading books on pregnancy now. Amanda could loan her a few.

Speaking of which—Amanda looked at her own house, and her stomach tightened. Quinn Davis had been a diversion, but she was home now, and she needed Gray. She needed comfort on the matter of sixteen-year-olds who couldn't live up to the image their parents set, not to mention thirty-five-year-olds who couldn't live up to the image their in-laws set.

Other than the gaslight at the head of the walk, the only other light came from the small room under the eaves of the garage, Graham's half of their home office. She could picture him at his drafting table, one foot propped on the rung of a stool, his knee bent, elbows bracing his arms, steadying the hand that sketched his plan in the narrow shaft of light cast by a gooseneck lamp. Computer equipment was lined against the wall to his left, but it would be idle. He had bought it in deference to the three associates and a business manager who worked at his office in town, and it was state-of-the-art and fully networked. So was Graham. He could work with CAD programs as expertly as every new graduate from design school. Given a choice, though, he worked by hand.

He would definitely do that on a night like this. He would be hungering for some pleasure, *any* pleasure, though it meant taking solace in work rather than his wife.

But she was a fine one to talk. She escaped into work, too.

Things were eroding. *They* were eroding. Not even the caress of the soft night air on her face when she slid out of the car could soothe the sting of that.

With a tired breath, she looked up at the night sky, so beautiful and star-filled, so devoid of answers. She didn't know why she and Graham couldn't have a child. They had so much going for them.

Righting her head, she was about to go inside when she caught a movement on the Cotters' front porch. It was the tip of a cigarette, glowing a deep orange on the uptake. Karen was there.

Taking this last, small, diversionary measure before facing Graham, Amanda crossed the cul-de-sac and followed the cigarette smell over the grass to the porch.

"Don't say anything," Karen warned softly. She was backlit, deeply shadowed. "I'm only having one."

Amanda settled onto the step beneath hers. "You've been so good. You had it licked."

"Only one. That's all. What's the latest on Quinn?"

Amanda would have preferred to ask what had triggered the need to smoke, but the therapist in her was beat. "He's sober."

"Is he being expelled?"

"Expelled? Lord, no. He's being suspended from the

team for the rest of the season." She wasn't betraying a confidence, but was simply correcting a rumor that was wrong. The truth was public knowledge.

"Suspended from playing baseball? Is that it?"

"Yes."

Karen stared out at the night. Quietly, she said, "That's the same punishment as the other two boys got. I'd have given Quinn more. When you're in a leadership position, the standards change. We expect more then."

"What does Jordie have to say?"

Karen put the cigarette to her mouth and pulled on it. Her answer followed a narrow stream of smoke. "Not much. At least, not to us. He raced out of here soon after he heard. God, do I hate this age."

"Ours? Or theirs?"

"Right now, theirs. I hate the secrecy. It makes you wonder what's really going on."

"Do you think Jordie drinks?"

"No, but I wouldn't have said Quinn did, either. So what do I know?" She took a longer drag on the cigarette, but if it was meant to relax her, it failed. Her voice remained tight. "I do know one thing, actually. Gretchen's pregnant. I took her a batch of cookies. Close up, it's clear as day."

Then Amanda hadn't imagined it. There was some satisfaction in that.

"She's seven months along."

"Seven? She didn't look that big."

Karen snorted. "No doubt the baby will be as willowy as she is."

Amanda did the math. "If she's seven months along, she conceived in October. The carpenter was around then replacing the porch roof."

"Uh-huh," Karen said, "and after the roof, he built shelves in one of the spare bedrooms, then he added support beams under the master bathroom for a Jacuzzi. The plumber and the electrician were both around for a while getting it hooked up."

"A *ménage à trois?*" Amanda asked, tongue in cheek. Comic relief was in order on a day like this. "So who's the father?"

"I don't know."

"Did you ask?"

"I didn't dare." When she took another drag of the cigarette, curls of smoke rose from her lips to her nostrils. "We're not exactly pals, Gretchen and me. My husband's the one who's her pal. He's the one running over there to shovel snow or stack wood or put on storm windows. I should send *him* over to ask."

"Maybe he already knows," Amanda said, being facetious as she and the other two women used to be on the issue of their husbands and Gretchen. It was common knowledge that Gretchen would talk to their men.

Now though, defensive, Karen pulled back. "Why do you say that?"

Amanda paused before replying. "I was thinking that one of the men working there might have winked or made a suggestive comment—some man-to-man kind of thing to imply he was getting it on with Gretchen. Do you think she'll be moving?"

Momentarily appeased, Karen returned her elbows to her knees. "Not soon. She told me she was decorating the nursery. There were paint spatters on her shirt."

Amanda could picture it. She would do the same thing if she were pregnant. She had dreamed of decorating a child's room more times than she could count—one color here, another there, stencils for a border, a big rocking chair. She had been superstitious enough to wait, not that waiting had done any good. So maybe she ought to go ahead with it. Maybe a sign of commitment was needed. She could paint, buy furniture, hang mobiles. She could fill shelves with fuzzy animals, and if it broke her heart to pass a room like that every day of the week, was it any worse than passing a room filled with cartons that should have been unpacked and disposed of years before?

Those cartons contained remnants of their premarriage lives, each clearly labeled with Graham's name or hers. There was no merging of a couple here. Amanda wondered if, taken metaphorically, that was the problem.

Karen drew on the cigarette a final time before stubbing it out on the underside of the step. "Georgia's due back tomorrow. I wonder what she'll say to all this."

"She'll be worried about Allison drinking."

"I mean about Gretchen. Of all the possible suspects, Russ is the one with the greatest opportunity."

Amanda would have said that Russ respected Georgia too much to cheat. Only that implied Lee didn't respect Karen—which he didn't, but rubbing it in wouldn't help. Besides, who was Amanda to pass judgment? Sure, Lee had a history of cheating. Sure, Russ spent his days in Gretchen's front yard, so to speak. But Graham had been in that house last October—an hour here, an hour there. If they were listing suspects, Amanda had to include him.

Chapter Five

The house was silent. Graham usually had music on—something soft, often bluegrass, perhaps Alison Krauss or Darrell Scott, both of whom they loved—but there was nothing playing tonight. Nor was there any sign that he had eaten. The kitchen was pristine.

Once, not so long ago, Amanda might have come home from working late to find that he had dinner on the stove. He knew how much she loved the homey feeling of that. Her life before him hadn't had much hominess in it, and she treasured it.

She could have used a little hominess now. Especially she could have used that sign of caring.

But he hadn't made dinner.

Which was fine. She wasn't hungry.

The phone rang. She waited, hoping that Graham would pick up in his office. By the fourth ring, when he didn't, she answered it herself.

"Hello?"

Her sister-in-law Kathryn launched right in. "Gray called Joe, and he called me. I'm sorry about the baby, Amanda. Are you okay?"

What she was just then was annoyed. She didn't know why Graham had had to call his brother so fast. "I'm fine."

"Next time, it'll take. Three's a charm."

It certainly was for Kathryn. She had three children, three dogs, three weeks' vacation from a three-day-a-week job. Amanda envied her. She envied the other O'Learys, too. Life just seemed to fall into place for them.

Things weren't so easy for Amanda and Graham. She couldn't begin to think about the next time yet.

"Don't be discouraged," Kathryn was saying. "You'll have that baby. O'Learys always do. So, cheer up, sweetie, okay? But that's only one of the reasons I'm calling. The other is to remind you about Sunday. Everyone's coming here at three. Is that okay?"

"Sure."

"No birthday gifts. Mom doesn't want gifts."

"I know."

"And you'll bring a trifle?"

"Uh-huh, made with Paddy whiskey, to your grandmother's specifications." One didn't make an Irish trifle without Irish whiskey. Amanda had learned that the very first time she had met the O'Leary clan. One didn't *eat* Irish trifle—at least, not in an O'Leary household—without toasting Paddy.

"Mom will *love* that," Kathryn said. "Did she give you the recipe?"

"No, MaryAnne did."

"Ah. Well, that's okay. MaryAnne gets it right. You know not to use Cool Whip, don't you? You have to whip real cream, or it isn't perfect, and you have to do it yourself. Fresh. Canned stuff won't do. I tried taking *that* shortcut once and, believe me, you can taste the difference. I've made that trifle a hundred times, so if you have any questions, give me a call. Otherwise, I'll see you Sunday at three?"

"We'll be there."

Amanda hung up the phone, wishing with all her heart that her mother-in-law's birthday was any weekend but this one. It wasn't that Amanda didn't like Graham's family. She adored his sisters and brothers and their spouses and children. The problem was Dorothy. Kathryn's exuberance notwithstanding—Kathryn's *manipulation* notwithstanding, since she had been the one to say who would bring what—Amanda wasn't at all sure that Dorothy would be pleased to know that she was the one making the O'Leary family trifle.

Dorothy had never accepted Amanda. It was almost as though she blamed Amanda for the breakup of Graham's first marriage, though in fact that marriage had been over and done well before Amanda and Graham met. Even the lengthy process of obtaining an annulment from the church was completed before that day in Greenwich.

If Amanda were Catholic, Dorothy might have felt differently. Barring that, having an O'Leary baby would help. But it was easier said than done.

Feeling weary and weak, Amanda went through the darkened hall into the living room and dropped into the nearest sofa. It was a deep, cushiony one, different from the tailored pieces her mother favored, and when she and Graham had been furniture shopping, she had fallen in love with it on sight. His love for it had been more physical; he had gone from sofa to sofa, plopping down, sitting this way and that to assure a generous fit; but the outcome had been total agreement on their parts.

She sank back now as he had then and let the cushions envelop her. She didn't turn on a light; the darkness pillowed her mind as the sofa did her body. She was as brain-tired as she was bone-tired. She wanted Graham. She just wasn't sure she wanted everything that went with him right now.

When she heard the kitchen door open, she told herself to be grateful that her husband cared enough to come down from his office when she returned.

"*Mandy?*" he called.

"In here."

She heard his muted footfall on the adobe tiles in the kitchen, then the hardwood of the hall. They stopped at the living room arch. Had she looked back, she knew she would have seen no more than a handful of inches between the top of that arch and the top of his head. She had watched him there before, had watched from the very sofa she sat in now. She had watched him approach with a hunger in his eyes that translated to sex right here on the Oriental rug. They had made love in most every room in this house. Not lately though. Lately, they did it in bed, every forty-eight hours on the days when she was ovulating and most likely to conceive.

Now she didn't look back, didn't move an inch.

"Are you okay?" he asked with such welcome gentleness that her eyes filled with tears.

"Uh-huh."

"Want some tea?"

"No. Thanks." Rolling her head on the cushion, she extended a hand. She didn't want to argue. She loved Graham.

Seeming to appreciate the gesture, he closed the distance, took her hand, and brought it to his mouth as he sank into the sofa by her side. His lips were warm against her fingers.

"Were you working?" she asked, nestling in, feeling his warmth envelop her.

He tucked her hand to his heart and stretched out his legs. "I tried. I wasn't inspired. So I took a walk. I just got back and saw your car."

"I didn't see you." She should have passed him when she'd been driving down the street.

"I was in the woods. Went right through the graveyard. Didn't see any ghosts."

They had a running joke about those woods, which began behind the Tannenwalds' and stretched for acres through conservation land. The area wasn't only lush with hemlock and fir, oak, maple, birch, and every imaginable kind of moss and fern. It was also rich in history, starting with gravestones so old that the markings on them were nearly indecipherable. That led Amanda and Graham to provide their own comical and often irreverent embellishments, for which they told each other that the ghosts of those good folks would be after them one day, hence the joke.

There had been houses in those woods once, too, and the unknowing hiker could easily tumble into an old stone cellar hole. Worse, a foolhardy one might try to climb the only structure that remained erect, a tower built of the same rough fieldstone that formed low walls through the woods. It stood forty feet high. Each of its four sides tapered from a width of twelve feet at the bottom to five at the top. The stairs that had once filled the inside were gone, leaving a dark receptacle for wind-blown leaves in various stages of decomposition, though neither of those things discouraged climbers. The outside walls, slanting in, were rife with toeholds.

The tower had as many stories woven around it—dead animals inside, dead *people* inside—as the gravestones had jokes, though none was based on fact. No one quite knew whether it had been built by Native Americans or by early settlers. Nor could anyone say for sure that it was haunted. All they knew was that those who managed to climb up couldn't climb down. It happened again and again, and not only to children. Rescue teams had to bring in ladders to help adults down as often as not. Worse, for each climb made, for each *rescue* made, the stones grew more shaky. A recent minor earthquake had dislodged a few, making what remained more precarious than ever, but there was nothing to be done. Whenever the town manager suggested razing the tower, the citizenry inevitably made such an uproar that the issue was tabled. The general sentiment was that if there were ghosts, this was their rightful spot.

Amanda gave the smallest smile now at Graham's attempt at humor. "You took your chances walking through there at night."

"No more than you took walking into that school. Is it settled?"

"Quinn's punishment, yes. His problems, no. He has them, Gray. That wasn't a happy kid I saw sitting there tonight. I told the parents I'd like to talk with him. I told them I'd even meet with him somewhere away from school. No one would know that we weren't discussing a peer leadership issue."

"They refused?"

"Totally."

"That's frustrating for you."

"Yes."

He pulled her even closer with a sure arm around her back, and she felt herself falling in love all over again—in love with the largeness of him, the warmth, the way he smelled, the way he knew what she needed. In that single instant, there was no tension between them. There was nothing of the world to put them at odds.

"You sound tired," he said softly.

"I am."

"Sometimes I think it's me."

"What do you mean?"

"That you don't want to talk to me."

"Why do you say that?"

"You could have called this afternoon. I was waiting." His voice remained soft, but the words were pointed. "You're not the only one with an investment in this, you know."

She angled away so that she could look up, bracing her hand on his ribs now, but his features were dim. "Investment. That's such an impersonal word."

Angling farther way, he met her gaze. "It's become that. Something impersonal. A project. I never expected it to go on so long. We should have had a baby by now. I don't understand why we don't."

That quickly, they were back where they had been earlier. Now, though, she was more tired and more defensive. She had struck out with Quinn's parents. She feared doing the same thing with Graham. "It's not like we haven't tried to find out," she cried softly. "What do you want me to do?"

"I want you to get pregnant," he said. "Didn't they say anything during the last try?"

"Like what?" Amanda asked, turning to face him

head-on. "I would have told you if they'd said something. It was a totally positive, totally routine procedure. They measured my egg follicles by ultrasound and said the time was right. Everything looked *good,* they said."

Pushing up, Graham went to the window. After a minute of staring into the dark, he returned, this time to the opposite sofa. With six feet of Oriental carpet and a large, square coffee table between them, he sat forward with his elbows on his knees. "I only asked, Amanda. I'm feeling frustrated."

"You didn't ask. You accused."

"No. I did not. If you heard that, it's your problem."

"It's *our* problem," she said. Turning her head away, she closed her eyes. She didn't want to think. About *anything.*

"What's next?" he asked.

She didn't answer. The thought of starting another cycle—another round of Clomid, another month of BBT charts, dipsticks, and breath-holding—turned her stomach.

"They said it might take three tries at artificial insemination for it to work," Graham said, sounding as though he were trying to get a grip by reasoning aloud. "We have one try left. There's still ICSI or IVF."

On another night, Amanda could have described each of the last two procedures in detail. She and Graham had become experts on the choices. Right now, though, she couldn't bear to even think the words behind the acronyms.

"No," she said softly.

"No, what? No to the third try?"

Amanda couldn't move. Her limbs were leaden, her heart heavy, her voice thin. "No to all three."

There was a long pause, then an alarmed, "No to all three? What in the hell does that mean?"

She opened her eyes, trying to think what it meant, but the only words that came were, "I'm tired."

"Of this? Of me?"

"Of *me*. Of my life like this."

"You're giving up?"

"No. Taking a break. I need a rest."

"*Now*? Geez, Amanda, we can't stop now!"

"For one month, Graham. One month. It won't matter in the overall scheme. Maybe it'll help. Like when you're trying to lose weight, you follow a diet so closely that your body shuts down. If you break the diet for a day or two, eat totally different things, it can jolt your system enough to get it to start losing weight again."

"Since when do you know about diets?"

"Since I've been on Clomid and gained eight pounds."

"Where?"

"Nowhere now. I lost them. But I had to work at it."

"Did Emily okay that?"

"No. It was no big thing. I just watched what I ate."

"Amanda, you're either under a doctor's care or you aren't. You should have told her."

Amanda folded her arms. "Fine. I'll tell her tomorrow, but if you think that's why I haven't conceived, you're out in left field. By the way, Gretchen *is* pregnant. Karen went over there and asked. I wasn't wrong. I know what I saw."

He didn't respond.

"We were trying to figure out who the father could be."

Graham remained silent.

"I can't see your face," Amanda said. "Are you shocked? Dismayed? Worried?"

"Worried? About what?"

"That someone may think it's yours."

"What are you talking about?"

"She's seven months pregnant. That means she conceived last October. You were working with her then."

"I did her landscape plan."

"You were in her house."

There was silence, then a low, "I don't believe what you're suggesting."

Angry that he didn't just come out and deny it, she said, "If the shoe fits . . ."

He was off the sofa in a flash. "I'm going to forget you said that," he told her on his way to the door. "I'm going to forget it and forgive it, because I can almost understand why it came out. You grew up in a house where parents cheated. That was your mother speaking just now."

"Gretchen's pregnant," Amanda repeated, on a roll and unable to stop. "She didn't do it on her own. So where'd the baby come from?"

"I have no idea. I don't know who she sees. I don't watch what she does."

"She doesn't date."

"How do you know? She could be seeing someone in town."

"She's home every night."

"So? Babies are conceived in daylight."

"You know what I mean."

"I do, but you don't have to *date* to conceive. It could happen in five minutes in a hallway somewhere—a hit-and-run accident—a spur-of-the-moment fit of passion."

"Precisely."

An icy silence came from the archway. It was followed by an angry, "You don't know anything, Amanda. You don't know what Gretchen wants or who wants her. For all you know, that's Ben's baby. For all you know, he banked his sperm. For all *you* know, *she* had artificial insemination and it took." He walked off.

Amanda didn't move. The minute the silence settled in, she heard the echo of her words and knew that Graham was right. That had been her mother speaking. Amanda had grown up with accusations, and most had been valid. Both of her parents had had any number of lovers, taken in retaliation for the other's infidelity. To this day, Amanda didn't know who had been the first to stray. At least, she didn't know the truth of it. She had heard arguments aplenty, as though every indiscretion that followed could be explained by that first affair.

Had she been a therapist working with her parents, she would have recommended that they divorce. When trust was so eroded as to be unsalvageable, there was no hope for love.

But she hadn't been her parents' therapist. She had been their daughter, feeling the pain of each new battle.

Now, here she was, accusing her own husband of infidelity when she didn't have cause. Graham was one of the most loyal people she had ever known. Indeed, it was one of the things that had drawn her to him. In his entire life, he'd had one relationship before her. It had been long and monogamous. That was the O'Leary way—and another selling point for Graham. His siblings were as solid as they came, free and generous in outward shows of affection, genuine in their caring. Not a single one had been divorced except Graham, and that was no blemish on his record. Amanda knew the circumstances of his marriage to Megan. Megan was the girl next door; they had been childhood friends; he had been faithful the whole time they were married. He would have been married to her still if she hadn't backed out.

Even knowing this, Amanda had never questioned Graham's love for her. It was lust that concerned her. She knew his needs. She had been their object, though not lately. Lately, what they did in bed was deliberate and prescribed. There was no spontaneity, no carefree passion.

And across the street was Gretchen Tannenwald—alone now, definitely a man's lady, and looking like Megan in ways that Graham and Amanda had often joked about.

Joked about. With Gretchen pregnant, Amanda wondered whether the joke was on her.

Immediately she chided herself. That was definitely her mother thinking. But how to stop those thoughts?

Wondering where Graham was, she went into the kitchen. He wasn't there, or in the bedroom upstairs. She even checked what was supposed to have been the children's rooms, but they were empty.

Part of her wanted to go out looking. He was probably in his office.

The other part needed to protect herself from his coldness. Entering the small den beside the bedroom, she stretched out on the sofa, pulled an afghan up to her chin, closed her eyes, and shut down her mind. She breathed deeply, inhaling and exhaling in the kind of even rhythm she hadn't felt all day. In time, there on the sofa, she fell asleep.

* * *

Graham didn't wake her up. He was waiting in the kitchen Wednesday morning, though, his mouth a hard line, his large hands wrapped tightly around a coffee mug. Grave green eyes locked on her the minute she appeared.

Chapter Six

Before either of them could say a word, the phone rang. Though Amanda was closer, Graham pushed back and reached it first.

"Yeah," he said. Seconds later, his face lit up. "Hey, how's it goin'?"

Amanda shoved her hands into her pockets. She knew that look, knew that tone. She hadn't seen much of either lately. She missed them.

"What's up?" he asked, the light in his eyes already dimmed. He turned away and said a quieter, "Not now. . . . Yeah. . . . How about noon?" He listened, lowering his head. "I can't. I have an appointment then. One? . . . Okay." He hung up the phone and turned back. His eyes held a challenge.

Who was that? Amanda wanted to ask when he didn't look like he was about to say. But asking would have made her sound suspicious. And being suspicious was her mother, not her.

So she ignored the call and said instead, "You should have woken me. I would have come to bed."

"Just as well you didn't. I was annoyed. Still am. I

don't like being accused of things, Amanda, particularly not things like that. I don't cheat."

"I know."

"Could've fooled me last night."

"I'm sorry."

"It was your mother's tone of voice. Honest to God, it was. I've never heard that from you before. It scared me. I didn't marry your mother. I married you. I don't *want* your mother. If you're going to be like her, we have a problem."

"We have a problem anyway," Amanda said, because her mind was clearer after a night's sleep. In the few minutes she had just spent in the bathroom, she'd had an overview of things.

"Yeah," Graham muttered. "Infertility."

"No. How we're dealing with it. This is the first problem we've had to face together. We're not handling it very well."

"I am. You're the one who wants out."

She bowed her head. Taking a bolstering breath, she looked up. "Not out. I just want to pull back from constantly thinking about a baby. We need to focus on *us* again for a few weeks."

He stared at her. She tried to identify his expression, but it was one she didn't know. It might easily have been anger, or disappointment or disdain.

"I'm not giving up on having a baby," she insisted softly, urgently. "All I'm saying is we need to give it a rest for a bit."

Graham put his hands on his hips. "So what do I tell my family? I was hoping to bring good news to my mother's party."

"Me, too. But we can't. And frankly, I feel worse for us than for them. This isn't their life. It's ours."

"They want this baby for us."

"Yes, but they're not us."

"They are. They're me. I can't separate myself from them."

"No," she said pointedly. "You can't."

He gripped the counter flanking his hips. "Meaning?"

"Meaning, none of us can separate ourselves from where we came from. Not completely. If I sounded like my mother, it wasn't voluntary. I didn't mean to do it, Graham. You know how I feel about her."

"Yeah, but I thought I knew how you felt about me, too—you used to trust me."

"I do trust you."

"You accused me of fathering Gretchen's baby."

Amanda sighed. "I'm sorry. I was upset. Look at it from my point of view. Sex has been work for us for months now. It's not inconceivable that some men going through something like that would be tempted to find fun elsewhere."

"I'm not some men. I'm your husband. I'm insulted that you'd even *think* I'd cheat."

"I said I was sorry."

"Do you know how that made me feel?"

At that moment she only knew that he was making her feel like a heel. "Can we get *past* this, Graham? Good *God,* injured innocence doesn't become you."

"What does *that* mean?" he asked, indignant now.

"It means I've apologized more than once, I've said I trust you, and you're *still* going on about it. If you're innocent, drop it."

Graham drew himself straight. His eyes were cold. "If?" Holding both hands up, he set off. "I can't deal with this." He was across the room and out the door before she could think of what to say.

* * *

Several minutes later, sitting in her hotel room, with a pot of coffee on a tray on the desk and a warm cup of it in her hand, Georgia called home. She imagined the scene when the first ring came—Tommy spooning up milky Froot Loops, Allison all but choking on her wheat toast in her rush to get the phone, Russ beating her to it by putting out a leisurely hand from where he stood at the stove, frying eggs.

"Hello?" he said.

She smiled. "Hi. I knew you'd get it. Who's having eggs?"

"Me. Not that I didn't offer a little protein to our progeny— No," he said to the side, "they do *not* kill you, Allie, not according to the latest studies." He listened to something Georgia couldn't make out, then chuckled.

"What did she say?" Georgia asked.

"She said to wait a week. The next study will say something else. Smart kid."

"Cynical kid," Georgia said. "What happened last night?"

"Not much."

"About Quinn."

"Lots of talk."

"Is she okay?"

"Sure is."

"How about you? Did you have a good evening?"

"Sure did. Aren't you supposed to be at a breakfast meeting?"

"They moved it back half an hour. I can still make my plane. If there's a problem, I'll call."

"I may not be here. I'm meeting Henry for lunch." Henry Silzer was Russ's editor.

"Oh. I didn't know."

"Me, neither. He called last night. He had an urge to get out of the city and give his expense account a workout. He loves having lunch at the Inn."

So did Georgia. "I'm jealous. Have a nice lunch. Can I talk to Allie?"

"She's shaking her head. Ooops, there she goes, out of the room. *Why can't you talk?*" he called, waited, said, "She says she has bed-head and needs to fix her hair."

"Then Tommy."

"Sorry, he left before she did. He was pressing his mouth. I hope that wire didn't pop out of his braces again. I'd better go check. Can't wait to see you, sweetie. Fly safe."

Hearing nothing then but the silence of her hotel room, Georgia hung up the phone.

Karen cooked pancakes for breakfast. She added a cup of fresh blueberries to the batter, not so much because blueberries had been on sale at the market, or because the children loved them, but because Lee didn't. He liked his pancakes plain.

Yes, and she liked her men trustworthy. People didn't always get what they liked.

"Where's the face?" Julie asked from her elbow, sounding and looking totally dismayed as she stared at the cooking pancakes.

"No face today," Karen replied. "No time."

"You never have time anymore."

"I do." She had time. What she lacked was patience. Arranging blueberries to make a happy face with eyes, a nose, and a mouth took more than she had.

"You didn't do faces last time, either. Can I do that?"

"They're a little tricky to flip. But okay. Here." She manipulated the child's hand around the spatula and helped her flip a few. "Good job. Now eat. Yours'll be getting cold. What're you guys doing?" she asked the twins, who were reaching syrupy hands into each other's plates.

"Trading blueberries," Jared said. "His are bluer."

"His are fatter," Jon added.

"Be careful. You'll make a mess. Agh," she cried when a glass of juice went over. Grabbing a dish towel, she mopped up the spill. While she was at the table, she glanced at Jordie. He had his head buried in the sports section of the paper.

"Anything interesting?" she asked.

He grunted something she couldn't make out.

With a frustrated sound, she returned to the stove. Moments later, Lee came in. He was dressed for work in a sports shirt and khaki slacks, which still made him more dressy than most of his employees. His hair, though, reflected his need to be a part of the group. It was newly lightened, so that it was more blond than sandy. He had gelled it, finger-combed it, left it.

"Morning, morning . . . morning, morning," he said, passing the children en route to his own seat. Once there, he tugged the sports section from Jordie, who promptly picked up his plate, put it in the sink, and left.

Karen poured Lee's coffee and, with a thud, set it down behind the paper. "Are you guys gonna want more pancakes?" she asked the twins, who mumbled what sounded enough like a "no," meaning that everything left in the pan was for Lee. She filled a plate and, with another thud, set it down behind the paper.

"Jon, Jared, wash those hands before you leave this

room. Hair time, Julie." She gestured toward the bathroom.

She brushed the child's hair, pulled it into a ponytail, and tied on a blue ribbon to match the blue dog on her shirt. From the foot of the stairs, she called up to remind the twins to put the permission slips for the class trip in their backpacks. "All set?" she asked Jordie when he ran down and past her. "Have a good day." The only answer she got was a nod on his way out the door.

"Thanks, Mom," she murmured under her breath. "Good breakfast, Mom. Have a nice day yourself, Mom." Feeling a wave of despair, she returned to the kitchen.

Lee was engrossed in the paper. She stared at him for a minute of pure annoyance, thinking that if something was amiss with Jordan it was his fault, given the example he set. Lee thought about Lee. When he wanted a section of the paper, he took it, whether or not someone else had it first. He might be warm and fun with the children, but he did it at his own convenience. When he wanted silence, he got it. When he wanted out, he went. Jordie was taking after him, all right.

She took the batter bowl from the stove to the sink and glopped what was left down the drain. Setting the bowl down none too gently, she ran water into it. It was full by the time she was back with the pan and spatula. She thrust them under the water and began to scrub.

"Something wrong?" Lee asked.

"No." She poured elbow grease into the work.

"What are your plans for the day?"

She had no intention of telling him her plans. Some

were on the calendar. If he was planning mischief, let him worry about the others.

"Karen?"

"The usual." She rinsed the pan. "Will you be home for dinner?"

"Yes."

She'd heard that before, with every bit as much conviction, but he had no compunction about changing his plans. Her efforts to provide a family dinner weren't high priority for him. Dropping the rinsed pan on the draining board, she glanced over her shoulder at his plate. It was still half full. "Are you done?"

He pushed shreds of pancake around with his fork. "I wish you'd left blueberries out of mine. You know I hate them."

Before he could say another thing, she whisked the plate out from under him and dropped it in the sink.

"What is the matter with you?" he asked, and for an instant, she wanted to deny that anything was. She was a peacemaker by nature. Rocking the boat wasn't her way.

But lately she had noticed things about Lee that were all too familiar—such as wearing a new cologne to cover up the scent of a woman, and working out at the gym to have an excuse for coming home newly shampooed. He was missing dinner at least once a week, and had shown up at the twins' Little League game late with no excuse at all. Worse, he was both happier lately and less demanding sexually. Those two things didn't fit, unless he was having an affair.

That thought alone was bad enough. But if he was having an affair with Gretchen—their *neighbor*—it would be one indignity too many for Karen.

Holding the dish towel tightly, she turned to face

him. "Gretchen's pregnant. Do you know anything about that?"

"Gretchen? Gretchen next door?"

Karen held her temper. Gretchen wasn't a common name. They didn't know any other Gretchens. At least, Karen didn't.

"Gretchen's *pregnant?*" Lee asked.

He did look genuinely surprised, though that didn't give her any comfort. Gretchen had said that the father didn't know. She had said that he had other obligations. Lee certainly fit that bill.

He frowned. "Since when is she pregnant?"

"Since October."

"Wow. No kidding." He was frowning at Karen now. "Why are you angry?"

"I'm not angry. I'm worried. Tell me the truth. Did you touch her?"

"Me? She's *Ben's* wife."

"Susan was Arthur's wife. Annette was Don's wife. Besides, Ben's dead. That makes Gretchen fair game."

He pushed back his chair and stood. "Are you accusing me, Karen?"

"No. I'm just asking."

"Well, the answer is no. I didn't touch Gretchen. What in the world would make you think that I did?"

She would have apologized and shrugged off the suspicion if she hadn't smelled that new cologne even now. But even *aside* from that, there were other hints. "You're always talking about her. You're always running over there to see what she needs."

"She's alone. And we're neighbors. You ladies have treated her like a pariah, when her only crime was marrying someone whose first wife died. I don't think that's a crime. I feel bad for her. So I help her out.

There are certain things women can't do by themselves."

"Like making babies."

He raised his voice. "Like fixing leaks under sinks. Or unstopping toilets. Come on, Karen. I do those things for you. Do you think she ought to struggle to do them herself?"

"Can't she hire someone?"

"Why should she if she's in a neighborhood with men who can help? Russ and Graham have helped her out, too. Are you asking them?"

"No. You're the one I'm married to. You're the one whose kids I worry about."

"The kids have nothing to do with this."

She thought about that. With measured words, she said, "They sit here listening, while you rave about that painting on her wall."

"It happens to be beautiful."

"To hear you tell, it's also erotic and seductive."

"So's half of what's on TV," he argued. "Isn't it good to talk about it? Get it out in the open? Let the kids know they can tell us anything? Isn't that what parents are supposed to do nowadays?"

It was. But Lee went too far with that picture—*so* far that the line blurred between the picture and Gretchen herself. At least, it did in Karen's mind.

"Hell," Lee scoffed, looking like an angry teenager with his spiked hair, "our kids need to learn from *one* of us that there's passion in life."

Karen recoiled. "I'm passionate."

"About causes. Not about men. You're never the initiator."

It was true. She felt a moment's guilt about that, then caught herself. Lee always managed to paint her as the problem, but she wasn't letting him off the hook this time. "No," she said quietly, "I don't initiate. I don't have to. You always get there first. Not lately, though. That makes me wonder."

"I'm waiting for a sign from you."

"You never did before. You came home from work with two things on your mind—sex and the Mets. I wish I could be as carefree as you at the end of a day, but my day doesn't end that neatly. I have a million things to do around here."

"Be grateful you don't work."

She bristled. "I *do* work."

"You know what I mean."

"No, I don't. I wish that for once you'd give me credit for something. You have a good life here, Lee. I do for you in ways that not many women do for their husbands. If I 'worked,' as you say, you'd get less. And still you risk it all by fooling around on the side."

"That's over," he said, standing straighter. "I made a promise to you, and I've kept it. Have I given you cause to doubt?"

"Not lately," she lied, because she didn't want to lose the focus. "Not until Gretchen."

"I haven't touched Gretchen."

She stared at him, desperate to believe him but not daring to. She had been let down so many times before.

Lee threw a hand in the air and thundered, "You're amazing! No matter what I do, no matter what I say, I can't please you. I could take vows of *chastity,* and you wouldn't be happy."

"Shhh," she said with a pointed glance at the door.

"God damn it, I'll yell if I want to. Kids should know that their parents argue. They should know that mothers make accusations that they have to take back, and you will take this one back, Karen. Mark my words. You'll take it back. *That's* a promise."

He went out the door, just as a crestfallen Julie came in. "Where's Daddy going?"

"He had to go to work."

"He didn't kiss me goodbye," the child said in a hurt voice.

Nor me, Karen thought, wishing she could feel the hurt. After years of disappointment, though, she was numbed to that. It was a sad state.

Amanda knew the minute she arrived at school that rumors were flying. Students were talking in huddled groups, shooting glances her way as she came from the parking lot. In the minute it took for her to leave home issues behind, she imagined they knew her every foible.

Can't have a baby.

Works with kids because she can't have her own.

Those who can't do, teach.

Of course, that wasn't what they were saying. "Okay, guys," she said, approaching one group. "What did you hear?"

There were five boys in the group, all freshmen. "Did Mr. Edlin really call the police?" one asked.

"No. The police know nothing about this."

"Same difference, if he's being kicked out of school," said another. "It'll be on his record forever."

"He's not being kicked out," Amanda corrected. "He's being suspended from the team. If he completes next year without an incident, his file will be clean."

"His parents are suing the school," a third said.

"I haven't heard anything about that. Mr. Edlin will be talking about this during first-period assembly. He'll tell you what's true and what isn't."

"What about what's *fair* and what isn't?"

"He'll talk about that, too. Okay?"

"Okay."

Continuing on into the building, she dropped her things in her office. She had to call the fertility clinic with the bad news. She also had to call Graham, but the thought of *either* conversation opened a gaping pit in her stomach.

Those calls would wait. She had others to make—namely to Maggie Dodd, to make sure that nothing about Quinn's situation had changed, then to counselors at the district's two middle schools, whose students might also be aware of what had happened. She wanted to attend the first-period assembly, then had to be back for a second-period meeting with a student, and that was all before ten. The rest of the day promised to be as busy, which would be a blessing.

While Amanda finished up with her first student, and used the few minutes before the next showed up to check her computer for a message from Quinn, Georgia wrapped up her breakfast meeting at her Texas hotel, collected her bags, and climbed into a cab. It had barely gone two blocks when it came to a standstill behind a long line of traffic. Within minutes, the traffic had piled up behind as well, and drivers and passengers alike were standing by open doors, looking off down the street. *An accident*, one said. *Construction*, said another. Georgia didn't care what it was, as long as she didn't miss her plane.

While Georgia was sweating it out in the Texas heat, Karen did a little sweating of her own. She knew the drill—knew to look through pants pockets, through papers on the desk, through file folders, under socks. She pulled out recent credit card bills and searched for suspicious charges, pulled out recent phone bills and singled out unfamiliar repeat numbers. There were plenty of both—truth be told, more strange charges and calls than ones she knew. Where to begin?

He paid in cash and reached the room early, but he didn't mind the wait. Anticipation was foreplay. He grew more aroused as the minutes passed.

The room was one of the new ones hidden way at the end of a primrose path, but it was as quaint as those closer to the Inn, built nearly a century before. This one was done in lilacs and blues, with large wicker chairs whose cushions matched the draperies and quilt, a king-size four-poster with the trademark stuffed frogs squatting near the pillow, and an oversized, glassed-in Jacuzzi standing in clear sight.

It was the perfect setting for a tryst, replete with a check-in desk in its own separate space. Anyone noticing his car at the end of the lot behind the Inn would think that he was simply eating in one of the many small rooms that served lunch. That gave him a neat alibi.

It was the perfect setting for a tryst, all right—though he didn't think of what they were doing as that. They had been at it for too many months for that to apply. An affair, then? Yes. But it was more. It was a relationship. He cared for her. She was vital to his peace of mind.

A soft knock came at the door. He was off the bed in an instant, pulling it open, feeling something inside him speed up when she slipped inside. He took her mouth before the door was fully closed and, with its click, pressed her to the paneled wood. She tasted of mint. He delved deeper, wanting to get to the essence of her, but her mouth alone couldn't offer that. Needing to be inside, he unzipped himself and pulled her short dress to her waist. She wore no panties.

Grinning against her mouth, he murmured, "That's my girl," and entered her with a long thrust. He put his head back then, closed his eyes, and held still, concentrating on the pleasure in his groin. She was tight. He liked that about her. She hadn't had many men in her life. He liked that about her, too. She began the tremulous little sighs that said she was totally aroused, and he liked that, too. Wanting to hear more, he slipped his hand between them and finger-stroked her until he simply couldn't hold himself still any longer. All it took then was a single, slow thrust. She cried out with her release, seconds before he did.

Moments later, he undressed her. With his eyes on her body, he undressed himself and the bed, then drew her down to the lilac sheets. When she was properly spread, he touched her. Her breasts were full, her belly gently rounded—and he liked her this way. He liked voluptuousness in a woman. It spoke of an age-old femininity.

"You're so beautiful," he whispered against one swollen breast. He drew in her scent, then her nipple, suckling strongly until her hips came up seeking his. Sitting back, he fitted her to him, watching her this time, thinking that he had never been with a woman even half as alluring. She climaxed with another cry, and still he watched. There was sensuality in the way she arched her back, turned her face to the sheets, put a hand on her breast.

His climax was every bit as intense this time. Heart

pounding in its aftermath, he grinned. He stretched out on his side and pulled her around to face him.

"How are you feeling?"

"Better."

"Is the doctor satisfied?"

"Yes."

"This isn't the one here in town, is it?"

"God, no. I'm not dumb."

He smiled and ran his thumb over her mouth. "No. You're not." He traced the straight line of her nose and the gentle curve of her brow. She was a blonde. He had always been partial to blondes. "How much time've you got?"

"Not long. Someone'll notice if I don't get back soon. They assume I'm at the market."

"You are. This is nourishment."

She smiled at that, but he saw the question coming, deep in her eyes even before she had it out. "Did you talk with her?"

"What did I tell you last time you asked?"

"That it was a delicate situation. But so is this."

"She's my wife. She came first chronologically. But it isn't just her and me. There's family involved. I'll talk with her when the time is right."

"That could take a while."

"It won't. Things are heating up. Come on, cookie. Don't pressure me. I get enough of that at home. I need you to be my escape."

She searched his eyes. "But you do love me?"

"You know I do."

She studied him for a minute, then smiled.

Chapter Seven

Shortly before the school bus was due that afternoon, Amanda rounded the curve and approached the cul-de-sac. Her workday wasn't done; she had to be back at school later that afternoon for two parent meetings. But the students had left, and she was tired. She was hoping that a break would revive her.

Actually, she was hoping that Graham would be home. They hadn't talked since he had walked out early that morning. Each time she thought of him, she felt a gaping hole in her middle.

But his truck wasn't in the driveway. She could see that from down the street.

The sky was overcast, but clouds couldn't hide the fact that the trees were a bit fuller, the grass a bit greener, the tulips a bit taller than they had been the day before. The world was blooming, even if she wasn't—and, Lord, she did feel static. She hadn't seen movement in any of three forty-minute sessions with students, six other shorter meetings, and as many e-mails.

Not one e-mail had come from Quinn. She had

talked with his mother, though—had initiated the call herself—but Marjorie Davis wasn't any more receptive to her today than she had been the night before. *Every boy experiments with liquor,* she claimed. *It's part of being a teenager. The school has overreacted terribly. I want you to stay out of it.*

Amanda kept seeing Quinn's thumbs rubbing, rubbing, rubbing, but there was nothing more she could do unless the boy came to her himself. That helplessness, combined with the day's stasis and the fact that she wasn't pregnant, made her feel infertile on every count.

Apparently, though, she wasn't the only one with weighty thoughts on her mind. In clear view of the cul-de-sac now, she saw Karen sitting at the curb, her shoulders hunched, waiting for the school bus. She was about to wave when Georgia's car came up behind her, back from the airport and Texas.

Amanda pulled into her own driveway, then walked to the street and waited at the end of the Langes' driveway. She felt a wave of envy when Georgia climbed from her car, every bit the businesswoman in sleek black and white, with her short, dark hair tucked behind her ears, jewelry that was simple but strong, and a confident gait. Granted, Amanda didn't look good in black and white. Her coloring was entirely different, as was the nature of her work. She needed splashes of warmth—something lime or periwinkle or red, her favorite. This day she wore a peach blouse and slacks. It was an outfit she normally liked. Watching Georgia approach, though, she felt nowhere near as consummate a woman.

"God, you look good," she said when Georgia joined her. "Half a day on a plane, and you're still totally together. How'd it go?"

"It went well, I think." Georgia gave her a hug and

held her close for a minute. "Russ told me about the baby, Amanda. I'm so sorry."

"Me, too," Amanda said, grateful for the support. Friends always had been her lifeline, growing up in a house with no siblings and parents who didn't get along. Friends were her lifeline still.

"What's next?"

"I don't know. Gray and I need to talk. So far, we've both been too upset." Hitching her chin toward Karen, she started down the sidewalk. "Did you hear about Quinn?"

"Oh, yeah," Georgia said, falling into step. "Not that Allie would say much. Or Russ." She lowered her voice. "Jordie plays baseball with Quinn. Was he involved?"

"Not that I know of."

"Karen looks a little worse for the wear."

She did, indeed. If Georgia was black and white and Amanda was peach, Karen was taupe today, and faded at that.

"She's feeling frustrated," Amanda said under her breath as they cut across the circle.

"We need another trip to Canyon Ranch, just the three of us again. I keep telling her that, but she says she's too busy. It'd pick her up."

"Mmm, I don't think so."

"Uh-oh," Georgia murmured. "Lee again?"

"Lee. Jordie. Quinn. Gretchen. It's been a tough twenty-four hours."

"Gretchen?" Georgia asked. "What's wrong with Gretchen?"

Karen caught the last comment and said a wry, "Nothing that two more months and another eighteen years won't solve."

Georgia frowned. "I don't follow."

"Didn't Russ tell you?"

"Tell me what?"

"That Gretchen's pregnant," Karen said. "Ah-ha. He didn't tell you. I wonder what that means."

"What *are* you talking about?"

Amanda took pity on her and explained. "Gretchen is pregnant. We found out yesterday."

"Pregnant?" Georgia looked from Amanda to Karen and back. "I was under the impression she didn't go much of anywhere."

"She doesn't."

"Then does someone come here?"

"Not that we've noticed."

"So who's the father?"

Dryly, Amanda said, "That's the million-dollar question. No one seems to know."

"Has anyone asked?"

"I came close," Karen offered, "but she didn't take the hint. She did give a couple, though. She said that the father didn't know, and that he had other responsibilities. Those qualifications fit any of our husbands."

Georgia laughed. "*Our* husbands? Cute. Our husbands wouldn't fool around with Gretchen."

"They talk about her enough," Karen said.

"All men talk," Georgia reasoned. "That's the nature of the beast. Talking about women—eyeing the pretty ones—that's what they're about. Actually *doing* it is something else. Besides, you're talking about the woman next door. None of our men would be that dumb." She settled down on the curb. "How did Lee react when you told him?"

"He seemed surprised. But he helped her out a month ago when her water heater burst. She would have been six months pregnant then. How could he not have known?"

"The same way we didn't," Amanda said. "All it takes is a big sweater or one of Ben's shirts to hide something like that. She's small for seven months."

"Seven months," Georgia echoed. "That means it happened in October. Who was around then?"

"Carpenter, plumber, electrician," Amanda said.

"And Russ," Karen added.

Georgia's immediate reaction was a flash of irritation, but sympathetic to the pressure Karen was under, she decided instead to indulge her. Rather than denying the suggestion, she chuckled. "Well, he certainly is around." She glanced back at her car, alone in the driveway. "Or should be. He was meeting his editor for lunch. They must be having a good talk."

"I asked him twice about Gretchen," Karen said, "once before I talked with her and once after. He swore he didn't know a thing about the baby."

"Then I'm sure he doesn't," Georgia decided. If Russ had chosen not to tell her that Gretchen was pregnant, it was because he didn't think it was important, or because he didn't know who the father was, or because he had been sworn to secrecy by one of the other men. Hell, Graham could as easily have fooled around with Gretchen as Russ. Graham had worked with her last fall, and he and Amanda were having a nightmare of a time.

Of course, Lee was still the one with the history of cheating, though Georgia wasn't spiteful enough to remind Karen of that. Instead, grateful for the approaching rumble of the school bus, she said, "Russ thinks gossip is for women. He prides himself on not playing that game, and he's right. When you come down to it, there's no reason why any of us has to know who fathered that baby. It's Gretchen's business. Not ours."

"We hope," Karen murmured as the school bus rounded the curve. It was a large yellow box on wheels, shiny and new as school buses went, carrying the two creatures who were nearest and dearest to Georgia's heart. She remembered waiting just like this when first Allison, then Tommy, returned home from kindergarten, then first grade, then second grade. They were older now, coming home from ninth and fifth grades, respectively, but the excitement of catching that first glimpse of them never quite went away. This was what she missed when she was gone.

Brushing off the seat of her pants as she rose, she scanned the row of windows until she saw what looked like one, then the other, of her children moving up the center aisle. With the squeal of brakes, the bus came to a stop. The doors clattered open. Karen's Julie was the first off, then the twins. Then came Tommy and Allison, giving Georgia hugs, telling her they were glad she was home, alternately demanding her attention as they walked off toward their house—and then came Russ, driving down the street, returning late from his lunch.

Surrounded by her crew, Georgia didn't give Gretchen's pregnancy another thought, and wouldn't until later that night.

Gretchen stood at the dining room window behind sheers that began with gathers at the sill by her hip and ended with the same just under her eyes. Even with the swelling limbs of a towering oak in her yard, she had a clear view of the three women out by the curb.

She always saw them. It was as if a bell rang in her head when they gathered, as if some spiteful being wanted her to see what she missed. She had always wanted to have female friends. When she married Ben, she had thought she might find them here. She was wrong.

Give it time, Ben had said. *They don't know you. When they do, they'll warm up.*

They didn't warm up, neither while Ben was alive, nor when he died and she was alone. Oh, they stopped by from time to time, much as Karen had done the evening before. But there was little genuine warmth, and no friendship bloomed. It might have helped if she had been outgoing, but she had never been that. Worse, she felt intimidated in the presence of these women, each so accomplished in her own way. They had their own little group, and she was an outsider. She was unworldly, uneducated, and ill-bred.

You are my beauty, Ben used to say, and coming from him, she believed it. Coming from him, beauty referred to things beyond the physical. He made her feel beautiful inside.

Ben had been one of a kind. But Ben was dead, and here she stood, hiding behind the dining room sheers, envying her neighbors their friendship. She would have given just about anything to go out and join them. Amanda was the closest to her age and seemed the gentlest, but what did Gretchen have in common with her? Amanda had a Ph.D., for God's sake. At least Georgia and Karen had been through pregnancies. They would be able to tell her that the contractions she felt were normal, that the pain in her hip each time she rose from a chair would go away, that having a baby was the most awesome thing, and that anyone who tried to tell her she couldn't do it herself should be shot.

But she couldn't go out there. She wasn't welcome. They wanted June, and she wasn't June. They wanted a contemporary of Ben's, an older woman, a mother figure. They wanted someone who was easy and gentle and wise.

They wanted someone ugly, someone their men wouldn't look at twice, but Gretchen couldn't accommodate them there, either. Her looks had been her ticket out of a life of squalor in rural Maine. Her looks were all she had.

Well, not anymore. She'd had Ben for a time. Now she had his house and the things in it. She had an investment portfolio. And she had a baby growing.

Smiling at that thought, she slid a slow palm over the swell of her belly. Her baby. All hers. One day in the not-too-distant future, *she* would be out there at the curb waiting for the school bus. Would the women accept her then? She didn't know. Perhaps by then she wouldn't care. Taking her baby places, she would meet other mothers. They would become friends. They would be more open-minded, she suspected. They certainly wouldn't stand out there in clear view of her, speculating on the identity of her baby's father. Oh, yes, that's what they were doing, of that she was certain. Karen had come to her house last night with a purpose, and it wasn't delivering cookies. She wanted to know with whom Gretchen had slept.

Let her worry, Gretchen decided, deeply annoyed just then. Let her sweat it out. Same with the others. If they couldn't find it in their hearts to show her a little compassion, she didn't owe them any in return. Let them wonder which of their precious husbands had fathered her child.

Turning away, she went through the front hall into the living room. Carefully, lest she jostle the baby and cause pain for them both, she lowered herself onto the sofa, slipped off her shoes, and folded up her legs. The painting hung on the opposite wall. Focusing on it, she let the tension seep away.

La Voisine. It had been a wedding gift from Ben, purchased in an art gallery in Paris during their honeymoon, and for that alone it would have held a special place in her heart. But she also loved the painting itself. She had loved it from the minute she had first seen it hanging on the gallery wall in its sculpted gilt frame. The artist wasn't a master; he wasn't even dead yet. But he had captured a contemporary scene in the soft pastels and gentle brush strokes of the Impressionist school, making it the most romantic, most sensual, most idyllic thing Gretchen had ever seen.

The subject was a woman clipping roses from a trellised vine. Her dress was yellow with gentle scallops at the neck and wrists; a sunhat hung down her back. She was on the far side of a white picket fence that separated her yard from the viewer. Her house and those beyond it were built of stucco, with lavish greenery climbing their sides. At the end of the narrowing street was the ocean.

What made it so sensual? Gretchen wondered. She had spent hours sitting before it, and she had yet to come up with a definitive answer to that question. There was no outward suggestiveness, certainly no nudity. The woman was full-breasted, so the simple swell of her breasts, uplifted with the rise of her arms, might have done it. Or it might have been the touch of pink on her cheeks, or the rosy tint on faintly smiling lips. Either one gave her radiance. Or it could have been the wisps of blond hair that had slipped from a loose topknot and curled around her face, or the subtle hint of sweat on her neck and throat. Gretchen marveled at the way the artist had done that. More than once she had gone right up to the painting and touched those luminescent dots, half expecting her fingers to come away damp.

Sweat was sensual. Then again, the sensuality of the piece could have come from nothing more than the faraway look in the woman's eye.

Gretchen identified with that faraway look. It was the look of a woman whose thoughts were of the kind of love that she had herself spent most of her life dreaming about. For a short time, she had found it with Ben. He had made her feel just as sensual, just as radiant as the woman in the painting. He was one of a kind.

For a short time, she had thought there was another like him. But she had been wrong. And that was fine. Her baby didn't need a father. It had a mother who would love it—a mother who could support it and offer it a stable life.

Ben's sons weren't going to be happy when they learned she was pregnant. Both grown, both married with kids, both older than Gretchen herself, they were upset enough that Ben had left her as much of his estate as he had. This would give them new cause to make noise. They would want to know who the father was. They would suggest she had been involved with whomever it was before Ben's death. They would talk about morals and call Gretchen a slut.

She had been called that before. Tensing up at the thought, she drew in a deep breath and refocused on *La Voisine.*

Self-contained. That's what the woman in the painting was. Self-contained. Perhaps that was what Gretchen identified with. Ben had always said that *she* was self-contained. And she had heard it before him. Self-contained—distant—aloof. People often saw her that way.

But self-contained was a euphemism for alone, and Gretchen knew about that. She had been alone from the time she was eight, when her father had come to her bed in the night and her mother had blamed her for luring him there. Self-contained was a cover for frightened, which was how she had spent so many of the years after that.

But no more. She was moving forward. Ben had given her his name. He had given her a taste of love. He had given her financial security. She liked to think he had given her this baby, too, and in a roundabout way, he had.

Amanda's parent meetings were more productive than those with students earlier in the day had been. During the first, she convinced a couple to let her meet with their daughter, a junior who was showing signs of stress on the matter of going to college. During the second, she convinced a newly separated couple to seek outside help for their son, a freshman, whose grades had tumbled since the separation. In both instances, watching the interaction of the parents gave her insight into the students' home situations, and hence greater understanding of the students themselves.

She was feeling better when she left school today, but her self-confidence fled when she arrived home and found that Graham hadn't returned yet. He had left a message on the answering machine, though, in a neutral voice that gave her no hint of his thoughts.

"Hey," he said. "I'm on my way to Providence. I got a call from a potential new client this morning. The guy's building an indoor mall, and he wants someone to design and plant an atrium in the middle. It could be an interesting job. I'll be with him for an hour or two. Then it'll take me a couple of hours to get back, so don't wait on me for dinner. I may be late. See you then."

The message was left only half an hour before, which meant that he was right. He would be back late.

There was also a message from Emily, in response to the brief one that Amanda had left earlier that afternoon. "Hi, Amanda. I got your message. I know you're disappointed, but we're far from done. Give me a call tomorrow and we'll plot the next step."

Amanda erased the message. The last thing she wanted to do was to think about Emily or the clinic. The *last* thing she wanted to do was to anticipate more of what she'd just been through. There were other options—adoption, for one. She wouldn't need Emily or Clomid or impersonal technicians to help with that.

Exhausted, she ate a bowl of cereal for dinner, then went to the den, stretched out on the sofa, pulled up the afghan, and turned on the television. She spent most of the next two hours channel surfing, finally staying put on a program about wolves and their young. By the time it was done, the room was dark.

Turning the set off, she lay quietly, waiting for Graham to come home.

It was nearly ten when the truck came down the street and turned into the driveway. She lay in the dark with her eyes open, listening, waiting, following his movements in the kitchen, then the hall. He would be going through the mail on the credenza there. He didn't call out a hello.

In time, he climbed the stairs. She held her breath when he came down the hall, and looked straight at him when he appeared at the den door. She was in darkness, and he was backlit. She couldn't see his face.

Either he couldn't see hers, or he didn't want to talk.

Not ten seconds later, he went on to their bedroom. She heard him in the bathroom. She heard him in the closet. She heard him climb into bed and click off the light.

And still she didn't move.

"Allie?" Georgia said from the door to her daughter's room. "You've been on the phone all night."

Allie held up a hand and said something into the phone that Georgia couldn't make out. Then she hung up. "It was Alyssa."

"Is this about Quinn?"

"Nuh-uh," the girl said, scooping her hair back with the thumb-and-forefinger gesture that all the girls used. "The prom. Mom, there's going to be an all-night party. Can I go?"

"All-night party? This is the first I've heard about a *prom*. What prom?"

"The freshman-sophomore one. You knew there was one."

"Yes, but last I heard, you refused to go."

"I changed my mind. A bunch of us are going."

"With whom? I mean, with dates?"

"Kind of, but not really, if you know what I mean."

Georgia didn't, but she could guess. "A group of you—mixed group—not paired up."

Allison lit up. "Yeah. But we want to spend the night at Melissa's."

"Just girls?"

"No. All of us."

"I thought Melissa and Quinn were a number."

"They are. The rest of us aren't."

"And Quinn's parents are letting him go to an all-night party after what happened yesterday?"

"What happened yesterday doesn't have anything to do with anything. It was the coach getting hot under the collar."

"Because Quinn showed up drunk."

"He wasn't drunk. He'd had one drink."

"Sloshed. That was the word you used last night."

"I was wrong. Can I go, Mom?"

"No."

Allison's face fell. "Why *not?* Everyone else is going. Do you know how humiliating it'll be if I can't?"

"You mean to say that Alyssa's mom okayed this?"

"Well, not yet. But she will."

"Uh-huh. She will if you say I okayed it. But I can't, Allie. You're fourteen. That's a little young for an all-night prom party, especially with what happened yesterday."

"There won't be any drinking."

"Why do you need to spend the night? What's wrong with coming home at midnight? I'd even give you until one. Dad or I could pick you up then."

Allison looked horrified. "We're taking a *limo,* Mom. We're not having *parents* drive us."

"Who's paying for a limo?"

"We're splitting it. There are ten of us. It won't come to much." The phone rang. She snatched it up. "Hello?" She listened, then covered the receiver and said to Georgia, "I have to take this call."

"Is your homework done?"

"Almost. I'll finish right after this." Her eyes grew wide, her voice urgent. "Please, Mom."

Feeling that she'd been dismissed by a child too young to be dismissing anyone, but trying to respect her daughter's right to privacy, she said, "Okay. But no all-night party. I may give on the limo. I'll have to talk with your dad. But no all-night party."

She left the room and looked in on Tommy. He was sprawled on his bed sound asleep. She used to be able to rearrange him, but he was too big now. So she settled for turning off the light, and went off in search of Russ.

He was in his office, typing the last of his column. Resting her chin on his shoulder, she read from the computer screen: *"The trick is knowing when you're beat. Sometimes all the lint-picking in the world can't right the wrong you did, so you go back to square one. Start over again, even when it galls you, even when you don't have the time or the hot water, even when you're low on soap."* She eyed him sideways. "What's the problem?"

"A tissue goes through the wash cycle and shreds all over the clothes," he murmured as he continued to type.

"No problem there," she said. "You just run the wash through again."

". . . *wash through again,*" he finished with a flourish

and grinned at her. "I did learn that this week. Knowing when to cut your losses is Life Lesson Four-twenty-two. Goin' to bed?"

"I thought I would."

"I just have to proof this and fax it in. Go ahead. I'll be quick."

She took a bath, powdered herself, brushed her teeth and hair, lightly moisturized her face. Dimming the bedroom lights, she stood at the window and looked out just as Graham's truck came down the street.

"Hi ya, cutie," Russ called from the door. Closing it carefully, he crossed the carpet, slipped his arms around her from behind, and nuzzled her neck.

"Did Allie mention a prom to you?" Georgia asked.

"No," he murmured against her nape. "Mmm, yes. I think."

"She wants to go to an all-night party."

Russ turned her around. "Shh," he whispered and took her mouth. "Not now. I want you now."

She could feel that, and she wasn't immune. Slipping her arms around his neck, she gave him her mouth, then, in bits and snatches, the rest of her until they were naked in bed with their limbs entwined. He had always been an avid lover. Sixteen years of marriage hadn't diminished his need. Her own had become refined. She liked the emotions involved in making love with Russ, just as much as the physical act. She liked knowing that this was her husband, her anchor, her home. She liked restaking this intimate claim.

As "welcome homes" went, it was a good one. He was hungry and easily satisfied, and if she failed to climax, that was fine. He was asleep within minutes. She took pleasure in that. Watching Russ sleep, seeing the small smile on his face, the looseness of his features, the utter limpness of long arms and legs, was as satisfying to her as an orgasm.

Russ was even-tempered. He was calm and serene. Looking at him now, she could see all of those things. He was content with his life—so much so that there were times when she wondered whether he missed her when she was gone. He said he did, but only at her urging.

"Did you miss me?" she'd ask.

"You bet."

"I have to leave again Monday." She always half hoped that he would tell her he was tired of that routine.

But he hadn't yet. Instead, he smiled. "I'll keep the home fires burning."

"I don't like being gone so much."

"But you love what you do."

She did love what she did, but it struck her now that Russ loved what she did, too. He might miss her, but he managed quite well while she was gone. He had adapted quite nicely to running the house, making daily decisions, reading the newspaper at the kitchen table in the middle of the morning or lying out in the yard with a paper and pen, doing his work that way. With the kids in school all day, he had freedom and flexibility. Take this day. He had gone to lunch with his editor and returned late, though Georgia would never have known that if she hadn't come home when she had.

So how many other things didn't she know? How many other times was he gone from the house with no one to answer to? Was he fooling around with Gretchen? Was he spending his afternoons in the comfort of her house? Worse, was she spending her afternoons *here?*

Georgia didn't think so. There would be signs. Besides, Russ was too hungry for her when she returned from a trip to suggest he was getting that elsewhere.

He was her husband. He didn't cheat.

Not now, at least. But if she stayed on the road, what would be in five years? Allison would be away at college. Tommy would be driving himself around. And Russ? When the custodial demands of parenthood eased, and he didn't have things like tissue shreds in the wash to fill his time, would he be lonely and bored?

She wasn't quite sure.

Karen always let out a sigh of relief when the house settled down for the night. Julie had been asleep for an hour, but the twins, who were far worse in the noise department, had finally dropped off. Jordie was still awake, but it was only ten. He wouldn't think of going to sleep at ten. His door was closed, but she could see the light underneath.

She knocked quietly, then opened the door and looked in. Jordie sat on the floor with his back to the wall, his knees bent, and his headphones on. He didn't look up, obviously hadn't heard her.

Grateful for the moment, she studied him. Looks wise, he had taken after Lee from the start. Now adolescence was giving him length before breadth, which meant that he was ropy and lean. But he had the same chiseled features as his father—the same square jaw, straight nose, blue eyes. He also had the same thick hair. Jordie's was sandy and long; Lee's was blond and spiked. Karen didn't care for either style, but hair was the least of her worries. Jordie frowned too much. Here he was, doing it again now.

He looked up, stared at her for a minute, then freed up an ear. "What?"

She smiled. "I was just looking in. It's getting late."

"Is Dad home?"

"Not yet."

"Where is he?"

"At the office. They're moving files and machines into the space they just took over. He had to supervise. I thought I explained that at dinner."

"But what's taking so long?"

"I don't know. I guess there's lots to move and set up."

Jordie looked like he didn't buy that—and Karen didn't either, but what could she do? As alibis went, it was a plausible one. She knew that Lee had taken new space, expanding into the offices that a small law firm had recently vacated. He had been complaining about the noise and dust for weeks.

"Have you called him?" Jordie asked.

"No. I figure the less I disturb him, the sooner he'll be home. Did you want him for something special?"

"Me? No." He returned the headphone to his ear.

She raised her voice. "Jordie?"

Scowling, he moved the headphone away again.

"Is everything okay with Quinn?"

"What's okay? He's off the team for the year."

"How's he handlng it?"

"Fine. He always handles things fine."

"Are you angry at me?"

"No."

She waited for him to say more. Something was definitely eating at him. But she couldn't get him to talk if he didn't want to. So she said, "Okay. I'll let you get back to your music. Is your homework done?"

"Yes."

"Good night."

He returned the piece to his ear.

Feeling useless, she backed out and closed the door. Lee should have been the one to talk to him. Boys that age needed their fathers. But Lee wasn't good at talking. Lee was only good at playing.

Back in her own bedroom, she got ready for bed, turned out the lights, and opened the front windows wide. Then she climbed into bed and lay in the dark wondering where Lee was, listening for his car. She heard Graham's truck as he drove in. It had a distinctive sound. She heard the chirp of a cricket and the snapping of underbrush in the woods behind the houses. Night creatures were at play, though whether human or animal, she didn't know.

Then Lee's Miata came purring down the street, and in a split second, she imagined his having parked on the far side of the woods, hiked through to Gretchen's, then hiked back and driven around. Granted, the woods were deep, and the timing of the sounds she'd heard was wrong. Still, given the growing list of questionable calls made from his cell phone, she figured he could be devious.

Turning over, she pulled up the sheet and closed her eyes.

Lee stayed downstairs for a while. When he came up, he got ready for bed and climbed in. "Karen?" he whispered as he always did, testing to see if she was awake and aware of when he'd come home.

As she always did these days, she remained silent.

Chapter Eight

Graham was gone from the bathroom when Amanda went in the next morning. The shower door was wet, the towels askew. She opened his closet with her heart in her throat, fearful that he might have packed up and taken his things, infinitely relieved when she found everything there.

She showered, dressed, and did her makeup and hair, all the while assuming he would be gone from the house by the time she was done, and wondering how she felt about that. When she went downstairs, though, he was in the kitchen, leaning against the counter with his ankles crossed. Despite the pose, there was nothing relaxed about him. His knuckles were white around a mug of coffee. His hair was damp, his eyes dark.

"Hi," she said with a cautious smile.

"You didn't come to bed last night. That's the second night in a row."

The gauntlet thrown, she said, "I fell asleep. You didn't wake me." She had woken several times on her own, wondering, waiting, fearing. She needed a sign from him that he didn't blame her for their not having kids. She needed a sign that he loved her and wouldn't *dream* of going to another woman.

At this moment, though, all she wanted was peace between them. The tension was starting to fester. It was so like the charged atmosphere she had grown up with—and so unlike what she thought she had with Graham—that she couldn't deal with it.

So she asked, "How did your meeting go?"

"It went fine. Did you talk with Emily?" His voice was tight. Apparently, he wasn't going for peace.

"Yes. I told her I'd call her in a month."

"What did she say?"

"She said that was fine."

"Did she agree with you about taking a month off?"

"She understood what I was feeling."

"Then she agreed?"

Amanda couldn't lie. "No. She would just as soon go ahead with the third try, but she said that it wouldn't hurt to wait a month."

"I'm with her on going for the third try now."

But the mere thought of it made Amanda's head buzz. "I can't, Graham. I can't go right on. I need a break."

"Is this about you? Or about you and me?"

"Me," she said. But it was fast becoming the other.

Graham knew it, too. He shook his head and looked away, downed the last of his coffee, and set the mug in the sink. "I'm going back to Providence this afternoon. I may be late again."

It used to be that late nights weren't allowed twice in a row, but they were becoming more and more common. On this day, it was unfortunate. Amanda needed to sit over dinner with Graham and talk.

But Graham didn't say another thing. He went out to the breezeway, letting the screen door clatter behind him. It was silent by the time Amanda reached it, but she gripped the handle nonetheless and watched while he backed the truck from the driveway and took off.

Not knowing what to think or do, she stayed there until the school bus came down the street. As soon as it headed out again with two Langes and four Cotters on board, she went outside. She intercepted Georgia, who was returning from the curb.

One look at her, and Georgia slipped an arm around her waist. "Have time for a cup of coffee?"

Amanda shook her head. "I have to get to school. I just need a sympathetic ear for a minute first." And Georgia's was a good one. She was a role model of sorts, having been married three times as long as Amanda had. Amanda wanted that longevity for herself and Graham.

"Is it the baby thing that's getting you down?"

"Whose?" Amanda asked dryly. "Mine or Gretchen's."

Georgia smiled. "Yours. For starters."

"Yes, it's getting me down. Graham and I are hitting a wall on what to do next."

"What do you mean, hitting a wall?"

"Disagreeing. We never used to do that."

"Disagreeing about having a baby?"

"No, about how to go about doing it. And about Gretchen. I did something awful, Georgia. I suggested that maybe he was the father."

"You didn't."

"I did," Amanda said in self-reproach. "Here I try to teach students not to make accusations they'll regret, and I went and did it myself. He isn't the father. I know that. But I wouldn't be human if I didn't wonder whether he hates what sex has become as much as I do. It used to be so great. Now it's prescribed and programmed. There are rules and regulations about where, when, and how often. Talk about lack of *spontaneity.* But Graham likes spontaneïty. So, no, he isn't the cheating kind, but I don't know the male psyche. Or maybe I do. Lust is a big thing for men. Physical urges. Momentary highs. So maybe Graham got swept up in a moment's passion when he was working with Gretchen last fall. Did I ever tell you that his first wife looks like her?"

"No."

"Megan's hair is more pecan than blond, but her features are so similar—heart-shaped face, procelain skin, wide-set eyes. Her mother became as Irish as possible when she married her father, but the woman was of strong Scandinavian stock."

"Is Gretchen?"

"She sure looks it. I mean, rationally speaking, I *know* Graham wouldn't fool around with her. He's a totally monogamous guy."

"So's Russ, but I have to confess I gave it a thought myself last night. Karen's right. He's around here all day. So maybe he's a rag-amuffin. But if he turns me on, he could just as easily turn on Gretchen."

"Russ is not a ragamuffin."

"He isn't exactly George Clooney."

"Right. Russ is more the norm. I like his looks. He has appeal."

"Well, his appeal sure beats that of the electrician," Georgia remarked. "Nathan is seventy-three and has emphysema. I can't picture him with Gretchen. What do you think about the others?"

All four houses in the cul-de-sac called on the same servicemen. "The plumber got married last summer and is totally starry-eyed. The carpenter is a born-again Christian. Do I see either of them with Gretchen?" She shook her head.

"That leaves Lee."

"A distinct possibility."

"He was supposed to have turned over a new leaf."

Amanda sent her a doubtful look. "So what do I do about Graham? I need a break from this. I've asked for a month. How do I convince him?"

"You know what you'd tell clients."

"I'd tell them to talk it out. But I just *think* about talking to Graham about this and I get tied up in knots." She couldn't imagine Georgia being that way. She wished she were *half* as well-balanced as her friend. "It's depressing. I love Graham. I've always been able to talk to him. But this is different. Are there ever times when you can't talk to Russ?"

"Yes. When we're distracted. When he's hung up on a deadline. Or when we're both rushed. Like this week. I missed the Quinn thing. They've all moved on and don't want to discuss it. Is it really over?"

"For now, I guess."

"I worry about drinking."

"Allie's fine. She's solid."

"So is Quinn."

Amanda was silent, judging how much to say. "Maybe not the way we thought."

"You know more?"

"Only that he has issues." She couldn't say more without breaching a confidence. "You and Russ must have talked about the drinking thing before."

"We have. We generally feel the same way."

"Are there any things that you and Russ are uncomfortable discussing?"

"His brother. The guy is shady. He owns a car dealership in Michigan and lives way above what we would assume a car dealer makes, but any time I say that, Russ hits the roof. He says it's his brother, and he loves him, and it's none of our business how he pays for what he buys. I guess it isn't. Be grateful Graham's brothers are clean."

"Oh, they are that," Amanda said. "I like all of Graham's siblings. His mother's the problem."

"When's her birthday party?"

"Sunday. I'd be looking forward to it, even only to see the others, if it weren't for this latest setback. What if we don't ever have a baby, Georgia? If his family is on our backs now, what'll they be like if a baby never comes?"

"Don't worry about that. There are other ways of being parents."

"Like adoption. I think we should consider it."

"Does Graham?"

"He thinks it's premature. He thinks we need to exhaust all the options for having our own first. My worry is that by the time we do, it'll be too late . . ."

Georgia tried to avoid end-of-the-week travel whenever possible, but this time it couldn't be helped. Executives from the company courting hers wanted a tour of the Florida plant. The only day they could make it was Saturday.

Killing two birds with one stone, she scheduled a full day of meetings with her management team in Tampa on Friday. Such visits were standard; she was the spirit behind the company and a perfectionist, which meant that she wanted things done well at all levels. She wasn't foolish enough to micromanage. She had staff to do that. But her physical presence made a difference, which was why she tried to visit each major office and plant once a month.

Her flight out wasn't until late afternoon on Thursday, and there was her own office in Danbury to visit before then. Still she had lingered with the children before putting them on the bus, then lingered with Amanda before she too drove off, leaving her with the same dreadful qualms she had each day she traveled—qualms that inevitably involved visions of terrorists opening fire while she was waiting for her plane, or the plane crashing. She was about to go in and let Russ cheer her up when the milkman came down the street, his truck creaking with age. It had been weeks since she'd heard that sound. It evoked thoughts of a simpler, safer time.

The Langes and the Cotters had been using the same dairy for years, but Pete usually came in the late morning. Georgia was surprised to see him so early, and was doubly surprised when he stopped at Gretchen's first. He hopped out of his truck with his metal basket and ran up the walk.

The milkman. That was an interesting possibility. He was in his forties and had a family. But he certainly looked eager. When it came to the Langes and the Cotters, he customarily put their orders in the hinged box by the back door. But he went into Gretchen's house and stayed for several minutes. Georgia watched until he reappeared before she went into her own kitchen. Russ was at the table, hidden behind the paper.

"I didn't know Gretchen used the dairy," Georgia said.

He lowered a corner of the paper. "Hmm?"

"Since when has Gretchen been using our dairy?"

"A while. She came over one day and asked for the number. Why?"

"He was in there a while. So maybe Pete's the guy."

Russ rolled his eyes.

Georgia said, "Why not Pete?"

Russ raised his brows and studied her over his glasses. "He has a full day's worth of deliveries to make. He doesn't have time to fool around with customers. Besides, she wasn't using him last October. It wasn't until January that she asked for the number."

Georgia was bemused. "You remember that."

"I do," he said without apology. "I was showing her all the super things Pete brings, and I pulled the last of the Christmas roll from the freezer. We were joking about how it had to be stale. I let her have a taste."

"She was tasting ice cream here in our kitchen?"

"For two minutes. It was snowing outside. She didn't stay long. Didn't do anything more than unbutton her coat. I think it was Ben's coat. It was big." He continued to look at her over his glasses, daring her to make something of the visit.

Instead, she was struck by how adorable he looked with his hair all messed up and his wedding band conversely neat on the long-fingered hand holding the paper. Opting for now to trust and believe, she went over, popped a kiss on the thinnest spot at the top of his head, and gave his shoulder a squeeze.

Karen spent Thursday morning repairing books at the elementary school library. As volunteer chores went, it wasn't mentally demanding. She was grateful that there were other mothers working with her. They talked about this, that, and the other, nothing earth-shattering but enough to keep her from brooding.

She and Lee were barely talking. Self-righteously indignant, he claimed to have been deeply offended by her suggestion that he had fathered Gretchen's child. He had actually marched defiantly to Gretchen's that evening to ask who the father was. He told Karen that Gretchen wouldn't say.

But Karen hadn't been at Gretchen's. She didn't know for sure what was said or done. If Lee wasn't fooling around with Gretchen, though, he was doing it with someone else. Karen would bet money on that.

She returned from school this day at noon and was sitting on her front steps, soaking up the warmth of the sun as an antidote to her emotional chill, when the mailman drove his Jeep down the street and parked. He leaned sideways to sort through his tray, filled his arms with mail, and slipped from the Jeep.

He put the O'Learys' mail in the box at the end of the drive and did the same with the Langes'. He walked the Cotters' mail over to Karen, asked how she was, remarked about the lilacs nearing bloom, and, with a salute, continued on toward the Tannenwald house.

Karen was sorting through the pile on her lap when the mailman called out a greeting to Gretchen, who came right down the driveway to meet him. She was wearing a pretty tunic top and slacks, with what looked to be Italian sandals on her feet. Any one of the three items were fine enough to have come from Saks or Neiman Marcus. Karen didn't shop at either store, not for herself or for the kids. But Lee had bought high-priced items at both, and not for himself. After seeing the charges on his credit card bill, she had checked labels in his closet. She had checked for cuff links that might have been new; naturally, since young techies didn't wear cuff links, there were none. Nor was there a new wallet.

Someone was benefiting from his largesse. She wondered if Gretchen wore a necklace hidden under her tunic, or earrings under the swing of that pretty blond hair, or a sparkly bracelet under her cuff. She was holding a manila envelope as she talked with the mailman. A bracelet might easily have slipped toward her elbow and out of sight.

The mailman was shorter than Gretchen and more round than a man who lugged mail up and down walks each day should be. Of course, he didn't always walk. Normally he drove from mailbox to mailbox, leaning out of his truck at each. Karen wondered why he had chosen to walk today. It could be that he had an abbreviated afternoon route and therefore time to spare, or that he wanted the spring sun or the exercise. It could also be that he wanted Gretchen.

There were smiles and several minutes of a conversation that Karen couldn't make out. Gretchen handed him the manila envelope and took a thicker one from him, plus smaller pieces. When one letter fell to the ground, Gretchen reached for it, but the mailman retrieved it first. He handed it over, smiled, and returned to his truck.

The mailman. The physical disparity between them didn't rule it out. Karen had seen tall women with short men. She had seen slim women with chubby men. Who could account for tastes?

Lee, on the other hand, was sinfully handsome. A woman could hate his spiked hair and still see that. He and Karen had been a handsome couple on their wedding day. Then life had grown complicated, what with children and work, and Lee's affairs had taken their toll. They made her feel inadequate and unattractive.

Turning, she went into the house and fixed a peanut-butter-and-potato-chip sandwich. She didn't care if it was starchy. She needed comfort food.

The sandwich helped only marginally. Back in the car, she headed to the home of the woman in charge of the all-school graduation party that was thrown by the town for its seniors each year. Karen and she would work together for several hours, going through the list of local stores that could be counted on to make donations for the event. Then Karen would head home in time for the school bus to arrive.

Needing more comfort than the sandwich brought, she vowed to keep an eye out for Amanda. Amanda was a sure bet to give comfort.

Karen wanted to ask her about the mailman. While she was at it, she wanted to know what was in the manila envelopes that were coming and going next door. She figured that Amanda had a stake in all this. After all, if Lee wasn't the father of the baby, even money said it was Graham.

Amanda immediately shook her head when Karen waylaid her as she climbed from her car later that afternoon and mentioned the mailman as a suspect. "Dominic? I can't believe that he'd have the courage, much less the desire to impregnate Gretchen."

"Because of his looks?"

"Because his mother is the center of his life."

"How do you know?"

"I've talked with him. I was outside one day when he came by, and he was looking so down in the mouth that I asked what was wrong. He lives with his mother. She's a semi-invalid, and he's her major caretaker. He was upset that day because she needed to have dental work done and he didn't have the money. The only alternative was to pull her teeth, and that was upsetting him."

"A fine son," Karen murmured. Putting her hands on her hips, she looked around the cul-de-sac. "Does Graham know anything?"

"I don't think so."

"Did he ask Gretchen?"

"Not to my knowledge."

"Russ did. So did Lee. Isn't Graham curious?"

Amanda was still for a minute. Then, softly, she said, "Karen, I don't think it's Graham. If he didn't ask, it's because he didn't think it was important."

"I'd say it's important."

"Okay. What did Russ and Lee learn?"

"Nothing. She wouldn't say who the father is. Maybe she'll tell Graham." Her voice grew hushed. "Oh. Look. There she is."

Gretchen came around the far side of her house with the garden hose in hand. When she glanced their way, Amanda raised a hand in greeting. Gretchen nodded, turned her back, and began watering her beds.

"That wasn't terribly friendly," Karen murmured. "She's toying with us."

"It may just be that she feels awkward."

"Because the baby's father is one of our husbands?"

"No. Because we're together and she isn't our friend."

"And whose fault is that?" Karen asked, raising a hand to wave at the paperboy, who was riding his bicycle down the street, his basket filled with the local weekly. "Hey, Davey," she called, then told Amanda, "I worked with his parents on last year's Christmas bazaar."

"Hey, Mrs. Cotter," Davey called back, but he had stopped in front of the widow's house and was holding out the paper while Gretchen crossed the grass.

"He may be towheaded and adorable, but I don't think he's a suspect," Amanda murmured, but she was entranced watching the widow. When Gretchen smiled, as she was doing at the boy, there was a definite warmth to her. And a shyness. Amanda had never noticed that quality before.

The paperboy glided toward them with one foot skimming the pavement. He offered a paper to each.

"I haven't seen your parents in a while," Karen told him. "How are they?"

"They're fine."

"Tell them I say hello."

"I will," he said. He sailed off, tossing a paper onto the Langes' front steps with a deft overhand lob and heading down the street.

As a matter of habit, Amanda opened the paper. She sucked in a sharp breath when she saw the headline.

Chapter Nine

BASEBALL STAR SUSPENDED AFTER DRINKING INCIDENT, read the headline, and the article went on to relate, in exact detail, the events of Tuesday.

Amanda murmured a soft, "Oh *no.*"

Karen had unfolded her own paper and was reading the same piece. "Well, it *is* news."

"Not like this. It's not even on the sports page. Talk about being pilloried."

"When you're a star, you have to take the good with the bad."

All Amanda could think about was Quinn Davis nervously rubbing his thumbs and forefingers at the meeting the other night. He wasn't all calmness and confidence. A kid who was in control didn't show up at baseball practice drunk. Given the vehemence with which his parents had tried to sweep his offense under the rug, this front-page exposure wouldn't sit well with them. Amanda could only begin to wonder how it would sit with Quinn himself.

She had no sooner stepped inside her kitchen when the phone rang. It was Maggie Dodd, as concerned as she was about the article. Yes, school officials had been asked about the incident, she said, but they hadn't given out details. Apparently those had come from the baseball coach, members of the team, and Quinn's friends.

Amanda and she were talking about possible fallout when Maggie put her on hold to take another call. When she came back, her voice was tight. "Quinn's parents. They're livid. They want to know how their son could be smeared this way."

Part of Amanda agreed with Karen's earlier, rather blunt assessment of the situation. In the four years that she had been reading the *Woodley Weekly,* there had been numerous front-page articles praising one Davis or another. This was the flip side of that coin, inevitable in some regards. To some extent, it *was* just news.

The other part of her—the counselor—worried about Quinn. "Let me call them," she suggested to Maggie. "I'll go over there to talk if they'll let me."

They wouldn't. "That would be a waste of our time, Ms. Carr," Quinn's father said. "You could have helped us the other night. But you aren't on our side."

"It isn't about taking sides," Amanda reasoned. "It's about doing what's best for Quinn. My concern right now is for him. Has he seen this article?"

"Of course he has. He couldn't miss it. His friends have been calling. *Our* friends have been calling."

"Is he all right?"

"No. But that's not your concern."

"It is. It's my job. It's my *nature.* I'd really like to talk with him."

"We'll handle it. Thank you." He hung up the phone.

* * *

Amanda felt helpless on the matter of Quinn. She wanted to talk it over with Graham. His instincts were good. He could reassure her or make a suggestion. It would be a neutral subject they could discuss.

For a minute, she thought her wish had come true. Graham called shortly after she hung up the phone with Quinn's father.

"Hi," he said cautiously. She could hear that he was in the truck. The reception had that hands-off quality.

"Hi. Where are you?" she asked, as she often did, wondering whether he was two, ten, or twenty minutes away. This time, though, her voice held the same caution as his, which made the question sound distrustful.

His voice reflected that. It was harder, closed to discussion. "Just now heading for Providence. I'm running way late."

She let a beat pass. "Will this be every day?"

"I don't know. It's a good job. It helps fill the time when you're at school."

"I'm not at school every night."

"Well, Tuesday you ran back."

"It was important."

"So is this." He swore. Amanda heard the angry honk of a horn, then Graham's angry voice. "That bastard just cut into my lane, smack in front of me at seventy-five miles an hour."

"You don't usually drive that fast."

"I'm running late."

"Was it a bad day?"

"Just busy."

So much for conversation. "When will you be home?"

"Ten, eleven."

"Okay. Have a good meeting."

"Yup."

Amanda hung up the phone thinking of all the things she could have said, *should* have said—all the ways she might have gotten him to talk more. But this Graham was a stranger to her. She didn't know how he would react to the things she said. She didn't know how the things she said would even come out. Perhaps it was better that she didn't even try to open up.

Sex might do it. They had always related on a physical level.

Although not in recent months.

But her period was ebbing, and she refused to think about the clinical aspects of baby-making, so maybe passion had a chance.

At least, that was what she was thinking when, later that evening, she bathed in bubbles, creamed her body with scented lotion, put on one of the slightly indecent nightgowns Graham had bought her during their earliest, randiest days, and climbed into their bed. As olive branches went, it was a fair one.

She lay nervously in the dark, glancing at the clock every few minutes from ten o'clock on. It was after eleven when Graham came in. She heard him come up the stairs and waited for him to come into the bedroom. Instead, he went into the den and turned on the television. At midnight, she went to the door and looked in. He was sleeping.

Wake him up, part of her cried. But she couldn't. If he was in the kind of mood he had been in on the phone, he wouldn't be receptive to seduction. That would leave her feeling foolish and more unwanted than ever.

So she crept back to their bedroom and lay in the dark trying to clear unhappy thoughts from her brain, sleepless until sheer exhaustion finally took its toll.

She was awake at six-thirty the next morning, when Graham came into the bedroom. He went to the closet, took out clean clothes, removed the ones he had slept in and tossed them in the hamper, then headed for the bathroom. She listened to the sound of the shower and for a split second thought to join him there—then lost her nerve.

"Hi, cutie," Maddie said when Amanda walked into her office.

"Hi, cutie," Amanda said right back, but went straight to her computer and e-mailed Graham. "Are you there?" She knew it was the coward's approach. But if it worked for the most reticent of her students, it might work for her.

After one student session and ten minutes wandering the halls looking for Quinn, she got a reply. "I'm here," he wrote. "What's up?"

"We need to talk," she wrote back, sent the message, then spent thirty minutes in the teachers' lounge talking with Quinn's English teacher. The boy had been in her class that morning looking for all the world as if he didn't have a care in the world. Had he been prepared? The teacher wasn't sure. The assignment had been parts of *King Lear,* and they had watched a theater video during class.

Graham's answer was waiting when Amanda returned to her office. "Fine. Talk."

"Are you angry?" she typed in.

His response came in as little time as it took for

him to receive, read, and reply. "Yeah, I'm angry. This isn't the way our marriage was supposed to be."

"Our marriage has been great," she wrote back, underlining and bolding the "great." "This is our first problem."

"Are you referring to the baby thing or the trust thing?"

"Both," she typed and had barely started reading transfer reports when his answer came back.

"But there is no issue of trust in the baby thing."

"Yes, there is."

"How?"

She thought about how to answer while she wandered the halls during a break in class. Some of her best student contacts had been made during this kind of wandering. Visibility was important. Availability ran a close second.

There were no breakthroughs in the halls this time, though she did see Quinn. He was laughing with friends and seemed fine. He didn't look her way, but then, she didn't expect him to. He was avoiding what he couldn't handle.

Was she? She prided herself on being older and wiser than her students, but being evasive with Graham was not terribly mature.

So she returned to her office and wrote him her deepest fear. "What happens if we can't have a baby? Can I trust that you'll still want to be married to me?"

"I love you," Maddie said.

Smiling sadly, Amanda gave the bird a treat. "You're a sweetie."

"Treat, sweet?" the bird asked.

"Treat, sweet," she answered and offered another treat. Then she went back to her computer.

Graham's answer came within minutes. "That's such an insulting question," he wrote, underlining and bolding the "such."

"But I know how much you want children," she typed back. "I know how much your family does. Your family means the world to you. I'm not sure I do."

"It's the choice thing again, then?"

"No. Just me needing reassurance. I haven't been feeling very feminine lately."

"Well, I haven't been feeling very manly. It doesn't help when you sleep in the den. Makes me feel like you don't want me."

"Who slept in the den last night?" she wrote back, then sent an instant follow-up. "E-mail sucks. That's going to come across the wrong way. I'm not accusing you. It's just that I don't know what you're feeling."

"Rejected," he wrote back.

Her heart ached. "Can we have dinner tonight? I'll pick up steaks and a salad, and we'll talk."

While she waited for his reply, she met with another student, then ate lunch in the cafeteria with a group of juniors she was advising on a community service project. She spent an uneasy thirty minutes back in her office making notes on the student meetings she'd had that morning, before Graham responded to her invitation.

"You don't talk. You accuse and withdraw."

"That's what I learned," she wrote back, and nearly erased it. She could blame her parents all she wanted, but that wouldn't help her own marriage. At some point, she had to take responsibility for her actions. That said, what she'd written did help explain why she did what she did. So she left it and added, "Help me change, Graham."

His response came within minutes. "I'll be home for dinner."

Graham resisted thinking the word "divorce," but having been through it once, it was an irrevocable part of his vocabulary. If his marriage to Amanda fell apart, that would make him a two-time loser. Coming from the family he did—coming from the religious background he did—it would be an emotional blow from which he might never recover.

Besides, divorce was so far away as to be laughable. He loved Amanda. They had hit a rocky stretch. That was all.

He wished he knew what to do. Everything about her said that she wanted to be left alone, so that was what he had done. If she wanted to sleep alone, fine. He was giving her space. He didn't like it, but he didn't see that he had a choice. He wasn't demeaning himself by crawling to her, especially if she was having second thoughts about their marriage. Maybe she wanted out like Megan had. Maybe there was something wrong with him in the husband department. Maybe there was something wrong with him in the *man* department.

What had she said—that e-mail sucked because things came across the wrong way? Lately, when it came to Amanda, that was the story of his life. He could talk about anything and everything with his brothers without worrying about who was taking him how, but with his wife every word counted—not only counted, but came out too harsh. So much was at stake.

Now they had a date. They would talk over dinner. He wished he could take a crash course on communicating with his wife before then. He wished he was better at marriage.

He was good at work. He had more of that than he could handle. Had Amanda been pregnant, he would have refused the Providence job. As appealing as it was—as professionally challenging—it was going to be time-consuming..

But Amanda wasn't pregnant, so he was grateful for the demand on his time. He worked at the office until late Friday afternoon, then went home because, when all was said and done, he wanted to hold Amanda. But she wasn't even there yet.

He was of half a mind to go back to the office. He didn't want to look overeager, didn't want to open himself up for disappointment if she wasn't on the same page he was. But he loved the house, and there were things to do here:.

He was washing the truck when Jordie Cotter walked over. "Need some help?"

"Sure." Graham tossed him a cloth. "Wipe close around the edges of the lights. Dirt gets stuck there. I got most of it with the hose, but if you want to check, that'd be great. Hey. Isn't there a game today?" Local parents came out in large numbers for Friday afternoon baseball games. Graham often stopped by the field himself, particularly now that he knew the players through Jordie.

Jordie's mouth went flat. "Today was just practice. The game was yesterday. We lost."

"Bad?"

"Twelve–three."

Graham grimaced. "Ouch."

"It's because we lost Quinn," the boy charged. "Edlin should've considered that when he suspended him. Did Amanda go along with the suspension?"

Graham wasn't committing Amanda one way or the other. "I don't know. But something had to be done. Kids can't just be showing up at practice drunk. So the team's pretty bummed out?"

"Yeah." Jordie wiped the taillights with a passing effort. "The tower lost more rocks."

"I know. I was out there the other night." He and Jordie shared a love of the woods that had started soon after Graham and Amanda moved into the house. Jordie had been ten, eleven, even twelve, leading Graham to the tower, sitting with him at its base. Together, they had speculated on its origin and created more than a few outlandish theories.

It had been a while since they had gone into the woods together. More than once, though, Graham had seen Jordie head in there alone.

"Think it'll fall?" Jordie asked now.

"It hasn't so far."

"Do you know about Gretchen's baby?"

Scrubbing at crusted dirt on the running board, Graham shifted gears. "Actually, yeah. Found out the other day."

"What do you think?"

"I think it's cool."

"I mean, like, who was she with? Who's the father?"

"It could be anyone. We don't know who Gretchen sees."

"She doesn't see anyone. I heard my mom talking. She thinks it's my dad."

Graham stopped working and looked at the boy. "Who'd she say that to?"

"Herself. She talks out loud when she's angry. You know, kind of slams around, muttering. I heard her this morning. She was making the beds. They were arguing about it the other night. She didn't accuse him to his face, but she came close. Do you think he did it?"

"No," Graham said as he knew he should. Jordie talked to him in ways that he didn't talk with many adults, perhaps because Graham was always honest. But this was Jordie's father they were talking about, and nothing had been proven. "He loves your mother."

"That hasn't stopped him before," Jordie muttered, and it struck Graham just how far he had come from the boy who had gone with him into the woods. He was leaning against the back of the truck now with his eyes on the widow's house. "She's lookin' out at us right now, y'know."

"No. Actually, I didn't know that."

"She stands in the dining room looking over the curtains."

"Maybe she feels you looking at her."

"What does she want with us?"

"Same thing anyone wants from a neighbor. Or a neighborhood."

A small red BMW came down the street. Jordie took one look and was transformed. "Oh wow," he exclaimed. "Look at that car!"

Graham looked. He saw a kid who looked too young to drive, in a car that he sure as hell hadn't bought himself. "Who is that?"

"Alex Stauer. Hey, I gotta run." He passed the cloth back to Graham, and did just that. Within seconds, he had squeezed into the backseat of the car, and the car had swung around the circle and zoomed off down the street.

Graham was looking after it when Lee Cotter drove up. "Was that my kid?" he called out the window.

"Yup," Graham said and returned to his work.

Lee parked and walked over. "That was quite some car."

"Driven by Alex Stauer. Wasn't he one of the boys suspended from the team along with Quinn?"

"Sure was."

"Think that was his parents' idea of a consolation prize?"

"It's his mother's car. She has a little wild streak," Lee said with a smirk that was a bit too familiar.

"How do you know that?" Graham asked and, in the next breath, held up a hand. "Don't answer. I don't want to know. Then if the wise guys get me and hold a flame to my balls, I won't have anything to say."

Lee chuckled, then sobered. "Speaking of which, I'd appreciate it if you'd downplay any talk about me and the widow." When Graham shot him an innocent look, he said, "Karen's making noise about it. She thinks I fathered that baby."

"Did you?"

"Would I tell you and give the wise guys a weapon?" Lee asked. "Just stand by me on this one. It used to be that I could show Karen I loved her by having another baby or two ourselves, but the last time I tried that, we ended up with three."

"You could've stopped at the twins."

Lee grimaced. "There was a small thing after the twins. I had to do a little more convincing."

Graham felt a wave of dislike. "Karen deserves better."

Lee chuckled. "All women do, but, hey, that's how it

goes. She's got her house. She's got her kids. We do the vacation bit twice a year. She does pretty well in the overall scheme of things. So cover me with Gretchen? Ask Amanda to get Karen off my back on this?"

Graham wasn't doing any such thing. Even if he approved of what Lee was doing, which he didn't, he had many more important things to discuss with his wife.

Amanda stopped in the center of Woodley for food on her way home from work. She picked up two filet mignons at the meat market, a head of fresh Bibb lettuce, a huge beefsteak tomato, one fresh pepper in each red, orange, and green, and the makings for Graham's favorite raspberry vinaigrette. When she drove down the street of the cul-de-sac, she didn't do more than glance at Gretchen, who was watering her flowers again, or wave quickly at Karen, who was on her front porch. Her eyes gravitated to Graham, who looked so normal and lovable, polishing his truck with a towel, that she actually felt shy.

She caught his eye when she climbed from her car.

"Need help with the bundles?" he asked.

She shook her head, gave him a quick smile, and went inside. She set the dining room table using the fine china, crystal, and silver they had received as wedding gifts. She rinsed the steaks, patted them dry, and put them on a platter. She made the salad, then the dressing. She was about to go to the bedroom to freshen up and change clothes when the phone rang.

Fearful that it was a business call for Graham, which would be totally unwelcome at this juncture, she picked up and said a rushed, "Hello?"

"Amanda? It's Maggie. We have a suicide."

Chapter Ten

Suicide. Amanda sucked in a breath. "Who?" she asked, but she knew. She was already conjuring up Quinn's face. When Maggie Dodd confirmed it, Amanda exhaled loudly. She closed her eyes and pressed a fist to her forehead, as though that might erase the images there, but she wasn't being spared.

"He hanged himself in the locker room," Maggie said. "The janitor had run into him there earlier, right after the team finished practice, and told him he ought to go home, too. Quinn asked if he could stay there for a little while to do his homework; he said it was where he concentrated best. Mr. Dubcek felt sorry for him after the hullabaloo over the suspension, so he allowed it. He left and went about his business. When he got back an hour later, he found Quinn. He tried to revive him, but it was way too late."

Way too late. The words echoed with a finality that chilled Amanda to the bone. Yes, for her the failure to conceive a baby was a kind of death, but it was nothing like this. Quinn Davis was fully formed. He was a living, breathing human being. He had a name, a face, a personality. He was totally viable in the world, and given his athletic prowess and leadership skill, was a productive member of the community.

"Dead," Amanda whispered, aching with impotence. "I knew he wasn't what he seemed, but I didn't imagine this. Are you sure it was deliberate?"

"It was deliberate. He left notes for his parents and his girlfriend."

Amanda let out another loud breath. Suicide was as bad as it got. "To feel that kind of pain . . ."

"We didn't know, Amanda. None of us did. But right now we have to think ahead. He was known and loved. Even students who weren't his friends will feel this. For most of them, it'll be their first brush with mortality."

Amanda was the psychologist. She knew what Maggie was talking about and should have been the one saying it. But she was in shock.

"Fallout," she managed to murmur. That was the concern. Extreme fear, deep depression, even copycat suicides—they were the nightmare of a school psychologist. That thought brought her to her senses. "Who knows about it?" she asked Maggie.

"His family. His friends. Two of them were waiting for him at the house when we called. They'll have told others by now, and word will spread fast. What do we do?"

Amanda allowed herself one last stunned exhalation before pushing aside thoughts of Quinn himself and focusing on those he had left behind. "Get the crisis team together. This is what it's for." As she said it, she was pulling her Filofax from the briefcase she had dropped on a kitchen chair. The list was there, with phone numbers. "We need to meet to discuss how to deal. Whatever students the grapevine doesn't reach tonight will hear about it in the morning. Can Fred stay?"

"He's planning on it. Send everyone to his office."

Amanda's mind was in operational mode. "There's a grief counselor I'd also like to call. She led a seminar on school suicide that I attended last fall, and she doesn't live far from Woodley. It's usually better for kids to be with people they know at times like this, but she's a wonderfully warm and approachable person. I'd like her on hand. I'll call her after I've called the others."

"What can I do?"

"Call the heads of the departments and have them call their teachers. If they can all meet with us at school tomorrow, say at nine, we'll be able to fill them in on the meeting tonight."

"When will you be here?"

Amanda glanced at the clock on the wall, only then seeing counters strewn with the makings of a romantic, conciliatory dinner for Graham.

But a student was dead. Work crises didn't get any worse. He would have to understand.

It was nearly six. "Give me a few minutes to call the team. How does seven sound?"

She had barely started making her calls when Graham came up the back steps. She met him at the door, refusing to see the bouquet of wildflowers that he had picked from what he called his "private stash" at the back of the yard.

"I just got a call. Quinn Davis committed suicide."

Graham dropped his hand, the flowers forgotten. His face paled. "*Killed* himself?" he asked in disbelief.

Amanda nodded, feeling the reality of it full force. "He hanged himself, Gray. In the locker room at school."

Graham remained disbelieving. "Quinn Davis?"

"He was smart," she said, listing all the reasons this should never have happened. "He was good-looking. He was athletic. He was personable. He had everything to live for. His only blemish was a single drinking offense, and the police weren't even involved with that."

Graham pushed a hand through his hair and exhaled, releasing remnants of optimism and hope, much as Amanda had done when she had first learned of the death. "But it was a public thing, being banned from the team," he said, trying to reason it out. "And the paper made such a big deal of it. They said he lived and breathed baseball. So, he killed himself for missing six games? Would six games have mattered in the overall scheme of things? Would he remember those six games when he was playing in college? Or after, if he made the pros?"

Amanda put a hand to her stomach. Her insides were knotted. "There was more. Something deeper. If he and I had been able to connect, I might have known what it was, but it's too late, now. He's gone."

"Oh, Mandy," Graham said and took her in his arms. "You can't blame yourself for this."

She didn't say anything at first. It felt so wonderful to be held, to be the object of Graham's warmth again, that she simply breathed it in and savored the comfort until, yes, guilt got the better of her. She let her arms drop and stepped back.

"Quinn is—was a leader. The thing now is to make sure no one else holds him up as a hero and tries what he did."

"There's no rationale for that."

"There's no rationale for suicide, period." She folded her arms. "It's frustrating. Here *we* are, trying so hard to bring a child into the world, and another child takes himself out, just like that. It isn't fair, Gray."

"Lots of things aren't," he muttered. Walking past her, he put the flowers down and stood with his hands on the counter and his back to her—and suddenly she wanted to talk about all of it. She wanted to talk about who deserved what, and what it took to be a good parent, and the fact that she and Gray would be the best parents ever. She wanted to talk about the things that could ruin relationships and how to nip them in the bud. She wanted to talk about the dreams that seemed to be going up in smoke.

But she didn't have time. She had more calls to make, then a meeting to attend. Attend? Conduct. How Woodley High handled this crisis was her responsibility. As the one in charge, she felt a tremendous weight.

"I'm sorry about dinner," she said.

He waved the concern away but didn't turn. "I have work to do anyway."

"I don't know when I'll be back."

"Neither do I."

"Then you aren't working here?"

"No. I'll go to the office. I concentrate better there."

"The periwinkles are beautiful."

"It was a thought. We almost had it."

The last phrase caught her. It had so many levels of meaning that if she dared think about them, she would be totally depressed. Easier to concentrate on the calls she had to make.

"Later, maybe?" she said as she picked up the phone.

"Sure," he said. But he didn't sound convinced.

Even though Graham understood the crisis, he resented Amanda for leaving. She was walking out on him at a time when he needed her. Yes, he knew death was the ultimate tragedy. Yes, he knew they could talk later. *Yes*, he knew he was behaving badly.

But knowing was rational. His feelings weren't. Again, he felt rebuffed.

Angry at that, he waited until Amanda had driven off, then walked across the street and around the yard to Gretchen Tannenwald's back door. He didn't see the Russian olive trees that he had planted in a sea of pachysandra, or the shag carpet of juniper, or the dogwood. He didn't even see the rough-hewn bluestones that he had placed as a path around the house. Single-mindedly, he knocked, then rang the bell, tempering his impatience only when he saw Gretchen approach.

She didn't smile when she saw him. "I was wondering when you'd come," she said and opened the door.

He entered the kitchen. "I don't follow."

"Russ and Lee have both been here."

"Yeah, well, the question is running rampant around the circle. Me, I figure I don't need to know. How're you feeling?"

"I'm okay."

"Anything need doing?"

She thought for a minute, then shrugged. "No. Not now. Can I get you coffee? A Coke?"

"No, thanks. I can't stay. I took my chances coming here. Someone will see and talk." He was thinking about Karen. For that matter, Lee wouldn't hesitate to spread the word if he could benefit from it.

"If I'm not making demands on anyone," Gretchen asked, "why is it so important?"

"Because trust is fragile," he said. Bowing his head, he rubbed the back of his neck. Then, sighing, he looked up again. "Listen, I don't know what the others said. But please yell if you need me."

Pressing her lips together, she nodded.

He held her gaze for a last minute, binding her to the agreement. Then, fishing his keys from the pockets of his jeans, he trotted down the steps, retraced his path through the yard and across the circle, climbed into his truck, and headed for town.

Karen watched Graham leave Gretchen's. She didn't honestly think that he was having an affair with Gretchen. She thought it was Lee. But why was Graham running over there the minute Amanda left home?

Karen was wondering what that meant and, in any event, whether Graham had learned anything, when the telephone rang. She picked up the receiver, but Jordie had answered on another extension. Someone was already speaking to him—not quite shouting, not quite crying, but certainly upset, enough so that she didn't recognize the voice. She would have had to be dense, though, not to get the gist of the message.

"Quinn did what?" she asked in the middle of the conversation.

"Killed himself, Mrs. Cotter. They found him in school."

"*What?*" she cried.

"He was unconscious," said Rob Sprague, rationally enough now so that she could recognize the voice. Rob was on the baseball team with Jordie. And with Quinn.

"He took pills?" she asked.

"Tranquilizers. His father takes 'em all the time. Some of the guys were supposed to meet him at his house. They were there when the cops came. Everyone's meeting there now, Jordie. Want me to pick you up?"

Karen couldn't believe it. Even in spite of the drinking incident, even in spite of the newspaper article exposing it, she wouldn't have thought that Quinn Davis was anywhere near troubled enough to kill himself.

"Jordie?" Rob asked.

Karen was thinking that if a boy like Quinn had done something like that, her own son, who was much more vulnerable, might be—when she heard a small sound behind her. Jordie stood at the door, looking so lost, his face ashen and his eyes haunted, that she hung up the phone.

"I think we ought to check this out," she said. "It may be rumor."

Jordie was shaking his head even before she finished. His Adam's apple bobbed, seeming too large for his neck, when he gave a convulsive swallow.

"Why would Quinn kill himself?" she asked. "He was happy. He was successful."

Jordie shook his head again, but his eyes looked glazed now.

She went over to him, unsure of what to do. Had he been younger, she would have held him in her arms. But it had been years since he had allowed that. So she simply reached out to touch his face.

He stepped back and looked away, frowning now, seeming to be trying to make sense of something. Then he headed for the door.

"Where are you going?" she asked.

He didn't answer.

She followed him out to the garage. "Jordie, let's make calls. Let's find out what's what. Let's verify this story."

But he had mounted the ten-speed bicycle that he hadn't wanted to be seen on of late because it had only two wheels instead of four, and was heading down the driveway. "What do I say if Rob calls back?" she asked. "Where will you *be?*"

His voice sailed back on the warm evening breeze. "Quinn's."

Georgia was behind the wheel of her rental car. She was returning from the Tampa airport, where she had picked up the two men representing her would-be buyer. One was a vice president, the other the CFO. She was driving them back to the hotel prior to a dinner meeting and, tomorrow, a full day of meetings and facility tours, when her cell phone rang.

"Hello?"

"Mom." It was Allison, sounding frightened this time. "Quinn killed himself."

"He did what?" Georgia asked, more alarmed by the girl's tone than her words. Kids—teenagers—used words like "killed" to mean a dozen different things.

"He slashed his wrists. Mr. Dubcek found him like that. It was way too late to do anything."

Georgia started to tremble. "Are you serious?"

"I *am*. Brooke just called. She said it was a big gross mess. But he's dead, Mom. Quinn is dead."

"Dear Lord," Georgia murmured. Unable to concentrate on the road, she ignored the existence of the men she was trying to impress, and pulled over to the side. "Oh, Allie. I'm so sorry. Why *ever* would he do that?"

"Brooke said it was the article in the paper."

"What article?" Georgia asked, feeling out of it again.

"His suspension was the lead story in the *Woodley Weekly* yesterday. Brooke says he was so embarrassed that he couldn't bear it, but Melissa says his parents were the ones who couldn't bear it. She was on the phone with him last night, and they were walking in and out of his room talking about boarding school and lawsuits." Her voice broke. "He's gone. *Forever.*" She started to cry.

"Shhh," Georgia said, feeling the girl's shaking body even over the phone. "It's okay, honey. Everything'll be okay."

"It won't," the girl sobbed. "I saw him this afternoon. I was talking with Kristen and Melissa in the hall when he came over. He wanted to know what time Melissa's hair appointment was. She was having her hair cut when he did it. I guess he wanted to make sure she wasn't around. And then he left her a *love* note. He said it wasn't her fault. But if he loved her enough, he wouldn't have done it. How can someone . . . *do* that, Mom?"

How to answer, knowing that her words would be taken as gospel? "Most people can't, honey. We don't know why Quinn did. All we know is that he wasn't as strong as we thought. Sweetie, is your father there with you?"

Allison sniffed. "He went over to the Cotters', to see what he could find out."

"Have you talked with Jordie?"

"No. This is so bad. I can't tell you how bad it is."

"Death is."

"No. For Jordie." Her voice grew frantic. "Mom, last Tuesday? When Quinn got drunk? They were drinking vodka. Jordie was the one who gave them the bottle."

"Oh, God."

"Only you can *not* tell anyone about that. Swear you won't. Jordie would never talk to me again if he knew I told you. But you see how this is *so bad?*"

Georgia could barely begin to imagine the guilt that Jordie had to be feeling. "I do see. Where is he now?"

"He went over to Quinn's. The team's there. Mommy, what do I do?"

For starters, Georgia wanted to cry, *get your father back in the house with you.* She couldn't believe that Russ had left the child alone, even for a short time. Allie needed comfort. She needed reassurance.

She needed her mother—that was what she needed. The horror went beyond Quinn's death to the larger issue of mortality. Yes, Allison knew about death. She had lost two grandparents in the last few years—grandparents whom she had known and loved. But Quinn was her contemporary. Thinking about his death, she would think about her own. That was scary for a fourteen-year-old girl who was just on the verge of blossoming. She was looking forward to life. She had dreams.

"The first thing you do," Georgia said, "is to go get your dad and give him a hug. Tell him you need him there with you."

"I mean, do I go over to Quinn's?"

"Not tonight. Not unless the other girls are going.

Quinn's parents must be in shock. They don't need a crowd."

"So what happens next?"

"His parents will make funeral plans—"

Allison shrieked at the word "funeral."

Much as she wanted to, there was no way Georgia could shield her from this. It would be a growing-up experience for her daughter. "The plans will include a wake. That's when you'll be able to pay your respects to Quinn's parents." Georgia angled her watch so that she could see the time. "Listen, honey, I can still catch a flight out of here tonight. You go get Daddy, while I make the arrangements. I'll call back as soon as I know anything, okay?"

"Okay."

"And make sure your brother's okay. Okay?"

"Okay."

"I love you, honey. I'll be home soon."

"I love you, too, Mom."

Georgia had tears in her eyes when she ended the call, and for the first time in minutes remembered her passengers. Her eyes flew to the man on her right, then to the one in back. In a split second, she remembered all that was riding on their visit. They had to be impressed with the efficiency of the southeast regional office, but they also had to be impressed by her. She had to come across as a professional. Being a mommy cut into that.

But it couldn't be helped.

"I can't stay," she said. "There's an emergency at home. It doesn't happen often, but when it does, there's no getting around it."

"One of your children lost a friend?" asked the vice president.

"He killed himself," Georgia said, feeling a jolt just saying the words. "She's very upset."

"Isn't your husband there?" asked the CFO.

"Yes, but I need to be there, too." She put the car in gear and resumed driving. "I'll drop you at the hotel and make calls from there. I'll have my district manager take over for me tomorrow. He'll be able to show you everything I would have." After checking her side-view mirror, she pulled out.

"But we've come to see you, not your manager," the vice president said. "You're a vital part of the package."

Package. It was such an impersonal word. Georgia wasn't a package. She was a parent. And, yes, she was a company president, but right now that was the least of her concerns. Not that she was telling these men that—at least, not as bluntly.

As she drove on, she mulled over her response. Finally, she said, "This isn't our first meeting. Even before today, you knew who I was, how I talked, what I looked like. You've read everything there is to read on me. You've done credit checks and criminal checks. Family is something else. It's a matter of priorities. Yes, my husband's back home with the kids, but life doesn't get much worse than death. If I can't be there for my kids now, I've blown it. So," she said, detesting the business in that instant as she never had, "I'm sorry you've come this far to see me, but I do have to leave."

It was close to midnight when Amanda got home. Emotionally drained, she climbed into bed and backed up to Graham's spine. She sensed that he was awake, but he didn't speak. Nor did she. She had been speaking for hours, and the next day promised to be no better. She didn't allow herself to think about their problems. Didn't allow herself to remember that at this time the month before, she had been gearing up to start on Clomid. Her mind closed up to all but the quiet warmth of his body.

Even then, though, she didn't sleep well. The next day was going to test her as a counselor in ways she had never been tested. Her stomach couldn't forget that. It jiggled nervously every few hours.

At five-thirty on Saturday morning, she got up. Graham was in the bathroom when she stepped out of the shower. His hair was disheveled and his eyes tired, but standing there in his boxer shorts, all broad shoulders and long, tapering body, with nothing but compassion in his stance, he was a dear sight.

"How are you?" he asked gently.

She began toweling herself dry. "Tired."

"What's the plan for today?"

"Teachers are coming in at nine. I want to talk with them—tell them exactly what happened and how much or little to tell the kids. Ann Kurliss, my grief specialist, will go over what the kids will be feeling and how teachers should handle it. The school doors will be open all day, and the teachers will be there on a rotating basis. We've told them things to look for in the kids who come by. The crisis team will be there to work with the ones who seem particularly distressed."

"What do you tell kids about something like this?"

"Not much. Mostly you listen." Setting the towel aside, she reached for her underthings. "They need to be free to air fears. We have to give them permission to do that, and to grieve. They'll tell us what they need. We have to listen and adapt as best we can."

"When's the funeral?"

"Monday morning. Class attendance will be voluntary for the day." Grabbing another towel, she scrubbed at her hair.

"I'd have thought they'd suspend classes," Graham mused.

"Some people wanted that," she said from a bent-over position as she wrapped the towel around her hair, then swung up. She felt more refreshed now. Stronger. Talking with Graham—feeling that he was an ally—made the difference. "We spent a long time hashing it through. Every student at Woodley knew who Quinn was, but not everyone knew him. Those students wouldn't necessarily go to his funeral. The fear was that if we suspend classes, we elevate him to hero status. Given how he died, we can't do that." She began with her makeup.

"Any more news on why he did it?"

"No."

"No word from his parents?"

"Nothing."

Graham smiled sadly. "We can't blame them. They are who they are. Many a kid's had worse and didn't resort to suicide." His smile faded. "Who's to say we'd do better?"

"Me," Amanda said, watching him in the mirror between strokes of mascara. "We'd do better."

"You think so?"

"Don't you?"

"I used to. But we haven't been doing a good job of much lately."

Frightened of where he was headed, Amanda insisted, "We have. We're hanging on."

"Shouldn't we be doing more than that?"

"Sometimes in situations of crisis that's all you can do."

"Are we in crisis?"

It was a minute before she capped the mascara and said, "Yes." She met his eyes. "We need to talk, but I can't do it now, and if today's as bad as I think it might be, I won't be able to do it tonight."

"Because you'll be at school late? What about tomorrow?"

"I'll probably go there in the morning. The afternoon's your mother's party."

"Do you still want to go?"

"Of course."

"You'll be wrung out."

"I'll be fine."

"You always talk about keeping an emotional distance from your job. It isn't working."

"No," she conceded, because she didn't want to fight about it. "But if not now, when? This is temporary."

"Good thing we gave up the baby bit," he said and returned to the bedroom. "That would have been one complication too many."

She followed him. "We haven't given up. We're taking a breather. Taking a breather. That's all."

He stopped moving, put his hands on his hips, hung his head. After a minute's silence, he drew in a loud breath and raised his head. "Can I make you coffee before you leave?"

"Yes. Thank you. I'd love that."

Graham vowed to spend the day at the office. Since it was Saturday, he would be the only one there, which meant more concentrated work. He was in the process of drawing preliminary designs for the Providence project and was eager to lose himself in it. This creative phase was the part of his job that he loved the most.

Today, though, it didn't hold him past noon. His mind began wandering and wouldn't stop. He felt restless and impatient. He didn't see anything new or exciting appearing on his computer screen, which was a blow to his professional ego. Dissatisfied, he turned off the machine at two, stayed at the office only long enough to check out the projects on which his associates were working, and then headed home. He made one stop along the way, for a dozen flats of impatiens.

A short time later, wearing his grungiest T-shirt, shorts, and work boots, he took the flats to the front yard and began to plant. He had been at it for an hour, building up a sweat in the sun, when Russ came out with two beers and sat himself down on the grass.

Graham took a long drink. The beer was cold and refreshing. "Where are the kids?" he asked as he pressed the beading bottle to his temple.

"Tommy's at a friend's. Allie's at school." Russ gestured toward the beds. "You should let Will's guys do this. Planting's their thing."

"This isn't planting. This is gardening. Gardening is personal and therapeutic. Besides"—he looked off toward the woods—"I'm not good for much at the office."

"Yeah. It's lousy about Quinn."

Graham nodded and took another drink.

"How's Amanda holding up?" Russ asked.

"She's tired. But this is her job. Lately, she's been feeling out of her element. So this is good."

"Out of her element, like with the baby stuff?"

Graham nodded. "And my family. Even me." He shot Russ a self-conscious look. "Excuse the self-pity, but I can't seem to get away from it. I feel like—" He stopped, frowned, struggled to put his finger on the worst of it. "I feel like I keep trying to do what's best in life and the same thing keeps knocking me down."

"What thing?"

Graham shrugged the question off. He didn't need to bare his soul—or his ego—to Russ. Yes, they were friends. But this was personal.

In the next minute, though, the words spilled out. "My first marriage. Do you know much about that?"

"Only that it ended amicably."

Cautiously, Graham asked, "Amanda didn't tell you anything more?"

"She said that the woman was a good friend of the family, but she only told me that to explain why your ex came here one day delivering a birthday present for you from your mother. Naturally, I asked more," Russ said with a self-deprecating smile, "but Amanda wouldn't give. Hey, what wife likes talking about her husband's first?"

"Megan's more than a good friend," Graham said. "She lives right next door to my mom."

Russ frowned. "Odd, for an ex-wife. When did that happen?" he asked, genuinely curious, truly innocent.

That made it easier for Graham to talk. He didn't have to defend anything, since Russ was clearly in the dark. "All my life. Megan and her family lived in the house next door. We grew up together. Aside from my siblings, she's the oldest friend I have. We played together and studied together. We were sweethearts as soon as we knew what that meant. We dated through high school and college. Everyone just assumed we'd get married, and we did. First weekend after graduation."

"Wow," Russ said with a bemused smile. "So why didn't it last?"

"It did for six years. Then she told me she was gay."

Pulling back, Russ huffed out a startled breath. "Whoa. Talk about unmanning a guy."

Graham had to chuckle at the way he said it. "Oh yeah."

"And you had no inkling?"

"Not at the time of our wedding. We'd gone to different colleges. She roomed with her lover the last two years. I thought they were just good friends."

"But she was your lover, too."

"Definitely."

"Was she good?" Russ asked in a man-to-man voice.

"You aren't taking notes, are you?" Graham asked, only half in jest.

"Nah. I'd like to know about the fertility thing—what a man feels about that—but this is personal. Just me, chronically nosy."

Put that way, how could Graham resist? "Megan was good when she wanted to be," he said. "There were times when she wasn't into it as much. I just assumed all women were that way." Until Amanda. With Amanda, the chemistry had been raw and constant—until the process of making a baby had gummed things up.

"Knowing how she was," Russ asked, returning Graham's thoughts to Megan, "how could she go ahead with the wedding?"

"Very easily. And I can't fault her for it. Part of her wanted to be married to me. It would have made her life simpler. Her family could never have accepted what she was. Marrying me would make everyone happy."

"Everyone but her. Did you feel where she was headed before she asked for the divorce?"

"I knew she was withdrawing. I felt that. She stopped sharing things. She was managing a little bookstore in town, and spent more and more time there. She probably could have gone on living that way for a while, if I hadn't pushed the issue."

"The *gay* issue?"

"The kids issue." Graham sputtered out a laugh and looked away. "Ironic, isn't it?"

"What?"

"The same thing's hanging up Amanda and me. So, what is it with me and women when it comes to having kids?" He looked back at Russ. "It's like it's the kiss of death."

"No. Not with Amanda. She wants kids, too."

"She wants to take a break from trying, that's what she wants. Know how that makes me feel?"

Russ looked horrified. "Take a break from sex?"

"No," Graham said, then rethought the answer. "But it might as well be that. Know what infertility treatments do to spontaneity?"

"I can imagine."

"Take your imaginings, and make them ten times worse—only this is not for a column, Russ. This is me needing to vent."

"Agreed," Russ said.

"Everything rigid. Everything on a schedule. Everything timed by body temperature and time of the month, and that's not even *touching* on the business of donating sperm for artificial insemination—then add no baby to that." He scowled. "I feel about as virile as I did when Megan made her announcement."

"But if Amanda's taking a break from trying for a baby, isn't sex better?"

"You'd think it would be. Only we've argued ever

since." He stopped, embarrassed. "I shouldn't be telling you this."

"That your marriage isn't perfect? Whose do you think is?"

"Yours."

"Are you kidding? Did I ever tell you that Georgia considered leaving me once?"

"I don't believe that."

"It's true. It was before we moved here. I was piecing together a professional life, not too well, and I wasn't happy with myself. I took it out on her."

"How?"

"I was moody. I was impatient. I was demanding. And critical. About petty things. Y'know?"

"What'd she say?"

"That I wasn't being fair. That it wasn't what she'd bargained for. That she'd just bumped into her old high school flame and that he was everything I wasn't right then."

Graham sat straighter. "She *said* that?"

"She did. She also said that she loved me and wanted to make our marriage work."

"Geez," Graham breathed. "Didn't you worry about the high school flame?" He would have been devastated if Amanda had said something like that to him.

"It was a wake-up call. I got my act together."

"Do you ever worry about what she's doing when she's on the road?"

"With men? No. I trust her."

Graham was about to ask whether the trust went both ways, whether Georgia worried about what *he* was doing when she was gone. He was thinking of Gretchen, but better sense told him not to go there.

Russ said, "Every marriage is tested."

"Tested. Good word." Graham tipped back the bottle and took another swallow. Righting his head, he thought about the challenge. "So right now she's overwhelmed with the Quinn thing. That was bad timing, coming on the heels of the other."

"The timing's never right with things like that."

Graham grunted. He set the bottle on the dirt and twisted it in until it stood on its own. Then he put his elbows on his knees and pushed his hands through his hair. "Somethin' else to think about, though. Another bucket of cold water. I mean, when I think about sex, I think about the way it's been for the last year—which is good," he said out of loyalty to Amanda—and the fact was that during those orgasmic seconds he forgot everything but the pleasure. "But it's for the sole purpose of having a baby. We have to get past that."

"Have to start over again," Russ advised.

"Recapture the feeling."

"Prioritize. Georgia's always talking about that. Prioritize."

So what were Graham's priorities? There was sex, Amanda, kids, and work. Not necessarily in that order.

In what order, then?

Amanda had to come first. Without her, none of the other three worked. He wanted to have sex with Amanda. He wanted to have kids with Amanda. And, sure, he could design backyards, shopping mall atriums, office parks, even highway roadsides without Amanda. But what would be the point of that? What would he do with the money, if not spend it on Amanda and their kids?

Amanda was the one thing that his priorities all had in common. She was the linchpin on which the others depended.

Yes, he hated it when she was distracted. When she pulled into herself and shut him out, it brought back everything he had felt when Megan had announced herself gay—inadequacy, humiliation, impotence. If Amanda couldn't understand that—if she couldn't apply her own skills to him enough to see where he was coming from—if she couldn't do some prioritizing of her own and place him first—if, damn it, she couldn't give him the benefit of the doubt when it came to Gretchen and her baby—there was no hope for their marriage.

That said, no one was going to tell him he hadn't tried.

When Amanda came home after a long day at school and an even longer evening at the funeral home, Graham brewed her a cup of tea and ran her a bath. She was nearly asleep before her head hit the pillow, but he held her close—and found satisfaction in it. For the first time in weeks, he wasn't angry that the passion wasn't there. For the first time, he was content just to be there for her—whether she knew it or not.

Chapter Eleven

Amanda didn't know that for the first night in a week she had slept in the arms of the person who meant the most to her. At some unconscious level she must have felt the comfort of his embrace; mentally, though, it didn't register. She was simply and completely exhausted, coming off hours of hearing sorrowful stories from students too young to be telling them, but the suicide of a friend opened a Pandora's box of guilt. One student confessed to having cheated on an exam, another to watching his mother and her lover, another to snorting coke—any one of the indiscretions seemed, in the perpetrator's eye, far worse a crime than coming to baseball practice drunk, for which Quinn Davis had been punished and subsequently died. Amanda did her best to separate the two, arguing time and again that Quinn's punishment had not forced his death. She sent a number of students to the religious advisors on her crisis team, but the weight of their stories stayed with her.

Thus, burdened even in sleep, she awoke in Graham's arms thinking that he was in bed with her to ease his conscience, holding her out of guilt. That easily, she found herself thinking like her mother again.

Struggling against it Sunday morning, she slipped out of bed while Graham still slept and made the trifle for his mother's party. She brewed a fresh pot of coffee and set the Sunday paper on the table, but by the time he woke up, she was heading for the shower, then back to school.

Watching her go, Graham wondered if there had been something subconscious in his sleeping late. Sleeping was better than dealing with the unease between them.

It was, of course, the coward's approach and not at all what he had planned after talking with Russ. Ashamed of himself, he vowed to be more proactive. It wasn't until afternoon, though, that he and Amanda were together long enough for any kind of serious talk, and then he couldn't get her going.

"The trifle looks good," he tried. "Thanks for making it."

She smiled politely. "You're welcome."

A while later, he said, "I thought about calling Mom this morning. But I decided against it. I figured I could wish her a happy birthday in person."

"I tried calling from school," Amanda said. "She was in the bath, so I left a message."

"You're a better daughter-in-law than I am a son."

"No. I'm just desperate."

"Desperate?"

Another polite smile. "To make her like me."

"She does like you."

Amanda gave him the kind of look that said he was lying and knew it. Not knowing what to say to that, he said nothing at all.

* * *

Arriving at an O'Leary affair was a physical thing. There were loud shouts and hugs, enthusiastic back-slapping and boisterous greetings. Amanda had been included in the ritual since the first day she had come with Graham. He had warned her that first time, and still she had felt overwhelmed. But she had loved it. The raucousness was everything she hadn't experienced as a child. She adored the genuine outpouring of feeling, the easy show of affection.

It was all there this time, too. Today the difference was in her. Totally aside from Quinn's death, which weighed heavily on her, being with Graham's family—being with Graham's *prolific* family—brought back the issue of the pregnancy that wasn't. She smiled and laughed and hugged and was hugged in return, but she heard thoughts and imagined words. She felt as though everyone *knew*—as though everyone blamed her, since the problem they were having in conceiving couldn't possibly lie with Graham.

Determinedly, she immersed herself in the festivities, led by the hand of one child or another into one room or another. She had always been drawn to the toddler brigade, which meant that the children she had played with during the first years of her marriage were now six, seven, and eight. They adored her, and understandably so. More so than the other adults, she was willing to read to them, to play card games, or fall for corny jokes.

"You are the prettiest aunt," one niece said, clinging to Amanda's side, looking up with a gap-toothed grin. "I don't *want* you to have kids. I like having you all to myself."

What to say to that? Amanda couldn't begin to

think. The trifle came out well, though the *mmmmms* were inevitably directed at MaryAnne, who—in all fairness—had masterminded the party. If Dorothy even knew that Amanda had made the dessert, she wasn't letting on. She made no mention of it during either of the times that Amanda sought her out to chat. Rather, she babbled on about the Garden Club or the Historical Society or even Megan, all subjects that she knew Amanda wouldn't want to discuss.

Still, Amanda was unfailingly polite. She smiled and nodded and asked as many questions as she could. Dorothy didn't ask a single one in return. Eventually the conversation between them died.

Malcolm O'Leary came to her rescue the second time. "Sorry, Mother, but I'm stealing my sister-in-law away. *Joseph,*" he called to one of the nephews, "come talk to your grandmother." Putting a large arm around Amanda's shoulder, he steered her off.

"Where's Graham?" she asked. She had barely seen him all afternoon.

"Playing volleyball out back. Good thing Mother has a big yard. We needed it when we were kids, and we sure need it now. How are you?"

"Great," Amanda said with a smile.

"That's not what Gray says. He says you're taking this last setback hard. We all feel terrible, Amanda. I know how much you want a baby. I can imagine the frustration you're feeling."

Amanda doubted that. "Well, it'll come in time."

"I heard about a great guy in D.C. He works with women who can't get pregnant. I'm told he's booked solid, but we did the screens for his sister in Hartford. One call from her, and you'd be in quick. What do you say?"

Controlling herself, Amanda said, "Did you run this past Graham?"

"Yeah. He said I shouldn't mention it, but hell, Amanda, if they can't figure out what the problem is, maybe you should see someone else. I'd be glad to make a call."

"Thanks, Malcolm, but we're working with someone good."

"Well, let me know if you change your mind. Graham is dying to be a father."

A short time later, she heard the same words, this time from Megan Donovan, Graham's first wife. One of only a handful of outsiders invited to the party, she knew all of the O'Learys and was treated like one of them.

To her credit, Megan was sensitive to the situation. She always came late, left early, and kept a low profile out of deference to Amanda. This day, she gave Amanda a warm hug, told her she looked beautiful, asked about her work as Dorothy hadn't. In turn, Amanda asked about Megan's business, a small bookshop that was struggling to survive against the competition of large chains and on-line stores. Megan answered freely, knowledgeably, interestingly enough to make Amanda think—and not for the first time—that she liked Megan a lot. That was before Megan lowered her voice and raised the issue of children.

"Gray says nothing's happening."

"Not yet," Amanda said with a smile and a hopefully final, "but it will."

Megan didn't let it go. "It must be hard on you. I know how much Gray wants kids. That was the one thing that marked the beginning of the end for us. I kept putting it off. I kept giving him one reason after another why we should wait. I finally ran out of excuses."

"The situation is different with us."

"Can I help?" Megan said.

Amanda frowned in amusement. "I don't think so."

"I mean, if it's a question of donating eggs or renting a uterus for nine months . . ."

Amanda was silent in the car. She had a splitting headache, a knot in her stomach, an ache from having produced so many unwilling smiles, and a bad taste in her mouth.

Graham was as silent, but simmering. She could feel it the minute he turned off his mother's street. They hadn't gone two blocks when he said, "Do you hate my family?"

Her eyes flew to his. "No. Why?"

"You were struggling to be pleasant. Anyone could see that."

Amanda stared out the windshield. There were so many things she wanted to say. So many things she wanted to *yell*. She didn't know where to begin.

"What's wrong with my family, Amanda?" he asked.

"Nothing."

"Then why do you have so much trouble being with them? You have a headache. I can see it in your eyes. Why does my family give you a headache? Noise? Commotion? Laughter? I thought you liked all that."

"I love it. I just feel different from them."

"Look, I know my mother isn't the warmest person in the world—"

"She is," Amanda interrupted. "She's warm to everyone but me."

"You're upset because she didn't thank you for the trifle."

Amanda turned to him then. "I'm upset about lots of things. Probably the least is that she didn't thank me, because I made that trifle while there were far more serious things on my mind, and it was just plain rude of her. I mean, don't *you* think it was rude?"

He brushed the question aside. "My mother is old. She isn't modern and isn't adaptable. We knew before we married that she wouldn't be easy. She's no worse now than she ever was."

"My needs have changed. I need more from her. I need her to be supportive."

"About the baby? She can't be supportive, Amanda."

"Maybe not. But you can." She grew beseechful. "Where were you all afternoon? You left me on my own to deal with the subject of why we can't have a baby and whose fault it is and what we're doing about it. Do you know that Megan offered to be a surrogate mother?"

"That was sweet," Graham remarked.

"She's your ex-wife!" Amanda cried. "What kind of soap opera would it be if we let her do that? It's one thing if a woman's sister does it, or even her mother, but an ex-wife? But back up a step. What makes her think my uterus is the problem? Why do they *all* think I'm the problem? Emily doesn't. She says it might just as well be you as me. Did you tell them that? Or did you just tell them that I keep losing babies—like I'm the shortstop you got in a trade, and I keep dropping the ball in the family baseball game?"

Shocked by the ugly sound of her voice, she went still.

They drove on in silence for a while.

When she felt she was in control again, she said more slowly and quietly, "I don't hate your family. It's just that when I'm with them, I lose you."

"You don't lose me," he scoffed.

"You're never with me. We're not connected. You're always talking with a brother or playing with a nephew or giving a sister or a sister-in-law garden advice. *Or* talking with Megan."

"I wondered when we'd get to that," he muttered. "Christ, Amanda, Megan is my oldest friend. I've known her all my life. We parted on the best of terms. I like seeing her. And I like seeing my family."

Amanda grew silent again.

"Do you want me to go see them by myself from now on?"

She closed her eyes. He was missing the point. "No."

"What *do* you want?"

She wanted him to make her pregnant, that was what she wanted. She wanted him to look at her like she was the center of his universe. He used to do that. At the party today, he hadn't looked at her at all.

"Tell me, Amanda."

"I want you to help me with them. Help me feel less isolated. Stand with me, not somewhere else like you're ashamed to be with me. *You* be the one to tell Malcolm that the man he heard about that's so great with infertile women may not be appropriate for us, since I am *not* infertile. Take my side. Help me. Support me." She took a quick breath and looked at him. "Better still, tell them to mind their own business. Having a baby is between you and me. They shouldn't be involved at all—and don't say that they care, because I know they do, but it isn't making things easier for me. They're all telling me how much you want a baby, like I can snap my fingers and make it happen. I know you want a baby. I don't need them telling me. What happened to respecting people's privacy? What happened to not discussing personal things in public?"

"Your family worked that way," Graham said. "Mine never has."

"Maybe they should. Maybe you need to let them know that I come first in your life. Unless I don't."

He shot her an angry look. "Is this a race now? To see who comes first?"

Amanda shook her head. His look had chilled her. She had never thought to be on the receiving end of something like that.

"It is," he decided. "You want me to choose—my family or you."

"Never. I just want you to act like a husband."

"I'm trying. I'm trying. I'm doing the best I can in a bad situation. But your being jealous of Megan and my family doesn't help. Your being jealous of Gretchen doesn't help, either. You want me to act like a husband? Then act like a wife. *Trust* me."

Naturally, when they returned to the cul-de-sac, Gretchen was in her front yard directing a misty stream of water toward the tulips. With the last rays of the sun putting a rainbow in the mist, making the entire picture idyllic, the widow suddenly seemed the embodiment of everything that was wrong with their lives.

How to discuss that without fighting? Graham didn't know. So he followed Amanda into the house and respected her apparent desire for silence.

* * *

Amanda awoke Monday morning with a lingering headache and a sense of dread. She tried to drum up positive thoughts, but there weren't many to be had on the morning of a teenager's funeral. She took Graham up on his offer that she shower first and thanked him when he was waiting with her towel at its end. She appreciated the fact that he didn't leer at her body, but kept his eyes on her face, and she wasn't so immersed in thoughts of what the day would hold not to see his concern. He asked what he could do to help, and, when she suggested it, he readily agreed to drop off several dozen doughnuts in the teachers' lounge for those arriving early.

Then he put on a suit.

"Do you have a meeting?" she asked. He occasionally dressed for a client, but he hadn't done it in a while.

"A funeral," he said. "I want you to know I'm there in the back."

It was a minute before she understood what he was saying and then, without intending to, she burst into tears.

"Ah, Christ," he murmured, drawing her close. "That was supposed to make you feel better."

It did. She had been stoic and strong through the whole ordeal with Quinn, keeping a stiff upper lip even during gut-wrenching times of self-doubt when she felt that she could have single-handedly prevented his death if she had only collared him in the hall and dragged him into her office, or pushed a little harder with his parents. She had been strong for everyone at school, bearing the brunt of people leaning on her. Now Graham was giving *her* someone to lean on. In doing that, she let down her guard, and when that happened, the tears came.

She didn't fight them. Rather, she slid her arms around his neck and held on until the agony waned. Then, drawing back, she looked up into eyes that were a fathomless green.

"Thank you," she said and put a soft kiss on his lips. Feeling the first tingle of true arousal that she had felt in months and having neither the time nor the know-how to deal with it, she stepped back, gave the mirror a dismayed look, and returned to the bathroom to redo her face.

The funeral was held in the white-steepled church in the center of town, and if anyone thought twice about the fact that the deceased had taken his own life, it didn't show. The flowers were lavish, the photographs of Quinn plentiful. Students sat with students, though many of their parents were there. Obligated to sit with the faculty, Amanda spotted Graham only once. He was gone by the time she left the church.

She held the image of him with her during the day, and it was a comfort. Though the atmosphere in the school corridors was subdued, there was only a handful of teary-eyed students dropping into Amanda's office. Quinn's closest friends had forgone school entirely and returned to the Davis house after the burial. Sports practices and a lacrosse game had been canceled out of respect for Quinn.

By three, the school buses had left and the grounds were eerily quiet. What few stragglers remained sat on the ground in small groups. Amanda sat at the bottom of the tall front stone steps for a while, and two girls did come over to talk. They didn't say much, just seemed to want to be near an adult who might be more comfortable with death than they were.

Amanda stayed with them until they left. Returning to her office, she sat there a while. Fred Edlin dropped by to thank her, and to compliment her on how well the crisis team approach had worked. "Write it up," he advised. "Every school system in the country ought to have something like this."

Amanda thanked him, but the fact was that with recent school tragedies having been highly publicized, many school systems did have crisis teams. It wasn't a new concept, and what she had done wasn't worth documenting.

Besides, she didn't want acclaim. She simply wanted to help the students she had been hired to help. The fact that the team had worked this time gave her a deep sense of relief. Quinn's death was still too raw—and too personal for the counselor in Amanda—for her to feel much satisfaction.

"Good job," Maddie crowed as soon as the principal had left.

"Thank you," Amanda said and removed a treat from the bag under the cage. It was snatched from her hand the instant she offered it.

"Sweet treat."

Amanda smiled sadly. "It's so simple to please you. I think that's the delight in having a pet. Easy to please. Uncomplicated. What you see is what you get." She turned at the sound of footsteps in the hall.

"Heeeere's Johnny," said Maddie and, sure enough, Mr. Dubcek appeared at the door. He had been at the funeral wearing a baggy brown suit, and had changed back into his usual green work pants and shirt, but his face was dolorous.

"How was things today, Mrs. O'Leary?" he asked in his rusty voice.

"All right. The shock is wearing off. It'll be a while before the reality sets in—the finality of death." She would continue to work with the faculty to look for warning signs in those students having the most trouble coping. They were keeping a list. Everyone agreed that being proactive would be better this time.

The old man's furrowed brow grew even more so. "Fifty years of working here, and this never happened to me. We had kids getting sick and fainting dead away on the floor. We had seizures. You know, epileptic. We had kids die in cars and one in a plane crash. We had kids kill themselves at home. But never here before. I shouldn't'a let him stay here. I should'a sent him home."

Amanda smiled kindly. She understood the guilt. Indeed, she did. "If Quinn was determined to kill himself, he'd have found another way. If you'd sent him home, he might have gone out into the woods and done it there. It would have been a lot longer before anyone found him."

"But if I'd come back right after he did it, he could have been saved. The paramedics said so."

"Believe me, I've been asking myself many of the same questions. If I'd gone out and dragged him in here, instead of sending him an e-mail—if I'd shared my concerns with the administration or with his coach—if I'd told his parents that he was in enough pain to hurt himself—but none of us knew that. We had no idea what he planned. It was the last thing any of us expected from a boy with so much going for him."

The janitor pressed his mouth shut and shook his

head. "Waste. A terrible waste." He returned to the hall.

"Fuck it," Maddie said.

"Oh yes," Amanda replied with a sigh.

She stayed at school until five, mostly answering the phone and talking with parents who were worried about their own children and unsure of how to deal with them. One of Quinn's teachers stopped by. He, too, was thinking back, looking for signs, wondering what he might have done differently.

In time, she locked up and headed home. The sight of Graham's truck in the driveway was warming, as was what she saw when she crossed the breezeway on her way to the kitchen. There in the backyard, on a carpet of grass, against a background of hemlocks and pines, stood the wrought-iron table with its two pretty chairs. The table was set with linen mats and napkins, wineglasses, and candlesticks.

Touched, she went into the kitchen. Graham was reading the directions on a box of rice pilaf. On the counter were the steaks they were to have eaten Friday night.

"I thought we'd try again," he said. Setting down the rice box, he opened the refrigerator, took out a bottle of wine, filled two waiting goblets, and handed her one. "It's been a while."

She nodded. In recent months, when she had been so frantic to conceive that she had taken to reading stories on the Internet, she had refused to take so much as a sip of anything remotely alcoholic. "For what good *that* did," she murmured and held her glass out to his.

"To life," he said.

Given the few days it had been, given the few *years* it had been, Amanda couldn't have said it better. "To life." They touched glasses. She sipped hers and let the wine linger on her taste buds while she inhaled the bouquet from the glass.

"You look better," Graham said.

"I don't feel so raw."

"Any major problems after the funeral?"

Still somewhat pensive, she said, "No. Not with kids. I worry about some of these parents. They're so bright and so opinionated. One mother stopped me at the funeral and had nothing good to say about Quinn's parents. She insisted that no child of hers would ever self-injure. When I said that children who come from all kinds of homes do it, she denied it. I'm sure she'll be all closed up if her daughter needs to talk about Quinn. So the girl will go to friends, who don't have any more answers than she does."

"But they'll get comfort from each other, won't they?"

"Yes. Knowing other people feel the same is a help. I like to think it's a help when people like me are available. Not that I have answers, either. But I'm an adult. They can lean on me."

Graham frowned. "You need a break."

"I'll get one next weekend. But being there for the kids helps me, too. I'm feeling just as bad as they are."

"You need to draw lines, stay a little bit apart."

"That's hard, with something like this. I can't *begin* to imagine what Quinn's parents are feeling."

"I can," Graham remarked, sounding suddenly desperate. "It must be something like what I felt when you got your period last week. We lost a baby. All the hopes and dreams and plans we'd had went right down the tubes."

Amanda would have chosen different words. The image he painted was graphic and harsh. "We'll have other tries," she said softly.

"You seem content to wait."

"No. Not content. Never that."

"Are you going to want to start again in a month?"

"Want? No." She wanted to make a baby the usual way. "But I will."

He held up a hand. "Hey, if this is for my sake, you shouldn't. A baby is a lifetime commitment. If you don't want it, let me know."

"And then what?" she blurted without planning to, but the question had been festering in the back of her mind for days, weeks, months. She would have taken it back when his eyes went cold, but just as teenagers needed to know how death happens, she needed to know this.

"Do you *not* want kids?" he asked, seeming hurt. "Has it been for me all along?"

"I want them. I've told you that. But what happens if they don't come?"

He looked confused.

She hurried on, just weary enough from the ordeal of the past few days to be reckless. "What happens if there's never a baby? What will you feel?"

"Not having a baby isn't an option. I can't consider it yet."

"I can. I do. All the time. I lie awake at night worrying. What if there's *never* a baby? What happens to us then? Will you blame me? Will you blame yourself? What will your family think? What will they *say*? Will they push me farther away than I already am? How much *do* you want a baby? Is it a necessary part of your psyche? Tied up with masculinity? If we go through another round of artificial insemination and then move on to in vitro and still don't conceive, what then? Will you still want me, or will you want to try with someone else?" She caught her breath and swallowed hard. "I think about these things all the time, Gray. They *haunt* me."

He didn't speak. She looked to his expression for a hint of his thoughts, but they were an enigma. His mouth was a flat line through his beard, though she didn't know whether he was angry or merely troubled. His green eyes were dark and wide—startled—though she couldn't tell whether he was feeling cornered, or simply surprised by her questions. As for his silence, it could have meant either that he didn't know the answers, or that he knew them and didn't want to say.

When a sudden knock came on the frame of the screen door, both of them jumped. Amanda looked quickly back. It was Gretchen Tannenwald.

To his credit, Graham didn't fall over himself to get to the door. He didn't move at all. Amanda was the one to do it.

Wondering how long Gretchen had been there and what she had heard, Amanda cautiously approached the door. The closer she got, the more she could see that something was wrong.

Innate civility bade her to open the screen, but it was womanly intuition that put the concern in her voice. "Is something wrong?"

"Yes," Gretchen said, her voice trembling. "I need Graham."

Chapter Twelve

I need Graham.

Every one of Amanda's worst fears suddenly surfaced. In that instant, she was convinced not only that Graham was the baby's father, but that he and Gretchen were wildly in love. That Gretchen's eyes—*huge* blue eyes—had moved past her to Graham gave credence to it all. The woman looked desperate.

Desperate? Amanda got a grip on herself. Not desperate. Frightened.

Graham came forward. "What's wrong?"

"I, uh, I think—I know someone broke into my house," Gretchen said in something of a monotone, clearly upset but reining in the fear. "There's been damage. I just got home and saw. I don't know if that person is still there."

A break-in. Amanda would have laughed in relief had she not been startled. Break-ins didn't happen in Woodley, and certainly not on a street like this where someone was always around.

"Theft?" Graham asked, sounding startled, too.

"Damage. To Ben's art. M-my art. I didn't put the

alarm on. I knew that you were here, and the Langes, and Karen Cotter. I—I didn't even lock the back door. I only went to the store to get fruit. I wasn't gone more than thirty minutes."

Amanda had been home herself for nearly that long. She hadn't seen anything unusual or odd in the street when she'd driven up. But an interloper might have come through the woods.

Graham went out the door, gently easing Gretchen aside as he passed. "I'll check."

When Gretchen started to follow him, Amanda caught her arm. She felt a trembling there. "Let him go alone. Just in case."

Gretchen swallowed. "Maybe he shouldn't. He could get hurt. Maybe I should just call the police."

But she looked too shaken to do anything, and it was Amanda's husband who was taking the risk. Drawing Gretchen into the kitchen, Amanda made the call herself. She gave the police the information they needed, and then led Gretchen back outside. They went down the driveway and waited on the sidewalk, in clear view of Gretchen's house, albeit safely across the circle. Graham had been gone long enough for Amanda to become concerned.

Julie Cotter was playing on her steps with a doll, while the twins, Jared and Jon, sailed around the cul-de-sac on scooters. None of the three seemed to think it unusual that Amanda was standing on her front walk with Gretchen Tannenwald. Other than a wave from Julie, the children paid them little heed.

It occurred to Amanda to send them inside. Being right there, they would be hostage material should a madman run from the house. But she decided that was an absurd thought. Besides, she was there, and

Gretchen was there. That would make it five to one.

Of course, if he had a gun, the numbers wouldn't matter.

"I'm sorry," Gretchen said, standing close enough to Amanda to suggest that she might have had similar thoughts. "I disturbed your evening. But I didn't know what else to do."

"Don't be silly," Amanda said gently. "That's what neighbors are for. Was anything stolen?"

"I don't know. I saw the picture in the front hall and ran out. I probably could have called the police from there. But I only wanted to get away."

"I'd have done the same."

"I don't have a car phone. Or I'd have called from the car."

"You did the right thing," Amanda assured her, but her worry was deepening. She had visions of Graham lying in a pool of blood, having been attacked by an assailant who had been hiding in a closet. Then again, it was possible that Graham was simply making a thorough sweep of the house. After all, he knew his way around. He had been there before. They both had, many times, at the invitation of Ben and June.

Gretchen put her slender hands together in front of her mouth. She was taller than Amanda by half a head, but seemed waiflike, even with her height and the bulge in her belly. Seeing the latter, Amanda felt a wave of envy that was nearly palpable.

Determined to ignore it, she asked, "What kind of damage was done? Paint?"

"Slashing," Gretchen said from behind the edge of her hands.

Again, Amanda saw Graham hurt. "God."

"I've been getting phone calls where no one answers. I figured it was one of Ben's sons. But I don't think they'd destroy something their father loved. And I don't see them sitting in the woods waiting for me to leave the house."

Amanda had met the sons a number of times. Though they were closer in age to Graham and Amanda than Ben had been, she far preferred Ben. He'd had an easygoing way about him. Same with June. The sons were more driven.

Focused intently on the house, Amanda jumped when she felt a warmth against her right hip. "Julie," she said with a breath of relief, putting her hand on the child's head, "you scared me."

"Is something wrong?" Julie asked.

"I don't think so," Amanda said as lightheartedly as possible.

"Why are you standing here?"

"We're just waiting for Graham." Slipping an arm around the child's shoulders, she gave her a quick squeeze, then let her go. The message, of course, was that Julie should turn and go back to her front porch.

"Can I wait with you?"

"Don't you usually help your mom with dinner?"

"She did it already. I asked if she'd read with me, but she said she couldn't. Only I don't know why not," Julie said with added feeling. "She's just *sitting* there."

"Maybe lost in thought," Amanda said lightly, though she could easily imagine what Karen's thoughts might be. Chances were no small part of them was focused on the woman standing on her left. "Maybe needing rescue. Go rescue her, sweetie."

Julie crinkled her nose. "She'll tell me to play with Samantha." Samantha was the doll, which sat neatly propped on the Cotters' front steps. "She's always telling me that. Where *is* Graham?"

"He's at Gretchen's."

"Why?"

"He's doing her a favor."

Julie slid Gretchen a curious look. Concerned that the questions might start getting uncomfortable, Amanda was relieved when the child said, "Oh. Okay," and skipped off.

"You're good with her," Gretchen remarked, though her eyes were focused on her house.

"She's easy to be good with," Amanda said, then murmured, "Where *is* Graham?"

"Where are the police?" Gretchen responded.

Both questions were answered in the next minute. Graham came out the front door of Gretchen's house just as a cruiser rounded the bend.

Relieved, Amanda ran to join him. Gretchen stayed close beside her.

"There's no one inside," he said when they met on the walk. He waved the cruiser over. "I went through the whole place. The only damage I saw was to paintings."

"Paintings?" Gretchen asked, sounding more frightened than ever. "More than just the one in the front foyer?"

"There was that one, and two in the living room."

Gretchen broke away and ran up the front steps. Swearing softly, Graham went after her. Amanda wasn't about to be left behind. She followed, right in through the front door, past the painting that hung in the front hall and now had a single slash through its center, and on into the living room.

Gretchen stood with a fist pressed to her heart, staring at the painting on the wall. Tears trickled down her pale cheeks. Amanda glanced back at the other painting that had been damaged, but the difference was startling. Far greater damage had been done to *La Voisine* than to either of the other paintings. Here the slashing had been vicious, leaving the subject that Amanda had known to be a breathtakingly beautiful woman nearly unrecognizable.

The police called from the front door.

"In here," Graham called back. When they appeared under the living room arch, he greeted both men by name, shook hands with each, and made the introductions. Their faces were familiar to Amanda, though she had never formally met either one. The older of the two, Dan Meehan, was fiftyish and easygoing. His partner, Bobby Chiapisi, was easily twenty years younger and obviously newer to the force. He wore his uniform starched; his manner matched it.

Directing them to *La Voisine,* Graham explained what he knew.

"Whew," said Dan. "Someone was angry. So it's this painting and the other two." He turned to Gretchen. "Anything else?"

Gretchen made no effort to wipe the tears from her face. She looked weak—"destroyed" was the word that came to Amanda's mind. She couldn't help but feel for the woman.

"I don't know," Gretchen whispered. She lowered herself to the sofa without once taking her eyes from the painting.

"I didn't see anything when I walked through the house," Graham said, "but I only looked for the obvious. Nothing was knocked onto the floor. There didn't seem to be any ransacking. Gretchen will have to go through to see if anything was taken."

"I wasn't gone very long," she said flatly.

"How long?" the younger officer asked, firmly gripping his small pad and pen.

"Twenty minutes. Maybe thirty."

Dan looked at Amanda and Graham. "And no one saw anything?"

They were shaking their heads when Karen came to the living room door. Julie and the twins were close behind, their eyes wide. "What happened to that painting?" she asked, gesturing behind her, but catching her breath when she looked ahead. "Oh my."

"We've had an intruder," Dan said. "It's Mrs. Cotter, isn't it?" At Karen's nod, he said, "Do you live nearby?"

"Next door."

"Did you see anyone coming or going in the last hour?"

"Just Gretchen." She didn't take her eyes from *La Voisine*. "What a mess."

Georgia and Russ materialized behind her. "Why are the police here?" Russ asked, seconds before his eyes, too, went to the painting. Graham approached them to explain, while Dan knelt in front of Gretchen. Thinking that she seemed pathetically alone sitting there on the sofa with her tear-streaked face, Amanda sat beside her.

"Would you like to see if anything else was taken?" the officer asked.

Gretchen shook her head. "The only things worth taking are my ring and earrings, and I never take them off." The earrings were diamond studs that matched in size and shape the central stone in an elegant wedding band.

"Would there be money anywhere to take?"

"No." She changed her mind. "Yes. But I don't care about money. They can have money. But why would they do *this?*"

"Do you have any idea who might have done it?" he asked. Gretchen shook her head. "Who has a key to the house?"

"The door wasn't locked."

"Is there a boyfriend in the picture?"

"No."

"The father of the baby?"

"No."

"No, what?" the man prodded gently.

"The baby's father wouldn't do this."

"Perhaps if you gave us his name—"

"There's no need," Gretchen said with quiet determination.

Feeling uncomfortable, Amanda asked the officer, "Can't you dust for fingerprints or something?"

"We will." He shot a glance at his partner.

Bobby Chiapisi looked unhappy. "If there were prints on a knob, they're probably gone. Half the neighborhood's just come in these doors."

Sure enough, Allison and Tommy were there, and before anyone could say much of anything, Lee appeared behind them. "What'd I miss?" he asked, then saw the painting. "Omigod."

His distaste looked real enough to Amanda. Still, she might have liked to know where he had been for the last hour and who could vouch for him.

Dan Meehan pushed himself to his feet, then straightened the rest of the way. "The thing to do is to let Mrs. Tannenwald go through the house to see if anything else has been touched. It could be we just have an art pervert."

"This was the only thing in the house that mattered to me," Gretchen murmured.

Not knowing what to say, Amanda simply put a supportive hand on her arm.

"The best I can suggest," the older officer said with regret, "is that you call your insurance company."

For the first time, Gretchen looked directly at him. "Can they replace the painting?" she asked, sounding angry—and Amanda was proud of her. Any fool could see that the painting had sentimental value.

"No," the policeman answered. "But they'll send out their investigators and an adjuster. You'll get money to buy a new one."

Amanda took one look at Gretchen's face and, quietly but firmly, said to the man, "I don't think she wants a new one. This one had special meaning. Whoever did this has stolen that from her. The best you can suggest," she used his words, "is how the department can track down the culprit and find out why he did what he did."

The man looked duly chastened. "Yes, Mrs. O'Leary. We'll try to do that. We'll get cruisers out on the other side of the woods and canvass the houses over there to see if anyone noticed anything strange. We'll put extra details on this area. We'll do what we can."

"Thank you," Amanda said.

Amanda was the last of the women to leave the house. The police were still inside with Gretchen, as were Graham and Lee. The others had dispersed. The only child in sight was Jordie, who was watching the drama from his front porch, with an arm high on a post. Despite the cruiser's glaring presence, the cul-de-sac was quiet.

As soon as Amanda neared the sidewalk where Karen and Georgia stood, Karen asked, "What were you doing in there so long?"

"I went through the house with Gretchen to see if anything's missing. I felt bad for her. If it'd been me, I wouldn't have wanted to do that alone. Not after someone had been in my house. It was a creepy feeling."

Karen arched a brow. "Being in her house?"

"Knowing that someone else had been there doing awful stuff with a knife. If I were Gretchen," Amanda said, trying to put herself in the woman's shoes, "I'd be wondering what he touched and what he thought and whether he was hiding out somewhere nearby and planned to come back."

"Think underwear," Georgia remarked. "What if he opened drawers and touched things? Can you imagine? I feel dirty just thinking of it."

"'Violated' is the word I used," Amanda said, reflecting on the bits of talk she had exchanged with Gretchen during the search.

Karen was less sympathetic. "She has an alarm. She should have used it."

"Do you use yours?" Georgia asked.

"No. I can't with the kids. They'd be locked out or locked in. It'd be a mess." She returned to Amanda. "So did she find anything missing?"

"No. She didn't think he'd gone upstairs. She said nothing looked like it had been touched there. He couldn't have been inside for long. She wasn't gone for long." The air was mild, but Amanda wrapped her arms around herself for warmth. No matter that Gretchen wasn't her favorite person in the world, no woman should have to face this. Sleeping in that house tonight was going to be a challenge. "I keep seeing the scraps of that canvas hanging every which way off the painting. Whoever did that was sick."

"Did she take it down?" Georgia asked.

"No. Graham asked if she wanted him to, but she said she'd do it later."

"Well, I won't miss that painting," Karen remarked. "It was trouble. So. Who do you think did it? I can't imagine it was a random thing."

"Not quite," Georgia said.

Amanda agreed. "Whoever entered the house had a mission. That painting was the target."

"Then it wasn't theft," Georgia reasoned, "which means that whoever did it bears a grudge." She slid Karen a crooked smile. "We have you on motive."

Once, they all would have laughed aloud, Amanda realized. They would have been of like mind and shared humor. They would have been a team, particularly where Ben's lovely, young, blond-haired wife was concerned.

Karen didn't smile now, though. "Ha-ha," she said soberly, then, "Did you see the way Bobby Chiapisi was looking at Gretchen?"

"He wasn't," Georgia replied.

"Precisely. He wouldn't look at her. It was like he wanted to be anywhere but there."

Georgia scowled. "You think that he and Gretchen . . . ?" She shook her head.

Amanda agreed with her. "I've seen him around town. He wasn't avoiding her. He's like that all the time—stiff, formal, starchy, awkward."

"He's the right age," Karen said. "He's single. He's always standing right out there in the open, manning the traffic light in the center of town. She could have seen him. He could have come on to her." Her brows went up. "Wasn't he part of the police detail on the day of Ben's funeral?"

"He might have been," Amanda said, though she didn't actually remember.

"The department is small," Georgia said by way of agreement.

Karen seemed satisfied with the possibility. "So"—she turned to Amanda again—"did you go upstairs with her?"

"Uh-huh."

"Was the bedroom pretty?"

Amanda thought for a minute. "Pretty? Enough so. Seductive, no."

Georgia returned to the intruder angle. "Should she be staying alone there tonight?"

"I asked her that," Amanda said. "I asked if there was anyone else she could stay with—family or a friend. She said there wasn't."

"I'm not having her stay at my house," Karen declared. "Neighborly concern is one thing, but having her down the hall would be pure suicide."

There was a heavy silence.

Karen waved a hand, as if to erase the words. "Oh my. That was an unfortunate slip of the tongue. Let's not go there."

But how not to? Amanda thought. All three of them had been at a sixteen-year-old boy's funeral that morning. It put vandalism into perspective.

Apparently agreeing, Georgia said, "Allison is shaky. When she's home, she sticks to me like glue." She glanced at the Cotters' porch. "How's Jordie doing?"

Karen followed her gaze. "He's quiet." Her voice dropped. "Let me see if I can talk with him." She set off, but before she had even reached the steps, he disappeared into the house. She stopped, hesitated, then more slowly followed him inside.

"Now *there's* a problem," Georgia breathed. "Mother and son do not get along. Some of it has to do with the age. But why is it so bad with them?"

Amanda didn't answer at first. She didn't like analyzing friends, and the fact was that she hadn't been inside Karen's home watching the Cotters in action since Christmas.

But she trusted Georgia. She wanted to share her thoughts and get feedback. So she set off down the driveway, heading for the Langes'. Georgia was beside her by the time she hit the sidewalk.

"I think there's tension in the house," she said. "I think things aren't good between Karen and Lee. Kids pick up on that."

"Has Karen said anything to you?" Georgia asked.

"No. But you've heard her talk."

"She sounds bitter. There's no sense of humor. No laughter. No gossip. No *give*."

"Only suspicion."

"She didn't used to be like that," Georgia said, validating Amanda's memories. "This must be hitting too close to home. Do you think Lee's the father of Gretchen's baby?"

"I don't know." Amanda was truly undecided here. "Gretchen didn't react one way or another when he arrived. I was watching her. She didn't react to Bobby, either. I cannot imagine it's him."

"Probably not," Georgia said. In front of her house now, they sat down on the curb side by side. "But it makes me think, y'know?"

"About Bobby?"

"About Russ. I'm gone a lot. Oh, I don't think he fooled with Gretchen. I don't think he's that lonely. Not yet."

"He loves you to bits," Amanda argued.

"Yeah, but there's a limit to that, too. I saw part of a column he'd written. It was about the loneliness of the stay-at-home parent. He'd printed it out and thrown it away, but without folding it or crumpling it up or anything, like maybe he wanted me to see it."

"Did he submit it to the paper?"

"No. He would have shown it to me directly if he had. That's the deal. He always shows me things that are at all about us."

"Why'd he toss it out?"

"Good question. Because it's too revealing? Not manly enough? All I know is I was happy I came home early."

"Did things get messed up with your buyer because you left his men in Tampa?"

"Yes. But it was worth it. Allison needed me. Tommy did, too, because he knew Quinn enough to feel sadness—or shock—or fear—or whatever it is he's feeling. He can't express it. But he likes my being there. He keeps saying it."

Amanda admired Georgia. The woman hadn't needed schooling in psychology to understand her family and its needs, and she did that on top of being a successful businesswoman. Even now, at the end of the day, she looked clean and chic in her tailored slacks and blouse, with her neat, short, straight hair.

Amanda worked in a local setting. Georgia's world was far broader, and while Amanda didn't aspire to that, she was awed by her friend's potential. "So, is this company going to buy you out?" she asked.

"The lawyers are negotiating. Mine says they'll make an offer. The question is whether I can live with their terms. They want me to stay on for three years, basically doing what I've been doing, but on a salaried basis. That would mean just as much travel as I've had. I don't know if I want that. I may just want out."

"And if you tell them that?"

"They may want out, too. They seem to think that I single-handedly run every aspect of this company and that without me it would fall apart. Hey, it's flattering. But it's dumb. I mean, who are we kidding? The company would survive without me. But *they* want me there because they know I care and would jump into action if something went wrong, and they'll keep me there until someone in their own organization learns the ropes. I just don't know if I want to be the teacher."

"What if they do want out? Are there other buyers in line?"

"Two possibilities, but this is the one I want. It's a good company. If they bow out, it'd mean starting the dog-and-pony show all over again, and I'd hate to do that. But I can't see jumping from the frying pan into the fire. I mean, if I'm selling the company to get off the road, and then I find myself back on the road, only answerable now to someone else, that stinks."

Finding the sentiment familiar, Amanda smiled sadly. "A lot of life does."

"The baby thing?" Georgia asked.

"That's part of it."

"And Graham?"

Amanda nodded, looking out across the street toward

Gretchen's. It was twilight, the denouement of a long day.

"Still not talking?"

"Well, we are. We're starting to."

"What about sex?" Georgia asked.

Amanda shot her a quick glance and laughed. "Trust you to cut to the chase."

Georgia put an arm around her and said quietly, "I wouldn't with everyone. I just care more about you and Graham than I do about some. You listen to people's problems all day. So who listens to yours?"

"You."

"I'm listening."

With dusk spreading blue shadows about, Amanda felt less exposed than she might have in broad daylight. That made it easier to speak. "He holds me at night. There's a wonderful warmth. I lie there and imagine we're old people just seeking comfort. Only we aren't old, and we want more."

"If you want it, what's the problem?"

Amanda tried to put it in words. "It's like there's a block. Like when we think sex, we get tense. Like sex has become a conditioned reflex."

"But it wasn't always that way."

"God, no," Amanda said with feeling. "I adore his body. He totally turns me on." Her eyes crossed the street again, as the men emerged from Gretchen's house and stood on the porch. Gretchen had turned on the lights. Amanda focused on Graham. "I mean, look at him. He's tall, dark, and handsome. Can anything be more clichéd than that—or more alluring? I love his eyes. I love his smile. I love his *beard.*"

"Russ tried to grow one once," Georgia mused affectionately. "Poor guy. He thought it'd make him look cool, only it came in motley. I have to say, Graham's is a good one."

"And his touch," Amanda went on, because she was into it now—the confiding, the sharing, the venting. "He knows how to make love. He's considerate and gentle. He senses needs and reads moods. He knows how to please a woman." She stopped short, exhaled. "That's who he is. And I respond to it and become someone I want to be."

"It sounds perfect."

"It was. Right up until the past year. When we make love now, we aren't ourselves. We aren't even who we want to be. We're just going through the motions."

"You're still thinking about the baby."

Determinedly, Amanda said, "Not this month. I'm not thinking. I'm not counting. I put everything away, all the paper and stuff, out of sight, out of mind. I'm not taking my temperature or popping pills or running to the clinic." She released a helpless sigh. "But it doesn't seem to matter. It's like we can't move on. Like we forgot how to enjoy each other that way. Like we can't make that . . . make that final . . ."

"Commitment?"

That was it. "Yes."

"Commitment to the future?"

"Yes."

"Looking at the big picture and wondering what'll happen."

"*Yes.*" Amanda smiled her gratitude. "Thank you for understanding."

"I try. It's hard for me to imagine what it's been like for you. I had babies when I wanted them." There was movement across the street as the four men came down the walk toward the police car. More softly,

Georgia said, "You don't really think Graham is Gretchen's guy, do you?"

Amanda heard what Georgia didn't say. "Because she came looking for him just now? That did cross my mind. But if I were her, I'd have done the same thing. Graham is good in situations like that. He's calm and clearheaded."

"You didn't answer my question," Georgia chided.

"No, I do not think he fathered that baby."

"Then who did?"

"She's not telling," Russ said an hour later. "Her lips are sealed."

The three men were shooting hoops in the Langes' driveway under floodlights mounted on the roof of the garage. Graham stole the ball from Lee and pivoted away when Russ tried to block his approach to the basket. He aimed and let the ball sail. It went through the basket touching nothing but air.

"Good shot," Lee said, getting the rebound and dribbling a bit.

Russ pushed his glasses up his nose with a forearm, then watched the others with his hands on his hips. "I'm surprised the cops didn't prod. You can't blame them for wondering about the baby's father, when she's so close-mouthed about it. We're living in an era of domestic abuse."

"Speak for yourself," Lee said as he began a layup shot.

Graham easily stole the ball, dribbled around on the far side, came in fast, jumped, dunked. He made the rebound himself and lobbed the ball to Russ.

"You know what I mean," Russ said, catching it but not moving. "If she won't tell who the father is, and someone went in there destroying the painting that her first husband—whom she loved—whom she worshiped—whom she idolizes to this day—bought her, it stands to reason that the father of the baby may be green with envy."

Lee gestured toward the ball. "Are you gonna stand there talking or play?"

Graham tried not to smile. Russ wasn't an athlete. He wore the requisite tank top and baggy nylon shorts, and he was sweaty and disheveled. Between that and his height, a passerby would think he was the star of the team. In truth, he liked the camaraderie far more than the game. At Lee's gibe, he passed off to Graham.

Graham dribbled in place. He liked the sound—that rhythmic *boom boom boom*—always had. It took him back to his childhood, playing for hours with his brothers. It was a normal sound, a predictable sound, a controllable sound.

Putting out an arm to ward off a lunge by Lee, he asked, "So who'd want that picture destroyed?" He dribbled out of reach and around the driveway. "My money's on one of Ben's sons. They wouldn't give her the time of day when Ben was alive, and they were downright rude to her when he died. I'm surprised they didn't contest the will." He took aim and shot. The ball bounced off the rim.

Lee went in for it. "They wanted to. I convinced them not to." He caught it and put it up. This time it went in.

Graham took the rebound leisurely. Behind him, Russ asked Lee, "Do you talk with them much?"

"Once in a while. They're nice guys. We used to talk stocks and bonds when they came visiting Ben and June."

"Whose side is the lawyer on?" Graham asked. Poised for an outside shot, he aimed, jumped, put a victorious fist in the air when the ball went through the net.

Lee grabbed the ball. "Deeds?" He faked a pass to Russ, who put his hands out to catch nothing. Then he spun around and executed an uncontested layup shot. He let Graham take the rebound. "Deeds is on the brothers' side. But he's a wuss. He wouldn't want to go to court. Wouldn't know what to do with himself there."

"So, what do you think?" Graham asked to the rhythm of that comforting *boom boom boom.* "Think either of the sons would damage that art?"

"Themselves? No."

"Would they hire someone to do it?"

"Maybe."

"Can you ask if they did?"

Lee laughed. "Why? It's done. Over. Gone."

Graham shot the ball at him harder than he would have if the guy had shown an ounce of compassion. Lee caught it. Graham wasn't surprised. The man had the reflexes of a fox.

"What if it wasn't them?" Graham asked. "What if it was someone else, someone who might just break into your house next, only when your wife is right there?"

Lee put the ball on his hip and stood there with his eyes on Graham's. He didn't say a word.

Graham was appalled. "Christ, why don't you just divorce her? If you dislike her that much, get the hell out. Let her off the hook. Let her get on with her life."

"Why? It works for me. We have a home. We have a family. There are still good times."

"So what happens when the kids leave home?" Russ asked. "I think about that a lot. Seven more years, and it's just Georgie and me. What are you gonna do when it's just Karen and you?"

"Ahhh," Lee said, shrugging off the question and making an underhand pass toward the basket. "It'll never be just Karen and me."

Graham was annoyed enough to let the ball just bounce off into darkness. "Okay. Forget Karen. What about *you*? Are you happy living this way?"

"Yes. I'm happy. I provide for her, and she's busy. That gives me the freedom to do what I want."

"So freedom's the key?"

"For me it is. I can't live without it. Karen knows that. She accepts it."

"And the kids?"

"The kids love me."

Graham wondered how long that would last. He'd heard Jordie. There might be love, but there was also a whole lot of resentment. No child should have to live with that. Not in his own home. For whatever differences Graham had with his mother, he couldn't fault her there. His parents had been deeply in love. He wanted that for his own children.

What if there's never a baby? Amanda had asked. *What happens to us then? If we go through another round of artificial insemination and then move on to in vitro and still don't conceive, what then? Will you still want me?*

The thing was, she was only looking at one side of the coin. He could as easily turn the questions around and ask what *she* would do if there was never a baby. The doctors had no proof that the problem was hers. Despite what his well-meaning family insisted at every turn, the problem could well be with him, and if that was the case, she might be the one to turn away. He could argue that it had started already.

It was an unsettling thought.

Had they been alone, he might have shared it with Russ, gotten a little encouragement, felt a little better. But Lee was a different story. Graham wasn't sharing personal stuff with him.

Having lost his taste for the game, he said a sudden, "I gotta go," and walked off into the dark.

Chapter Thirteen

Despite the dark cloud hovering in the back of Gretchen's mind, Tuesday broke sunny and warm. Spring scents rose from the cul-de-sac in wisps. Up at dawn, she brought several of the first lilacs inside to perfume her kitchen. She had cut an armful of tulips—red, pink, and yellow—and had put them in vases around the house. She hadn't put any in the living room. She hadn't gone in there since the men had left the night before. Instead, she had set the alarm, gone to her bedroom, and cleaned the place top to bottom. She had washed every washable piece of clothing and had made a pile of others to be dry-cleaned. Though she still didn't think that anyone had been in her room, she wasn't taking any chances. She had worked too hard to take the dirt from her life to allow even the tiniest speck of it in.

She was thinking about that now, sitting in a rocker on the porch. It was barely seven-thirty, and the neighborhood was melodic. Bird sounds came from lawns and trees, bee sounds from rhodies, kitchen sounds from open windows. Georgia came around the side of her house with an arm around Allison's shoulder in a way that Gretchen would have given *anything* for from her mother when she was fourteen. Lee opened his garage door, went inside with Julie, and began rummaging about noisily.

All was quiet at the O'Learys' house, as it so often was. They were trying to have a baby. Graham had told her that, and Gretchen was rooting for them. She would like it if they had a child close in age to hers. That would be a bridge.

As though conjured up by the thought, Amanda emerged from the breezeway. She wore a shirt and pants the color of celery, and looked attractive and petite in ways Gretchen had never, ever been. Opening the door to her car, she put her briefcase inside. Rather than following it in, though, she started down the driveway. Gretchen fully expected her to join Georgia and Allison, who sat now on the curb. She was startled when Amanda headed *her* way.

Her heart began to pound. Amanda had been kind yesterday, but there was no cause for her to return. She wondered if Graham had sent her, and if so, why.

"Hi," Amanda called from the head of the walk and continued straight on up.

"Hi," Gretchen called back.

"How are you?"

"Fine."

Amanda stopped at the foot of the steps. "Are you feeling less shaky?"

"Some."

"Did you sleep?"

"A little. I alarmed the house." Gretchen paused, waiting for Amanda to nod, say something short and sweet, and leave. But she didn't. She stood there at the bottommost step with her hand on the rail, looking at the flowers in the nearby beds. So Gretchen asked, "Would you like coffee or something?"

Amanda shot her a small smile. "No. Thanks. I've had too much already. I have to get going to school."

"Then"—a brainstorm—"some tulips? I cut some before, but there's lots left. I could cut some for you to take to school."

"Oh, you don't need to do that."

"You don't have tulips."

"Funny thing about that, with what my husband does for a living."

"I wasn't criticizing," Gretchen put in quickly. The last thing she wanted was to offend Amanda. "He put other things in your yard that are just as pretty. Tulips would have cluttered it up. I love your yard."

Amanda smiled. "Thanks. I like yours, too."

"Your husband is very talented." She looked across the street just as Graham appeared. Loping off the breezeway, he strode toward his truck. He raised a hand high in a generic wave their way.

Holding her hands in her lap, Gretchen let Amanda be the one to return his wave. Watching Amanda watch her husband climb into the truck and back out of the driveway, she felt a great wave of envy. "You're lucky to have him."

When the truck disappeared around the curve, Amanda looked back at her. "You're lucky to have a baby coming. We'd like one, but it's taking a while." Her eyes touched Gretchen's stomach. "How are you feeling?"

"Fat," Gretchen said.

"Fat is beautiful when you're pregnant."

"It doesn't feel it."

"I think pregnancy is the most beautiful state a woman can be in."

Gretchen didn't have to be a friend of Amanda's to imagine her thoughts. "I'm sorry. It must be hard for you seeing this."

Amanda didn't respond. Instead, she climbed two steps, put her back to the rail, and held on. "Is the baby active?"

"Yes. At night, mostly. That's what was the hardest last night. I'd be sleeping, and a kick would wake me, and I'd remember what happened."

"Any thoughts on who the vandal might be?"

Gretchen shook her head. Needing to think about something else, she looked across at Amanda's yard. "You have mountain laurel. I don't have those. I used to love them. They were all over the place where I grew up."

"That was in Maine?"

"Uh-huh. Can't you hear it in the way I talk?"

"Only once in a great while," Amanda said with a gentle smile. "A word here and there."

"I work at that."

"Why? Maine's a pretty way to talk. Whereabouts was it in Maine?"

Gretchen grew uncomfortable. "A small town. A no-name place. Too small for a map."

"If you'd asked Graham, he'd have been glad to plant mountain laurel for you."

"He suggested it. He said mountain laurel was acid-loving and would go with my conifers, but I told him no." When Amanda gave her a puzzled look, she explained, "Bad memories."

"I'm sorry."

Gretchen shouldn't have said anything. "It was a

long time ago. Well, not so long ago. But it feels it. Anyway, it's history."

She stopped talking and looked away. In the next breath, though, she heard Ben's voice saying that the women in the neighborhood would like her once they got to know her. Amanda had taken a first step by crossing the street today—and Gretchen desperately wanted to air her fear. At least then, if she was found dead in her kitchen, the police would know where to look.

"My family was not very nice," she blurted out. "Bad things happened in that town. When I left, I just left. I didn't tell anyone where I was going. There are times I worry they found out anyway."

Amanda frowned. "Weren't they at your wedding?"

"Oh, no," Gretchen said. "That was one of the reasons we got married in Paris." She saw what was either surprise or doubt on Amanda's face. Resigned, she added, "I know you all thought Ben married me on impulse. But he didn't. We planned it out. We knew that his sons wouldn't be happy with us and wouldn't come if we invited them, and I didn't want my family invited at all."

Amanda came up another step. "Do you think one of them might have slashed the painting?"

"I don't know. But I keep getting silent calls. I don't think it's Ben's sons, and I don't have any other enemies. Except my family." She watched Amanda closely, looking for revulsion. "Sick, isn't it, to say that about your own family?"

But Amanda seemed more worried than revulsed. "I've heard worse. If you tell the police, they'll check it out."

"But if they do that, my family will know where I

am. I mean, maybe they already do, if they're the ones making the calls. But then again, maybe they don't, and in that case, I don't want them finding out."

"I see your point." Worried still, she asked, "About the phone calls—do you have caller ID?"

"No. Ben wasn't into things like that."

"It's easy enough to hook up. You could buy something today."

"Hi, Amanda!" called Julie Cotter as she ran across the lawn. "I'm getting a new bike."

"Are you?" Amanda asked, taking the girl under her arm.

"My daddy's gonna put on training wheels. But he has to put the bike together, and he can't find the right tools."

"Oh dear."

"Can I stay here with you?"

"For a second or two. Then you have to go to school, and I do, too. Want to show Gretchen your teeth?"

Facing Gretchen, Julie bared a grin that was toothy enough to show a big gap in front. "Two teeth out?" Gretchen asked.

The child nodded.

"That's nice."

"Are you having a baby?"

"Yes."

"My mommy says it has to have a father."

Gretchen swallowed. "Uh, right now, it just has me."

"My mommy says it *has* to have a father."

"It does," Gretchen said, figuring that would be the only way to quiet the child. She braced herself for the next question.

But Julie only looked adoringly up at Amanda. "Maybe if you come over later, we can put the bike together faster."

Amanda shot Gretchen a conspiratorial look. "Tell you what," she told the child. "If your dad has trouble, we'll get Graham to help. He's better at things like that than I am. Okay?"

"Okay."

"You'd better go now. The bus'll be here soon."

Julie ran off, and Amanda turned to Gretchen. "I'd better go, too. Will you give me a call if there's any problem?"

Gretchen had said that she would, assuming the offer to be a figure of speech, albeit a kind one. She didn't expect to be in need of help as soon as that afternoon. But that was when the next problem arose.

Unfortunately, Amanda was at school and Graham was at work later when Gretchen's doorbell rang. Coming from the kitchen, she looked out over the dining room drapes. Two strange cars were parked in front of the house, both late enough models to preclude either one having been driven by a family member of hers.

A man and a woman stood on the doorstep. She didn't recognize either one, and opened the door only because the screen door was locked.

"Mrs. Tannenwald?" the woman asked. "We're with the company that insured your husband's art."

"My art," Gretchen said quietly. "I did not call you."

"No. We received a call from David Tannenwald. He wanted an appraisal of the damage." David was the younger of Ben's two sons, though he was still ten years older than Gretchen.

"I don't know why he wanted that done. The paintings belong to me." She thought of something else. "How did he find out about the vandalism?"

"I don't know. I just know that we got a call. We also got a call from his attorney, Oliver Deeds. He agreed that an appraisal was in order."

The male half of the team said, "We want to see the damage, take some pictures, ask you some questions."

Gretchen didn't want her house entered, particularly by these people. But the rest of her things were insured by them, so she didn't want to offend them. Besides, if they saw the damage for themselves, they could report it back to David Tannenwald and Oliver Deeds. She didn't want to see either one.

So she would let these people in to see the painting. But she was no fool. She had learned not to trust. "Do you have identification?"

The woman looked annoyed. "We're with Connecticut Comprehensive."

Gretchen didn't speak. Nor, though, did she reach for the lock. She simply stood there and waited until finally, with a grunt, the woman dug into her purse and the man into his pocket. Only after she had studied their identification cards did she unlock the door.

Stepping back, she let them enter. With a minimum of talk, she showed them the painting in the foyer and the two in the living room. They stood looking at *La Voisine* for a while.

The woman said, "Odd. This was the least expensive of the three."

"Yes. But it held the most meaning for me."

"We can't reimburse you for meaning."

"I haven't asked you to reimburse me for anything."

"Are you saying that you're not filing a claim?" the man asked.

"I don't know. I probably will. That's what my husband would have wanted. That's why he insured the pieces."

The man raised his camera and focused. "Who else has seen these?" The shutter clicked.

"The police. My neighbors."

"No," the woman specified. "Before. Who else knows that they exist?" There was another click, then another.

Gretchen was mystified. "Anyone who's walked in here in the last two years."

"Can you give us a list?"

"No. There were dozens of people here for the funeral. I didn't know them." She stepped back when the man indicated he wanted to photograph the painting from where she stood. He took several more shots, then turned to photograph the other, less damaged painting in the room.

"All right," the woman said with a sigh. "Let's start with frequent visitors. Can you name them?"

"Why?"

"Because it might help us assess whether you have a legitimate claim."

Gretchen was growing uncomfortable. Yes, she had seen identification cards that looked legitimate enough. But something didn't feel right. "I don't understand. This art was insured. Now it's ruined. Does it matter who did the damage?"

"Very much," the woman informed her. "If you did it yourself, we owe you nothing."

"If I what?"

"If you did it yourself—"

Gretchen was appalled. "Would *I* do this? Would I destroy something I loved?"

"I don't know what you'd do and what you wouldn't."

"I loved this painting. It was the best thing my husband left me. I would never do anything to it. I feel sick every time I see this."

"We're only trying to assess the extent of your claim."

Gretchen was furious. "I think you should leave."

"This is a necessary process. If we leave, someone else will have to come. It's all part of filing a claim."

"I think you should leave," she repeated, not knowing what else to say.

From the door came the sound of a throat being cleared. "Excuse me?"

Gretchen looked around to find Oliver Deeds standing awkwardly under the arch. He was a mid-level partner at the law firm that Ben had used, and had served as the executor of the will. Just Gretchen's height, he wore a dark suit and nondescript tie, though that wasn't what made him seem older than the forty-something she knew him to be. He was almost entirely gray, for starters, with the usual thin swatch of hair separating from the rest and sloping across his brow. He was also pale and looked overworked, if the strain around his eyes meant anything—and those eyes were sad. They were red-rimmed and made even more woeful by the slight downturn of his mouth. When he smiled, he could be good-looking, but he rarely smiled.

He wasn't smiling now. "Is there a problem?" he asked in a quiet voice.

"Yes," Gretchen said, because, after all, he was supposed to be her lawyer, too. "These people are from the insurance company, but I didn't call them. Can you ask them to leave?"

The woman apparently recognized him. "Mr. Deeds," she said in a resigned voice. "We were just trying to explain that this is all standard procedure."

But Gretchen had turned away from the door and was watching the cameraman. "That last picture you took wasn't of my art," she accused.

"I'm trying to put its location in context."

"No more pictures. I want you to leave." She shot a beseeching look back at Oliver Deeds.

"Perhaps if I walk through with him?" the lawyer asked.

"No. This is my house. No one has to walk through it but me. They've seen the paintings. They got pictures. The police made their report. The insurance company can work with that. I want you *all* to leave." She stood stiff and straight for a minute, then marched past the three of them and went to the door. That was when she saw Amanda pull into her driveway.

Shaking with anger, Gretchen marched out the door, down the walk, and across the street.

Amanda had barely climbed out of her car when Gretchen advanced on her looking stiff-backed and angry—and, for a split second, she had visions of a confrontation over Graham. But Graham wasn't around, and the three strange cars in front of Gretchen's house suggested something else.

"I didn't ask them here," Gretchen said, sounding more Maine in her upset. "I don't think they have a right to be here."

"Who?" Amanda asked.

"Insurance people. And Ben's lawyer. I asked them to leave, but they keep ignoring me."

Relieved that the problem had nothing to do with Graham—ashamed that she had even *thought* it—Amanda said, "Come," and set off for Gretchen's house. It had been a madhouse of a day at school, with parents still calling about their children in the wake of Quinn's suicide, teachers still wanting advice on how to deal with their students on the issue, and, on a more personal note, Jordie not showing for a meeting. Walking with Gretchen, Amanda felt useful.

She felt it all the more with each step that they took. By the time they reached the house, she sensed a new strength in Gretchen. Woman-to-woman, it was a gratifying thing.

Amanda immediately recognized Oliver Deeds. She had seen him coming and going in the wake of Ben's death. He was talking with the two who must have been with the insurance company.

Gretchen cleared her throat. The three looked up.

Feeling like she was part of a team, Amanda said, "I think that Mrs. Tannenwald asked you to leave."

"Are you a friend?" the woman asked.

The lawyer answered for Amanda. "A neighbor. It's Amanda O'Leary, isn't it?"

"That's right." She was surprised that he remembered. They had met at the funeral, where she had been but one of many mourners.

"These two are just leaving," he told Gretchen, and the insurance adjusters started for the door.

"Do you have business cards?" Amanda asked them and held out an expectant hand. When it held two cards, she passed them to Gretchen.

Gretchen took them, but her attention was on the

lawyer. "They said that David called you. How did he find out?"

"He got a call from one of your neighbors."

Amanda knew just which one. "Lee Cotter," she said on a note of disgust. Only when the name was out did it occur to her that Gretchen might not feel disgust, but something positive, for the man. She studied her face, seeing nothing either way.

"Why would Lee call David?" Gretchen asked Oliver.

"To tell him about this. Lee wanted to know if either David or his brother was involved. David was pretty upset."

So was Gretchen, if the set of her jaw meant anything. "Were they involved?"

"No," Oliver said. "They wouldn't hurt you."

"David told the insurance company that I might have done it myself."

"Did he really?" Amanda asked, astounded. "He obviously hasn't talked with you. He wasn't here to see the look on your face when this first happened." Dismayed, she went to stand in front of *La Voisine.* It was a sick sight. But something held her there, something Rorschach-like. Looked at a certain way, there seemed to be a pattern to the knife marks at the top, though, for the life of her, she couldn't interpret it.

Behind her, Gretchen told the lawyer, "That's the angle those two people were looking into. That's why they were taking pictures of other things. They were trying to get evidence against me."

"They won't anymore," Oliver said. "I'll make sure of it. Lee also told David that you were pregnant. You should have told me."

"Why? This doesn't have anything to do with the estate."

"I'm the executor. I'm supposed to be watching over you. I was surprised when David told me. I might have known more what to say."

"About what?" Gretchen asked. "This isn't David's business either."

Amanda glanced back at them just as Oliver lowered his eyes. Head down, he pushed the swatch of hair back from his brow. Then he sighed, looked up, aimed sad eyes first at Amanda, then at Gretchen. Quietly, he asked, "Should we talk alone?"

Gretchen said, "I trust Amanda."

After a silent beat, seeming emboldened in turn by her force, Oliver replied, "Fine. The pregnancy isn't sitting well with David and Alan. They think—"

"They think," Gretchen cut in to complete the thought, "I was having an affair with someone before Ben died. That doesn't surprise me. Tell them I wasn't. Tell them that if they don't drop it right now I'll sue them."

"Sue them for what?"

"I don't know. You're the lawyer. Libel. Slander. Whatever I can. I have the money to do it. If they smear me, I have nothing to lose."

Amanda wanted to look back at the painting. Something about the way it had been slashed was registering—like seeing animals in clouds. But she was fascinated by this side of Gretchen, who seemed vulnerable but determined, and wholly genuine. And the subject matter held her riveted.

"Are you dating the baby's father?" Oliver asked.

"That isn't your business, either."

"It would help if I could give them a name."

Gretchen gave a slow headshake.

Oliver ceded the issue. More gently, he said, "Forget David and Alan, then. You're right. It isn't anyone's business but your own—and mine, since I was Ben's attorney and he placed his trust in me. Do you need anything?"

"No," Gretchen said. Her voice was as firm as ever, but Amanda sensed a dent. "I'm fine."

The lawyer studied her for another minute, then ceded this issue, too. "Well, let me know if something comes up. I can take as much money from the trust fund as you need."

"I'm fine," she repeated.

He pressed his lips together and nodded. As he started for the door, he seemed to remember the paintings. He stopped and looked back into the living room at the two that had been slashed there. "Would you like me to hire a private investigator to look into whoever did this?"

"No."

"Would you like me to talk with the police?"

"There's no need. *They* don't suspect me."

"I don't either," he said. "I just thought a man's voice would help."

"She has one," Amanda said, coming forward at last. "My husband knows the officers who came here. He'll make sure they stay on top of the case."

Oliver looked oddly deflated. "Oh. Well then, okay. But if Gretchen needs anything, the estate is there for her."

He had barely let himself out the door when Gretchen rounded on Amanda. "The estate is there for me? It is not. It's there for Ben's sons. *That* man would take me to *court* if they asked." She made a sound of disgust, threw a hand in the air, turned away. In the next instant she turned back. "Ben said I could rely on Oliver. Fat chance. He's shown his true colors. I wouldn't be caught *dead* calling him."

She was already pale. Suddenly, though, she became even more so. She put a hand on her belly, drew herself straighter, took a deep breath.

Amanda, who had lived and breathed thoughts of pregnancy for the better part of the last four years, felt her discomfort. "What's wrong?"

Gretchen eased herself down on the sofa and gently rubbed the band of muscle that supported the baby. She breathed in and out, in and out.

"What is it?"

Gretchen released a slow breath. "Braxton-Hicks contractions. The doctor says they're normal. There. That's better."

"Are you sure? Can I get you anything—water or something?"

"No. Thank you. You've already done enough." Easing herself to her feet, she went off toward the kitchen.

Amanda wondered if she was being dismissed, and felt the same hostility that she had often felt from Gretchen. Then she caught herself and wondered if it was hostility, or a less negative aloofness, or even a simple wariness. Lord knew, given her lack of a relationship with the neighborhood women, Gretchen had cause for wariness now.

Wanting to make sure that she was all right, Amanda followed her into the kitchen. She walked in just as Gretchen was filling a glass of water from the dispenser on the refrigerator door, but Amanda's attention was drawn to the kitchen table. It was covered with papers and books.

"What's this?" she asked.

Setting her glass on the counter, Gretchen quickly gathered the papers together. "Nothing," she said, seeming more embarrassed than secretive.

But Amanda had seen something that surprised her. "That looked like French."

"I was thinking of learning it," Gretchen said quickly as she shifted the books and papers to the counter. "I loved hearing the language spoken when I was in France with Ben. It isn't so easy, though." She retrieved her water, took a sip, then seemed to remember that Amanda was there. "Would you like something—water—or pineapple juice—I have that."

"No. I have to get home. I have reports to write."

Gretchen walked her back to the front door. "I did get caller ID. I bought a box this morning. There haven't been any calls yet, though. But it was a good idea."

"It can't hurt."

"Thank you for coming over."

"I'm glad I could help. Three against one is unfair. Are you feeling all right now?"

Gretchen nodded and held open the screen. "Thanks again."

Amanda was feeling quite proud of herself as she walked across the street to her own house. Reaching out to Gretchen felt good on several counts. She was eager to tell Graham.

That was before he called to say he would be late for reasons that proved to be bogus.

Chapter Fourteen

Karen was standing on a corner of the porch, hiding a cigarette by her thigh, when Amanda came from Gretchen's house and crossed the street. She watched her warily, wondering what was going on. The more she wondered, the more uneasy she felt. Taking a final drag on the cigarette, she stubbed it out on the underside of the porch rail, then tossed it into the shrub bed as she headed down the steps.

"Mommy?" Julie called out from her bedroom window.

Karen called, "I'm running to Amanda's for a minute, sweetie. I'll be right back."

"But what about our pie?"

"I'll be *right back,*" Karen repeated, wondering what had possessed her to suggest that they bake. But she knew. The supermarket had been running a special on the plumpest blueberries she'd seen in a while, and—sucker that she was—she had thought her family might appreciate a home-baked pie. Julie would. So would the twins. Jordie probably wouldn't care one way or the other. He had been a walking zombie since Quinn's death. And Lee? Lee didn't like a blueberry pie any more than he liked blueberry pancakes.

But Lee was working late. Or so he said. She would never know if it was true or not. She could study the bill from his cell phone all she wanted, but it wouldn't tell her where he was when he made a call. She hadn't seen Gretchen's phone number on the bill, and their home phone line didn't give a breakdown of local calls. So maybe he was calling her from the office. That shed a new light on the idea of his working late. Phone sex was big. She read about it all the time. As far as she was concerned, it wasn't any less of a betrayal than the real thing.

Just as well that he wasn't here tonight, though. She had a list of parents to call about helping with the graduation lunch for seniors. She wouldn't have had time for Lee. She barely had time to bake a pie. She certainly didn't have time to be running to Amanda's. But she couldn't let it go.

Amanda was dropping a grocery bag and the day's mail on the kitchen table when Karen trotted up the back steps and opened the screen. "Hi, Karen," she said with a smile.

"Was that you I just saw at Gretchen's again?" Karen asked, sounding nonchalant about it, though Amanda suspected she was anything but. The lines running from her nose to the corners of her mouth were marked.

"It was."

"She had quite a crowd over there. Anyone I should know about?"

Amanda took a head of lettuce and a bell pepper from the bag. "No. Two of the cars belonged to insurance adjusters. The other was Oliver Deeds'. They were here about the paintings."

"But why did she come to get you?"

Amanda put the produce in the refrigerator. "She isn't used to dealing with people like that. She needed moral support."

"Are the insurance people involved in the investigation?"

"Only for the sake of processing a claim."

"She's asking for money, then," Karen remarked. "That puts a different slant on her talk about how much that painting means to her. It makes you wonder who committed the crime."

Amanda had taken a bunch of asparagus from the bag. She paused with it in hand. "What do you mean?"

"Well, she wouldn't be the first person to destroy something she owned for the sake of the insurance."

The insurance company had suggested a similar thing, but Amanda's gut said it wasn't so. She might fault Gretchen for being closer to the neighborhood men than to the neighborhood women, but she didn't take her for a scam artist. "Oh, Karen, I don't think she did that. She wasn't even the one who called the insurance company. David Tannenwald called them, and only after Lee called him."

"Lee?" Karen asked in alarm. "Why on earth would Lee call David?"

Amanda shook her head, shrugged, pulled a bunch of broccoli from the bag.

"So," Karen went on, "do they know anything? Are there any suspects?"

"Not yet. Graham left me a message earlier. He talked with the police. There haven't been any other break-ins in town. The people on the other side of the woods haven't seen anyone strange."

"What does that mean?" Karen shot back. "That whoever it was came from our side? From right *here?*"

Amanda tried to calm her. "No. It just means that they don't have any leads."

"What about fingerprints?"

"They dusted. But too many other people had handled the doors."

"How does Gretchen feel about that?"

"No suspects? Not happy."

"Is she going to push it?"

"Push the police? I don't think so. She's just heartsick about the painting."

"So do you think she'll move?"

"Because of this?" Amanda asked in surprise. "She didn't mention it."

"What does she mention?"

"The baby," Amanda said, because it seemed a positive thing to discuss.

Karen put a negative spin on that, too. "She talks about the baby, knowing what you've been through? That's selfish. And you keep going back for more? You've been there three times in two days. How come? Do you like her?"

As she put the veggies in the refrigerator, Amanda tried to verbalize what she felt. "I don't dislike her. I never disliked her. I never got to know her much. I thought she was aloof."

"Are you becoming friends?" Karen asked, sounding as though that would be a betrayal of the highest order.

Amanda understood where Karen was coming from. If she was married to Lee, she might agree. But she was married to Graham. Graham didn't have a history of cheating. Taking the high road—the one that her mother would not have taken—Amanda was working under the premise that nothing had happened between Gretchen and him.

"I'm not sure we're friends," she told Karen. "But there may be more to her than we know."

"Yeah. Husband stealing."

Amanda had actually been thinking about the fact that the woman was learning French. The idea that she did something like that in her spare time was far different from the idea that she sat around watching talk shows on TV.

But she didn't want to tell Karen about the French stuff. She didn't want Karen to find something negative about that, too. So she simply said, "Gretchen's a human being. She's a woman. She's been through a hard time. She could probably use our support."

Karen made a disdainful sound. "And you don't think her being vulnerable is an act?"

"Why would it be?"

"Because she may want allies. God, Amanda—wouldn't you do the same thing if you were in her shoes? What better way to put the wife off the scent than by getting so close that she simply takes the scent for granted?"

Amanda was totally put off. Yes, she wanted to be compassionate, but she didn't like Karen very much just then. "That's a cynical view," she warned as lightly as she could while still making her point.

"Well, she still won't say who fathered the baby. Why's she keeping it such a secret? If it was just anyone, wouldn't she say?"

Amanda took napkins and paper towels from the

bag. "I don't know. She may have reasons. She may be protecting someone."

"That's correct."

"Karen, that someone may be a man we don't know at all. There may be a whole other set of circumstances revolving around this baby's conception." She paused, thinking about what Gretchen had said about her family in Maine, wondering if there was more that she hadn't said. But Amanda wasn't telling any of this to Karen, either. "She may be keeping it a secret to protect herself. For all we know, she was threatened."

Karen looked as though she didn't buy that. "I'd be careful of her, if I were you."

"On the other hand," Amanda reasoned, reaching for the big brown grocery bag, "if I get to know her, she may confide in me."

"She may tell you lies, too."

Amanda folded the bag and sighed. "Well, it feels like the right thing to do, showing her a little compassion. She didn't ask for someone to ruin that painting."

"Are you doing this to please Graham?"

"No. I'm doing it to please me. Lately, all I seem to feel is helpless. Like I have no control. With Gretchen, it's like I'm *doing* something. Taking control of something. Reaching out. *Helping* someone. That's refreshing. Y'know?" She thought about Quinn. She had felt totally useless in his instance. Then she thought about Karen's own son and the appointment he had missed that day. Appointment? Meeting. They were keeping it informal. Quiet. Certainly confidential. "How's Jordie?" she asked gently.

"He's fine," Karen said, but those facial lines deepened. Her voice held an edge that went beyond simple conversation. "Why do you ask?"

"He was Quinn's friend. Lots of the others have dropped in to talk. They're having a tough time getting back to routine."

"Jordie's fine. He's upset. But he's fine."

Calling home from Kansas City a short time later, Georgia knew that Allison was feeling down the instant she heard her voice. Just that morning, she had been with her daughter at home. They had talked, and talked well. Given the events of the past week, though, her imagination went wild. "What is it, honey? Did something else happen?"

"I just had a fight with Jordie. He says that everyone's gone back to the same old same old, and it's like nothing ever happened, only Quinn is gone. But what're we supposed to do, Mom? No one's forgetting Quinn. Kids are still talking about him. But we still have classes, and there's other stuff going on. You can't talk about death *every* minute."

"Did you tell him that?"

"Yes. He said I was cold. Am I cold?"

"No. You're one of the warmest people I know."

"Jordie is so out of it. Like, you talk to him sometimes, and he doesn't hear. He thought Quinn was the greatest thing in the world. But the guy *killed* himself. Would the greatest thing in the world kill himself?"

"No."

"Like, Quinn was a nice guy, okay? I'm the first one to say that. He was smart. He was a great baseball player. But he wasn't perfect." She snorted. "So how do I get that across to Jordie?"

"Have you tried just telling him outright?"

"Sure. He says I don't know what I'm talking about. Then he turns around and walks away. I mean, like, we're all suffering, but he just walks away. How can you be friends if he isn't there when you need him? Isn't that what friends are about—*being* there when times are rough?"

"I'd say so," Georgia acknowledged with more than a little guilt. She wanted to be there for Allison, and not only as a mother. Allison was on the verge of womanhood. Georgia wanted them to be friends. Yet here she was, away again.

"Dad says that there's a pride thing involved with men, and that I have to come at it from the side, but I don't know what that means, and if I don't know what it means, how can I do it?"

"Talk with Amanda. She'll know what to do."

"Well, I would, but lately she's over at Gretchen's all the time."

"Not all the time," Georgia said.

"Okay, maybe not, but she was there a little while ago. Does that mean Gretchen's an okay person to be with now?"

Hearing her daughter put it that way, Georgia felt guilty. "She's always been an okay person to be with."

"You never liked her."

"I never got to know her. Maybe that's what Amanda's doing. I think that's good. Amanda's good about things like that. Go talk with her, honey. She'll help you with Jordie."

"I wish you were here."

Georgia did, too. Her lawyer was with her this time around. They were working out the last of the contract terms. A deal could possibly be sealed within the week, assuming Georgia agreed to remain at the company's helm. That was the single most troublesome part of the deal, as far as she was concerned. If she balked, they would be back at square one, starting negotiations all over with another company. After all the time and effort that she had invested in this one, she hated the thought of that.

I wish you were here.

Georgia felt the old, familiar tugging, and she had left home only that morning. "Me, too. But it's a short week, Allie. I'll be back tomorrow night. Put your dad on, would you, honey? I want to say hi."

"Hi," Graham said.

Amanda's heart lifted at the sound of his voice. "Hi. I was wondering when you'd call. Are you on your way home?" She was making dinner, anxious to talk. She felt a need for Graham that had nothing to do with being comforted for not conceiving or failing to prevent a student's suicide. This need had to do with the future. Their future. She couldn't deal with a blank screen anymore.

But Graham said, "Actually, I'm headed in the opposite direction," and the lift she had felt vanished.

"Providence again?"

"No. Stockbridge." He had landscaped a museum there earlier that spring. The project was such a plum and the design so beautiful that it was already framed on the wall in the office over the garage.

"I thought Stockbridge was done," Amanda remarked.

"So did I. They're still making noise about my fee."

"They approved it. It's in the contract."

"I know. But they're saying that all the other subs came in over budget, and they just don't have the money. So I'm making my case at a meeting of the board."

* * *

Graham didn't go to Stockbridge, though what he'd said about it was true. The directors of the museum were indeed making noise about his fee, which not only included designs for both landscape and hardscape, but their execution by Will's crew, with on-site supervision by Graham. Forget expertise and a quality outcome. In time alone Graham's investment had been substantial, which was what he had told the board in a conference call that afternoon.

No. This night he was going to have dinner with his brother Peter, but Amanda had been so paranoid about his family lately that he preferred not to mention it. He also preferred that the rest of the family not know they were meeting either. So he had chosen a spot on neutral ground, a diner that was an hour's ride for them both. Peter had agreed to secrecy even without knowing its cause. He was that kind of guy—which, totally aside from his being Graham's brother, was why Graham had sought him out.

They met in the parking lot, hugged, and went inside, where they slid into a booth at the back and both ordered meatloaf and beer. They exchanged newsy little tidbits until their stomachs were filled and the beer had mellowed them out.

Then Graham said, "I need to talk with you about the family. I don't know how to handle them."

"About the baby thing?" Peter asked, as perceptive as always.

Graham let loose with all the frustration that had been building for weeks. "They keep talking about it. They keep asking about it. They keep talking about how Mom wants me to have a baby, like I'm deliberately letting her down. They keep making suggestions about one thing or another that we ought to do to conceive, like we're sitting around doing nothing, like our medical advice is no good."

"They're concerned. They're trying to be helpful."

"Well, it's not working. It's coming between Amanda and me. Marriages can be wrecked by family interference. This is a tough time for us. She's feeling pressure about the baby. Now she feels pressure about this, too. She thinks I'm taking sides."

"Are you?" Peter asked, just as Graham had done dozens of times in the last few days.

"I don't know. I don't want to. But if she's feeling pressure about the family, think about what I feel. The pressure's worse on me. You all are my past. You're where I came from. You mean the world to me. I respect your opinions. But I'm married to Amanda. She's my present. She's my future." Once again, he heard the echo of her words. *What if there's never a baby? What happens to us then?*

Quietly, Peter said, "You don't look convinced, Gray."

Graham opened his mouth to deny it, but the words wouldn't come. He thought about that, thought about what was really on his mind. Finally, looking away, feeling a sense of dread, he admitted, "I'm worried. The whole baby thing has torn us apart. I don't know if we can mend things."

"They're that bad?"

"No. But they were always so *good* for us. I don't know if we can get back to that point."

"Do you love her?"

He looked at Peter. "Yes."

"Why?"

"Why. What do you mean, why?"

"What do you love about her?"

Graham sat back, wondering where to begin. Without planning it, he conjured up his very first view of Amanda, six years before on that hillside in Greenwich. In an instant, he was back there in time and the image was fresh. "I love her smallness. Her delicacy. She's so feminine." Embarrassed, he added a quick, "I mean, it's not like Megan wasn't. But Amanda is feminine in a different way. Because she's small, I feel big. Masculine." That was one of the first things he had felt. Given his marital history, it mattered to him more than it might to another man, and he wasn't apologizing for it. Returning to that Greenwich hillside, he felt the comfort now. "I love the way she's petite and fragile-looking. I love her legs. I love the way her hair curls."

"Those are physical things," Peter said.

Graham disagreed. "Not entirely. There's an attitude involved. She tries to pull her hair back so it's neat and smooth, only it won't stay. I love that. It's like there's this wild streak in her that just can't stay put no matter how much she tries."

Peter smiled. "Does it come out in other ways?"

Feeling pride, Graham smiled back. "Oh yeah. We used to go mountain climbing a lot. I mean, she'd trip over the rocks, but she'd always come up laughing. Same thing with kayaking. She'd overturn the kayak more than anyone else, but it didn't get her down. She's klutzy, but she's adventurous. She likes trying new things. I love that about her. But then there's the sensitive side, y'know, with her work?"

"I've seen her with nieces and nephews," Peter said. "She's always been wonderful with them. I've never seen her in action at school."

"I have," Graham said, remembering those times clearly. "It's like she knows just the right tone to set, and it isn't always the same. Some kids need a soft approach, some need a street-smart one. She manages to convey what's right, even if she isn't saying much." Being of the up-front and out-there school himself, Graham never failed to marvel at that. "She's book-smart. But she's also intelligent, in a commonsense kind of way, if you know what I mean. I like that about her." He thought of something else. "The first time I ever saw her, she had a red thing around her hair in back. You couldn't see much, just a flash now and again." He smiled. "I like the way she looks in red."

Peter chuckled. "A true adventurer."

But Graham was back on that hillside again. The red thing wasn't the first thing he'd noticed that day. Nor was it her blond hair. Or her shape or size. Frowning at his coffee mug, he tried to verbalize his thoughts. "I think," he began slowly, because saying it aloud felt weird, "I think that the first thing I loved was the way she looked at me. There were a bunch of us planting shrubs, but she was looking at me. Even aside from the masculine thing, I felt special. Like I was the only one there. She made me feel like that lots of times."

He looked up to see if Peter was laughing. Will might have laughed. Same with Joseph or Malcolm. But Peter was serious, pensive.

"You say you 'used' to do things like mountain climbing and kayaking. Don't you still?"

"We haven't in a while."

"Why not?"

"No time. We're both busy with work. We also

worry about doing something that might hurt her conceiving." He felt his forehead tighten. "Conception has become the single most controlling thing in our lives." He studied Peter, waiting in silence for the priest to praise him for that.

But the priest said, "Having babies is only one part of a relationship."

Graham snorted. "Tell that to Mac. Tell it to James or Joseph or Will. Tell it to MaryAnne and Kathryn."

"I will if you want. I'll do what I can to help. You know that, Gray."

Graham did. That was why he had wanted to see Peter. But it wasn't a simple matter of talking with their siblings. "The thing is that I *know* they love me and want me to be happy. It's not a malicious thing on their part. But it's making a bad situation worse. I didn't face any of this when I was married to Megan. You all knew her. She was family even before I married her. Amanda is so different—from you all and from Megan. There isn't the automatic comfort level when we all get together, so I feel torn, with Amanda on one side and my family on the other. How do I find a balance?"

Peter didn't answer. He seemed to be thinking.

Graham said, "The answer is that we have kids and there's no problem. But what happens if we never have kids? Will they blame it on Amanda? Will they keep her at arm's length? Will they let me live with that? Because if they don't—if they keep harping on the baby thing—they'll back me into a corner. I don't want to have to choose between Amanda and them."

"I hear you," Peter said. "What do you want me to do? Want me to talk with them?"

"No. Not unless they bring it up."

"And then what?"

"Tell them to ease off," Graham said, then let loose with all he'd been thinking for weeks. "Tell them to mind their own business. Tell them I'm a big boy—that I know more than they do about fighting infertility—that I want a baby but that their nagging won't help. Tell them that if they really want to help they can make Amanda feel like she's one of us. Ah hell, Peter, tell them whatever you want. They'll listen to you."

"What about Mom?"

"I'll handle Mom," Graham said. He didn't know how, but he would. That decided, he had only one more request of his brother the priest. It was probably the single most pressing reason for his seeking Peter out. "Tell me it's okay if we never have kids."

"Oh, you'll have kids. If it doesn't happen biologically, you'll adopt."

That wasn't the point. "Tell me," Graham specified, "that it's okay if Amanda and I don't have kids of our own."

"It's more than okay. If children don't come, it's God's will." Peter paused. His voice lowered. "That's my view. What's yours?"

Amanda was writing reports at her desk in the office over the garage when the phone rang. "Hello?"

"Graham O'Leary, please."

"I'm sorry, but he isn't here. Who's calling?"

"This is Stuart Hitchcock calling from Stockbridge. I wanted to thank him for spending the time with us this afternoon. I've always been on his side, and he made his case well. I wish we could have given him an answer when he called, but seven of the ten board members had evening plans, so we could only meet until six. We'll be meeting again next week. Will you tell him that if we have any other questions, we'll call him then?"

Wondering where her husband was tonight if he wasn't in Stockbridge, Amanda said that she would.

Chapter Fifteen

By the time Graham got home Tuesday night, Amanda didn't want to know where he'd been. She heard him come in, but she was settled as comfortably on the sofa in the den as one could be when in the midst of a very private war. She knew she should get up and confront him, but she was too angry, too disappointed, too frightened.

The best she could do was to write out Stuart Hitchcock's message and present it to him at breakfast the next morning. He read it, then stood for a silent eternity focusing on that condemning piece of paper. Finally he raised his eyes.

To his credit, he did look guilty. "I was with Peter," he said quietly. "I had to talk with him. I didn't think you'd appreciate that."

Amanda might have. Of all the O'Leary siblings, she most trusted Peter. But that wasn't the issue. That wasn't what was making her feel so let down. "You lied."

"I didn't feel like I had a choice."

"You always have a choice," she insisted, because

when it came to being truthful with each other, they *did* have that choice. Conceiving a baby was something else.

He didn't say anything, just stood there looking conflicted—and she was conflicted herself. Part of her wanted to hug him, wanted to tell him that it was all right, that she understood, that she loved him anyway. The other part didn't want to bare her heart and soul without knowing first what he felt.

When it looked like he wouldn't tell her that, she said, "If trust is the issue, this doesn't help."

"Trust? Oh, God. Are you still on the Gretchen vein?"

"I'm on the what-do-we-mean-to-each-other vein. You still haven't told me how you'd feel if we never conceive."

He looked suddenly desperate. "We'll have a baby. Somehow or other, we will."

Amanda didn't know what "somehow or other" meant, and as for that desperate look, it could have been from not wanting to give a more honest answer, which didn't make her feel any better.

"I have to get going," she said, slipping the strap of her briefcase onto her shoulder.

Between that time and the instant when she went out the door, he had more than enough opportunity to say, *Wait. Let's talk. I want to live the rest of my life with you no matter what. I'd never, ever look at another woman. You're the one I love.* But he didn't.

Amanda immersed herself in work with the help of a flurry of calls from parents. Sandwiched around three meetings with students, they kept her on the phone for most of the morning. One mother was worried about her daughter's falling grades as the end of the year approached; another wanted to know whether her son's acting out at home was normal for a senior. One was concerned about the bad influence of his son's friends; another wanted to alert Amanda that she and her husband were divorcing and that their daughter was upset. Several still called about the suicide issue, wanting to know that the school remained vigilant.

Amanda was the consummate professional through it all, until Allison Lange appeared at her door. It was late morning. Like so many of the students who sought her help, the girl looked unsure of what she was doing.

In this instance, though, Amanda was immediately concerned. She was personally involved with Allison in a way that didn't apply to the other students. She also knew that Jordie and Allison were tight, and that Jordie was suffering. She had e-mailed him again this morning, but had gotten no reply.

Drawing Allison into her office, she closed the door.

"Hi, cutie," said Maddie.

Amanda said a more direct, "You look like you need a friend."

Allison didn't smile. Seeming uncomfortable, she looked at the parrot. "My mom keeps saying I should talk with you. I was going to go over to the house last night, but then everyone would have seen me." Her eyes met Amanda's before skittering away. She approached the bird cage. "I mean, like they wouldn't have known what I was going there to talk with you about, but I would've felt so guilty, y'know?"

"I love you," Maddie told her.

"Guilty?" Amanda asked, joining her beside the cage.

"Talking about Jordie."

Amanda tucked a long swathe of hair behind the girl's ear and left a gentle hand on her shoulder. "I'm concerned about him, too. I think he's . . . struggling with lots of things."

"*Lots* of things," Allison said, looking at her then, seeming relieved that Amanda saw it, too, as though that gave her permission to open up. "I can hardly *talk* with him anymore. It's like he's a different person. He won't say much of anything. Then he snaps at me when I ask what's wrong. He walks around here like he doesn't want anyone coming *near* him." She paused, dead still now. "Except he isn't here today."

That would explain why he hadn't answered Amanda's e-mail. "Is he sick?"

Allison spoke even more quietly. "He wasn't this morning. He was on the bus with all of us and got off with the rest of the high school kids. I saw him come inside. Only he wasn't in math class last period. No one's seen him since the end of first period."

"No one?"

"I asked all our friends. They don't know where he is. He's been as weird with them as he's been with me."

"How about you? Do you have any idea where he is?"

The girl shook her head.

Amanda's first thought was that Jordie had taken sick and been sent home. It was the most benign explanation and could be easily confirmed by a call to the school nurse.

On the other hand, if it wasn't the case and if Allison was there when she learned it, the girl would be more upset. So, holding the phone call off a minute, wanting to ease Allison's worry, she said a confident,

"He's probably at the nurse's office. Or was. He may be home now."

Allison shook her head. "I called. Twice, in case he was in the bathroom. There's no answer."

"Then it may be that the nurse kept him here until she could locate his mom." She paused. Allison was every bit as sharp as Georgia, every bit as thorough. "Tell me you've been to the nurse's office."

The girl's guilty look said that she had. "Just to the door, but I couldn't see inside. The bell rang, and I didn't dare hang around."

"Where are you supposed to be now?"

"Study hall."

Amanda wrote out a pass. "Give this to the proctor, so that you don't get in trouble."

"What do I say if someone asks why I was here?" Allison asked.

Amanda was used to the question. Students liked her. They just didn't want to be seen with her.

In this instance, though, she didn't see why a simple version of the truth couldn't work. "Your friends know I live next door, and they know that your mom's out of town. So just say that you talked with her last night, and that she asked you to give me a message."

Allison took the pass. "What are you going to do about Jordie?"

"First, I'll check with the nurse."

"What if he isn't there?"

"I'll try him at home. He may have just arrived."

"What if he hasn't?"

"I'll try to reach his parents."

"I don't want him getting in trouble because of me. It's just that . . . I worry about . . . the other, y'know?"

Amanda nodded. She worried about the other, too.

The "other," of course, was Quinn's suicide. Jordie had been Quinn's friend, though they were more different than alike. Quinn had been a top student; Jordie struggled. Quinn had been starting shortstop on the baseball team; Jordie usually warmed the bench. Quinn had been president of the sophomore class; Jordie was an apolitical freshman. If Amanda had to put her finger on the one friend who might copy Quinn, Jordie was it.

Jordie wasn't at the nurse's office. The nurse hadn't seen him at all.

He wasn't at home. Or if he was, he wasn't answering the phone.

Amanda enlisted Maggie Dodd's help in quietly making sure he wasn't elsewhere on the grounds of the school, without alerting the students to the problem. They checked the boys' locker room. They checked backstage in the auditorium. They checked every last study carrel in the library.

While Maggie continued to look, Amanda tried Karen's car phone, but the best she could do was to leave a message. Same thing at Lee's work number.

Suffering visions of a bloodbath at home, Amanda cleared the next few hours, got into her car, and drove to the cul-de-sac. Neither of the Cotters' cars was there, which meant that they were away from the house as opposed to being dead inside. Appeased on that score, though now envisioning a nightmare of things Jordie might have done to himself alone, she sought help.

Graham wasn't there. But Russ was home—or supposed to be. His car was in the driveway and the back door was unlocked, but when she went into the kitchen and called his name, even went into his office, he wasn't there. That left Gretchen. Thinking only that she wanted backup should something be dreadfully wrong, Amanda went across the street and rang the bell.

Gretchen looked pleased to see her, though puzzled.

Amanda was in the process of explaining the situation when Russ appeared behind Gretchen. He wore his usual T-shirt and shorts, and was only as disheveled as he normally looked, for which reason Amanda didn't give his presence there much thought. Besides, whether or not Russ was fooling around with Gretchen wasn't a first-priority worry right now. Finding Jordie was.

Russ went to the Cotters' house with her. They tried the bell first, then knocked. When no one appeared, Amanda took a key from the hiding place that Julie had shown her and unlocked the door.

"Jordie?" she called from the front hall. "Jordie? It's Amanda!"

In the echoing silence, she shot Russ a frightened look, then followed him in a fast search of the house. He seemed to understand that time was of the essence. If Jordie had done something to himself, minutes might make the difference.

Finding nothing at all on the first floor, they went up the stairs. They looked in Jordie's room, then Lee and Karen's. They checked the twins' room, Julie's room, and all of the bathrooms. They checked closets. They checked the attic. They checked the basement.

When they reached the backyard, Gretchen joined them. They were standing there talking about where the boy might be when Karen pulled up. Climbing from the car, she left a tentative hand on the door. "What's wrong?"

Amanda approached her, staying calm. "Jordie isn't at school. He checked in for homeroom period, but he left sometime after that. We searched the school. I thought maybe he was here."

Karen was pale, though whether more so than usual was hard to tell. She stared blankly at Amanda, shifting the blank stare to Russ when he joined them, then Gretchen.

Amanda didn't know what to make of her reaction. Given what had happened the week before, if Jordie were *her* child, she would be terrified. Karen looked numb, though Amanda didn't know whether it was because she was frightened and didn't know what to do first, or because she simply didn't know why they were making this into a big deal.

Feeling guilty about the possibility that she had indeed jumped to conclusions, Amanda said, "I tried calling you. I tried calling Lee. I left messages. I was worried."

"Why?" Karen asked.

"Jordie's taken Quinn's death hard."

"But Jordie was only one of Quinn's friends," Karen said in that same frozen way. "Why do you assume Quinn's death would hit him harder than anyone else? Why do you assume the worst? Why did you leave school and drive all the way here?"

"Karen, this is your son. He's my neighbor. I know him. I'm concerned."

Karen darted glances at Russ and Gretchen before returning to Amanda. Less frozen now, she looked almost angry. "Well, there's no need for worry," she declared. "Jordie's fine. He's doing fine with Quinn's death. I talked with him about it. He's doing fine."

If Jordie was fine, Karen was in denial. Amanda would put money on that.

Russ would, too, judging from the challenge in his voice. "Do you know where he is?"

"Actually, yes," Karen said. "He's with Lee." She reached into the car, pulled her keys from the ignition, and shut the door.

Amanda was startled. "In the middle of the school day? Did Lee pick him up? Did he tell anyone at school?"

Karen set off for the house. "I don't know what Lee did. I wasn't there. But if Jordie isn't at school, he's with his father."

"Did they plan that?"

"Yes. They did. I'm sure Jordie just needed to talk." She kept going for several seconds, then turned suddenly with a look of horror. Again, her eyes touched on the other two before homing in on Amanda. "You don't have the whole *school* out looking for him, do you?"

"No."

"Ahh. Thank God. That's the last thing we need, everyone thinking he's on the verge of committing suicide when he's perfectly fine." She went on toward the house. "I'll call Lee. I'm sure he did tell someone, and it's a screwup on the school's end. I've worked there enough to know how awful they are with things like this." Over her shoulder, now, she said, "Jordie is fine. Go back and tell everyone that he's *fine.*"

Jordie wasn't with his father, though it was another hour and four cigarettes before Karen learned it. It took her that long to get through to Lee. The good news was that she didn't have to wonder if Lee was with the widow, since Karen had been with the widow herself at the time in question. The bad news was that Jordie was missing.

"So, where is he?" Lee asked angrily.

"I'm sure he's with friends," Karen said, because it had to be that. This wouldn't be the first time Jordie had gone off with friends without telling Karen or Lee. He'd never done it during school before, but that was part of growing up, growing bolder, growing defiant and rebellious. He was with friends. No doubt about it.

"Did Amanda check that out?" Lee asked. "Did she look to see if any other kids were missing?"

"I assume she did."

"Assume? You didn't ask? That would have been the first thing I'd have asked."

"*You* didn't ask anything, because *you* weren't in the office. Where were you?"

"Out to lunch."

"The truth at last," Karen muttered.

"What in the hell does that mean?"

It meant that he was blind to her needs and to those of their children, and unaware of the toll that their private war was starting to take on all of them. It meant that when a man's credit card was charged for a visit to an obstetrician, and that man paid the bill even when the man's wife hadn't visited said obstetrician, there were answers to be had. But this wasn't the time. First things first.

"I'm just worried about Jordie," she said. "I'll start calling his friends."

"Let me know one way or the other, will you?"

Karen agreed, but it wasn't until another hour had

passed that she was able to make any calls. She had to wait until the school bus had deposited Julie and the twins at the cul-de-sac, before knowing that Jordie's friends who didn't have practice would be trickling home—and that was assuming they went home as opposed to somewhere else.

She managed to reach a few, but Jordie wasn't with them. They all thought he had gone home sick.

Karen had horrible visions, not the least of which was that the police had picked Jordie up and were holding him in jail. It was absurd, of course. They couldn't possibly know about the knife.

Frightened now, she called Lee again. "I have a bad feeling."

"That's not unusual. You're a worrier."

"This is different. He's been strange lately."

"He's an adolescent. That's how adolescents act."

"What if it isn't that? What if it's something else?"

She heard a long silence, a muttered curse, a resigned sigh. "Fine. I'll come home. Make more calls, will ya? He has to be somewhere."

Amanda couldn't let it go. She didn't think Jordie was with Lee. She didn't think Karen knew *where* he was. She had worked with parents who refused to see that their children had serious problems. Quinn Davis's parents were a prime example.

Haunted by that thought, Amanda did her detective work as quietly as possible. She learned that Jordie had been at school until ten that morning, but that no one had seen him since. She kept at it in a nonchalant way, asking a friend here, another there, the baseball coach, his Spanish teacher. By the time she exhausted her resources, it was nearly five. She gave Karen a call.

Karen said a fast, frightened hello.

"It's me," Amanda advised. "Has he shown up?"

There was a frustrated release of breath. "No." And a tense confession. "He wasn't with Lee after all. I must have confused it with another day. We figure he's with friends."

Amanda didn't figure that at all. She felt an awful dread. "Have you called the police?"

"The police? Why would we call them?"

"To tell them Jordie's missing."

"He hasn't been gone long enough to be considered a missing person."

"That may be true to the letter of the law, but this is a small town," Amanda reasoned. "The police know about Quinn. They might—"

"This isn't the same," Karen cut in. "This isn't the same at all. Jordie hasn't done that. He wouldn't do that. Not Jordie."

Amanda gentled her tone. "I know. But there are other ways of expressing grief. If he's really upset and not thinking straight—"

"Why are you *harping* on this, Amanda? You're getting all worked up, and he's probably just off with friends. If that's the case, you can be sure he isn't in Woodley. If he's with friends, they'd be fooling around in Darien or Greenwich, even Manhattan. So what would calling the local police accomplish, besides getting a report of the search printed in the papers next week and mortifying Jordie? That was what did it to Quinn. Let's face it. That article drove him to kill himself. If he hadn't been publicly humiliated, he'd be alive today. Why are you carrying on about the police? I don't know what you want."

Amanda was stunned. She didn't think that a single

suggestion was "carrying on." But Karen was clearly upset. So she responded calmly. "I'm concerned about Jordie."

"And I appreciate that," Karen said. "But we have to remember where you're coming from. You weren't able to save Quinn, so you're feeling guilty. Guilty and—and gun-shy. You're jumpy. You're making something out of nothing. I understand this, Amanda. But Jordie's all right. I'm telling you. He's all right."

Still, Amanda couldn't let it go. Yes, she felt guilty about not helping Quinn, but the stakes with Jordie were higher. Totally aside from living two doors away from his family, she knew him. She had counseled him. So perhaps she was imagining a greater problem than there was. But with the worst-case scenario having proven a reality with Quinn, she couldn't just sit back and do nothing.

As soon as she finished talking with Karen, she left school. Once she was in her car, there was no doubt whom she needed to call. It didn't matter that she'd left the house in a huff this morning, or that she and Graham hadn't talked all day. He had a stake in Jordie, too. He had a rapport with the boy that was independent of Karen and Lee. He was the one whose opinion Amanda valued most.

He wasn't in the office, but she reached him on his cell phone. After explaining the situation, she asked, "Do you think I'm getting alarmed over nothing?"

To her relief, Graham was nowhere near as complacent as Karen and Lee. "No. You know Jordie. So do I. If Karen and Lee aren't worried, they should be. I sure would be if he was my kid."

Amanda felt a tiny fist squeeze her heart. In the space

of an instant, she was back to picturing their baby, desperate to hold it in her arms, desperate to pass it to Graham and see the light in his eyes.

With an effort, she put the image aside. "I don't understand Karen. How can she just wait?"

"It isn't just her. It's Lee, too. Maybe they feel that not knowing is better than knowing the worst."

Amanda could identify with that. Hadn't she felt that way about Graham at times? Wasn't it one of the reasons she hadn't confronted him? Hadn't pushed? Hadn't made him answer her questions?

"But if the worst can be prevented?" she asked, forcing herself to focus on Jordie again. "I'm going over there now. Maybe I can convince them to do something. If you were Jordie and you were going through a rough time, where would you be?"

"Not with friends," Graham replied. "Not Jordie. He's on the fringe of the group. I can't imagine him finding solace with friends, unless there's a whole other group we know nothing about."

Losers, Amanda was thinking.

"Losers," Graham said. "Cruel term, but they're the ones who'd look up to Jordie."

Amanda knew the school population and who palled around with whom. "I haven't seen Jordie with any kids but the usual ones. So where would you go if you were him and you were upset?" She knew where she'd go if she were Jordie. She would head for the woods. He liked walking there. He had told her that. He liked the darkness and the mystery. He liked the silence. The peace.

Graham didn't venture a guess. Rather, he said, "I'm on my way to an appointment in Danbury, but my gut tells me I should turn around and meet you at home."

Amanda would have given him a hug if he'd been there. They had always been of like mind in things like this. He was concerned where concern was due. It was one of the things she loved about him. "Jordie may be safe and sound, in which case we'll laugh about this later. But I'd rather be safe than sorry. Quinn's suicide is too real to me to take anything for granted. I don't want to take chances with Jordie—and please don't remind me that I'm supposed to keep a professional distance. It would be impossible for me to do that here."

"I know," Graham said quietly. "That's one of the things I love about you."

Tears came to her eyes. It was a minute before she managed a whispered, "Thank you," and another minute before she would have been able to say more, but by that time, broken static said they were losing the connection. She barely heard Graham tell her that he would see her at home, when the line went still and the main menu appeared on the face of her phone.

She drove on, as eager to see her husband as she was to talk with Karen and Lee. When she arrived at the cul-de-sac, the only sign of anything even vaguely amiss was a sky full of clouds overshadowing the lushness of May. The Cotter twins sped around the circle on their scooters, while Julie rode more sedately on her new bike with its training wheels. At the Langes', Tommy was tossing a ball into the pitch-back that was propped against the garage door, while Russ coached on the side.

Amanda parked and started toward them. Russ met her halfway between the houses.

"Anything doing?" he asked in a voice low enough that his son wouldn't hear.

"Not yet." She glanced at the Cotters' house. For all outward appearances, there was nothing at all amiss.

"About before, over at Gretchen's," Russ murmured, turning his back on his son and lowering his head. "I know it probably looked weird, my being there. I'd just gone to ask how she was feeling, and then you came along. I couldn't have been inside more than five minutes."

"Look at me, Amanda!" Julie Cotter called, and they both looked her way. Continuing to pedal, but keeping her widened eyes on the sidewalk before her, she took both hands off the handlebar for a fraction of a second. Grabbing hold again, she looked up and grinned triumphantly.

"Look at you!" Amanda told her. "Good girl!" More quietly, she asked Russ, "Did you father that baby?"

"No."

"Then there's no reason I should question your being there. Besides, all that is about birth. This isn't." Worriedly, she glanced at the Cotters' front door. "They're so afraid of embarrassment."

"If it were me, I'd have called in the troops."

"You and Gray, both. And me. I'm going over to see if I can light a spark." Giving his arm a squeeze, she set off. She went around to the back door and let herself in. Karen was on the phone. Lee was leaning against the counter with his arms folded and his ankles crossed.

Amanda looked at him and raised her brows.

He shook his head. His mouth was tight.

"Do you have any idea where he is?" Karen asked into the phone. She listened, sighed, sounded cross. "Well, if he does show up, would you please tell him to give me a call?" Seconds later, she hung up the phone and turned to Amanda. "He wasn't at baseball practice, but that figures. The rule says you can't play ball on a day when you haven't been in class." She leaned back against the wall, pressing her fingertips to her mouth.

"No clues?" Amanda asked Lee.

"Nah," he said and pushed off from the counter, snatching up his keys along the way. "I'm going driving."

"Where?" Karen asked in alarm.

"Anywhere my friggin' son might be," he said and slammed out the door.

In the silence left behind, Karen dropped her hand. She looked furious. "This is his fault. Kids can see through their parents. Jordie's old enough to know what his father's doing. He may not be screwing Gretchen, but he's sure doing it to someone else." She returned her fingertips to her mouth. Her eyes held Amanda's.

"Does Jordie know names?"

Karen shrugged.

"Would he run away because of it?"

"He hasn't run away," Karen said through her fingers, though they were trembling now. Amanda could see that.

Coming close, she put a hand on Karen's arm. "Call the police."

"No."

"They can be on the lookout."

"We don't need the police. This isn't a police matter. Get the police involved, and it won't end here."

"Why not?" Amanda asked, suddenly wondering whether there was something she didn't know.

"No reason," Karen said quickly. "I just think calling the police is overkill."

"If we figure that he left school at ten, he's been gone for almost eight hours."

"He'll be hungry soon. He'll show up. I'm making shepherd's pie. That's his favorite."

"Mom?" came a call from outside and, seconds later, Jared's nose was pressed to the screen. "Jon ran into me. He did it on purpose."

"Tell him I said to apologize."

Jared turned and yelled at the top of his lungs, "Mom says you have to apologize." Through the screen again, this time in a normal voice, he said, "We're hungry. When's supper?"

"When I make it," Karen said. "I'll do it soon."

Amanda said, "If Lee's out driving, I'm going walking."

"Walking where?"

"The woods."

"Jordie wouldn't be there."

Amanda disagreed, but she wasn't about to argue. "It won't hurt to look there just in case. I'll keep my cell phone in my pocket. Will you call if he shows up here?"

Karen swallowed, suddenly teary and unsure. "You don't think he'd harm himself, Amanda, do you?"

"No. But I think he's hurting."

"Have any of the other kids done this?"

"Disappeared? They may have. The thing is that I really want to find Jordie."

"Are you more worried about him than about the other kids?"

Amanda considered that for a minute, then nodded. "He has a lot to handle. You said it yourself, Karen.

He has to be aware of what's going on between Lee and you. He's old enough to feel conflicted."

"Conflicted?"

"Wanting to take sides. Not wanting to take sides. Praying that things are fine between you and Lee, but not buying it. Feeling frustrated and helpless."

Karen clasped her arms around herself. "Do you think he's suicidal?"

"No. But I think I'd like to check out the woods before dark. That gives us about two hours. Do you want to come?"

Karen shook her head. "If he finds out that I was worried enough to think he's in there and then go in after him, he'll hit the roof. No. I'll stay here and make more calls." Turning her back on Amanda, she reached for the phone.

Amanda returned home for a quick change into jeans and a jacket. No matter how warm the days were in May, the evenings got cool. Plus it looked like there would be rain before long.

Tucking her cell phone into a pocket, she left the house just as Graham drove up. He was out of the truck in an instant, joining her without a word. Seeming to know exactly where she was headed, he fell into step. Crossing through the yards between Karen's house and Gretchen's, they entered the woods.

Chapter Sixteen

They walked for several minutes without talking, Amanda behind Graham. The path was narrow but defined. Whatever might have grown there had long since been trampled, leaving little but the needles and leaves that had fallen the autumn before. The ground was damp after winter's snow and spring's rain, muting the sound underfoot.

The forest was eerily quiet, what with the heaviness of the air absorbing extraneous sounds. The cloud cover seemed more dense as they passed under evergreen fronds and hardwood branches, full with fresh, new leaves. Amanda almost imagined that the forest was holding its breath, waiting for something to happen, and the feeling heightened her own apprehension.

Even the red squirrels that lived there were quiet, with none of their usual hissing and chattering. If they were chasing each other over patches of moss and up one tree to the next, they did so with only the merest patter. Birds flitted higher up. The rustle of branches attested to that, along with the occasional whistle or trill, but those, too, were muted—not silent, simply muted in the thick air. It was mating season, after all.

Amanda thought about that as she followed Graham, with his sure step, his neat logger's beard, his firm body encased in a polo shirt and a pair of jeans. She loved seeing him this way. He was in his element in the great outdoors, and this qualified as the great outdoors. Though only ninety minutes from Manhattan and a mere ten from downtown Woodley, the town forest was a world in and of itself. The fear that she felt for Jordie couldn't dull the sense of place. Even under thickening clouds in torpid air, the forest was alive. Amanda wanted to think that was a good omen for the boy.

"Jordie," Graham called out into the woods. More quietly, he said over his shoulder to Amanda, "He always talks about the tower."

She was on the same wavelength. "If he's here, that's where we'll find him. The fact that it's been declared off-limits wouldn't keep him away."

Graham grunted. "If anything, it would heighten the attraction. Same with the lore. And he knows it all." Abruptly he stopped walking. Coming up against him, Amanda held on to the back waistband of his jeans. He cupped his mouth. *"Jordie?"* They both listened for something other than an echo. Graham called out again, directing his voice left, then right, but there was no response. "Even if he's here, he won't answer," he murmured.

"That doesn't mean he doesn't want to be found," Amanda said.

Graham shot an understanding glance over his shoulder at her. Along with the understanding was concern—and warmth. Reaching back, he took her hand in his and set off again. The path began to climb, a gentle but noticeable incline.

Amanda had to walk quickly, even trot to keep up with the pace he set. Her stride was shorter than his, but she was used to it. "This reminds me of Mount Jefferson," she said, welcoming the diversion from worrying about Jordie. "Remember? It started to snow, and we had to race back to the hut."

"You skidded most of the way. Fell a whole lot. You were black and blue for days."

"But we made it." She let the memory soothe her. "I've missed you, Gray."

In a single fluid motion, he turned, caught her up, pulling her against him, kissed her soundly on the mouth, set her down, and, still holding her hand, went on. Amanda was totally turned on. In the next instant, though, she remembered why they were hurrying through the woods with the light fading fast.

"Jordie," Graham called out again. *"Jordie."*

"What if he's hurt himself?" Amanda asked.

"Let's cross that bridge when we get to it."

"We talked, he and I."

Graham gave her hand a squeeze. "I figured that. When was the last time?"

"A week ago yesterday."

"Before Quinn."

"Yes."

He held her hand more tightly, giving her a silent boost. They were five minutes into the forest, another ten yet to the tower. They continued on, sharing the sense of urgency, ever vigilant for a sound that might tip them off.

Amanda trotted to come alongside Graham when the

path widened enough to allow it. "We haven't hiked in ages. Why, Gray?"

"Too busy. Too preoccupied." He shot her a look. "Doin' okay?"

"Doin' okay." It was their stock exchange when they hiked.

"I mean, physically," he said with an intimate glance, and she knew just what he had in mind. She was done with her period, and for the first time in months, she wasn't taking medication to increase the production of eggs.

She liked his concern. She also liked the absence of anger in his voice. "Better," she said, though she was growing breathless from the pace. "It's like I'm reclaiming my body." She felt a raindrop on her arm, then one on her nose. "Oh dear."

"Yeah," Graham breathed. "It's starting. *Jordie,*" he called, then muttered a frustrated, "Where the fuck is he?"

"There's the tower," Amanda said, spotting the palette of multitoned gray fieldstone that stretched obelisklike through the softer, more giving boughs. Though sketched in local lore as timeless and strong, it had grown ragged with age. Stones had cracked and fallen out, many during the earthquake the year before. The tower continued to stand forty feet high. Now, though, its slanted sides, narrowing as they rose, were pockmarked with bulges and dents.

Amanda stumbled on a tree root that lay over the path. Had she not been holding Graham's hand, she would have fallen.

"Easy," Graham said, tightening his hold without slowing.

"Do you see him there?"

Graham's voice pulsed with the pace he kept. "We're coming in from the wrong side. If he's there, he's on the other side."

Amanda said again, "What if he's hurt himself?" She had visions . . . visions . . . of rounding the tower and finding a rope . . .

"Don't think it," Graham murmured, setting her behind him when the path narrowed again.

The rain picked up, creating a patter overhead. Releasing her hand, Graham began to trot. She did the same. She didn't try to look ahead, didn't try to see anything but Graham's back. This, too, she was used to—and if a die-hard feminist were to take her to task for enjoying following after her husband this way, she would argue that said die-hard feminist didn't know the joy of following Graham. He was coordinated. For a man who stood six-foot-three and weighed a solid one-ninety, he was graceful and deft. He moved with a confidence that she found to be reassuring—whether they were trying to outrun the weather, trying to beat the clock, or trying to overcome unsettling mental images of Jordie on the other side of the tower.

The path veered to the right and curved around. Amanda didn't have to look beyond Graham to know that the tower loomed higher. She felt the enormity of it, heard the difference the rain made hitting fieldstone high above. Her shirt had grown damp. Tendrils of hair were escaping from the scrunchy in back and curling wildly in the drizzle.

They emerged into a clearing. The tower stood twenty feet from them. A dozen feet wide at its base, it narrowed to less than half that at the top. A makeshift fence of weak plywood slats circled it, but as deterrents went, it was lame. It had been bent in spots and broken through in others. If Jordie had climbed it, he wasn't the first.

"Jordie?" Graham called as they continued around to the far side. He stopped short, looked up, then started walking, more slowly now.

Amanda was right beside him, her head tipped back. She had seen him too. Any relief she felt that the boy was alive was tempered by the precariousness of the situation. He sat on an incline at the very top of the tower, dressed in a dirty T-shirt and jeans, barely visible against the deepening gray of the day. His legs hung over the side, giving more of an illusion of comfort than his hands indicated, as they grasped the rock on either side of his hips. He could as easily fall backward into the hollow tower and down those forty feet as fall forward. With the rocks growing wet, accidental slippage was a real fear.

"Jesus, Jordie," Graham called, breathing more heavily now that they had stopped. "You scared the living daylights out of us! Your parents are looking all over. They're terrified." Under his breath, he said to Amanda, "Give 'em a call."

Pulling the cell phone from her pocket, she punched in the number with shaky fingers. When nothing happened, she looked closer. "No service. I don't believe it."

Graham expressed frustration with a guttural sound. "Our fault," he said without taking his eyes from the boy. "We voted against letting them put an antenna up here." He raised his voice. "The weather's not gettin' better, Jordie. Think you can come down?"

It wouldn't be that easy. Amanda knew it, but she wanted Graham to take the man-to-man approach first. If Jordie were of a mind to come down, he might find it more palatable to do so at the bidding of a man than a woman.

Of course, wanting to come down was one thing. Being able to do it was something else. Climbers didn't come down from the tower on their own. They always needed help. That was part of the lore.

Jordie didn't move. In Amanda's eyes, he was starting to fade into the rocks. "Is he alive up there?" she whispered in horror.

"Oh yeah," Graham said. "He blinked." He raised his voice. "How'd you get up there? Did you climb up the back side? Maybe we could talk you down."

Amanda made out the tiniest headshake.

"Why not?" Graham called. "You could be the first to do it. There's nothing to be accomplished by staying up there."

Jordie gave the smallest nod.

Amanda and Graham caught in simultaneous breaths when the boy let go of the stone with one hand and reached underneath his T-shirt. They stood perfectly still when the hand emerged with a small pistol.

"Where in the hell did you get *that*?" Graham yelled.

Jordie didn't answer. Nor, though, did he point the gun in any particular direction. He just let it rest in his lap as a message that he possessed an element of power over them after all.

"It's Lee's," Amanda murmured. "Karen mentioned it." She raised her voice. "You don't want to use that, Jordie. It's unnecessary. Nothing is that bad."

Jordie didn't argue. He simply continued to stare out at the forest.

Amanda moved closer to Graham. As wet as his shirt was growing, a warmth came from beneath it.

She didn't stop this time to remember other instances when she had sought his warmth out in the wild this way. Now, she just swallowed. "How do we get him down?"

"We don't. It's too dark and too slippery. The rescue squad gets him down."

"I'll run back."

"I'll go. I run faster. You stay here and try to get him talking. You do that better than me." His eyes met hers. He touched his fingers to her mouth, followed them with his eyes for the space of a second, then set off.

His absence was sudden and visceral. Amanda felt it deep inside. Looking up at Jordie, she had to work harder to distinguish him from the stones. It was a typical spring rain, steady now but mercifully gentle. Pushing back wet strands of her hair, she moved closer.

"I wanted to talk today," she called up. "I e-mailed you several times."

"Where'd Graham go?" Jordie called down in a distrustful voice.

"To let your parents know where you are. They've been beside themselves with worry."

"I'll bet," he muttered.

She might not have heard it if she hadn't been expecting it. Jordie had issues with his parents—it didn't take a counselor to see that. Amanda had the added advantage of knowing Karen and Lee. She also knew what it was like growing up with battling parents, knew what it was like to feel a churning in her stomach each time she walked in the door of the one place that was supposed to be a haven.

"They love you," she called, but the rain suddenly fell harder, and her voice didn't carry as far. Sheltering her eyes with both hands, she put more effort into it.

"Why the tower, Jordie? Do you really want to spend the night up there?"

He didn't respond.

"Talk to me," she called, because that was key. He needed to vent and curse and share his fears. On the parent front, she knew where he was coming from. On the Quinn front, she could commiserate. She had to be closer to him, though. She wanted to be sitting beside him.

Going forward, she climbed through a hole in the fence and went to the side of the tower where the rocks served as steps.

Jordie called out a warning. "Don't come up."

"I can't talk to you from down here," she called back, testing the rock with one hand and a foot. The granite was slick, but her hiking shoes had good treads. Scraping the soles free of wet leaves, she raised herself onto the first step. Grasping the stone above with both hands, she steadied herself and moved up another two steps. One foot slipped. She caught herself, held still for a minute to let the pounding of her heart ease, then rose another eight inches.

"I'll jump if you come," Jordie called.

He didn't mention using the gun. That was good.

She couldn't see him now. He was on the other side of the tower. Increasingly, between the rain and dusk, she had trouble seeing even the rocks above. She could feel them, though. Her hands led the way.

She raised her left foot to the next stone, found rocks to grasp with her fingers, climbed up. The incline of the tower gave her help with gravity. Her right foot found the next step. Her palms closed over rocks to the right and left. Heart racing faster with each step, she rose higher.

"Amanda?" Jordie called, sounding as though he wanted to know where she was and couldn't decide whether he was frightened or angry.

"If you jump," she called back, "I'm apt to fall, in which case my death will be on your conscience." She was apt to fall anyway. The ground was growing farther and farther away. The thought was chilling.

"If I'm dead," he charged, "it won't matter."

"You don't want to die." She had to believe that. "There are too many things in life you love."

He didn't respond.

Taking shallower breaths, ignoring the fear she felt, she kept climbing. Oddly, the higher she went, the easier the stones were to find, but that was part of the lore. The tower gods hooked you and pulled you up, it was said, and Amanda was ready to believe it. Her foot slipped as it had below, only she was higher now, making it more dangerous. She cried out, braced herself for a fall, miraculously found her footing again. Several more steps, and she nearly slipped again when, groping for a hold, her shoe knocked out a rock. She didn't fall this time, either. But she did hear the dislodged rock tumble over stone to the ground. The sound was not reassuring.

About halfway up, she reached the point of no return, where, according to legend, she couldn't have gone back down if she'd tried. Reaching it now, she wasn't sure whether it was the cutoff between further adventure or sheer terror. She certainly felt the last. She didn't look down, didn't look up other than to search for handholds. Gripped by that terror, she told herself she was an imbecile—told herself she should have waited for the rescue squad—told herself that she was absolutely, positively going to die. But Quinn was dead, and Jordie was up there with a gun, and even if she had wanted to turn back, it was too late. Physically, she couldn't do it. She had no choice but to keep going, finding one foothold after the next, climbing higher and higher.

"Jordie?" she called in a shaky voice when she sensed she was nearing the top. She refused to think of how high she was, refused to think of how far she would fall. "Are you still there, Jordie?"

The derisive sound he made came from a spot not much higher. "Where would I go?"

Like his threat to jump rather than shoot, the self-derision was telling. She wanted to think he realized that he'd made a mistake but didn't know how to right it.

She continued to work one foot after the other until her hands reached open space. Her stomach dropped at the void. For a split second, she was dizzy. She may have even whimpered, though the sound of the rain swallowed it up.

"You're crazy," Jordie said.

Climbing a step higher, Amanda said a high-pitched, "You and me, both." Bracing her hands on the top circle of stones, she had moved her feet high enough so that she could bend over that top row and rest her legs, but, for the life of her, she didn't know what to do next. Her knees were shaking. Her stomach was twisting. She was calling herself every kind of fool for having done this.

Jordie must have heard the element of panic in her voice, because he said, "There's a ledge to stand on about two feet down on the inside."

She eased a leg over and groped blindly—lower, then lower—until her shoe touched the ledge. It didn't feel any too wide to her, but it did seem sturdy. Carefully, she slid the other leg over. She held on for a minute, bent over the top. Gingerly, she inched sideways until she reached Jordie.

He was soaking wet. Though the light was dim, she could see that—and the fact that he was no longer holding the gun. That was some relief, along with the fact that visibility was so poor now that she couldn't make out the area below the tower. Pretending that they were only three feet off the ground, she carefully slid a leg over and straddled the rock.

"Graham's going to kill me," she said, because it was the first thought that came to mind. "These stones are treacherous. I'm not good at treacherous things." With a bit of leftover breath, she asked, "Where's the gun?"

Jordie didn't answer.

"I don't want it accidentally going off."

"I know how to use it."

"I'm sure you do," she said. What she didn't say was that any *moron* could point a gun at his heart, pull the trigger, and make his point. She wasn't giving him any ideas.

"You shouldn't've come up here."

There was a cracking sound, then the thudding of another rock as it careened down the tower's side. Imagining that if enough stones fell out under their weight, the tower might just crumble and bury them alive, Amanda said in a mildly hysterical way, "I didn't want you feeling lonely." She repositioned her hands, one in front and one behind her. They were less than cemented to the wet granite, but the bracing made her feel marginally more secure.

"How do you know what I'm feeling?" Jordie asked. "You're not me."

"No. But this is what I do."

"Read minds?"

"Feel." She let that sink in for a minute. "Is it Quinn?"

Silently, he looked out into the rain and the fast-falling darkness.

"Quinn needed help," she said.

"I helped him," Jordie muttered bitterly. "I gave him the vodka. He said he wanted it for a party. I thought he meant a weekend party. I thought it'd be cool to go. So I told him my dad had a stash in the basement and wouldn't miss a bottle. I brought one to school."

"And you feel guilty about that."

In a rush of angry words, Jordie said, "If I hadn't given him the stuff, he wouldn't have been caught drunk, and if he hadn't been caught drunk, he wouldn't have been punished, and then there wouldn't have been anything in the paper, and he wouldn't have killed himself."

"Oh, Jordie. It wasn't just the piece in the newpaper. It was other things."

"Yeah. Like his parents. At least they were together."

She couldn't miss his meaning. "Your parents are together."

"Barely. They fight all the time. If that's what together means, I don't want it."

"All marriages have rocky times."

He looked at her then. Even as dim as the light was, she could see his incredulity. "They *hate* each other."

Amanda felt shades of the familiar. Years of agonizing over her parents' relationship hadn't produced any answers. She had finally learned to let it go, though that was more easily done intellectually than emotionally. "Whether or not they do, they love you kids. Do you doubt that?"

Jordie didn't answer. Instead, turning half around in anger, he blurted out, "Why was he with Gretchen?"

There was a grating sound from below, a minuscule shudder, the clatter of what sounded like a cluster of small rocks tumbling down the side of the tower.

Amanda held her breath, didn't move, didn't say anything until the sound died without follow-up. In the aftermath, she imagined she and Jordie hurtling down the tower, bumping against the side just as the rocks had done.

Where is Graham? she cried silently, feeling like a coward but not caring a bit. *What was* taking *him so long?*

"You're not answering," Jordie taunted.

"I didn't know he had been with Gretchen," she managed. "Are you sure about that?"

"It won't have been the first time he's cheated on my mom. And don't tell me I'm wrong. I hear them fighting. I'll give you names if you want."

"Did he say he was with Gretchen?"

"No, but my mom thinks he was. She gets so angry, she scares me."

Amanda imagined she felt a tremor under her, a tiny aftershock, the resettling of the stones. Feeling an incipient nausea, she said, "I worry about that gun, Jordie. If you've stuck it in your waistband and it goes off by accident when these rocks shift again, I'd hate to think what it'd hit."

"It doesn't matter."

"It does," she insisted. Focusing on Jordie, because he was a more stable point of reference than the darkness behind her lids if she closed her eyes, she took a slow, deep breath. She needed to keep Jordie talking until help arrived. "How does your mom scare you?"

"She's someone else when she talks to him. I don't care what you say, she hates him, and it's Gretchen's fault. She should've moved away when Ben died. She didn't have any cause to stay, and if she did, she should've taken care of herself, instead of letting my dad and Graham and Russ fuss over her. If she hadn't lured them in, none of this would've happened."

"None of what?"

"My parents' fights. There were fights before, but they were okay before this."

"That's like saying Quinn killed himself over the newspaper article. It's too simplistic an answer."

Jordie sat there with his jaw tight, seeming to resist until the words just spilled out. "So why did he kill himself?"

"He was deeply troubled. He didn't have anyone to talk to. He felt pressure to succeed. It was just too much."

"Everyone feels pressure to succeed. That's what getting grades in school is about."

"He felt pressure to be at the top."

"Because of his brothers?"

"Possibly."

"But he was at the top."

"He felt pressure to stay there. The pressure grew. He wanted to succeed. He pretended to be confident and self-assured, when inside he wasn't feeling that at all."

Jordie thought for a moment. "So he killed himself because he wasn't perfect? How does that make the rest of us feel? We aren't anywhere *near* being perfect."

"And Quinn wasn't anywhere near perfect either.

But he felt such pressure to achieve perfection that he became helpless and gave up. His biggest problem was that the helplessness took away all his strength. But you're still strong, Jordie—you're still fighting. Quinn gave up. He *wasn't* strong."

"He was so. He couldn't have been all the things he was if he wasn't strong."

"Class president? Starting pitcher? Mr. Congeniality? Life is full of choices, Jordie. None of those things involved tough ones. The one time Quinn faced a biggie, he did it wrong. Death is not a good choice. Not when you're young and healthy. Not when you have potential. Not when people love you."

"It isn't that simple," Jordie muttered and looked quickly back toward the path.

Amanda heard the same sound he did, the thud of approaching footsteps. Seconds later, the beams of large flashlights converged on the ground below.

"Shit," Jordie muttered.

"Amanda?" Graham called around the ground level. *"Amanda?"*

"Up here," she yelled down. The only thing she could see of him was the yellow rain slicker he had put on, and that, only as the beams of other flashlights crossed his body. Suddenly, all of those beams were aimed up, hitting their eyes. Instinctively, she put a hand up to shield hers from the glare, but the movement caused a shift in the rocks. Grasping them, she screamed, *"Lower the lights."*

The lights lowered, forming a network on the ground.

"Jordie?" Karen called, clearly frightened.

Lee's voice followed. "What are you doing up there, Jordie?"

"Come down," Karen urged. "We can talk. We can work everything out."

There was more thudding from the woods, then another voice. "The squad's on its way." It was Russ. "Hang on, Jordie. They're coming."

"Amanda's up there with him," Graham said. "I'm going up."

"No," Amanda cried. "No, Gray. It isn't stable. Rocks were falling out when I climbed. If many more fall, we're in trouble."

"I'm in trouble anyway," Jordie muttered.

Amanda grabbed his wrist. "If you go, I go." She didn't care whether he was mortified, having everyone he cared about down below. She wasn't having him die of embarrassment. Not on her watch.

"You don't *get* it," Jordie cried in a hoarse whisper. "I *can't* go down. They'll kill me when they find out what I've done."

"The vodka? No one's going to blame you for that. You didn't make Quinn drink it."

"Not the vodka," he said in a panicky way. *"Gretchen."*

That quickly, something clicked in Amanda's mind. She saw the marks of a knife, forming the shape of words that might have been her parrot's favorite: *Fuck it.* "The painting."

"Yes," Jordie hissed. "I can't *stand* that painting. I can't stand *her.* I just want her to leave. My parents would be okay if she left."

It wasn't as simple as that. Amanda knew the havoc that distrust had wreaked between Graham and her, and there had been no cause. In the case of the Cotters, there was. Lee was having an affair, if not with Gretchen, then with someone else. His marriage had been in trouble before Gretchen arrived. Chances were that it wouldn't improve if she left.

At the clatter of more rocks, Amanda felt those under her shift. Her pulse raced. She waited for more movement, but there was none.

Down below, Graham swore.

"She was right," Russ told him, his voice just barely carrying up to the top. "Stay down. It's not safe."

"Gray?" Amanda called.

"I'm okay," he grumbled, but her attention swung right back to Jordie.

"I shouldn't've done it," he muttered in the same desperate way. "I was just so angry, and the phone calls didn't scare her off."

"Phone calls?"

"Just enough to spook her, only they didn't. It was stupid of me. Stupid. *Stupid.*"

She could feel the tension that radiated through his body in the wrist she held. She gave it a sharp shake. "Not stupid. Angry, yes. But anger's okay. You have a right to be angry, though not at Gretchen. You can be angry at your parents, because they're struggling to work some things out, and they're upsetting you. I've been there. I know how that is. I went through the same thing with my parents. I kept telling myself that I couldn't say anything, because that would only make things worse. So I drew into myself and was silent and moody, which made them more unhappy, and me angrier. It took me years to realize that I had a right to be angry—took me years to give myself *permission* to be angry."

In the rain, he was listening. "And then what?"

"I expressed the anger. I said what I was thinking."

"Did it make things better for them?"

"No. But I felt better."

There was more action below, the beams of floodlights, the approach of more people.

"Half the town's here," Jordie said in dismay.

"No. Probably just four men. They need that many to carry a ladder long enough to reach us up here."

"They'll put it in the paper, just like the stuff about Quinn."

"All they'll know is that we climbed up here and got stuck."

"I'm not going down. I can't. I know the insurance people were at Gretchen's. If they don't come after me, the cops will."

Relieved that help was at hand, Amanda spoke more calmly. "They won't. We'll work something out."

"Like make Gretchen forget her picture's ruined?" Jordie sneered.

"No. But it could be she'll understand what you're about, and why it happened."

"The cops are already involved."

"They won't be, if she refuses to press charges."

He snorted. "So then I just have to answer to my parents."

"And they won't feel even a little bit to blame? Think about it, Jordie. Think about what you felt with the vodka and Quinn. Your parents are going to be thinking the same way, once they get over their initial anger. You have to talk to them. You have to tell them what you're feeling. It may help them, Jordie. Think about *that* for a minute."

There were voices far below, the scrape of aluminum on stone, the extension of the ladder. There was a jiggling, a ratcheting, more scraping and squealing, until the top of the ladder settled against the stone on the other side of Jordie. Amanda held her breath, half expecting the top of the tower to fall inward under the weight. But it held.

"You have nothing to be ashamed of, Jordie," Karen called. "Absolutely nothing. Things sometimes happen that aren't your fault."

"We all make mistakes," Lee said.

But it was Graham's voice, spoken with greater quiet and extraordinary intent, that spoke to Amanda. "Hold on, babe. Hold on for me."

Her heart swelled and clenched. Somewhere through the rain she felt the warmth of tears in her eyes, but there wasn't time to dwell on that emotion. With a final creaking as the ladder took on weight, the first of the rescue team started up.

"What do I do?" Jordie asked Amanda.

"They love you," she said, holding his wrist as tightly as ever.

The ladder creaked; its extension pulleys jangled.

"Are you going to tell them we talked at school?" Jordie asked in a rush.

"No," Amanda answered, feeling an urgency to seal the deal before their time alone was done. "I told you that was confidential. Besides, you've told me much more up here than you ever did there. That's the stuff you need to share with your parents."

"About Gretchen? They'll go *apeshit.*"

"Not if you tell them why. Not if you explain."

"That's easy for you to say."

Yes, it was. It struck her just then, with help fast approaching, that lately she hadn't done a very good job sharing her own feelings and thoughts. She was a fine one to talk.

"It's the strong thing to do, Jordie," she said, though

she might have substituted her own name for his. "It's the grown-up thing to do." Releasing his wrist, she took his chin and forced him to meet her gaze. "You are strong. You're a fighter. You're a *survivor.* You can get through this, Jordie. I know you can." She held his eyes until the sound of a man's voice came from barely four feet away.

"Okay, Jordie, I'm going to grab hold of your leg and guide your foot to the ladder."

Jordie started to shake his head, but Amanda tightened her hold on his chin. "Yes," she whispered firmly. "Quinn was a coward. You aren't. Show them that, Jordie. I'm begging you to show them that."

For an instant, he looked like he wanted to argue. In the next instant, though, he seemed to let out a breath. He didn't quite nod, but she saw his acquiescence. Releasing his chin, she held his arm until he had both feet on the ladder. He looked up at her a final time.

"Go," she said. "I'll be down right after you."

She saw the rescue worker immediately beneath Jordie, close enough so that he couldn't fall or jump. In tandem, they moved down one step, then another. Before long, they were a body's length beneath her, then two. She was just starting to think that they were out of the woods when she heard the rumble of stone and felt a shift. This one didn't stop so fast.

Chapter Seventeen

In the space of a breath, as she slid forward and back on the slick granite, Amanda pictured Graham standing below and feeling unspeakable pain as he watched her die.

But she didn't die. Heart thundering, she rode the stone to a standstill. Beneath her, there was a commotion of voices. It was a minute before she was thinking cohesively enough again to look down into the grid of flashlight beams and wonder about Jordie. She couldn't see the ladder.

"How is he?" she yelled.

"Fine," said Graham, sounding closer than he could possibly be.

"Gray?" she cried.

"On the ladder, behind you and down, babe. Are you hurt?"

"No. Just terrified."

"You're gonna have to slide back to where you were."

"It isn't safe. The rocks are loose."

His voice came from a closer point. "We have no

choice." He shouted down, *"Shine the beam so I can see her,"* then gentled his voice again. "Move slowly now. There, babe. That's it."

Desperate to be where he was, which was surely a safer place, she inched backward. She didn't look anywhere but at her own two hands, which were soaking wet and cold with fear.

"Keep coming," Graham coaxed from close enough behind her that she started to cry. "Keep coming."

She felt his hand on her leg, guiding her carefully.

"Gentle, there. A little more. I'm putting your foot on the top rung. Lean forward now, honey, and swing the other leg over. Easy. That's it. That's my girl."

She did as he told her, grateful to be led. She was weeping softly, shaking all over, feeling tired and weak and sore—and frightened still, now for Graham, too. When she had both feet on the ladder, he guided her down one step after another, until his body surrounded her. Only then did she dare release her hold on the granite and grasp the sides of the ladder.

Graham pressed against her and tucked his chin into the curve of her shoulder. For a long moment he held her still. His breath warmed her ear. "Shhhh. Don't cry, Mandy. We're goin' down now."

Fearful that the slightest movement would topple more rock, they moved slowly, backing down carefully, one rung at a time. The ladder widened when they reached the next extension, then widened again a bit lower, but Amanda was only peripherally conscious of anything but Graham's voice in her ear. She didn't even hear the words, just felt the tone. It kept her legs working, kept her holding her own weight until he touched ground and swept her up in his arms. He carried her to the edge of the clearing, safely away from the tower and the others gathered there. Sinking down onto the wet earth, he enveloped her in his slicker and drew her in close, rocking her back and forth, holding her with arms that trembled.

Amanda didn't move. She was too tired, too content. The rain was no problem, since they were already drenched. Speech was unnecessary.

At some point, Russ came over to report that Jordie had broken a leg in the final tumble, but fortunately that was the worst of it. At another point, he came back to report that they had the boy on a stretcher and were carrying him out. At a third point, he returned to see if Graham and Amanda needed help.

At that point, Graham pulled Amanda to her feet. They didn't need help, he said. They were fine.

"Fine" was one word for it, Amanda thought, though that put it mildly. Jordie was safe; a tragedy had been averted. Amanda knew who had defaced Gretchen's artwork, and though she still didn't know who had fathered the baby, she knew with absolute certainty who hadn't done it. Graham hadn't. Being with him now, pressed close to his heart under the shelter of his arm, she felt the conviction of that.

She felt more, as they made their way back through the forest. She felt the psychic connection that had so drawn her to Graham at the start. She also felt the chemistry. It was back—back from the lab, where it had been stuck in a mess of tissue cultures, blood workups, tests, and medication—back to the heart-pounding, bone-deep thrill that had been such a steady part of their relationship before all that had come between them. It felt good to focus on those curls of attraction as they walked back through the rain—felt good to press against Graham's body and let his warmth become part of her again.

By the time they came out of the woods, the rescue squad had Jordie on his way to the hospital. A tiny voice in the back of Amanda's mind told her to see who had gone with him, who was left with the other children, how they all were faring.

She ignored that tiny voice. Graham filled her heart, and her senses. Selfishly, she pushed all else from her mind.

They were barely in the kitchen with the door closed behind them when he lifted her, set her on the counter, and took her face in his hands. His kiss had the taste of urgency. It said that he felt everything she did—but she had known that well before their lips touched. She was able to savor it and return it, clinging to his hair, then his shoulders.

"I love you," he whispered, lowering his mouth to her neck. At the same time, he unsnapped her jeans and tugged at the zipper. It was wet and resisted, but that didn't stop him. He managed to push a hand inside.

Amanda felt the heat rise even before he found his mark, and his touch sent it higher. She climaxed within seconds, a spasming that seemed endless. She was still in the last of it when he began pushing her pants out of the way, and she went to work releasing him from his own. He was heavy and hard; she would have explored that, if there hadn't been such a dire need to have him inside. His entry was magic. It was smooth and fast, creating aftershocks of her climax that drove her toward a second, and his was nearly as potent. One, two, three deep strokes, and he clutched her tighter and cried out in release.

He stayed hard even when the pulsing inside was done. Sliding his fingers into her hair, he took her mouth again, and for Amanda it was a reunion. She had missed the way his lips slanted over hers, the way his tongue searched and his teeth nibbled. She had missed the trail of his tongue on her neck and, once the slicker was pushed from her shoulders, her jersey was over her head, and her bra tossed aside, on her breasts. She cried out when he drew a nipple into his mouth, and, feeling a line of fire arrowing down, bucked against him when he suckled more strongly.

He began again then, stroking her inside while he used his hands above. Again they climaxed within seconds of each other—one igniting the next in an order neither knew.

The denouement was more leisurely this time, a slower return to awareness, a more spent embrace.

"Cold?" he asked in a raspy whisper.

She shook her head.

"But wet," he said.

She couldn't deny that, though the words were provocative. When he drew back and the slash of a wicked grin shot through his beard, she coiled her arms tighter around his neck.

"Dry me," she whispered.

During a break in the action, he went to a quiet window and gave her a call. She picked up after a single ring. She had been waiting.

"I can't get there tonight," he said.

She paused for a beat, then replied with a disappointed, "Not at all?"

"No. I'm needed here. There's no way I can get away."

"You said that wouldn't happen."

"I also said it was a delicate situation, and that was then. Now it's even more delicate."

"Why?"

"Complications. A turn of events."

"What events?"

He pushed a hand through his hair. He was frazzled enough not to want to go into detail. "We had a major trauma tonight. I'm picking up pieces. It's important."

"I thought *I* was."

"You are," he said, and then, because his body didn't stir at the thought of her and he felt guilty for that, he softened his voice. "We've been through this, cookie. You *are* important. But there's an order to things."

"I'm running out of time. If this keeps up much longer, the baby will be born."

"No pressure. Not tonight. I'm too drained."

"I feel pressure. Shouldn't you, too?"

He wanted to say that he didn't. He wanted to threaten to deny that the baby was his, if she didn't back off. Hell, he wasn't even entirely sure the baby *was* his. She was a hot little number. Quickies were her specialty.

But after the events of this evening, he wasn't in a threatening mood. Fear was a potent mellower, and he did feel mellow.

"I'll give you a call tomorrow," he said.

"How do I know you will?" she asked in a way that would have been a total turnoff even if he had been interested in her just then, which he wasn't. He wasn't being roped into something that didn't work for him. If the baby wasn't his, he didn't owe her a thing.

"Look, I'm not going to answer that. I can't talk now. That's it." Ending the call, he turned his back on the window and refocused his thoughts on the home front.

* * *

Georgia had planned to be home in time for supper, but her flight was delayed. She had barely turned on her cell phone and left the plane, though, when Russ called. She stood stock-still, just inside the terminal, while he explained what had happened. Once the initial horror passed, she began walking again, with growing speed as her sense of direction narrowed. If she'd had even the least bit of doubt about what she wanted when the plane had touched down, it was gone.

She wanted to be home.

Karen would have stayed at the hospital if she hadn't been worried about the other children. Allison was with them, and they were in bed when she got home, but they were awake and needing reassurance. She gave them that, tucked them in, and kissed them goodnight. Then she went down to the kitchen and called the phone by Jordie's bed.

Lee answered. "Hello?"

"It's me. How is he?"

"Pretty good. Here."

There was a moment's silence during the transfer of the receiver, then a subdued, "Hi."

"How's the leg feel?" she asked in as upbeat a way as she could.

"It's okay."

"Does it hurt?"

"Yeah."

"Did they give you something for the pain?"

"Yeah."

"That's good. You must be tired."

"A little."

"Jordie?" She didn't know where to start, there was so much to say.

"I'll be home in the morning," Jordie said in a way that summarily shut down discussion before it began. Karen didn't know whether he wouldn't talk because he was tired, in pain, or upset—or because he was just being Jordie—or because Lee was right there.

"I know, honey," she answered. "I'll be there to get you. I just want you to know that I love you."

Jordie was silent.

"Jordie—" Her eyes filled with tears. He was their son, and although he had behaved badly, it occurred to her that she and Lee hadn't done much better. Keeping the family intact was one thing; doing it at the expense of the children's peace of mind was something else.

"I know, Mom," he whispered brokenly. "Me, too."

"We have to talk," Amanda murmured a bit later. She and Graham had made love in the shower and again in bed. She lay now with her cheek on his shoulder, her hand on his chest, her belly to his middle, and her leg wound through his.

"Later," Graham whispered, barely moving his mouth. His eyes were closed, dark lashes resting on the tanned skin beneath.

"Talking's the key. We stopped doing it."

"For other reasons than this," he murmured with the ghost of a wry smile.

She touched his mouth. His lips were firm and puckered right up to kiss her fingertips, but that was the extent of his exertion. His chest rose and fell with healthy regularity, but his limbs lay long and inert.

"Why'd we stop?" she asked.

He was quiet for so long, still for so long, that she wondered if he was falling asleep. He had a way of doing that after they made love. Not her. Lovemaking stimulated her. Even now, when she should have been exhausted from her adventure with Jordie, she was wide awake.

"Life," he murmured.

"Life what?"

"Got in the way. We got caught up. Things came between." He drew in a deep breath, turned his head on the pillow, and opened his eyes to hers. "The answer to your question? I want you. If we don't have a baby biologically, we'll have one another way."

She studied his eyes. His gaze was direct. In its nakedness, she saw an unmistakable honesty.

At the urging of his arm, she lay her head down with an ear to his heart, and timed her breathing to match its beat. "What if things come between us again?"

"We won't let them."

"We weren't aware it was happening this time. How will we know another time?"

"We're experienced now. This was our first big blow-up, our first real test."

"I'm sorry I accused you of being with Gretchen. It's just that there she was, suddenly pregnant and I wasn't, and you did such a gorgeous landscape plan for her right around the time she would have conceived." When he didn't respond, she raised her head. His eyes were closed again. "Who do you think fathered her baby?"

"Don't know," he murmured.

"Think it was Lee?"

"Hmm."

That was a "could be," Amanda knew. She thought about the ramifications, in light of the talk she'd had with Jordie up at the top of the tower. "At least, if it was Lee, he might have an element of control over her. He could prevent her from going after Jordie for destroying the painting. Think he would?"

Gretchen waited until Thursday morning to make the call. She knew the number by heart. Though she had phoned Oliver Deeds only a handful of times, she had studied his number many more times than that in the awful months following Ben's death. He had been a backup for her then. She kept his number beside that of the local police. He had been a resource when she didn't know how to handle something, a source of stability, just as Ben had wanted. Of course, Ben couldn't have anticipated the strength of his own sons' reactions to what he had left her in his will, and the way that pulled Oliver in different directions at once.

"Fillham and Marcus," came the receptionist's singsong voice.

"Oliver Deeds, please."

"May I tell him who's calling?"

"Gretchen Tannenwald." She took a deep breath, turned away from the phone, waited.

He came on promptly, as was his way. His specialty was estates. A paper-and-pencil man, he lived and acted contracts and forms.

"Gretchen?"

"Yes," she said, rushing out the speech she had rehearsed, trying her best to sound independent and strong. "I won't take much of your time. I just wanted to tell you that I found out who damaged my paintings. It's someone I know, so I won't press charges. I'd appreciate it if you would tell that to the insurance company and to David and Alan."

There was a pause, then, "Are you saying you're withdrawing the insurance claim?"

"I never filed a claim. I never called them. You did that."

"You have a right to the money."

"What good's the money if I can't replace the painting?"

"Money's money. You have a baby coming. Do you need any for that?"

"No."

"You know I'll help."

"No."

He stayed quiet. She wanted to think that she had surprised him, which was pretty pathetic. Oliver knew her better than Ben's sons did. He should have known she wasn't in it for the money.

"So who did slash the art?" he asked.

"It doesn't matter."

"Is it someone you're seeing?"

"I'm pregnant. I'm not seeing anyone."

"Oh. I was just wondering. Gretchen—"

"That's all. I just wanted you to know that. Bye, Oliver."

Graham was still in bed, and it was nearly noon. He couldn't remember the last time he'd stayed in bed this long. Of course, he couldn't remember the last time they'd made love so much, and it wasn't over. Turning his head on the pillow, he saw the riot of Amanda's blond hair inches away. Her bare back and bottom nestled against his equally bare side. His arm was numb where her cheek rested, but that was the extent of his numbness. Holding her, lying so close, he felt the hum of arousal.

They had called in sick. Both of them. It wasn't a first, but it had been years since they'd done it last.

Turning onto his side, he drew her back against him with a satisfied sigh. Earlier passion had taken the edge off his need. What he felt now was the slower pleasure of a simmering heat, as blood worked its way to his groin.

She took in a deep breath, held it, looked over her shoulder, turned. "Hi," she said with a sleepy sigh that ended in a smile.

"Hi," he said, kissing her nose.

"Mmm. You haven't kissed my nose in months."

"You haven't looked so cute in months." She looked about twenty years old. Not that he had a thing for younger women. Well, maybe he did. He certainly liked Amanda's freshness.

Looking dreamy, she closed her eyes. Seconds later, they popped back open. "Did you call the Cotters?"

"Yeah. I called earlier. Jordie's fine. He stayed in the hospital overnight. I think they want him to see someone this morning."

"See someone. Like a psychiatrist?"

"I got that impression."

"From Karen or Lee?"

"Karen. Lee wasn't around. Maybe he was making the arrangements."

"Or out playing somewhere."

"He was pretty upset. He didn't fake that while the two of you were up there on the top of that tower."

When she held her breath, he knew she was remembering. He couldn't imagine it had been any more frightening for her than it had been for him. His first instinct, seeing her up there, had been anger. But it didn't last. She was the one who had stayed with Jordie, while he ran back for help. She had known what Jordie needed.

"You did good," he said softly.

She released the breath. "It was . . . redemption." She scrubbed his beard with her fingertips, then, spreading her palm over it, brushed her thumb over his mouth. "Karen and Lee have decisions to make."

"So do we," he said, because he didn't want to discuss Karen and Lee. He didn't want to discuss much at all—just wanted more of what was passionate and irresponsible and light. It was fun. They hadn't done it in too long a time. He had missed it. "I'm hungry. Do we have anything good in the house?"

"Actually," she said thoughtfully, "you have a choice of entrées. There's chicken, steak, or me. I'd have to defrost the chicken or the steak. Me is ready."

Rolling over onto her, Graham found that she was. He was already inside her when the telephone rang. They let it ring.

Georgia hung up the phone with a look of concern. "Are they all right?"

"They're all right," Russ said. "Trust me. They're all right. And don't go ringing their bell. They need time to themselves. You'd know that if you'd been here last night. Man, that was a scary scene."

It wasn't until ten that she had finally pulled into the driveway, and by then the drama was done. At least, the one in the woods was. The one involving the future of Beet Beer was about to come to a head.

The phone rang. Seeing the return number of her attorney, she picked up. "Yes, Sam."

"They won't budge," he said. "You're part of the deal. They want you to stay on for another two years. They're willing to give you that."

"Two, rather than three."

"It's something. It's certainly flattering."

"Flattery doesn't do much for me when I'm three hours away by plane and my kids need me," Georgia said, massaging her lower-back muscles. She was tired—tired of packing and unpacking, tired of pulling bags through airports and dashing from one gate to another to make connecting flights, and squeezing her body between two other passengers when the only free seat was in the middle—and all that was on *top* of emotional exhaustion, the tension of worrying about what was happening at home, the long-distance sessions with Allison, who was growing up too fast, and Tommy, who would be reaching that point soon—and even *that* was on top of Russ and his needs and her needs and the fear of what would happen if the separations went on and on and on. Never in her wildest dreams had she imagined that she would be standing here making a major business decision while her lovable dork of a husband pawed through a basket of laundry fresh from the dryer looking for the mate to one of Tommy's soccer socks—red stripes on white, except for the foot, which would be permanently gray from the playing-field dirt unless she bleached it. The question was whether there was bleach in the house. There were cartons of Beet Beer in the pantry. But Clorox?

She started to laugh. She didn't know what else to do.

Russ looked at her strangely.

Sam said, "I missed the joke."

She put a hand over her face. "No joke." Dropping

the hand, she took a deep breath that raised her shoulders, and let them settle. "So," she said into the phone as she held her husband's mystified gaze. "Here's the story. I want to be able to go to the market, buy bleach, and make my kids' socks good as new. Is that so terrible?"

Sam said, "No. But I don't know how it translates into legalese."

"That's the easy part," Georgia said, feeling a startling wash of calm. "The answer's no. There's no deal if it involves my being on the road. I'll work from here. I'll be accessible on the phone. But the traveling's done."

"It may nix the deal."

"Then make another," she said. "I want out."

By the time Friday morning rolled around and Amanda left for work, she was feeling as strong as Georgia. Spending a day with Graham had been a tonic, largely because of the kind of day it had been. It hadn't been an intellectual one. They hadn't gone into deep discussions about trust and communication, hadn't broached suspicion, hadn't gone *near* talk of Graham's family, and, other than Graham's early mention of it, had avoided discussing babies.

The day had been . . . earthy. They hadn't bothered to dress, because they didn't leave the bedroom for long. Twice they accessed phone messages, but didn't answer the phone in between. They kissed. They touched. They had made love more times than she could count, and lay close together for silent, sleepy hours. They showered together. They heated pizza from the freezer and ate it in bed. They danced to Doc Watson, boogying body to body, stark naked, across the bedroom floor.

It was sex, as pure, as raw as it had been at the beginning. It was new again and elementally physical. Passion washed away all that had come between them. They were alone together, their bodies in total sync. They were starting over again.

It was an incredible escape from the world—and Amanda would have done it again this morning in a heartbeat, if the voice of responsibility hadn't risen. She had a backup of meetings and calls; Graham had chores of his own. With the weekend nearly upon them, a single day of work seemed in order.

That said, he was a constant interruption. He e-mailed her every hour, called twice before lunch and twice after, and when she came home from school at four, he was waiting at the door with his bags packed.

Chapter Eighteen

For a split second, every irrational fear returned. But there was something about his grin—not an irreverent O'Leary grin, but an intimate Graham grin—that restored her faith. He let her use the bathroom. That was it. Within five minutes, they were in his truck, headed north.

The inn was called Frog Hollow. It was in the tiny town of Panama, in the northern reaches of Vermont, and while new, it was already widely known. Each room was different from the next, though the common theme for all was frogs. The grounds were lush, with a pond here and hiking trails there. A tiny country store sat directly across the street. In addition to the usual penny candy, it carried bite-sized Almond Joys.

As getaways went, Amanda couldn't imagine anything more ideal. She had only two complaints. The first, mildly countered by the five-star quality of the food, was that there was no room service, which meant that they had to dress and leave their room. The second, annoying in that it distracted her, was Graham's need to issue a throaty *frrrribbit* whenever she touched on any subject remotely serious.

He did it when they were talking about Amanda's thoughts about Quinn.

"Frrrribbit," he said.

"That's irreverent," she advised, though it did lighten things a bit.

He did it again when they were talking about how much they loved their work and, therefore, how easy it was to bury themselves in it when things were rough at home.

"Frrrribbit," he said.

She humored him. "You like things green. I know."

He did it yet again when they were discussing Graham's family.

"Frrrribbit," he said.

"Have you done that for them?" she asked with an arched brow.

And yet again when they were speculating on who, if not Lee, might have fathered Gretchen's child.

"Frrrribbit," he said.

"I—don't think so," she replied with such gravity that he was the one who laughed. In her own defense, she said, "It's an issue, Gray. That baby has been a catalyst for a whole lot of self-doubt. I want to know who the father is. Don't you?"

Collaring her with an elbow, he hauled her onto his lap. "I don't want to think about that. It isn't top priority right now. Neither is my family, or your work or my work, Jordie, or Quinn. Yes, we need to talk about these things. I don't think I fully understood what you felt when Quinn died, or what it's like for someone without siblings to face a roomful of siblings like mine. I can't completely understand why you all feel threatened by Gretchen, but it's good when you try to explain. Bottom line, though? None of that matters. What matters is us. That's what we lost sight of." His eyes grew a deeper green. "Know what I love most about you?"

She couldn't speak, simply shook her head.

"How different you are from where I'd been. I didn't want more of the same, Mandy." He pulled at his beard. "Why do you think I grew this?"

It was an interesting question. They had never discussed it. Nor had she analyzed it, though, Lord knew, she analyzed almost everything else to death. She had simply accepted Graham's beard as a handsome addition to his looks. "Defiance?"

"Simpler. I wanted to look different from them. I wanted to go a different way from them." He held her gaze. "I still do."

Amanda took him for his word. She didn't spend another minute of the weekend thinking about his family and the way it pulled him. But the breather was short-lived. They had barely started home Sunday afternoon when Graham's cell phone rang. It was Peter, calling to say that Dorothy had suffered a stroke.

There was no question of dropping Amanda off at home. She wouldn't have that. Dorothy was Graham's mother, and this was an emergency. She wanted to be with him for this.

Graham kept driving, retracing the route they'd taken north on Friday until they reached the southern tier of Vermont, when he connected to a highway that headed east of Woodley. The sense of fun and irresponsibility had ended with the initial call, but the closer they got, the more tense Graham grew. He phoned Will and learned that Dorothy had had the stroke at dawn. From Joseph he learned that she was awake and aware. Malcolm was the one to tell him that Megan had found her first.

Not knowing what to say to that, Amanda said nothing. She couldn't tell Graham that Dorothy would be fine, because she certainly didn't know that. All she could do—which she did—was to hold his hand to silently remind him that she was there.

It was early evening when they reached the hospital. Graham parked. Half running, half walking, they hurried through the lobby to the elevator. Thanks to detailed instructions from MaryAnne, they knew just which way to turn when they reached the sixth floor, though, had they come in total ignorance, they would have been hard-pressed to miss the O'Learys gathered outside one particular room.

Malcolm came to meet them just shy of the door. "She's okay. Impatient, actually. She doesn't want to stay here, but there's no way she's leaving until they do a battery of tests, and even then, she'll need help. Her balance is off. She's listing to the left. They suspect there was minor damage on that side."

"Minor," Graham echoed with caution.

"Minor," said MaryAnne as she joined them. "She was lucky."

Amanda didn't have to love the woman to be grateful. She felt the relief in Graham. "What caused it?" he asked.

"They don't know," Mac replied. "That's what the tests are for. It could be just a product of age."

"Is this a precursor of others, then?"

Having joined them, Peter said, "They'll medicate her to minimize the chance of that."

Graham sputtered. "That may be easier said than done."

Even Amanda knew how Dorothy hated taking pills.

Mac grasped his arm. "Well, she'll have no choice. Come on. She'll be pleased to see you. She keeps asking."

Entering the room, Amanda couldn't help but feel for Dorothy. She was a waif of a thing fading into the white of the hospital sheets. Even if the stroke had been mild and she wasn't seriously ill, it was clear she was badly frightened. The way her hand shook when she reached out to Graham attested to that.

He took her hand and kissed her cheek. "You look pretty good for someone who's just taken ten years off my life."

"Where were you?" Dorothy asked in a high child's voice. "You weren't at home. They called and called. It's a good thing Will had your other number."

Amanda followed Graham, leaning in, kissing Dorothy's cheek. "He's right. You look better than we feel. It was a long drive, worrying."

Dorothy gave her the briefest glance before returning to Graham. "They want me to stay here. I can't stay here."

"You have to," he said. "They need to do tests."

"Tests kill. That's what killed your father."

"No, Mom. Cancer killed him."

"It was the test. If he hadn't had that one—"

"If he hadn't had that one, he would have died anyway, only we wouldn't have known why until later. It wasn't the test that killed him."

"You believe what you want. I'll believe what I want."

"But you're wrong, Mom. Believe that, and you'll

only get more worked up. Tests are benign. They don't kill."

"Fine for you to say," she grumbled. "You're not the one having them. They're also saying I can't go home alone. They say I need help. But I can't ask my daughters to spend all their time with me. They have their own families to care for. My sister-in-law has a bad hip; she wouldn't be able to handle the outside stairs, let alone the inside ones. I'd ask Megan—Megan would do it in a minute—I'd still be lying on the floor at home if Megan hadn't gotten worried when I didn't bring in the morning paper—such a good girl—but Megan has the store. So who do I get to help?"

"We'll hire someone."

Dorothy looked appalled. "A *stranger*? I can't do that."

"How about a nurse?" Amanda offered gently. "They do this kind of thing. Some of them even cook and clean. It wouldn't hurt."

"You get one, then," Dorothy muttered. "It's your generation needs the pampering, not mine."

"Mom, Amanda has a point."

"She works. She wants someone else to clean and cook. If she didn't work, she could do it herself."

"But she does important work," Graham said. "She helps kids. Why should she give that up to keep house?"

Amanda saw the trap. Dorothy didn't waste any time tripping it. "She helps other people's kids. There's the shame."

A nurse appeared on the other side of the bed. "Time to go, Mrs. O'Leary." To Graham and Amanda, she said, "We're doing a CAT scan."

Dorothy shot Graham a final desperate look. Realizing that he wouldn't save her, she locked her jaw and let herself be wheeled away.

Graham was on the phone most of the night, going back and forth with his siblings about how best to handle Dorothy. The tests were inconclusive. More would be done over the next few days. Dorothy remained adamant against both the tests and the idea of hiring someone to help her at home, so much so that several of Graham's conversations did focus on the possibility of the family members taking shifts.

Sitting in the kitchen with him, listening to his end of the conversation, Amanda injected a whispered, "I can help her out after school each day," to which he gave her an appreciative smile and a speedy headshake.

She felt dismissed. And she couldn't blame him for it. Dorothy didn't want her help. That was a fact. She might put up with her daughters helping. She might put up with Mac's wife helping, or James's or Joe's or Will's. From the half of the conversation that Amanda heard, she knew those possibilities were being discussed. She also knew, though, listening to Graham's half, that none of his siblings considered her a suitable helper. They, too, knew how Dorothy felt. Graham might deny it, but they all knew.

Settling into the background, Amanda found herself revisiting the insecurities from which she'd been so free all weekend. It was as if a germ had survived the wash of the last few days and was now taking root again and starting to grow. If Graham was aware of it, he didn't bring it up. He was totally absorbed by his family, until the final call ended, and he and Amanda went to bed.

Once there, he held her with the same love she'd felt since coming down from the tower, but silence wasn't enough now. Passion couldn't kill this revived little germ. It was real. Amanda needed him to admit that. If life had indeed come between them in the last year or two, and the struggle to conceive was the major factor, Graham's family came in a close second.

She was tired of feeling like an impostor. She wanted to tell him that.

But she didn't. She didn't say a word. Dorothy was ill, and Graham was worried. This wasn't the time for a confrontation.

Come Monday morning, Karen was of like mind. This wasn't the time for a confrontation. Even at the best of times, she wasn't confrontational, and these weren't the best of times. Jordie would be wearing a cast for six weeks and seeing a psychologist for far more than that. The twins, aware of something amiss, though not sure what it was, were talking to themselves more than ever, and Julie was clinging. When Karen was in the kitchen, Julie was there. When Karen was in the laundry room, Julie was there. The only free time Karen had was when Julie was at school, and then Karen was doing work on one committee or another.

Amanda and Graham had taken time off, and why not? They had each other. They could forget that the rest of the world existed. Karen couldn't do that. If she wasn't at school, carrying on as though nothing at all was wrong, lest someone think that something was, she was haunted by indignity at home. She couldn't so much as drive down the street without praying that Gretchen wasn't staring at her with pity or disdain, and now it had as much to do with Jordie as with Lee.

Karen had disposed of the knife with its telltale bits of paint. She had wrapped it up, buried it in a bag of garbage, and taken it with the rest to the dump. So Gretchen wasn't pressing charges. Even if Jordie had confessed, there was no evidence.

Now, though, there was the gun. She wasn't supposed to see it. Russ had dropped it over that morning. It had been wrapped in a sealed bubble mailer addressed to Lee, but she hadn't been able to resist. The feel of it had tipped her off.

The kitchen door opened and Lee came in. The door clattered shut behind him. "I got your message. They said it was urgent."

Slowly, evenly, Karen drew the small pistol from her pocket. Keeping it at waist level, she aimed it at Lee, who frowned and took an instinctive step to the side. She followed him with the nose of the gun, feeling an odd power.

"What the hell are you doing with that?" he asked with his eyes on the gun.

"Russ brought it over this morning. I think it's yours."

"I don't own a gun."

She took a breath and went on. "I've seen it in your drawer."

"You're searching my drawers now?" he flared up, as she had known he would. He was good at shifting blame to avoid the issue.

But she refused to wilt. She knew what she had to say, had been practicing her response for days. "I fold your boxers and put them away. Sometimes I rotate them and bring the less-used ones from the back up to the front. The gun's been back there a long time. It wasn't a good place to keep it, Lee. It was too obvious. Jordie didn't have to look far to find it."

Apparently deciding that denial wouldn't work, Lee tried boredom. "It happened to have been the easiest place to reach for it if I heard an intruder in the middle of the night. Besides, how do you know this is the one Jordie had?"

"Because yours is missing. And we never did find the gun when we got Jordie down. It wasn't on him when they undressed him at the hospital. I thought you'd taken it from him, but Russ must have."

Lee's eyes went back to the gun. "Put it down. Guns can kill."

Karen nodded. Swallowing down bits of hysteria, she said, "This one could have killed our son. I had a nightmare again last night about that."

He held out a hand. "Give it to me."

"Not yet."

"What do you want with it?"

"To make a point."

He sighed, bored again. "What point?" he asked as though humoring a child.

Karen usually backed down at this stage. Lee was the one with the high-tech knowledge and the successful business. He was the one who was quick, smart, worldly. She couldn't compete with that.

But she was a mother, and he couldn't compete with *that.* So maybe the gun gave her strength. Or maybe she had been belittled one time too many. But she wasn't backing down. She had a point to make about the problems with their marriage. Three points, actually.

"Lies. Cheating. Violence," she said.

Still in the bored vein, Lee sighed. "There's no violence in our marriage. If you're claiming abuse, you haven't got a leg to stand on."

"It's subtle. It's silent. But it's taken a toll. It's gotten so it affects everything in this house. It's gotten so I can't think straight."

"See a shrink. I'll pay. I've said that before."

"A shrink won't help. I can't go on this way, Lee. I can't go on with the other women and the late nights and the anger."

He softened in an oh-so-familiar way. "You imagine things."

"No." Again she forced out damning words, but the gun in her hand reminded her that the situation was dire. "I've seen bills. There's no imagining that you're paying an obstetrician, because his name is right there, and more than once. Someone's seeing him every month, and it isn't me."

That unsettled him. "Were you looking through my desk?"

The cat was out of the bag, she thought in fear. He might excuse her for seeing something in his drawer when she was putting his shorts away. But he wouldn't forgive her for rifling his desk. He had always trusted her. That would be forever changed now.

But her *life* was forever changed. The past two weeks had seen to that. She felt the old fears—of being alone, being without Lee, being a nobody, being poor. The fears had kept her with him when she should have left, and they might have now. They were strong arguments.

But she couldn't go back. She *couldn't.*

"Yes," she said in a rush, "and don't try to turn things around and make me the devil, because it won't work this time. I don't believe in divorce. It terrifies me, and you know that, which is why I let you apologize and come back and swear that it's over between you and your mistress, but things aren't right between us, and the poison's spreading. I could live with it when it was just me, but now it's affecting the kids."

"The kid are fine," he scoffed.

"Lee," she cried in disbelief. "Look at *Jordie.* Look at what nearly happened to him. And to Amanda. And look what he did to *Gretchen.* He wouldn't have done that if you hadn't gone on and on about that painting. He wouldn't have done it if he hadn't thought you were involved with her."

"That's *your* fault," Lee charged. "It's your anger and suspicion. Jordie would have to be blind not to see."

Having come too far to turn back, she stared at him, thinking that he looked absolutely foolish with his blond hair spiked that way. "My *anger and suspicion* is a direct result of your lying and cheating."

He held up a hand. "Don't try to shift the blame back to *me.*"

"We nearly lost Jordie!" she shouted. "Doesn't that *chill* you?" She caught herself from yelling more. Amanda wouldn't yell in a situation like this. Neither would Georgia. They would be calm. They would speak with conviction, even when they were shaking with fear. "Don't even answer that," she said, as they would have. "I don't want to hear answers. I just want you to go and pack. The kids'll be home in an hour. I want you gone by then."

His expression turned blank. "What are you talking about?"

She swallowed. Amanda and Georgia would stick to their guns when they knew something was right, even if they had qualms. "I need you to move out."

"Are you serious?"

She nodded.

"Come on, honey," he said and started toward her.

She raised the gun.

He stopped, stared at the gun, then at her. "This is my home."

"Not anymore," she said quickly, fighting the force of habit, when she knew this was for the best. "I'll go to court, if I have to. I have copies of the bills. I have the name of a good lawyer. You need to leave, Lee."

Conciliatory, he patted the air with both hands. "You're upset. You're thinking of things that happened in the past. You're thinking about Jordie up on that tower. You were numb before. So was I. Now we're not, and the reality of it is hitting us."

"It's not only Jordie."

"Of course it's not. We all go through rough spells. This is one of yours. You're not thinking clearly."

"I'm thinking very clearly."

"Things become warped when you go through a scare like the one we had with Jordie."

Karen drew in a tempered breath. It struck her that she was tired of being talked down to by Lee. "I want you out," she said with deliberate care. "I don't care where you go, as long as it's away from here."

"But *why*?"

She didn't blink. "Chalk it up to one woman too many. You're with someone, Lee. I don't care if it's Gretchen you're seeing or someone else, I can't live this way anymore."

He looked like he was on the verge of denial. But she had evidence this time. She could see the knowledge of that in his eyes, when the fight suddenly drained away. "I'm weak, Karen. I make mistakes. They don't mean anything."

"Is she pregnant?"

"It doesn't matter. All that matters is our kids. And you."

"Why don't I believe you?" Karen asked.

"Because you're upset."

"No," she replied, feeling surprisingly little pain. "We don't matter to you. If we did, you wouldn't hurt us this way."

"But she doesn't *mean* anything to me," he pleaded. "And anyway, she's done. It's over. I learned my lesson when Jordie was up on that tower."

Karen didn't believe that either. He had sworn off philandering in the past, and more than once. In her eyes, he had no credibility left at all. "Pack. Now."

He was silent for a minute. Curiously, he said, "Or what? Will you use the gun?"

"Actually, I'm about to run it back to Russ. He'll know how to dispose of it." She lowered it, but didn't soften. She was feeling anger now—anger at being the butt of Lee's infidelity for too many years. That anger gave her the guts to say, "I don't need a gun. I have another weapon, and I'll use it. If you don't pack—if you don't leave—if you don't give me a good divorce settlement, I'll tell the children what you've done. You love them, Lee. I won't deny that. You love them, and they love you—even Jordie, who probably hates both of us as much as he loves us right now. But that's the deal. You leave and let this be civil, and you keep the love of your kids. Make trouble for me, and I'll make trouble for you."

It was a gamble, and she wasn't a gambler, so this moment was particularly difficult for her. She had never dared to challenge Lee this way, not even when he had confessed to earlier affairs—and part of her wanted the old apologies, the old making up. Part of her wanted to keep the status quo. It was safer. It involved no change and less risk. The devil she knew might be better than the devil she didn't.

But the past infidelities had affected only Lee and her. This one had affected the children. That made things different.

Amanda left school early Monday afternoon and drove to visit Dorothy. She hadn't told Graham she was going. She wasn't doing it for him, but for herself. She was hoping that if she made the effort—if Dorothy saw that she made it—the woman might soften toward her.

Again, a horde of O'Learys milled in the hall. There were grandchildren this time, armed with self-drawn get-well cards and other little gifts. They were being shuttled in and out of their grandmother's room a few at a time.

The children greeted Amanda with more enthusiasm than anyone else. She gave them appropriate greetings and hugs, then asked Sheila, James's wife, "How is Dorothy?"

"Not bad. They've had her up and around, and she does very well, but she's afraid she'll fall again."

"Have they done more tests?"

"Yes. It was definitely a mild stroke. There's no serious damage. Even the balance problem is better."

Amanda approached the door of the room just as Will's two oldest children came out. Ignoring the unsettled feeling in her stomach, she went in herself.

Dorothy's eyes were closed.

Amanda said a soft, "Hi. Have the kids exhausted you?"

The woman opened her eyes, saw Amanda, looked past her. "Where's Graham?"

"He couldn't come. He's meeting with a client in Litchfield. I just wanted to see how you were doing."

Dorothy gestured toward the group in the hall and closed her eyes again. "They'll tell you."

"They did," Amanda acknowledged. "It sounds as though the word is good. That's a relief." When Dorothy didn't respond, she looked at the drawings on the bedside tray. "Looks like you have some beautiful cards here."

"I have wonderful grandchildren."

"Yes. You do. With any luck, there'll be more."

Dorothy opened her eyes then. The accusation in them was at odds with the limpness of the rest of her. "Mac said you stopped trying. That won't make children."

"We didn't stop trying. We're just taking a rest."

"I never did that. I never wanted to. I loved my husband. Making children wasn't a chore."

Amanda didn't like her suggestion. But she didn't want to argue. So she smiled, nodded, said, "It was easier in the old days. I sometimes wonder if it isn't something in the air."

"Jimmy says Graham is frustrated."

"So am I. We both want children."

Dorothy's eyes went past Amanda again. This time she smiled. "Here's Christine." Joseph's wife. "It's good of you to come, Chrissie. You're so busy."

Oblivious to the undertone, Christine winked at Amanda before turning to her mother-in-law. "Never too busy to see you. How are you, Mom?"

That easily, Amanda fell from Dorothy's radar screen. She tried to take part in the discussion of Christine's work as an event planner, but what Dorothy was doing felt so obvious and unkind that she didn't last for long. Brooding on it when she left the room, she even blamed Christine. Christine could have asked Amanda about her own work, there in front of Dorothy. Amanda sensed Christine would have done it had Megan been there in her place.

Don't go there, she told herself. *It has nothing to do with Graham and you.*

The problem was that, in small and unwanted but hurtful ways, it still did.

Graham felt it that night, despite Amanda's efforts to mask it. She had made a delicious dinner, replete with wine and strawberry shortcake, which he loved. She gave him the neighborhood news—told him that Georgia had called the bluff of her buyer and was waiting to hear the verdict, and that Karen had kicked Lee out of the house. She told him how nice it had been being at school after the weekend they'd had together. She said she felt as though she had a private little secret that kept her smiling all day, had kept her strong through the pall that lingered in the halls.

But there was something she didn't say. It wasn't until later, after a call from Peter, that he learned she had been to the hospital. "Why didn't you tell me?" he asked, upset by her silence. They had agreed to talk. That was part of what the weekend had been about.

She made light of it by shrugging in a self-deprecating way. "It wasn't a fruitful visit. Amanda Carr strikes out again."

"Oh, Mandy. My mother is old. She's angry now, and scared. You have to consider all that."

"I know. But it's hard. Maybe I should start calling her Mom. Maybe she'd like that better. It just seems so . . . put on. I mean, she's not my mother, she's yours."

That thought stayed with Graham through the night. *She's not my mother, she's yours,* Amanda had said and had left it at that. She hadn't made him take sides, hadn't demanded anything of him where Dorothy was concerned. She accepted the fact that the woman was ill, and seemed willing to make allowances for her coldness.

But the coldness wasn't new. That was what ate at Graham when he got up Tuesday morning. *She's not my mother, she's yours* had become, in his mind, *She's not my problem, she's yours.* He liked the fresh start that he and Amanda had made. It had made everything that he loved about her seem new and real and strong, and Amanda had been an active player in all that. She was trying as hard as he was. When it came to Dorothy, though, there was only so much she could do. She could only take the first step so many times, before she gave up.

This isn't the time, he told himself. He would never transplant a mature sycamore during the height of the summer's heat, regardless of how pivotal it was to a project's success. Sycamores needed moisture—just as Dorothy needed coddling. Her stroke might have been mild, but these were precarious days for her. A better time would come. Driving to see her early that evening, he vowed to wait.

Dorothy had other ideas.

Chapter Nineteen

"Hi, Mom," Graham called as he turned into her room. He had bumped into Mac in the elevator and knew that the others had gone home for dinner. It was nearly six. Dorothy's own dinner lay half-eaten on the tray. She had the television on with the volume low, but her head was turned on the pillow. She was looking out the window. It would be a quiet moment, or so he thought. He had barely reached the bed—and she had barely turned and smiled—when Will bounded in.

"I was honking two trucks behind you," he told Graham. "Hey, Mom. How're you doing?"

"Better now that my boys are here," Dorothy said, sounding stronger now that another day had passed. "It's lonely sometimes. I start wondering if that's the way it'll be for me now."

Will eyed her askance. "To hear my wife tell it, there's been traffic jams here all day."

"Mac said the same thing," Graham put in, lest she make them feel guilty. "I'd think you would welcome the rest."

"No. I like my family here. Your girls were so

adorable," she told Will, waving a thin hand toward the bulletin board on the wall. "They sat here for the longest time making drawings."

Graham went over for a closer look. "Ah. There's Grandma in her bed. I see a nurse on one side." The large Red Cross on her cap was hard to miss, though he had yet to see a nurse wearing a cap. "Lots of machines. And who else?"

Dorothy listed her guests. "MaryAnne's there and Sheila. Some cousins. And your wife, Will."

Graham waited for her to go on. He saw a headful of yellow crayon curls that couldn't belong to anyone but Amanda, whom he knew had dropped by. But Dorothy was silent.

Conversationally, he said, "This looks like Amanda. Was she here?"

"She may have been. I'm not sure."

Will tried to cover for the slight. "They have you on medication. Things must be blurry."

Graham was annoyed at Will, *and* at Dorothy, but he let it go. *The time isn't right,* he told himself, and, instead, said, "I'm glad Amanda could drop by. There's been heavy pressure at school."

"Still with the suicide?" Will asked.

"That, and the season. There are lots of end-of-the-year issues."

"She shouldn't bother to come," Dorothy said. "Everyone else is here."

"She doesn't see it as a bother," Graham said and darted a quick, warning look at Will. "She's as concerned about you as we are."

"Well, it's different," Dorothy mused with startling breeziness for a woman so weak. "She doesn't have the connection. You know?"

"Hasn't been married to an O'Leary long enough," Will teased.

But Graham was offended. "What connection, Mom?"

"You know, honey. I mean, all the other children here. It's different for her."

"If it's different for her, it should be different for me. Do you think it is?"

"Gray," Will murmured, "not now."

Graham took a deep breath. Will was right.

But, damn it, Amanda deserved better.

As a concession to his brother, he made his voice quiet and calm. But he just couldn't let it go. "Amanda's trying, Mom. She'd like to help. She wants to be part of us."

"But she isn't," Dorothy said sweetly. "She's always been different. That doesn't mean we can't get along with her. Now that I think of it, she probably was here earlier, because she's always good with the children and they were especially well-behaved today."

Graham pressed his mouth shut.

Will said, "My children adore Amanda. She's going to make a terrific mother herself."

Graham could have killed him.

Dorothy said, "I'll have to take your word for that." She closed her eyes.

Graham looked at Will and mouthed a large, "Shut up."

Will mouthed back a bewildered, "What?"

"Oh, don't get angry at Will," Dorothy scolded. "He's only trying to help. You're so protective of that girl. You'd think she was made of fine china."

"Mom, please," Graham warned.

But, lying there in that hospital bed, Dorothy mus

have felt a measure of power in her situation, because she said, "I can see why you do it. There is something fragile about her. She's always been different from us in that, too. Megan wasn't. She was sturdy."

"Don't go there, Mom."

"She came over this morning with audiotapes. She even brought a tape recorder so I could listen. She thought of everything."

"Mom."

"She's a wonderful person. I never did understand what happened between the two of you."

"I told you what happened," Graham said.

"Gray," Will cautioned.

But Graham had had enough. If his mother was well enough and strong enough and sharp enough to demean his wife in the name of his ex-wife, Dorothy could hear what he had to say. "Megan's gay."

Dorothy stayed with her own train of thought. "She's doing so well with that store. I'm so proud of her. I like her partner, too. Brooke. Did I tell you that Brooke moved into the house with Megan?"

"Brooke is her life partner, Mom. They're lovers. Megan left me. Accept it."

Dorothy didn't blink. "I will if you will. But I'm sure it's still hard. Especially now, with all this."

"All what?" Graham asked, though he knew where she was headed.

"The baby business."

Will touched his arm, but Graham wasn't about to keep still. He might have preferred another time, but certain things had to be said. If Dorothy was strong enough to goad him, she was strong enough to hear it through. "I didn't want Megan's baby."

"I can understand why you'd say that."

"No, Mom, I don't think you can. I didn't want Megan's baby, because Megan and I were great friends, only we never did work as a couple, and that would have spelled disaster for a child. Megan did me a favor by ending that marriage."

"Don't say that."

"It's true. What I have with Amanda is much better. We're not just old friends whose families wanted us together so badly that we didn't think about anything else."

"You were lonesome," Dorothy said, and Graham didn't contradict her.

"Yes, I was lonesome. But I'd dated lots of women before I met Amanda, and none of them did anything for me until her. She was everything I wanted. I didn't just—just end up with her. I *chose* her."

Dorothy seemed mildly deflated, but she was far from done in. "So now she's making you choose again."

"Excuse me?"

"She's making you choose. It's either her or us."

Graham was astonished. "She's not doing that. You are."

"It isn't just me," Dorothy said with a flare of indignation. "It's all of us. Mac knows she isn't right. So do MaryAnne and Kathryn and—"

"Mom," Will broke in. "That's enough."

"Are you siding with him?" she asked. "Do you hear what he's saying?"

"He's saying he loves his wife."

"That's only for starters," Graham said. He was all wound up, letting loose with things that had been on his mind for far too long. "I'm saying that I'm with Amanda for life. I'm saying that she's the only mother I want for a baby of mine. I'm saying that it we don't conceive a baby ourselves, we'll adopt, and if that baby isn't welcomed by this family with open arms, we're outta here." He put a hand on the back of his neck, where the muscles were hard as steel. "Hell," he muttered, "I'm outta here anyway." He turned to the door and stopped short at the sight of Amanda, who obviously had just arrived. In the next breath, though, he was in motion again. "Come on, babe," he said and reached for her hand. "Let's make tracks."

Amanda took his hand, but she didn't move. Her eyes went from his angry face to Will's alarmed one to Dorothy's stunned one. She hadn't arrived more than two minutes before, clearly in the middle of the discussion. But she had heard enough to love Graham more than ever, to respect him more than ever, and to know that his relationship with his family was at stake.

"Mandy," he growled, "let's *go.*"

"Wait," she whispered. Freeing her hand from his, she went back into the room where she'd been an hour before. After an apologetic glance at Will, she said to her mother-in-law, "I was downstairs in the coffee shop. I knew Gray was coming and thought I'd surprise him. There's an Italian restaurant across the street. I was hoping he and I could have dinner there. He's been worried about you and worried about me and feeling pressure about lots of things he shouldn't have to."

"You had no business eavesdropping," Dorothy charged.

"I didn't hear anything I didn't know. I know that Graham feels passionately about his family. I also know he feels passionately about me. I've always loved him for both of those things. Making him choose between them would be a sin."

"*I'm* not making him choose."

"Neither am I," Amanda said simply. "I love his being from a large family. I accept them. I want them to accept me."

"We do," Will said.

Amanda shot him a sad little smile. "I think you want to. I think you try. But I also think you all walk on tiptoes about Megan." To Dorothy, she said, "I like Megan. I think she's a wonderful woman. I like to believe that she'll be coming over to our house with books from her store when we have kids, but Gray's right. She needed her space, and he needed something else. I just want to give it to him. If I'm different from what you wanted, I'm sorry."

"This isn't only about Megan," Dorothy blustered. "It's about having babies. Graham's been unhappy these last few months."

"So have I. What we've been through hasn't been fun."

Didactically, Dorothy asked, "Isn't there a message in that?"

"*Christ*, Mom," Will muttered.

Amanda didn't balk. She had an answer for Dorothy. "Yes, there's a message. The message is that life isn't always fun. If you were to ask Gray"—she smiled warmly—"he'd make an analogy to pulling out weeds. He'd say that the more time you put into pulling out weeds, the healthier your shrub bed, because the weeds suck away nutrients. In our case, the weeds are the little bits of dissension that come when you're trying to have a baby and can't, or when you're trying to get along with family and can't. Dissension sucks away the nutrients in a marriage. So we've been working to get rid of it. I trust that he loves me." How could she not, after what she had just overheard?

"And you trust that he's over Megan?" Dorothy asked, clearly doubting it.

Here, too, Amanda had an answer. "Yes. I trust him in that, too. So that leaves you all. I'm not asking him to choose. I'd never do that. But if you can't find it in your heart to accept me, the one who'll be hurt most by it is Gray. We both love him. Can't we keep that from happening?"

Graham was slow to calm down. "She is insufferable," he muttered as he strode down the hall.

Amanda had to walk faster to keep up. "Your mother is set in her ways. You haven't conformed to those ways. She's having trouble with that."

"She's rude and ungrateful. She's shortsighted. If she thinks our kids are going to want to be with her—if she thinks we're going to *let* them be with her—"

"We will," Amanda said, though not without the pang that came from four years of trying to make kids in the singular, let alone plural. "She'll come around. She's your mother, Gray. And she isn't well."

He snorted. "She was well enough to argue. But it's my fault," he said, finally slowing to a saner pace. "I should have set the record straight months ago. I should have done it *years* ago." He stabbed at the elevator button. "I'm sorry. I let you down."

Amanda slipped her arm through his. "You said what needed to be said just now. Thank you."

The elevator opened. It already held a handful of

passengers. Graham and she entered it and turned to face front, tabling the discussion until they reached the bottom floor. Rather than speaking then, though, Graham took her hand. Seeming almost shy, he said, "Are we doing dinner?"

"I hope so. There's nothing waiting at home."

"Italian?"

"Sounds good to me."

He paused then, looked down at their hands, raised vulnerable eyes to hers. "Did you mean it, what you said back there? The thing about trust?"

She nodded.

He studied her a minute longer. The green of his eyes grew deeper as confidence returned. Amanda was both humbled that she could affect that confidence, and gratified by its return. Graham O'Leary was a magnificent man. When he looked at her that way, oblivious to the people skirting them as though they were a sculpture in the middle of the lobby, she trusted him with her life.

Releasing a breath, he pulled her to his side, threw an arm around her shoulder, and led her through the hospital lobby and out the door.

Two hours later, in separate vehicles, since that was how they'd come, they returned to the cul-de-sac. Separated physically didn't mean separated by voice. They had been on and off the phone with each other during the drive. Slowing to a crawl now, Graham narrated.

"The night is dark," he said on a note of intrigue. "If there's a moon, it's hidden behind clouds, but we can't see even those, since there's no moon, so how do you know what's up there at all?"

"There are no stars," Amanda put in from her car. "That's the tip-off."

"Right. But there are lights down here. The Langes are all in. Georgia home, too?"

"Maybe permanently."

"And the Cotters. Subdued. No dancing shadows in the windows. No kids bouncing around. Think they'll be okay?"

"I don't know. It depends on Karen and Lee. She says they'll be fine. She says Lee won't fight the divorce, and rightly he shouldn't. As evidence of infidelity goes, she has him cold. He's moved in with his pregnant lover."

"At least she isn't Gretchen, speaking of whom, the house is dark."

"Wait," Amanda advised as her car inched forward, "wait . . . there. At the back of the living room. There's the light. What *does* she do in the library so late?"

"She studies," Graham said.

"Like French?"

"Like lots of stuff. She's taking correspondence courses to get a college degree."

Amanda stepped on the brake. That was a new take on the books on the table, and a nice one. "How do you know that?" she asked.

Graham's voice came back clearly. "She told me."

"Why didn't she tell *me*?" Amanda asked. What had Gretchen done instead? She had tried to hide the books.

"She feels intimidated by you. Come on, Mandy. Don't get in a huff."

"I'm not upset. Well, maybe a little. I mean, if she wants to be friends, why hide something like that?"

"You wouldn't. But she isn't as confident as you," he said as he turned into the driveway.

Amanda pulled in beside him. By the time she was out of the car, she had let go of the irritation that had surged briefly. Jealousy had no place in her relationship with Graham. He was loyal. He loved her. She had no cause for suspicion of anyone, and that included Gretchen.

But they hadn't been in the house for more than five minutes when the telephone rang. Amanda's first thought was that Dorothy had taken a turn for the worse after their visit. Judging from the look of alarm on Graham's face, he was thinking the same thing.

He snatched up the phone. "Yes?"

Amanda watched him, waiting for clues as he listened to the voice on the other end. He shot her a quick glance, but the look of alarm remained.

"When?" he asked tersely. Then, "Are you sure?"

When threads of a high-pitched voice reached her, Amanda's heart began to pound. If her own words to her mother-in-law had caused a setback—or worse, sparked another stroke, a stronger one this time—she would never forgive herself. Graham, she thought with fear, might not either.

"I'll be right there," he said and hung up the phone. "Gretchen's bleeding," he told Amanda. "She thinks she's losing the baby."

For a minute, Amanda did absolutely nothing. It took her that long to switch gears. Gretchen. Calling Graham.

But no, she cautioned in the next heartbeat. Not calling Graham. Calling this house and talking with Graham because he'd been the one to answer the phone. Just as he'd been the one who had worked with her and earned her trust, so that she had felt comfortable enough to confide in him about things like taking correspondence courses. Just as he'd been the one to show kindness, when Amanda and the other women had failed.

"We have to help her," he said. "We're right here, and we don't have kids that need watching. She trusts us. She has no one else."

Having let go of her suspicion, Amanda responded with friendship. "We'll take my car," she said, handing him her keys as she went back out the door. Counting on Graham to bring the car close, she hurried across the street. Gretchen was already at the side door, her pallor accentuated by the gaslight there.

Her voice was thin and tremulous. "I was fine. I was really fine. Then I stood up, and I felt a pain, and then there was blood."

Putting an arm around her waist, Amanda guided her toward the approaching car. "Did you call the doctor?"

"He told me to get to the hospital. I hate to bother you. You have other things to think about. But I didn't know who else to call."

"Is there pain now?"

"Contractions," she said in a higher voice, "but it's too early. The baby's too little." While Graham backed the car up, she clutched Amanda's arm and said in an urgent whisper, "Graham isn't the father. There was never, *ever* anything romantic between us. He's been a friend, but that's all. I was just angry, so I didn't say."

"I know." Amanda opened the back door.

"It wasn't Russ or Lee, either. I wouldn't do that to any of you." Clutching her middle, she closed her eyes.

Amanda held up a hand to stay Graham, who was

out of the car, wanting to help. When Gretchen began to breathe more calmly, they guided her into the car. Without forethought, Amanda followed her in and sat close by her side, giving her a hand to squeeze with each pain.

Graham drove quickly. There was only one hospital in the area. It was the one that he and Amanda knew intimately, the one that housed the fertility clinic. The thought of that alone was enough to trigger a jumping in Amanda's stomach. Determinedly, she focused on Gretchen.

"I won't lose the baby, will I?" Gretchen whispered at one point.

"Not if we can help it."

A minute later, she asked, "It can live at seven and a half months, can't it?"

"Definitely," Amanda said.

"But it'll be small. What if it isn't fully formed? What if there's brain damage? Or lung damage?"

"Don't think those things," Amanda begged, though she had thought them all herself and not so long ago. She hadn't been pregnant. But she had imagined being pregnant. Even imagining it, she had worried. So she knew what Gretchen was feeling.

"Why's it coming early?" Gretchen whispered. "Is something wrong?"

Amanda reassured her as best she could, though it was certainly a case of the blind leading the blind. "The baby may just be impatient." She tried to think of other benign possibilities. "Or ready. Maybe you miscalculated." That didn't explain the blood.

"I didn't. I know when I conceived." She sat back against the seat and whispered, "I've lost so much. I can't lose this."

"Here we are," Graham announced. Turning into the hospital lot, he drove straight to the emergency entrance.

Suddenly there were attendants opening the door, helping Gretchen out, settling her into a wheelchair. Her obstetrician—he was Amanda's own, though not her fertility specialist—was there, too, holding her shoulder, telling her that she would be fine.

Pushed to the side in the rush of medical assistance, Amanda felt a deep yearning. When Graham materialized beside her, she met his gaze. They didn't say a word, though the message was there. *It should be us, damn it. It should be us.*

Gretchen gave herself up into the hands of her doctor. She had trusted him from the first, largely because he exuded confidence, and he did now, too, even in spite of the bleeding. Confidence, however, didn't mean he didn't act quickly. She was admitted and prepped. She was wheeled into an operating room and given a spinal. They performed a cesarean section, which was just as well, since, lacking a partner, she had forgone Lamaze courses and would have been hard put to know how to breathe.

A sheet blocked her view of what was happening, but her obstetrician stood tall above it, and she watched his eyes. They were calm and competent, concerned for perhaps a minute or two, though that might have been Gretchen's imagination. Soon enough there was a smile in those eyes, and the unmistakable sound of a baby's cry.

"You have a boy, Gretchen," the doctor announced, "and he sure looks healthy to me. He sounds it, too. Listen to the little guy go."

Gretchen thought that *waaaa-waaaa* was the most

beautiful sound she had ever heard. Not knowing whether to laugh or cry herself, she did both, which meant that when they brought the baby to her, she could barely see him through her tears. But she saw enough. She saw a screwed-up little face, a tiny body, spindly arms and legs with the appropriate numbers of fingers and toes. Then they whisked him away, explaining that they wanted him examined, cleaned, and warmed in an incubator until they determined if there were any side effects of his premature arrival.

She wanted to ask what those might be. First, though, now that he was in good hands, she wanted to know if she would live.

"Live?" her obstetrician asked with a mischievous look in his eyes. "I haven't lost a patient yet to a little run-of-the-mill hemorrhaging. It's stopped. We'll just sew you up now. Live? You'll live long and well with that boy."

Gretchen liked the sound of that. Closing her eyes, feeling a tugging at her body but little pain, she let herself relax.

Amanda and Graham were at the window of the special-care nursery when Gretchen's baby arrived. It was swathed in blankets. The nurse held him up and mouthed the words. Amanda felt goose bumps and caught in a breath. "A boy. That's *so nice.*"

Holding her hand in the pocket of his jeans, Graham gave it a squeeze. "You'd say the same thing if it were a girl."

But Amanda was enthralled. "Look at him. He's so tiny."

"Is he okay?" Graham asked the nurse, who, given her salt-and-pepper hair and the ease with which she held the baby, was no doubt experienced at lip-reading, too.

With a reassuring thumbs-up, she carried him to the pediatrician waiting at the rear of the room.

Amanda watched until the doctor blocked her view of the baby. Then she looked at the other preemies. Babies born at this hospital with serious problems would have been transferred to larger hospitals, which meant that the ones left were small but healthy. She saw a pink cap, a blue cap, a trio of yellow ribbons. One incubator had a sign that read TIMOTHY. Another had a stuffed rabbit perched on the top.

"So," Graham asked, "who did he look like?"

"Not you," Amanda replied. "I've pictured your baby in my mind a million times. I've seen other O'Leary babies. This isn't one."

"Maybe he resembles Gretchen."

"Nuh-uh. O'Leary genes are dominant. O'Leary babies have a certain look."

"This one's just a preemie."

Amanda glanced up at him. He was either testing her, or teasing her. "Who do you think he looks like?" she asked.

"Ben."

She chuckled. "Mm. Both bald."

They were quiet for a while. Gradually the excitement of the night—the exhilaration of a new birth—faded. Amanda didn't have to look at Graham to know that he was feeling it, too. Standing there at the nursery window, knowing that they should have been looking at *their* baby by now, she felt the return of emptiness. She wondered if Graham was feeling that also—wondered if he was looking out at those babies in their incubators and thinking that some woman had managed to carry and bear each one. She wondered if Graham was thinking that he had married a dud of a woman. She wondered—

She caught herself midway, headed into the same old trap. Wondering was dangerous enough. Wondering, and then imagining, had gotten her in big trouble before. She couldn't just wonder. She couldn't just imagine. She had to *know.*

"What're you feeling?" she asked quietly.

He was silent for a minute. Then he put his hands in his back pockets. "Envy."

That was honest. She felt it, too. "What else?"

"Determination." His jaw showed it. "If we try once more, just once more, it has to work." His profile was strong—yes, determined. When he turned his eyes on her, though, they held something else. "Dread," he added. "Not a pretty word. But it's the truth. I'm not looking forward to starting it all up again. I don't want to lose what we've had the past few days."

"Hey, you two," called a gentle voice. It was Emily, their fertility specialist, coming toward them down the hall.

Amanda smiled in greeting, but didn't say anything. Neither did Graham.

Emily cocked her head toward the nursery. "Is this an attempt to get psyched up again?"

"No," Amanda said. "A neighbor's baby's in there. Are there any of yours?"

Emily pointed at the middle of the room. "Those three, the ones with the yellow ribbons tied to the handles. They're IVF triplets, two sisters and a brother. They're very small, but they're well." Turning away from the babies, Emily braced a shoulder against the nursery glass. "The downside of your problem is that we don't know its cause. The upside is that because we don't, there's lots we can try. The simplest is to up the dosage of Clomid."

Amanda wasn't wild about that idea. The lower dosage had made her hot, bloated, and moody, and according to the tests, the Clomid had worked. She had produced plenty of eggs. They just hadn't taken to being fertilized.

Besides, an increased dose of Clomid raised the risk of overstimulation of the ovaries and the development of ovarian cysts. She would have to be closely monitored for that, meaning near-daily tests at the clinic. Should a large cyst develop, it would have to be surgically removed.

"We can stick with Clomid and add an injection of HCG," Emily proposed. "That would be done on the fifteenth or sixteenth day of your cycle. It would trigger ovulation."

"Ovulation isn't my problem," Amanda said.

"No, but this would coordinate the release of the eggs from their follicles. Consolidate the firepower, so to speak. Or we can do multiple inseminations—artificially inseminate you daily or bi-daily. Or we can try Humegon, either alone or with HCG."

Amanda shuddered at the thought. Humegon had to be injected. It was awkward and painful. Moreover, since it caused a decrease in progesterone levels, progesterone injections had to follow the Humegon ones, all of which would precede the HCG shot. The whole thing was unpleasant. The side effects were reputed to be as bad as, if not worse than, the other.

"We can try IUI," Emily suggested, "or go directly to IVF. My point is that you do have options."

Amanda didn't want options. She wanted a baby.

Glancing at Graham, she saw that he did, too.

"I want you guys back in," Emily said. "What do you say?"

Graham didn't say a word. His eyes held Amanda's, seeming to say that he would go along with whatever she decided. More, they seemed to say that he was in it for the long haul. That gave her a measure of confidence.

She smiled at him, released a breath, then smiled at Emily. "I've had my break. I'm ready."

Gretchen barely slept. She was too excited to sleep, and also too uncomfortable as the anesthesia wore off, but she would only take the mildest painkiller. She didn't want to be doped up. She wanted to be out of bed as soon as possible and down the hall with her baby. She was all he had. If he was struggling in any way, she wanted to be there with him.

When she asked, they said he was fine. A nurse even wheeled him into her room, and she was allowed to hold him, but only for a short time. Her milk hadn't come in, and he wasn't ready to nurse. After wailing lustily at birth, he dozed peacefully.

But he was breathing. She looked closely for that. She touched his mouth, touched his nose and his cheeks, and felt their warmth. She whispered a kiss over the soft spot that pulsed at the top of his head. She laid a light hand on his little chest and felt its movement. She touched his palm and felt his tiny fingers close around hers.

He had yellowed some, which they said was normal for a preemie. He didn't have a lick of hair, and she couldn't see the color of his eyes. But he was surely the most beautiful baby she had ever seen. Holding him brought tears to her eyes and a rush of such emotion that it startled her at first.

"That's what motherhood's about," Amanda said when she stopped by at noon with a balloon bouquet. "At least, that's what I'm told. Have you decided on a name?"

"Not yet." She had chosen a name for a girl, but not a boy. She kept putting that off, thinking that maybe things would change and there would be a man to name the baby after. "I keep coming back to Benjamin. But if I did that, Ben's sons would go berserk."

"You do what you want," Amanda urged.

Gretchen loved her for that, as well as for coming to visit. It couldn't be easy for either Graham or her. "Do you hate coming here?"

"No. I love babies. Coming here reminds me how much."

"You'll have a baby. You're a good person."

"Those two things aren't always connected," Amanda advised, then tipped up her chin. "But we will. Somehow, we will. To quote Graham quoting Ralph Waldo Emerson, 'Adopt the pace of nature. Her secret is patience.'"

Gretchen let the words sink in. They were soothing. "You'll have a baby," she repeated.

"Well, you have yours. I told Georgia and Russ. They were excited. Is there anyone else you'd like me to tell?"

"No. There's no one." Her eyes shifted to the door and her heart skipped a beat. Oliver Deeds stood there, holding a vase of roses.

Chapter Twenty

Gretchen didn't want Oliver there. He was a reminder that Ben was dead, and that Ben's sons—technically her stepsons, absurd as it was—would be perfectly happy to put her out of the house and on the street with nothing on her back but the clothes she had worn when she'd first met Ben. She had a baby now. Somehow, she didn't think that would make a difference. They were a hard-hearted lot, these men who had been so close to her kindhearted Ben.

Amanda touched her arm and said a quiet, "I have to run."

Gretchen felt a moment of panic. "Don't. Please stay."

"I wish I could, but I have to get back to school. Is there anything you need?"

Gretchen shook her head. "Thanks for the balloons."

"No thanks needed," Amanda said, adding with the intimacy of a close friend, "I'll give you a call later."

Gretchen nodded in gratitude, feeling tears in her

eyes and a warmth deep inside. She had wanted a friend. She couldn't do better than Amanda.

But Amanda was suddenly gone, and Oliver remained, the lawyer from head to toe in his dark suit and his tense look. He took a step into the room. "The balloons are pretty. It was nice of her to bring them."

Gretchen brushed the tears from her cheeks.

"Are you all right?" he asked.

"Just fine. Amanda and Graham got me here last night."

"I know. I stopped at the house to see you this morning. Russell Lange saw me standing at the door and told me. You should have called."

"I can take care of myself."

"They said you had a cesarean section."

"Many women do. I can still take care of myself. And my baby."

Oliver looked away, brooding. When he looked back, a swatch of hair fell over his brow. "I saw him. They held him up. He's a handsome guy."

Gretchen remained silent.

"Listen," he began, but she found her voice and interrupted.

"He's my baby," she told him. "I have plenty of money. I can take care of him. If David and Alan want to cause trouble because I have a baby, I'll fight them. You can tell them that."

"They won't cause trouble. I won't let them."

"I don't need your help, either," she said, because she couldn't count on him. He was there one minute, gone the next. True friends weren't that way.

"Gretchen, I want to explain."

She held his gaze. "There's nothing to explain."

"I didn't abandon you. But you were a client. I shouldn't have done what I did. It was unethical."

Unethical? He was calling their baby *unethical?* He was calling the warmth he'd shown her—the gentleness and the caring, the *passion*—unethical? If that was the kind of man he was, she didn't want any part of him.

Her face must have shown it. Either that, or he just didn't care. He glanced at the vase he held, frowned, and came forward only enough to put it on the tray table. Then he returned to the door. She was thinking that he was going to leave just like that, without another word, in which case she would ring for the nurse and get rid of his flowers, when he turned.

"Have you decided on a name?" he asked.

"Yes." She did it that very minute. "Benjamin."

"That's a big name for such a little boy."

Benji wasn't. She would call him Benji. He might never know Gretchen's Ben, but he would be raised in the security of a home that the man had provided. Amanda was right. Alan and David didn't count. Gretchen could do what she wanted to do. She was her own woman. And she had friends now. She didn't need Oliver. For the first time in her life, she had friends of her own.

Graham refused to think about Emily, the fertility clinic, pills, bloating, moods, or masturbation. He refused to think about making a baby. For the first time, he understood what friends of his meant who waited long years to have kids so that they could have their wives to themselves. Sure, it was selfish. But what man didn't like being the sole center of a woman's world? Graham sure did. He liked having dinner with Amanda, and went out of his way to come home from work with plenty of time to spare beforehand. He liked watching her make dinner. He liked helping her with it.

He liked doing things with her, period. She was beautiful; he was proud to be seen with her. She was intelligent; he liked hearing about her work, which she shared more now that they were talking again. And she asked about his, wanting to know the kinds of details she hadn't in a while.

He loved the closeness. This was what would remain long after their children were grown and out of the house. When he thought about growing old, he saw Amanda and him on the porch of their dream vacation house. They might be sitting in rockers, or on the wide wood steps. They would be enjoying the soft sounds and the sunset. In time, they would go walking by the water's edge and pause to look for shooting stars.

They had lost this closeness for a while. He loved having it back. With Emily breathing down their necks, the trick would be making sure they didn't lose it again.

Amanda didn't want to think about Emily and the clinic, about pills, charts, calendars, and bated breath any more than Graham did, and the time of the year helped with that. With less than a month left of school, she was busier than ever, meeting with parents and students. Add faculty meetings, and community service assignments, and talks to rising seniors—and wanting to be home by four so that she had all the time in the world for Graham—and she had little time to think about this next fertility round.

Dorothy went home from the hospital on Thursday,

and Amanda strongly felt that they should visit her. Graham argued against it, preferring to let his mother stew for a while, but Amanda refused to let him become estranged from his family, so she dragged him along.

And then there was Gretchen. They drove her home from the hospital on Saturday, with the baby strapped neatly in the infant carrier that Gretchen had bought months before, and Amanda should have kept an emotional distance. She should have, because being around a new baby was an addictive thing. The smells alone—from the new wooden crib, from baby powder and lotion and baby wipes—made her ache with wanting.

She should have kept her distance, but she couldn't. She was drawn to the baby, in part because Gretchen wasn't much more experienced with one than she was, which made them co-conspirators of a sort—though the fact that he had been born six weeks early and was tiny would have given the most experienced parent qualms. Amanda took her turn changing diapers. She helped give Benji his first bath, and rocked him to sleep when Gretchen faded. But she wasn't the only one drawn here. Russ came by. Georgia stayed for hours. The neighborhood children rang the bell, wanting to look at the new baby. Even Karen was curious.

"I keep looking for resemblances," she reasoned, seeming to need an excuse for standing there with Amanda at the side of the crib.

Amanda didn't see any need for excuses. Karen was a caring person at heart. A seasoned mother, she would take pleasure watching a newborn—any newborn.

In fact, Karen was calmer than she had been in months. With Lee out of the house, her anger had ebbed, and without the anger, she was becoming the kind of woman Amanda remembered. Determined to make an independent life for herself and the children, she had booked a cottage on Martha's Vineyard for the week after school got out. Amanda thought it an incredibly brave thing to do.

Studying the baby now, Amanda said, "I don't see any resemblances."

"So if it isn't one of our men, who is it?" Karen asked.

Amanda had her theory, but she was waiting for Gretchen to feel comfortable enough to confide in her. It happened in a roundabout way. Amanda was there one evening the next week when Oliver Deeds dropped by again. If Gretchen's refusal to see him hadn't been a giveaway that their relationship was more than a professional one, the way he looked at the baby certainly was.

Graham saw it, too. He was holding Benji when Oliver appeared at the door. Having come from work, the lawyer looked the part, except for his eyes. Sad was one word for them. Uneasy was another, defenseless a third.

It was the first time Oliver had seen the baby close up. He tried to look past Amanda for Gretchen, tried to look for a place to put the gifts he'd brought, tried to look at the floor or the stairs or the door, but his eyes kept returning to the infant.

"Want to hold him?" Graham asked, and Amanda quickly relieved Oliver of his bundles. Before he could say no—before he could say much of anything—the small blanketed bundle was placed in his arms.

Oliver blushed. "I—I've never held a baby before,"

he said, but his arms took the right shape, and if the baby sensed a novice, he didn't let on. His tiny eyes were closed, his skin silky. "I thought they'd keep him at the hospital longer, being early and all."

"They checked everything out," Amanda said. "He was healthy, so they thought he'd be better off here."

"But he's so small," Oliver said. When the baby opened his eyes, he whispered a nervous, "Can he see me?"

"Only vaguely. Mostly he sees shapes."

The baby pursed his lips and batted a fist in their general direction.

"He'll be a thumb sucker," Graham said.

"So was I," Oliver remarked. He looked up quickly, reddening all the more, but he didn't attempt to qualify the statement. His focus returned to the baby. "He doesn't weigh very much."

"Five pounds, eight ounces," said Gretchen from the stairs.

They all looked around.

There was a moment's silence. Then Oliver spoke, his voice proud: "He's very handsome."

Gretchen nodded but stayed where she was with her weight against the banister.

"Does he eat well?"

She nodded again.

"Are you nursing him?"

"Yes. I need him now." She sent Amanda a look that held both demand and plea.

Gently, Amanda took the baby from Oliver and carried him to Gretchen, who went up the stairs without another word.

Oliver's eyes followed. Amanda couldn't help but see the yearning there. She had seen the same thing too many times in Graham's eyes not to know what it meant. She was trying to think of the most tactful way to raise the issue, when Graham said a blunt, "Where've you been all these months?"

To his credit, Oliver didn't try to deny it. "In the dark," he replied, his eyes back to being sad. "I didn't know she was pregnant until the art was vandalized."

"So you just . . . did it and disappeared?"

Oliver frowned. His Adam's apple moved above the neat knot of a tie that might have been gray, green, brown, or something in between. "It wasn't as simple as that."

"How not?"

"She was Ben's wife. She was a new widow. She was lonely and vulnerable. She was a client. I wasn't supposed to be drawn to her."

"But you were," Amanda said, feeling as peeved as Graham. The issue of Oliver's identity had been such a major concern in the last few weeks. If he had come forward sooner, he might have saved the neighborhood a lot of grief.

"I thought what we had was mutual," he said in his own defense. "I thought that if I backed off, and she took the initiative, it wouldn't be so bad. But she didn't call me either."

"She wouldn't have," Graham put in. "She isn't self-confident when it comes to members of the opposite sex."

Oliver met his gaze. "Neither am I."

Gretchen came down within minutes of Oliver's departure. The baby hadn't needed to nurse. She had only wanted to get him away from Oliver. Sitting carefully on one of the lower steps, she laid him on her thighs.

His eyes were on her. Hers were on Amanda and Graham. She wanted to see if they were disappointed in her, but all she saw was gentleness.

Amanda came to sit on the step below hers. "You should have told us."

"I couldn't. He had to do it."

"What happened?"

How to begin? She hadn't wanted it to happen. She hadn't planned it. "He was here a lot after Ben died. He had all the legal answers, and he knew how to handle Alan and David. He helped me with other things. I didn't even know how to balance a checkbook. Never had enough money to do that before Ben. Pretty dumb, huh?" she asked with a glance at Graham.

"I've been there," Graham said.

"He still is," Amanda said with a fond smile. "I'm the one who balances the checkbook."

Gretchen felt a little better. "It was one night. That's all. One night. I waited for him to call afterward, but he didn't. So maybe I should have called him. But I was sure he'd decided he wasn't interested. I didn't want to be hurt."

"I've been *there,*" Amanda said, darting Graham a quick look, but she didn't elaborate. She turned back to Gretchen. "Did you think of calling him over the winter?"

"A hundred times," Gretchen said. "A *thousand* times. I always lost my nerve." She touched the baby's cheek. He turned his head toward her finger. "I saw him a couple of times, but they were professional visits. He didn't seem inclined to want anything more. I wasn't showing then. Even when I started to show, I could hide it under a sweater."

"Do you love him?" Amanda asked, as Gretchen had done a dozen times.

"I thought I did at the time. I thought it was something mystical—like Ben handpicking the man who could take care of me." The words sounded pathetic to her. She could imagine how they sounded to Amanda and Graham. Quickly, she added, "I mean, it's not like I need a man to take care of me." Her voice dropped. "Only I didn't know that then."

"Knowing it puts you in a position of strength," Graham said, crossing the foyer to join them.

Gretchen didn't understand. She looked from him to Amanda.

"You're stronger now," Amanda explained. "You could talk things out with him. See what he wants. See if there's anything worth pursuing."

Gretchen was torn. "What if he says there isn't?"

"He won't," Graham said. "He's interested."

"How do you know?"

"I know."

"We saw how he looked at the baby."

"If it's just the baby, it's no good," Gretchen said. She needed someone to love her.

No, she caught herself. She did *not* need it. She wanted it. There was a difference.

"You'll never know unless you give it a shot," Graham said.

And that was what life was about, Amanda decided during one of the few moments when she let herself think about the next round of treatment. Taking chances. Giving it a shot.

She also decided that the most important thing was not letting the desire for what you want ruin what you already have. She had Graham. One look at Karen, with four children and a tough road ahead, and she realized how lucky she was. One look at Gretchen, who might or might not be loved by Oliver, and Amanda appreciated her marriage all the more. She had always felt that she had something special in Graham. With each day that passed, she realized she hadn't been wrong.

Graham couldn't get enough of Amanda. He had assumed that after the first flurry of passion following the crisis with Jordie, the hunger would ease. That it lasted through the debacle with Dorothy—that it grew through the pleasure of being with Gretchen and her baby—told him something.

Amanda had shown her mettle in the last few weeks. It was a total turn-on. She walked in the door, and he was hard. She drove down the street, and he was hard. Hell, she called on the phone to say that she was *about* to drive down the street, and he was hard.

"This is remarkable," he murmured against her throat after a rousing bout against the dryer. She had walked into the house, whipped off the sweater she had spilled coffee all over, and gone straight to the laundry room, and what could he do but follow?

"Not even a hello," she chided, but her legs were wrapped around his waist, ankles locked. She wasn't letting him go, though they had both already climaxed.

"You addle my mind," he said and took her face in his hands. Her lips were moist and rosy, her cheeks nearly as smooth and soft as that baby's across the street, but what got to him most—always—were her eyes. That hadn't changed. He doubted it ever would.

When she looked at him that way, like he was the center of her universe, his insides went nuts. "Have I told you lately I love you?"

She grinned lazily. "Mmm-hmm. But you can say it again."

"I love you. I love loving you. I love when it's just you and me. It feels new."

"It is. Back from the lost and found."

"But better." He believed that. They had made it through some rocky days. If couples were tested, they had passed. He sandwiched his hands between the dryer and her bottom. "Maybe we should play with it a while longer."

"What does that mean?" she asked, still lazy, still grinning, eyeing his mouth now.

"Maybe we should wait another month before . . . you know," he said, hestitant even to say the word.

Slowly, she shook her head. "I said I needed one month. I didn't say two."

"*I'm* saying two. I want two."

"That's because you like doing it when you want."

"It's because I'm scared," he blurted out, not quite realizing it until that minute. "Aren't you?"

Her grin faded. She took a breath. "Of course I'm scared. I'm scared that the same thing will happen, only it'll be worse, because this is our last try at artificial insemination. If it fails, we move on."

"I'm not just talking about failing at making a baby. I'm talking about *us*."

"I know," Amanda said, very sober now. "But there's no avoiding it. We could play for the next three months or the next three years, but we'd only find ourselves that much further from being parents. You want a baby. So do I."

"We could adopt. That'd take the pressure off. Sure thing, you'd get pregnant then."

"Not yet. I'm not ready to adopt yet."

He dropped his head back. "God, I'm not looking forward to this."

Amanda rubbed her forehead to his neck. "That's because the process is cold." She looked up, took his face in her hands, and brought his eyes to hers. Her voice was seductive. "We need to warm it up. I can do that. You don't need *Playboy.* I'll do it for you." Slipping a hand between their bodies, she touched him at the spot above where they were still joined, and that quickly, he wanted her again.

"Would ya?" he asked hoarsely.

"You bet," she replied.

They decided to go with a heavier dose of Clomid, a shot of HCG, and multiple inseminations. The deal with Emily was that they would call when Amanda got her period and drop by within a day or two for the medication, instructions on when to take it, and a pep talk.

Amanda didn't look at the calendar. She didn't have to. Her cycle was regular and prompt. She would get her period on Wednesday, call Emily on Thursday, drop in on Friday. Then she and Graham were taking off. He had made reservations for another weekend away, this time at an inn on the Maine coast. They were determined to keep the focus on their relationship, while they followed Emily's directions. They were doing everything together this time, from having ultrasounds, to keeping temperature charts, doing ovulation tests, producing sperm or injecting it.

The month before, she had remained in her chair for the better part of the day, not wanting to make any move that would bring on her period. This month, she dared it to come. It would mark the start of a new attempt to conceive. The sooner the better, she reasoned, and, intent on hastening it, she was on the go from the minute she reached school that morning until the last few minutes before she was ready to set out for home. The only reason she slowed down then was the sight of Jordie Cotter at her office door. His leg was still in a cast, but it was a walking one. He had a single crutch under one arm and a backpack over the other.

"Hi, cutie," called Maddie from her cage.

"Hey," Amanda said gently. "Come on in."

"You were leaving."

"I always have time for you." She gestured him forward. They hadn't talked since their night on the tower. "I think about you a lot. How's it going?"

"Not bad." Coming forward, he nudged his chin toward the cast. "I can't play, so it isn't a matter of warming the bench. Things like that are better. Others are weird."

"Weird, like with your dad?" she asked. She didn't believe in beating around the bush when something was so obvious. Kids saw through that in a minute.

"Yeah. With my dad. He's over a lot. He's even nice to my mom. Julie thinks they're getting back together."

"Do you?"

"No," he said, but he was pensive. "Too much has happened. I blame myself sometimes."

"Don't."

"They say that, too. They say they had problems for years."

"I think that's true. In any event, they're right. What happened between them wasn't your fault."

"Does Gretchen hate me?"

"No. Gretchen isn't a hater. Besides, she's too happy with her little son to think about it."

"But her painting is ruined."

"She'll find something to put in its place."

Jordie nodded. Quietly, he said, "I hope she does." He limped back toward the door. "Maddie's awful quiet."

Amanda sat against the edge of the desk with a hand by either hip. "She doesn't have any cause to swear. You're too calm. Is it going all right with the new therapist?"

He stopped at the threshold. "It's going okay. But he isn't you."

"What a sweet thing to say."

He turned. His eyes met hers, then shied away. Seconds later, he forced them back. "I owe you more. What you did that night was amazing." He was talking of their time together at the tower.

"I did what I had to. I needed it for me, as much as for you."

"Because of Quinn?" When she nodded, he said, "I miss Quinn."

"We all do."

"I won't ever forget the dates. Y'know, when he died and all. It was four weeks ago yesterday when he drank my dad's booze. It feels like a year."

"Four weeks ago today," Amanda corrected gently.

"Nuh-uh. It was a Tuesday. I know exactly where I was when I got the call saying he'd been caught. It was like the first thing in a whole chain."

Amanda didn't answer. He was right. The drinking

incident had occurred on a Tuesday. She was trying to figure out how she had confused the days, then trying to grasp what it meant.

It must have shown on her face, because Jordie asked a worried, "Are you okay?"

Amanda's heart was palpitating. "I am," she said, and asked out of sheer habit, since her mind had jumped ahead, "Need a ride home?"

"No. My dad's coming to pick me up."

Amanda was grateful for that—because she wasn't going straight home. She had a stop to make. Oh, sure, she had pregnancy tests at home, but she wanted one that was fresh.

She bought three. Each was made by a different company and worked a slightly different way, but each one could be used at any time of day, as early as the first day of a missed period, with accuracy over ninety-nine percent of the time.

She was shaking all over by the time she got home, and then botched one strip by wetting the wrong end. That left two. She did the first, waited the requisite five minutes, and saw a plus. Afraid to believe, she did the second, waited the two minutes that *it* required, and saw two magenta lines. Two meant pregnant.

She put the strips side by side on the bathroom sink. She washed her hands. She picked up the cell phone and punched in Graham's office number.

"It's me," she said when he answered. "You have to come home."

He was immediately frightened. "What's wrong?"

She swallowed and bit back her excitement. She wanted him to see the strips for himself. Wanted him to feel the disbelief, the surprise, the *ecstasy. We blew it, buster!* she wanted to yell in delight, because he'd missed the dates, too. She had no idea how they'd *both* done that.

"Nothing wrong," she said, careful to steady the shake in her voice. "I just have to show you something."

"Something good or something bad?"

"Good."

"Something big or something small?"

"Graham. Come home *now.*"

Ten minutes later, he drove down the street. Heart pounding, she met him at the door, took his hand, led him up the stairs and into the bathroom, and pointed at the strips. He stared at them, then at her. He approached them curiously, studied one, then the other. He looked at the boxes from which each strip had come. His eyes widened.

"Christ," he murmured on a thread of a breath and turned to her in excitement. "We did it?"

She nodded.

"But today—"

"Yesterday," she shrieked, unable to contain her elation a second longer. "We miscounted. I was due *yesterday*!"

"You're pregnant!"

"I'm pregnant!" Though the very best part at that moment was the joy in his eyes.

He swept her up off the ground and around, then held her in his arms so tightly that she thought she would burst with the excitement of it all. When he set her down, he put his face level with hers. "When did it happen?"

"One of the hundred times we made love in the last two weeks."

"But you didn't feel anything. No little spark. No woman's intuition."

She started to laugh. "How could I feel anything but *you*? That was all I felt those times. Just *you*."

And there was a message in that.

Barbara Delinsky recently took time from working on her next book to talk to us. Here are the excerpts from that conversation.

Q. How did you come to dream up *The Woman Next Door?*

A. This is just my kind of story. I write about real-life relationships such as ones I read about in newspapers and magazines, as well as things that I see firsthand. Well, lately I've read and seen lots about marriage—what makes some good and some bad, what makes some last and some end. It seemed a natural for me to devote a book to examples of the strains that test a marriage.

Q. What are some of those strains?

A. Work pressures. Family pressures. Fertility pressures. Infidelity. In *The Woman Next Door,* I touch on all four of these. The story takes place on a cul-de-sac in western Connecticut and opens with the discovery that an attractive young widow is pregnant. In the absence of a man in her life, the three other women living on the cul-de-sac are forced to consider whether their husbands might have fathered the baby. All three husbands have had the opportunity to be with the widow. But the will? As each of the three wives asks herself that, she looks reflectively at her marriage, her lifestyle, her goals, and her dreams. Though the widow is a viable character, she is first and foremost the catalyst for the taking-stock that the other women do.

Q. But the widow is *The Woman Next Door,* isn't she?

A. Yes and no. There may be more than one interpretation of the title. I'll let my readers decide. Suffice it to say that I conceived of this title before I had even plotted the book. It fit both the book and *me.*

Q. Okay. Explain that.

A. The one compliment readers give me most often is that I write about them or people they know, people they can easily conjure up. They say they can identify with my characters, because I write about average, everyday people. Well, that's because I *am* an average, everyday person. I grew up in suburbia, went to college, got married, had kids. To this day, publicists can't find a dramatic "hook" to use as a promo gimmick. I'm a down-to-earth, low-key, private person who does indeed live like the proverbial woman next door.

Q. *The Woman Next Door* was first published in the summer of '01. By now you've heard from many readers. What praise do they most often give?

A. They call it a page-turner. They say that they couldn't put it down.

Q. And on the other side, what criticism do they most often give?

A. Fortunately, the bulk of my mail is positive. Several readers, though, have had trouble with the idea that two of the women, in particular, might suspect their husbands of infidelity. They say that this is unrealistic. I'm not sure I agree. My husband and I celebrate our 35th wedding anniversary this summer, and I've never had any cause to question his fidelity—but that doesn't mean that my imagination hasn't played a time or two when he is working on a trial (he's a lawyer) and is in the office from five in the morning to midnight, day after day. Amanda and Georgia, of *The Woman Next Door,* are like me. They have no reasonable or just cause to suspect their husbands. Unlike me, though, they know that some man did sow his oats where he shouldn't have, so to speak. Their friend and neighbor, Karen, whose husband *does* have a history of infidelity, quite defensively points out the reasons why each of their husbands might have strayed. The seed of suspicion is thus planted.

Q. Does criticism of your work bother you?

A. It bothers me a great deal. Even the most petty criticism stings. As I said, though, my readers are overwhelmingly positive in their feedback to me, and I do love hearing from them. That feedback, in fact, inspired my newest book.

Q. O-kay. Explain *that.*

A. Several years ago, I wrote a book called *Lake News.* It was set in a small New Hampshire lake town and centered around a woman who grew up there and was forced to return when a scandal drove her out of the city. The woman's sister, Poppy, was a secondary character in *Lake News.* Poppy was confined to a wheelchair and ran a telephone answering service in this little lake town. In the course of *Lake News,* she had a phone thing with a terrific good-guy reporter named Griffin. She kept discouraging him from coming to town, though, because she didn't want him to know she was in a wheelchair. Well. Readers wanted to know more about Poppy and Griffin. More people commented on them than commented on Katherine Evans, my breast-cancer survivor in *Coast Road.* How could I not write Poppy's story?

Q. But Poppy is a paraplegic. You've just said that readers identify with your characters. Will her disability make that difficult?

A. No. *An Accidental Woman* is not about paraplegia. Rather, it is about bad things happening to good people, and how they deal. In that sense, it could as easily be about grappling with the aftermath of illness, unemployment, or terrorism. Besides, Poppy leads a very normal life. She has the same hopes, dreams, and fears as the rest of us. Lake Henryites do not see her as disabled. I doubt readers will.

Q. Was it easy going back to an old familiar town, one you've written about before?

A. Funny you should ask. I thought it would be *simple.* I thought, "How *nice* not to have to create a town from scratch." Then I discovered the downside to that thinking. Returning to Lake Henry, I had to make sure that things in *An Accidental Woman*—the people, the town center, the roads, the stores, even Thursday nights at Charlie's Café—were consistent with *Lake News.* My readers are astute. If there are mistakes, they'll catch each and every one.

Q. *An Accidental Woman.* Is the title based on Poppy?

A. Poppy and Heather. Heather is one of Poppy's closest friends. She got a single sentence in *Lake News,* but her arrest in the opening pages of *An*

Accidental Woman makes her a major player now. She is accused of involvement in an accident fifteen years before in which a man was killed. Regardless of her guilt or innocence, the charge alone is enough to wreak havoc with her life. In fact . . . oops, I can't say any more, or I'll spoil the story. I've worked too hard writing this book for that.

Q. Do you put research in the category of hard work?
A. No. I think of research as fun. But there was lots of it to do for this book. There were small things, like blind cats and the storage space in a Porsche. But there were also two biggies—spinal injuries and maple-syrup production. The spinal-injury issue clearly has to do with Poppy. As for maple syrup, *Lake News* took place in the fall and discussed the making of apple cider. *An Accidental Woman* takes place in late winter, when maple sap starts to run. Heather's significant other, Micah, is a sugarmaker. I had a wonderful time learning what he does.

Q. Hmmm, like maple syrup, do you?
A. Love it—on pancakes, baked apples, sweet potatoes, chicken. I've actually been running a contest on my Web site for the most creative maple syrup recipes, one per month. Readers have sent in some incredible ones. The winners are printed in the *Monthly Ledger.*

Q. So if other readers have recipes—or just want to drop you a note—how do they reach you?
A. Easy. Either via the Internet at www.barbaradelinsky.com or via snail mail at P.O. Box 812894, Wellesley, MA 02482-0026.

Within seconds of coming awake, Micah Smith felt a chill at the back of his neck that had nothing to do with the cold air seeping in through the window cracked open by his side of the bed. It was barely dawn. He didn't have to glance past Heather's body toward the nightstand clock to know that. He could see it in the purpling that preceded daylight when February snows covered the forest floor.

The purpling seemed deeper this morning, but that wasn't what caused his alarm. Nor was it any sound from the girls' room that caused him to hold his breath. They would sleep for another hour, he knew, and, if not sleep, then stay in bed until they heard Heather or him up and about.

No. What held him totally still, eyes on that inch of open window, was the sound of a car, moving very slowly down the snow-crusted drive toward the small house that Micah had built for his family.

Get out of bed, cried a silent voice, but he remained inert. Barely breathing, he listened. Not one car. Two. They inched their way closer, then stopped. Their engines went still.

Do something, cried that silent voice, more urgent now, and he thought of the rifle that was mounted high above the front door, out of reach of the girls. But he couldn't move—couldn't *move*—other than to turn his head toward Heather. She continued to sleep.

As he watched the swirl of her long dark hair, he heard the stealthy click of car doors—one, then a second. A patch of her pale shoulder showed through the tangle of her hair. He would have touched it if he hadn't feared waking her, but he didn't want that. Once she was awake, once she heard what he heard, once this moment ended, their lives would be changed. He didn't know how he knew that, but he did. A part of him had been waiting for this moment, fearing it for four years.

The footsteps coming toward the house were careful, making only the occasional crunch on the snow, but a lifetime of living in the New Hampshire woods had trained Micah's ear well. The house was being surrounded. He figured that his rifle wouldn't do much good. The people out there weren't intent on violence. And what was happening was inevitable.

A soft knock came at the front door. He quickly slipped from under the thick down and silently pulled on jeans. In seconds, he was down the hall and through the living room. He pulled the door open before another knock came, though Pete Duffy's hand was already raised.

Pete was second in command to Lake Henry's chief of police and was a friend of Micah's. The look of regret on the man's face did nothing to ease Micah's sense of dread as his eyes moved to a second man who stood just behind Pete. This man and the two women with him wore jeans and identical blue jackets that Micah knew must have law-enforcement initials on the back.

The man held out paperwork, along with his ID.

"Jim Mooney. FBI. I have a warrant for the arrest of Heather Malone on charges of flight to avoid prosecution."

Micah had always known that Heather hid her past. During those times when he had wondered what might have caused her secretiveness, involvement with the law had been the worst-case scenario. "Prosecution for what?" he asked the agent now.

"Murder."

A sharp breath escaped Micah—oddly, he felt relief. If murder was the charge, then there surely was a mistake. "That's impossible. Heather's incapable of murder."

"Maybe as Heather Malone. But we have evidence that her real name is Lisa Matlock, and that fifteen years ago she killed a man in California."

"Heather's never been in California."

"Lisa has," the agent informed him. "She grew up there. She was there until fifteen years ago, when she deliberately ran a man down with her car. She disappeared right afterward. Your Heather arrived in Lake Henry fourteen years ago and worked as a short-order cook, just like Lisa did in California in the two years before she left. Heather's face is identical to Lisa's, right down to the gray eyes and the scar at the corner of the mouth."

"There are millions of women with gray eyes," Micah said, suddenly aware of cold air on his bare chest, "and that scar came from a car accident."

"Not this accident. She escaped this one unscathed, but the man she ran down died—a man she tried to extort minutes before she ran him down."

"Extort?" Micah snorted. "Not my Heather. She's gentle. She's kind."

The agent was unfazed. "I need her to come out here. Either you bring her, or we go in."

Still Micah argued. "Eyes and a scar. What kind of proof's that?"

"We have handwriting samples," said the agent.

Micah read enough to know a little about the law. "That's not conclusive."

"I'd say you're biased."

"Same the fuck with you."

Pete stepped between the two men. Slowly and deliberately, he told Micah, "They have a warrant. That gives them the right to take her. Don't rile them, Micah."

A low light suddenly came on behind him, a lamp near the spot where the living room met the hall. Heather stood there. She had slipped on a robe and held the lapels shut with one hand while with the other she steadied herself against the wall. As she looked at the people beyond the door, her eyes grew wider.

Micah held up a hand to stop the two female agents who started forward, and instead went to Heather himself. Slipping his fingers into the hair at her nape, shaping his hand to hold her head, he searched her eyes for a sign of knowledge or guilt. All he saw was fear.

"They say you're someone else," he whispered. "They must be wrong, but they need you to go with them."

"Where?" she asked with barely a sound.

That wasn't the first question Micah would have asked if he had been in her shoes. He'd have wanted to know who they thought he was and why he needed to go with them. But she was a practical sort, far more so than he.

"I don't know," he answered. "Maybe to Willie Jake's office." He glanced over his shoulder at Pete. "They just want to question her?"

Before Pete could answer, the two women approached. "We need to book her," one told him before turning to Heather. "If you want to dress, we'll go with you."

Heather's eyes flew from one woman's face to the other, then in fear to Micah's.

"I'll take her to dress," he said, but one of the agents was already grasping her arm and reciting her Miranda rights. The moment would have been terrifyingly real even without Heather's eyes clinging to his.

Frantic to help her, desperate to do something, but realistic enough to know he was hamstrung, Micah glanced back at Pete. "Someone's gonna answer for this. It's wrong."

Pete came forward as the two female agents ushered Heather down the hall. "I told them that. So'd Willie Jake. He spent most of last night trying to talk some sense into them, but they have the warrant."

When Micah started after her, Mooney caught his arm. "You have to stay here. She's under arrest."

"Daddy?" came a soft voice from even farther down the hall.

Micah turned in alarm. It was Melissa, his seven-year-old daughter. In a voice that was as normal as he could make it, what with a growing panic, he said, "Go back to bed, Missy. Too early to get up."

But Missy, by far the more curious and bold of his two girls, padded toward him in her long pink nightgown. Her hair was as dark as his—and as thick and long as Heather's—but wildly curly. "Why's Pete here?" she asked, slipping a hand in Micah's but looking at Mooney. "Who's he?"

Micah shot a frantic glance at Pete. "Uh, he works with Pete sometimes. They have to ask Heather some questions."

"Now?"

"In a little while. I want you to go back to bed. Make sure your sister sleeps a little longer."

"She's awake. She's just scared to come out."

Micah knew it wasn't as simple as Star being scared or shy. He had long since accepted that the five-year-old possessed an odd adult insight. Star would know that something was desperately wrong.

"Then go back in and play with her. That'll make her feel better."

Missy smiled and released his hand. In the few seconds it took for her to step back and flatten herself to the wall, her expression turned defiant.

"Missy," Micah warned, waving her back down the hall, but before she could refuse, Heather emerged from the bedroom with the two female agents. She was dressed in jeans and a heavy sweater, the sheer bulk of which made her look lost. Her expression mirrored that. When she caught sight of Missy, she stopped short. Her eyes met Micah's for a single, alarmed second.

Missy was looking at the two agents. "Who're *they?*"

Micah said, "More friends of Pete's. Go on back in with Star, Missy. I need you to help."

Heather knelt by her side. "Daddy's right, sweetie," she said in a gentle voice. "Star needs you."

Missy slipped an arm around Heather's shoulder. "Where are you going?"

"Into town."

"When'll you be back?"

"A little later."

"Do you promise?"

Waiting for the answer himself—hanging his future on it much as the child was—Micah saw Heather swallow. But that was the only beat she missed. In the same soft voice, she said, "I'll do my best to be here when you get home from school." As she straightened, she pressed a kiss to the child's head. She closed her eyes, and a look of anguish crossed her face. Micah imagined that she held the kiss a beat longer than she might have. Sure enough, as she came toward him, her eyes were filled with tears. When she was as close as she could be, she whispered, "Call Cassie."

Cassie Byrnes was one of Heather's closest friends, and she was a lawyer.

Micah took her hands, only to find that the sleeves of the bulky sweater concealed handcuffs nearly as cold as her skin. Furious, he turned on Pete, who raised a brow in warning and nodded toward Missy.

"Call Cassie," Heather repeated—which was certainly the right thing to say, certainly the *practical* thing to say, though not what Micah wanted to hear. He wanted her to profess utter confusion, to insist that a mistake had been made, to protest her innocence. But yes, Heather was a practical woman. Given the fact of an arrest warrant, cooperating was the thing to do.

Still, the handcuffs offended him. A small person like Heather didn't have a chance of overpowering three agents, even with both hands free. Not that his Heather would think of fighting. In the four years that they had been together, he had never seen her lash out in anger at anything.

When the two female agents ushered her toward the door, he followed closely. "Where are you taking her?"

Mooney stepped in his path as the agents whisked Heather outside. "Concord. She'll go before a magistrate there this morning. She needs an attorney."

Go before a magistrate. Micah's eyes flew to Pete, who said, "They have to return the Fugitive Flight Warrant. Heather can choose to waive an extradition hearing and go back with them, or she can fight it. They can't take her back—can't charge her with murder or anything else—until they make a solid enough case that the charges are legit."

Micah wanted to know the how, why, and where of everything Pete was talking about, but he had more immediate questions, and Mooney was leaving. Following the agent out the door, he trotted barefoot down the steps, oblivious to the crusted ice on the wood planks, the snow on the drive, the subfreezing air on his near-naked body. As he trotted forward, Heather vanished into the back of a dark van. At the same time, two other men materialized from the woods and slid in.

Micah began to run. "I want to go with her."

Pete ran alongside him. "They won't let you. You'd be better going down with Cassie."

When the deputy pulled at Micah's arm and tried to steer him back to the cabin, Micah tugged free and ran on. He stopped at the closed door of the van, bent down, and flattened a hand on the window. His eyes met Heather's just as Mooney started the engine, and short of running alongside until the van gained enough speed to leave him behind, he had no choice but to stop. Straightening, he watched the van round a bend and disappear down the forest drive.

Suddenly, he felt cold inside and out. Turning fast, he started back toward the house. "Some friend you are," he muttered as he stormed past Pete.

The deputy ran after him. "They had the warrant for her arrest. What could we do?"

Micah took the front steps in twos, energized by anger.

"Look at it this way," Pete argued. "They have to *prove* she is who they say. You think anyone here's going to say she's someone else? No way. So they're going to have to dig up other people. That'll take some time, don't you think?"

What Micah thought was that *any* amount of time he was separated from Heather was bad. He wanted her with him, and not just for the girls' sake. He had come to depend on her gentleness, her sureness, and—yes—her practicality. He was a nuts-and-bolts guy who sometimes was so focused on the small details that he didn't see the larger picture. Heather did. She was his helpmate when it came to being human. She was also his partner when it came to maple sugaring, and the season was about to start.

Striding into the house, he shut the door before Pete could follow. Missy stood in the middle of the living room looking crushed, and though there was no sign of Star, Micah was sure she was nearby. He looked around the living room, behind and under the sofa, the chairs, the large square coffee table that he had built at Heather's direction, but it wasn't until he looked behind him at the bookshelves flanking the front door that he spotted her. She was on the bottom shelf, tucked in beside a stack of National Geographic magazines that were a stark yellow against the pale green of her nightie. Her hair, dark like his but long, straight and fine, lay over her shoulders like a shawl. Her eyes were woefully sad and knowing.

His heart lurched. It wasn't that he had stronger feelings for Star, just that he worried more. She had been an infant when her mother left—"left" being the word he used in place of "skidded off the road, went down a ravine, and burned up in the cab of her truck." He knew that Star couldn't possibly remember Marcy; still, he was convinced that she sensed the loss. Heather was wonderful with Star. Heather was wonderful with both of his girls. And now Heather had left, too.

Hunkering down, he caught up the child. Her arms and legs went around him as he straightened.

Not knowing where to begin, he simply said, "Everything's okay, baby," as he carried her down the hall to the room the girls shared. He set her on her bed. Like Missy's, it was a mess of gingham sheets, pillow, and down—Missy's pink, Star's green—all of which was Heather's doing again. "I just need you and your sister to get dressed while I make some calls. Then we'll have breakfast together."

"We won't wait for Momma," the child said in a sure little voice.

"No. She'll have breakfast in town."

"What'll she eat?"

He thought for a minute. "Eggs? Waffles? If we eat the same thing, it'll be like she's with us."

"Oatmeal," Missy announced from close by. "Oatmeal's her favorite. She'd be having that. But I can only eat it if it has lots of maple sugar on it."

"We have lots of maple sugar, so we're golden. Help your sister dress?" Micah said and, with a return of the urgency he had felt when the FBI van disappeared with Heather inside, he headed for the kitchen to call Cassie. Halfway there, though, he did an about-face and went back down the hall, this time to the spare room. He had to step over the girls' doll-house village to reach the closet, then had to push spare clothes aside to get to the shelves built in behind.

The knapsack was on a well-hidden shelf, out of reach of the girls. A drab brown thing, it was small and worn. To his knowledge, it was the only relic Heather had of her pre–Lake Henry days.

Tucking the sack under his arm—and refusing to consider what was inside—he went through the kitchen to the back hall. Jackets of various sizes hung from hooks at all heights; an assortment of footwear was lined against the wall. Stepping into the largest boots in the pile, he pulled on a jacket and stuffed the knapsack inside, then went out, down the back steps, and over the well-packed snow on an oft-trodden path. The sugarhouse stood several hundred feet up the hill from the house. It was a long stone building with a large cupola atop, through which steam from the evaporator escaped when the sap was being boiled down.

Nothing escaped it now. There was no sweet scent, no air of anticipation. The sugarhouse and woods alike were cold and still.

Feeling only dread, Micah slipped inside and went to the far end of the main room, where sugar wood was stacked high and deep. He pulled off three logs at a time. When he found one with a significant curve, he tucked the tattered bag into the pile, put that log back, then the rest. Brushing his hands off on his jacket, he left the shed.

Back in the kitchen, he called Cassie Byrnes. She gave him fifteen minutes to pick her up for the drive to Concord.

Fifteen minutes didn't give Micah much time to get his life in order. He and Heather had been a family long enough that he hadn't had to worry about who would take care of the girls before and after school. Thinking about his predicament now, he could conjure up only one name, one face for the job. Of all of the people whom he and Heather called friends, Poppy Blake was the one he trusted most.